Bettah Days

by Veronica R. Wells

Bettah Days

For Leanora and Linton

1927, Seven

Hilda's eyelids flew open abruptly, jarring the rest of her body alert. During the wait she had drifted into an accidental, restless sleep. The tree frogs and cicadas had been performing their nighttime symphony for hours and the creaks and cricks that characterized their modest home had settled. It was in the quiet of the house that Hilda stirred.

She looked over at her sister Olga, whose sweaty arm had been resting against hers, still sleeping soundly. Hilda kicked the covers away from her legs and jumped into a pair of slacks she had folded neatly at the edge of her bed. Though he'd come home hours ago, she knew her father was gone. By now, she assumed he was probably halfway to the post office where a woman with big, welcoming legs was looking out for him. Her school friends had been whispering stories of this woman and her father for months now. And tonight she was going to see for herself. She tried to move stealthily, placing her foot down in sections on the linoleum floor. But she wasn't quiet enough. A floorboard creaked under her weight and her youngest sister, Constantine, heard her.

She sat up in bed rubbing her eyes before asking, "Where yuh a go dis time ah night?"

Hilda sighed.

Her sister was just seven years old, a child. She wouldn't understand.

"Meh steppin out fah a minute." She tried to sound authoritative so her sister would just go back to sleep. But the girl barely listened to their parents. Hilda knew from the moment Constantine sat up, she would have company. By the time she finished the sentence, her youngest sister had kicked off her covers and leapt to her dresser to throw on a pair of pants of her own.

In vain, Hilda tried again. "Nah bodda puttin' no pants on. Yuh nah go wid me."

The thin, coffee-bean-colored girl stopped, slowly turned her head toward Hilda, then glared, narrowing her already beady eyes.

"Yes, meh ah go."

Her voice still had the smallness of a child but there was no denying the resolve behind it. Her biting words and slick tongue were the reasons their mother beamed with pride and their father found her intolerable. Realizing she'd lost, Hilda whispered for Constantine to hurry up and get dressed.

Once they were both ready, Hilda turned the knob slowly, not yet pulling the door open. She glanced back one last time to see that Olga was still asleep and then she and Constantine stepped out. The two tiptoed down the short hallway, calculating each step. Constantine gently slid her hand into her big sister's as they made their way past their mother's room. The duo crept through the living room, breathing in sync so as not to make any additional noises. Finally, they reached the front door. Hilda carefully tightened her fingers around the knob and turned it slowly. She heard the cylinder in the door tumble and she froze. When she didn't hear anyone stir, she turned again, opening the door. Jamaica's thick, damp night air barged into the house, pushing past the two huddled sisters.

Hilda put one foot out the door, keeping her body close to the frame. Constantine did the same. Once they both were on the porch, Constantine extended her skinny arm and short fingers to close the door behind them. Before she could reposition it, she saw the red embers at the end of their mother's cigarette. Her shoulders and spirit sank in disappointment.

Grace Ann stared at them, her face deadpan. Sitting on the porch swing facing the doorway, she cocked her head slightly in curiosity while her brow furrowed in anger. Despite the intimidating face, her voice came out as it always did, squeaky. In her earlier years it had been thin, but now, after decades of smoking, it was weighted with phlegm and punctuated by sporadic cracks.

"Yuh two chasin duppy? Wha unu doin outta yuh beds creepin' 'roun the house, suh?" Her hand shook slightly as she flicked the ashes toward the ground.

Hilda and Constantine remained speechless.

They didn't have to say anything. Grace Ann knew her daughters. She knew why they were up. She even knew why her husband had left the house. If her neighbors were awake, any one of them would have known where Theophilus was spending the evening. It didn't bother her. She had been telling herself this for so many years she couldn't remember whether it was true or not… She was just grateful and even indebted to Theophilus for taking care of their children and the outside ones, the ones she'd brought into the marriage, who were grown and gone now. There weren't too many Jamaican men who would have done that. If he wanted to have a woman or two across town, perhaps he'd earned that much.

Grace Ann pursed her trembling lips and used them to point toward the door, which Constantine was still holding open.

"Back tuh ya beds, nah!"

Hilda kissed her teeth slightly, just out of her mother's earshot as she nudged Constantine back inside.

When the adrenaline left their systems, Hilda, having failed at her mission, drifted off into a less than peaceful sleep. But Constantine laid awake thinking about their father. She only seemed to catch glimpses of him. If she were up early enough, just as the sun was rising, she'd watch him, in the stark white of his baker's uniform, leaving for work. After school, if he came straight home, she'd spot him outside, using the bucket of water to rinse away the last bits of flour that had grayed his large hands. She'd wish him a good afternoon and he'd reply with an air of apathy that sucked the sweet smell of his uniform right out of the air. Once he'd finished with the bucket, she washed the streaks of dirt off her thin legs and they'd enter the house together, their cleansing revealing an identical complexion. When he stepped inside the house, Theophilus went from baker to boss as Grace Ann busied herself, plating his food and setting his dinner in front of him. Theophilus spoke to Constantine outside because he was attempting to teach his children respect for their elders. But his wife was already grown, and as a result wasn't gifted such pleasantries.

It would be a lie to say Constantine or any of her sisters were conceived in love. Maybe a strong affection at best. Grace Ann and Theophilus's story didn't include moonlit strolls, ballads sung off-key, or a galloping of heart and head. Instead, the two were introduced through an older, mutual friend, a busybody who assumed they had something in common: children from failed relationships and both too old to be single.

Not disliking each other but not truly desiring one another either, Theophilus courted Grace Ann for six months. He found her attractive but not alluring. She found him stable but not sensual. There was little passion and no yearning to be together as much as they yearned to be settled. Theophilus, nearly forty, was tired of sleeping in different beds all over town, scrounging up meals as payment for services rendered.

And Grace Ann, then thirty-five, couldn't find stillness. Her right leg shook uncontrollably, attempting to shake off the worry of finding a man who would help her raise her children, Cissy and George. When she gnawed at her cuticles, she chewed on the idea of having a chance to redeem herself and find a husband who would finally make her an honorable woman. She chain-smoked, inhaling the notion that marrying for love was an option she could no longer afford.

It was a match, and eventually a marriage, made in anxiety, fear, and indifference.

Still, in the evenings, after Theophilus had sucked the marrow from the oxtail bones, he immediately reminded Grace Ann of another one of her wifely duties. And in the darkness, with an overflowing appreciation for a meal well prepared, an itch yet scratched, and a desire to keep her man, their arid union bore fruit.

The two never came together with the intent to produce a child, and each time Grace Ann presented their latest bundle to him, Theophilus deflated. His body must not have been in accordance with his mind because he only seemed to have daughters. His first child, the one before he and Grace Ann met, was a girl. And with her, three more had followed.

First, there was Hilda. Theophilus's shoulders slumped when he learned she wasn't a boy. But he figured there was still time for a son. Plus, this was a daughter he'd fathered within the confines of marriage. This child, unlike his first, brought respect to him as a man. So he loved her in spite of her gender.

Then two years later, there was Olga. He sneered momentarily when the doctor informed him that it was yet another girlchild; but he knew there was still time for a son, so he loved her too.

Theophilus was certain the next child would be the last. Not only was Grace Ann getting older, with the birth of each child, she was less and less preoccupied with satisfying him. This last child had to be a boy. Theophilus, who was far from religious, thought he'd try something different and ask God for a son.

But God failed him too. Constantine wasn't a boy. Where his hope for the future son had allowed him to be affectionate toward his other daughters, Constantine represented a finality, an end to the possibility of a male heir. And though she had not asked to come into this world, he resented her for doing so.

As a baby, having mastered the art of walking, Constantine toddled over to her father one day, reaching up, gesturing for him to lift her. He looked down at her as if she were a stain he'd just noticed on his pant leg. From that day forward, when Constantine thought about her father, that was the face she saw.

***

The next morning, Constantine's young body rebelled, protesting its inevitable rise. She listened as her mother moved about in the kitchen, preparing their cornmeal porridge and squinted her eyes shut as Olga attempted to coerce her out of bed. It wasn't until Grace Ann came into the room, issuing what Constantine knew to be an idle threat, that she got up.

All throughout school, the curtains of her eyelids threatened to end the day's production. It was only the dismissal bell and its promise of sleep, after her journey, that summoned the last bit of energy she needed to walk home.

When she arrived, she saw that Theophilus wasn't outside with the bucket. But when she walked up to it, to wash up, she noticed that the water was still a bit cloudy from his flour. She heard her father's footsteps moving across the linoleum floor inside and her heart fluttered. Constantine hurried to rinse her legs, face and hands before dashing through the front door.

Just as she suspected, her father, still in his uniform and overcoat, which he wore everyday, despite the island heat, sported his rare grin. The cane he walked with was propped up in the corner. Theophilus had no real use for it. Harkening back to his unknown and unacknowledged African roots, he used it because it made him feel more powerful, like a king. He looked up from his phonograph to see Constantine standing in the doorway. "Come girl. Wha' yuh feel like listen to tunight?"

"Meh nah haf no preference pupa, jus play somethin meh can dance to."

"So mi girl wan' dance huh?" Theophilus bopped softly in front of his record collection, surveying his choices.

Constantine slipped out of her shoes and ran back to her room to drop her school bag. As soon as it hit the floor, she heard the first chords of her favorite mento song, "Sly Mongoose." In stocking feet, Constantine raced back to the living room, freezing at the scene there. No matter how many times she'd seen her father shed his callous exterior as the fusion of Jamaican folk and American jazz music leapt from the speaker, she always stood and watched in awe. Theophilus, already working up a sweat, tossed his overcoat onto his chair, threw back his head, lifted his shoulders up and down repeatedly as he shuffle stepped in time to the music.

"Come Connie, Sam Manning nah sing all night."

Constantine imitated her father's movements, lifting and sliding her bony feet across the linoleum, stepping in time toward him. When the two were standing in front of one another, they lifted their shoulders together, leaning and rocking in an unrehearsed but familiar synchronization.

When sweat ran down the both of their backs and Constantine's cheeks ached from smiling, Theophilus transitioned into the smoother, sounds of American love songs.

In the hot, sweaty and euphoric aftermath of she and her father's dance session, Constantine, slumped in the other living room chair, clinging to the enchanting melodies of those love songs. Not only because they scored the times—the only times—she actually liked her father; but also because those records told the story of a life she wanted to experience.

She just didn't know it would be coming so fast.

1930, Ten

The night Hilda and Constantine tried to sneak out of the house seemed worlds away now. Hilda was eighteen with a child of her own. And when she left her parents's home to go live with her boyfriend, Olga was promoted to oldest child in the house, while Constantine remained the baby, except on the weekends. It was then that, a woman who they'd only seen in passing on the street, would drop their new, baby brother off at the house. Theophilus, who rarely held any of his daughters, was always the one to carry him inside, before handing him off to Grace Ann to watch. The boy's mother, out of a twisted sort of misplaced respect, never showed her face at their house.

Theophilus broke the news of the family's expansion three months after Roy was born. He came home, sat the family down at the table, and told them of his son's existence. There was no shame and he offered no further explanation. He managed to cut his eyes upward toward Grace Ann, anticipating a word or a glance from her. She would not give him one. Instead, she sat at the other end of the table, holding her head still, her eyes staring, unfocused past her husband's face.

In the privacy of their own bedroom, away from their daughters, Grace Ann had expressed her displeasure when Theophilus first learned his mistress was pregnant.

"Meh know is yuh who mek de muney but how de people dem look pon me knowing anudda woman carryin a chil' fah mi husband? Yuh shame me and de girls dem."

Theophilus, who had been avoiding eye contact, looking in the opposite direction, finally turned to face his wife.

"Yuh an' de girls dem can be shame 'ere in de 'ouse or yuh can be shame in de streets."

That was the last they spoke of it.

Constantine peered at Roy, bundled in his blankets and smiled warmly down at him. She knew this little brother wasn't her mother's child but she loved Roy anyway. Boy children were a novelty to her and being the former baby of the family, she relished the role of big sister. As Roy got older, Constantine would concoct impromptu lessons, which she would deliver diligently to her brother. And when it was time for the exam, she'd see how it had all been in vain. Then she'd sit the five-year-old down for as long as he'd stay still to lecture him in the same disappointed tones the nuns used with her classmates when they failed to grasp a new concept.

One Saturday, right before Theophilus came back with Roy by his side, Constantine started feeling ill. Instead of running around preparing the lesson for her little brother, she found herself shuffling around the house, sullen. She had no reason to be sad. But she couldn't seem to escape the cloud.

With each passing hour a slight, dull pressure weighed against her insides, starting from what she thought was the pit of her stomach and traveling to the opening of an area Grace Ann had dubbed her "jelly pum pum." The nickname only lasted until Constantine had started growing pubic hair. Then it was retired and given to Hilda's baby girl. Now any talk that had to do with her vagina was about maintenance and cleanliness.

Today, she was clean but experiencing a new, odd sensation. The pressure she felt wasn't stagnant. It lingered and throbbed slightly, almost issuing a warning, sounding the alarm that her body, emotions, and the bleached white drawers she was wearing were in the process of changing forever.

Later in the day, feeling a bit slimy in between her legs, Constantine went to the bathroom. She pulled down her panties, completely unprepared for the sight that awaited her. A dark, earthy-colored spot soiled the inside of her underwear. She stood, stunned for a few seconds, inspecting it, trying to figure out what it was. It was the color of a bowel movement without the smell or consistency. Once she'd gotten over the shock, she spent the next twenty minutes pouring water from the bucket and scrubbing. Constantine rubbed and rubbed, straining her little biceps. Every time she thought she'd gotten the stains out, she'd hold her underwear up to the light only to see that a mark, which she might have been simply imagining at this point, remained.

Finally exhausted, she relented, realizing that her underwear would never be that crisp, white color again. She threw the panties out, washed in between her legs, and put on a new pair. She felt clean for a couple of hours only to go back to the restroom and find a second pair ruined.

She didn't know what was happening to her. Ten years old and unable to control her bowels? She couldn't tell anyone about this. They would think she was going mad. Instead, throughout the day she just kept washing up, putting wet panties up against her skin.

At night, when it was time for her to go to sleep, she wrapped a wash rag around the crotch of her panties, put on her white nightdress, and climbed into bed. Constantine felt like she slept for five minutes before a stronger, sharper pressure from her abdomen woke her. She attempted to roll over and the slickness between her legs caused them to slip away from each other too quickly. She got up and rushed to the bathroom for what seemed like the thirtieth time that day.

Lifting her white nightdress, she found blood—red, watery blood—running down her leg. Seeing the life gush out of herself so strongly, she gasped. Constantine knew then that she was dying.

Losing this amount blood in a day's time was just too much for a child to survive. Constantine washed herself up again, wrapping the same rag around her underwear, and rinsed the still-wet stains out of her nightdress. She wrung it out as best she could and slipped back into it.

The nightdress clung to the mounds of flesh that had started developing months earlier on her chest. They didn't resemble the breasts her mother and sisters had, so everyone called them mosquito bites. This nightdress was Constantine's favorite, and now that she'd removed the stains, she figured it would be suitable as the last outfit she'd ever wear.

Constantine grabbed some old rags and went outside to the veranda to talk and pray to God before it was time for her to go.

Before she could thank Him for the short ten years she'd had on this earth, tears sprang to her eyes. She intended to go quietly so her mother wouldn't have to watch her suffer but the injustice of dying so young overtook her and she bawled. It was a cry full of fear and confusion. It was raw and almost animalistic, desperate and powerful at the same time. Hearing herself make these noises only frightened Constantine more. She curled up on the floor of the veranda, her body shaking. With each sob, fresh blood leapt out from between her legs.

After five minutes, hearing the strange yet undeniable sound of a child, her child, crying on her front porch, Grace Ann came running out onto the veranda to see Constantine crumpled on the floor. Before she could even wonder why she was outside in the middle of the night, she dashed to her side and knelt down to inspect her daughter. Grace Ann's eyes had gone wild with a mixture of fear and concern as she uncurled her daughter's twisted figure on the ground.

"Constantine, wha's de mattah?"

Another wail seeped out as Constantine thought about how to tell her mother that she was dying. She opted for softer words, describing what she had been experiencing all day, the constant blood, the constant washing. Grace Ann was silent throughout the whole story, her face easing as she recognized her daughter's perceived ailment.

"Meh nah mak it truh de night," Constantine concluded.

She lifted her gown to show her mother the blood running down her leg.

Grace Ann squirmed uncomfortably. It was a lot for a girl her age. Her sisters had started their periods much later. But these things were on no particular schedule. Now, everybody in the house was grown. With her lips turned slightly upward, her eyes softening, Grace Ann tilted her head back slightly and let out a short, burst of unsmiling laughter.

Constantine's fear and sadness immediately transformed into confusion. It wasn't the reaction she was expecting.

"Constantine, yuh nah die. Yuh jus seein your period."

With all of those women in the house, Grace Ann assumed Constantine would have learned about the menstrual cycle by proximity alone. This girl didn't even know to be looking for it. Grace Ann looked away from Constantine, ashamed of her oversight.

She should have done better but now she had to concentrate on getting Constantine off the porch before the little girl's blood stained the wood.

As she was helping her up, she stifled a chuckle. She had to admire this child. Even something as natural and burdensome as a period she managed to turn into an adventure.

She knelt down and kissed her dramatic daughter on the top of her plaited head as she led her back into the bathroom.

Constantine was relieved to know she wasn't dying but she wasn't exactly elated to learn that every month she'd feel this same pain and discomfort. Every month she'd lose enough blood to weaken a grown man. There would be no more hopping around during that time, no climbing trees and running after her little brother. She'd have to wear a sanitary belt and, as she quickly learned, too much movement left it unstable and insecure. And most importantly, now more than ever, she had to make sure she kept herself clean. Grace Ann warned her that she needed to wash at least three times a day when she was seeing her period. As she helped Constantine clean up her nightgown, Grace Ann stopped in mid-motion to tell her a rule, an understood fact of life, among all women: "If yuh can smell yaself, yuh know den da next person already smell yuh."

There were few things worse than having someone smell you. Your man could step out at night, your daughter could bear a child from a no-count man, and your husband could bring his outside child to stay in your home every weekend. But having someone smell you was the greatest shame.

Constantine emerged from the bathroom having been schooled and equipped with the knowledge of the ways in which she was beginning her gradual transition into womanhood.

Now that she was bleeding, Grace Ann had a new name for Constantine's vagina: "Fishy."

It was more of a warning than an actual descriptor. She was *never* to smell like this.

Once Constantine had gotten cleaned up and her sanitary belt was fastened into place, both she and Grace Ann drifted off into an uncomfortable sleep. Constantine, because of the throbbing in her uterus, and Grace Ann for the throbbing in her heart at the realization that her youngest was no longer a child.

She was entering the dangerous years. The same years that had tripped up Hilda. Grace Ann knew that in a short while her opinion and approval wouldn't be the only one her baby girl sought. All too soon, she'd be interested in the boys. And she knew, as all women do, that the boys would only cause her daughter heartache.

1931, Eleven

Though she would eventually grow to know the truth, at the time, Constantine truly believed the emergence of her period also marked the arrival of her womanhood. And just as her mother feared, when she started seeing her period, she started seeing the boys. The same boys who she had viewed as too stupid to pay any mind, with their idiotic games and streams of shallow insults, suddenly appeared less aggravating and more intriguing.

Ennis Tawkins was one of these boys. Constantine had known Ennis since they had started primary school together. And as long as she'd known him, no one had ever called him by his first name. To his teachers, peers, and eventually even his parents, he was just Tawkins, like he'd enlisted in the military at the age of eleven.

The formality suited him. Even as a kindergartner, when everyone else returned from recess disheveled, Tawkins kept his uniform spotless. In class, he checked and double checked his schoolwork, whispering to himself, before he turned it in. Whenever Constantine, searching for a brief distraction from her schoolwork, would look two rows behind her at Tawkins's desk, his eyes would never meet hers. Only the tight kinks on the top of his head were visible as he hovered over his work, the tip of his bright salmon-colored tongue peeking out between two thin, dark lips. Through the years, the two hardly ever spoke to one another beyond an occasional hello or inquiry about a test grade. They thought about each other frequently though, plotting constantly to outdo the other.

Every year, minutes before she and her classmates were sent home for Christmas break, their teachers would tape a piece of paper containing their academic ranking in the corner of the chalkboard. Constantine would maneuver her way through the throng of students crowded at the board, to see where her name had fallen on the list. She was always in one of two places, either right below Tawkins, in second place, or right above him, in first. After first grade, Tawkins never checked the list himself. Whenever Constantine walked away from the chalkboard, her sly smile or sour scowl told him exactly where he stood.

But Tawkins's intelligence and passion for perfection didn't keep him from being well-liked, particularly by the girls. Years ago, when they first started attending school, just two years removed from the nursery, an overzealous girl named Maybel claimed Tawkins as her boyfriend. And though he didn't protest initially, he broke up with Maybel three days later after she received low marks on her spelling test. He didn't want a girlfriend, not even a pretend girlfriend, who wasn't bright. It was ice cold. And while Maybel cried herself to sleep that night, the rest of the girls in their class, with the exception of Constantine, thought of ways to convince Tawkins that they were worthy of filling the vacancy.

By the time they were reaching the end of primary school, many of the students were preparing to take exams. These weren't like regular tests, or even finals. The results of these exams would determine whether or not a student would be allowed to continue on with their secondary education. So, much to the chagrin of his female classmates, Tawkins was focused on his lessons. The same was true for Constantine. She had had a couple pretend boyfriends for a few days as well. But she had outgrown that game. It was nothing but a popularity contest. Plus, she was convinced, now that she was seeing her period, she was too grown for those type of activities.

This year, like all the other years before, she would be competing against Tawkins to see who had the best scores. But this was also the year her wandering eyes stood in the way of her usual focus. From the very beginning of the school year Constantine noticed that when she'd look around the room, she'd meet Tawkins's eyes instead of the top of his head. They were eyes that were just a little too light brown for his almost blue-black skin. The first few times she caught Tawkins looking back at her, she brushed it off, thinking perhaps he was just letting his mind rest by staring at no one in particular.

But it kept happening.

Constantine kept turning around to gaze at him, curious to see what he was doing, how he was faring with his schoolwork; and more times than not, he was staring right back at her. Of course, once they'd locked eyes, Constantine immediately turned away so he wouldn't think she was looking intentionally. At first the looks were purely innocent. Constantine was just being nosy. But within a week's time, the behavior had become a compulsion. She had to look at him, to know if he was looking at her too.

When their eyes would meet, there was a weird magnetism. Her focus on surrounding objects blurred, his too-light eyes snapped into focus, and the thoughts swirling around in her mind slowed to a crawl as she stared. And he stared too. It seemed like those extended looks lasted several minutes. But after she deliberately pulled herself out of the honeyed haze, redirecting her thoughts back to her lessons, she'd find they were only seconds.

The two played the eye-contact sport for weeks. It got to the point that before she would even turn around, she knew when Tawkins was staring at her. She could feel his eyes studying the back of her head with the same intensity he had once devoted to his lessons.

In her eleven-year-old mind, Constantine assumed that the two of them would go on forever like that. It was clear there was a connection between them that didn't need words. Speaking of those fixed looks would only ruin them.

But Tawkins thought differently.

After weeks of staring, he sent his friend Lloyd Jones to play matchmaker. Though it hadn't occurred to Tawkins, Lloyd was perfect for this job. With his slightly rounded stomach and just enough rose in his mocha-colored cheeks, he looked the part of a Jamaican cupid.

After running the entire length of the recreational area to reach Constantine, Lloyd's white uniform shirt was weighted with sweat. And though he stood in front of her with something to say, he rested his hands just below the hem of his blue shorts, sucking wind. Once he'd collected enough air, he didn't waste any time with small talk.

"Yuh like mi friend Tawkins?"

Constantine, stunned by the question, jerked her head back in mock indignation. Trying to buy herself some time, she said the first word that wouldn't incriminate her.

"What?!"

The question was dangerous. She tried to display annoyance, but her face revealed the true nature of her emotions as she tried to craft an appropriate response. Wondering how he had known that she liked Tawkins, she thought maybe he'd seen them looking at each other. Still, it was none of his business. And in her irritation, she lied to him.

"No, meh nah like Tawkins."

It never occurred to her that Tawkins could have been the one who sent Lloyd over.

It wasn't until she saw Lloyd's look of confusion and then disappointment that she put it together. And just as she was about to open her mouth and offer some type of explanation, Lloyd took a deep breath and ran back across the yard, directly to Tawkins. Constantine watched helplessly from across the playground as Tawkins's shoulders slumped. He nodded briefly before looking right at her. She wanted to move toward him, tell him that she'd lied. But she was paralyzed. And within the next second, Tawkins turned on his heel and headed back into their classroom.

For the rest of the day, she didn't feel his eyes on her back. When she thought her intuition might be off, she turned around only to see the top of his head, hovered over his work.

That evening, as she went back into her room to remove her uniform, Constantine avoided the mirror, unable to face herself. If refusing dinner were an option, she would have opted out. But instead she ate her food without tasting it, speaking no more than she had to. Once she had cleaned her plate, she went straight to her room and lay across her bed, replaying the look of dejection on Tawkins's face earlier that day.

That night, lying in bed, listening to her sister snoring, Constantine thought of a plan to erase that look from his face. She'd wake up a bit earlier so she could part and braid her hair. While Constantine looked best in her favorite cotton dress and patent leather shoes, the nuns wouldn't even let her walk through the gate if she weren't wearing her white shirt and navy blue skirt. There wasn't much she could do with the uniform but she could wear last year's shirt now that it was tighter than it had been last summer. The shirt's snug fit would help her to showcase the breasts that were no longer mosquito bites. In the morning, she'd roll the waistband of her skirt under just a little to make it shorter and during their recreational period, she'd walk up to Tawkins and tell him straight to his face that she'd lied to Lloyd, that she did like him. By the time she returned home the next day, Tawkins would be her boyfriend. With thoughts of redemption on her mind, Constantine drifted off into a peaceful sleep.

The next morning she lathered her wash rag until suds ran down her arm, then scrubbed until her skin was nearly raw. To ensure that she smelled pleasant, she snuck into her mother's room and rubbed a bit of her khus khus perfume on the sides of her neck. Her old uniform shirt was tighter than she remembered, particularly under her arms. With the fabric so close to her skin, it was nearly cutting off her circulation but it would have to do. She tried to roll the skirt up around the waistband but her hips hadn't come in yet and the skirt kept slipping. Lastly, right before she walked out of the door, she brushed her teeth, hard, gagging on the toothbrush when she pushed it too far back as she brushed her tongue. Constantine steadied herself so she wouldn't vomit. Lastly, she carefully laced her shoes before heading out the door.

Before she even stepped into her classroom, Constantine scanned the room frantically. Up until today, it had been simply a place of learning. But now, it was a battlefield. Every move had to be calculated and carefully executed. As she slowly removed her supplies from her school bag and settled into her seat, Constantine rehearsed the lines she'd deliver later that day, occasionally looking up to see if Tawkins had walked in yet.

He hadn't. Five more minutes passed and Constantine dropped the cool act. She scanned the room desperately. With each person that walked in, she swung her head around, stretching the limits of an already too tight shirt, hoping it was Tawkins. A pang of nervousness rippled through her skin as she thought of the possibility of him not showing up today. Their teacher, Sister Carter, a pretty, young, shapely woman despite her habit and matronly robes, was heading to the board now. While the boys turned to watch Sister Carter's behind jiggle as she wrote, Constantine began to worry. Where was he?

Just as she started to call the roll, Tawkins strolled into the room, his demeanor the exact opposite of Constantine's frazzled state. He apologized to Sister Carter for his tardiness and took a seat. For as long as she'd been expecting him, Constantine couldn't even wait until he got settled in his seat before she turned around and glared at him, silently asking, *"Where the hell have you been?"* This time he looked right back at her with a stale expression. Even if his face wasn't as soft as it'd been before, at least he was acknowledging her presence. Just as Constantine was about to snap herself out of that familiar haze, she noticed the corners of Tawkins's mouth turn upward into a knowing smirk. Constantine's eyes widened, wondering what the sly smile meant. In her confusion, she hadn't realized that she'd completely turned away from the board. Sister Carter, who had just asked the class a question, called on Constantine to answer it, since she obviously wasn't paying attention. "Constantine, wha's yuh ansah?"

She turned around mortified, completely oblivious to the conversation that had preceded this public scolding.

"Meh sorry Sister Carter. Could yuh please repeat the question?"

"Constantine are yuh 'ere wid us today?"

Her classmates sniggered through their fingers. Constantine swiveled her body to face forward again but not before checking Tawkins's reaction. He wouldn't give her one and instead looked straight ahead, waiting for Sister Carter to resume the lesson.

He might have been able to concentrate, but the school day was a wash for Constantine. The whole morning all she thought about was what she was going to say in the school yard. She ran the scripts over and over in her head. She'd tell him that she lied to Lloyd because she wanted to keep -- whatever was going on between them--private and special. But then she thought that sounded too forward. She thought maybe she'd turn the thing back around on him and ask why he'd sent Lloyd instead of asking her himself. Or she'd just outright ask whether he liked her or not. Eventually, she decided a combination of the three was the way to go. She'd ask why he sent Lloyd over and then, just as he was stumbling, trying to think of his answer, she'd interrupt him dramatically to say that she'd lied, that she did like him. Then, as to not be too forward, she'd leave the part about asking to be her boyfriend up to him.

As soon as she'd decided on a course of action, she had a terrifying thought. What if she'd misinterpreted the whole thing? What if Tawkins didn't like her at all? What if Lloyd was just asking out of his own curiosity? He could have run across the yard and told Tawkins anything. Perhaps the look of dejection had nothing to do with her or her lie.

The doubt overshadowed all the feelings of excitement she'd felt that morning. As the day dragged on, the determination and confidence she'd had earlier seeped out of her. When their recess rolled around, all that was left was doubt and fear. So Constantine decided she wasn't going to say anything at all. Instead, she strolled staring at the shoes she'd polished specially for today, trying not to look at anyone, especially Tawkins. As the minutes passed, she steadily convinced herself that she'd fabricated the whole thing. Even though Tawkins was always looking at her in class, maybe that was just some type of weird habit that had nothing to do with attraction.

Constantine spotted the painted rock she and her classmates had used as a meeting point when they were young enough to still appreciate games like tag and hide-and-go-seek. She made a beeline toward it and used it not for recreation but for reflection. Before she sat down, she unrolled the hem of the skirt, which the nuns had failed to notice, and then smoothed the back of it, letting out a disgusted snort.

Then, just like something out of a melodramatic picture, she started singing the saddest song she knew, an American song: Ethel Waters's "Am I Blue." She hummed it first. Then whispered a few lyrics. And though the words hardly applied to her situation—Ethel was singing about a man who was actually hers before he decided to leave—it seemed fitting at the time.

> *Without a warning I found he was gone.*
> *Why did he do it, how could he do it?*
> *He never done it before.*
> *Am I blue? Am I blue?*

What started off as a muted hum had turned into something like a performance as Constantine, sang from her diaphragm, squinting her eyes to push the notes out. And just as she was immersing herself in the melancholy, rocking side to side as teardrops threatened to fall from her eyes, she felt a tap on her shoulder.

Mortified at the thought of anyone seeing her so emotional, she blinked back the tears before turning around to face the intruder. Whoever it was they stood directly in front of the sun and Constantine had to shield her eyes to make out the features. As she started putting pieces of the face together, she realized it was Tawkins. Her stomach lurched. Had Tawkins heard her singing that song? She tried to hold her face still as all the questions she had been longing to ask him danced through her head.

But even if she'd wanted to speak, she couldn't. So she just waited silently for him to say what he'd come all this way to.

"Constantine, yuh okay?"

She nodded and managed some words. "Meh do all righ'."

This was the first time she'd ever heard him say her name, or at least the first time it meant something to her. Her name in his mouth sounded different.

Constantine had always hated her name. She thought it was obnoxious, too long and too formal for a young girl like her. And it didn't go over all that well among her peers either. But hearing it cascade out of Tawkins's mouth, she had a new appreciation for it. She would have been satisfied reflecting on this sweetness a bit longer, but his next question halted her thoughts.

"Yuh did mean wha yuh say to Lloyd yestaday?"

She'd so convinced herself that Tawkins didn't like her that again she looked for words that wouldn't betray her true feelings. "Wha meh did say tuh Lloyd?"

"Yuh know, that yuh nah like me. Is dat true suh?"

His voice was strong and purposeful but even with the sun blocking the definition of his features, she could hear the slightest sting of rejection. Constantine sighed deeply. She couldn't avoid the truth any longer. She wanted Tawkins to know that she liked him. She just never imagined herself saying it out loud to his face. "No, it nah true." That was all she could manage. She wanted to say, "It nah true Tawkins. Meh like yuh," but she wasn't ready to say his name out loud yet. Her emotions would be wrapped around every syllable.

At her admission, Tawkins sighed, smiled fully, and then motioned for Constantine to scoot over so he could sit down on the rock next to her. "Good, because meh like yuh too. And meh wan ask yuh fi go steady."

It took Constantine a while to speak over the excited chatter flittering around in her head. But she figured this official request required a verbal response. So through a grin and a short giggle, she managed to say yes.

She had a real boyfriend. Not the ones she used to keep in kindergarten but a real boyfriend. She and Tawkins had made it official by holding hands for the rest of recess, away from the watchful eyes of the Sisters. Later that day, she shared the news with a couple of girlfriends. And later in the week, after she'd been holding the secret of Tawkins for three days, she decided it was time for her to tell her mother.

Constantine got home to find her mother in the kitchen putting the finishing touches on the escovitch fish, rice and peas, and the callaloo they were having for dinner that evening.

Grace Ann turned from the stove once she heard her youngest step in. The way she stood there, her fingers resting softly on her lips and her eyes darting upward and then back and forth, let her know the girl had something to tell her.

Constantine, who had yet to say good evening, picked at the imaginary dirt under her naturally gray nail beds. When she finally looked up, she saw her mother staring down at her, eyebrows raised, waiting for her to unburden herself.

"Mumah, yuh evah did like a boy?"

It never occurred to Constantine that Grace Ann might actually like her father. They fluctuated between cordiality and contempt. Instead, Constantine was asking if a boy had ever consumed her thoughts or sent pricks and surges of delight through her stomach that made her feel foolish and cherished at the same time.

Grace Ann knew what she meant, had even experienced it. She had those pleasant pricks with the father of her first two children, before she was a married woman. She had loved him and thought he felt the same about her. But the way the relationship ended, with her pregnant and alone, it wasn't a feeling she wanted any of her daughters to know. Love was too costly for a woman.

She was too late for Hilda. Grace Ann hadn't been firm enough with her. When she heard the whisperings and rumors of her sneaking around with the rusty-kneed neighborhood boys, she should have run her to church. Instead, she prayed for her in her own room and tried to issue warnings of trouble she couldn't save her from. But it had all fallen on deaf ears as Hilda was unmarried and pregnant with her first child just two years later.

Grace Ann thought she had at least a few more years to start talking about the boys with Constantine. But the child had a bad habit of rushing to be grown. And though she saw the newness and excitement in Constantine's eyes, Grace Ann looked at her at eleven-year-old, her last child, and also saw her being seduced, used up, and abandoned.

And instead of celebrating the exciting, new feelings she was experiencing, she interrogated her. "Why? Yuh does tink yuh like a likkle boy at school nah?"

At eleven, Constantine failed to pick up on the shift in body language and tone. She just knew her mother would be happy for her. Still, the news was too good to surrender so easily. She smiled sheepishly, directing her eyes to the floor, shrugging her shoulders, wanting her mother to work for this delicious secret.

Instead, Grace Ann pounced, almost hissing:

"Mek meh tell you somethin', now is no time fi be concerned bout de boys dem." Grace Ann narrowed her eyes, spittle spraying from her thin lips as she sputtered, each syllable more powerful than the last. "Dey are liars, and all dem wan do is get yuh into truhble. Yuh mek sure yuh keep yuh focus on yuh books. Yuh undastand?"

By the time she had finished her tirade, Grace Ann was wheezing. Constantine stood there, her bottom lip slipping away from her top one, allowing the shock to seep out of her system. Her mother was supposed to share in the frothing happiness she felt in having her first, real boyfriend. But Grace Ann's widened eyes, tight jaw, and desperate reach for the cigarette in the pocket of her house dress let Constantine know she would not.

Constantine's brow furrowed trying to categorize her mother's reaction. While she was certainly disappointed to know she couldn't share this moment with her, she wasn't upset. She pitied her. It was clear that she had never experienced this type of joy with a man. She figured it must be painful to watch her young daughter experience something so magical when she, in her old age, could not even imagine it. Constantine suspected that her mother was a bit jealous of her own child.

Of course that notion was absurd. Grace Ann knew full well what Constantine was feeling. And while she certainly wished she had more of her daughter's facety nature, she couldn't be envious of the pain that she knew awaited her and so she pitied her daughter as well.

The conversation set a precedent with these two. While Grace Ann thought she was doing her duty, protecting her daughter from imminent anguish, Constantine learned that when it came to matters of men and emotion, she couldn't come to her mother. A boundary had unknowingly been erected and while Constantine would surely need her mother's advice and expertise later on, she would always reference this conversation, remembering the vitriol in her words.

1936, Sweet Sixteen

Though Constantine couldn't have predicted it and Grace Ann surely wouldn't have believed it to be possible, the innocent childhood crush between Tawkins and Constantine blossomed instead of wilted during adolescence. In the beginning he brought her candy to school and they ate lunch together, holding hands under the table. Then, once they were a bit older, Grace Ann begrudgingly allowed Tawkins to take Constantine out to the beach and to the track meets at their school.

Constantine mocked Tawkins's military rigidity, tickling him when he was concentrating too hard or suggesting they go for a walk when the pressures of his young life seemed too great. And once things were properly put into perspective they went back to studying, taking breaks to kiss as they read the week's lesson. There was still the undeniable competition between the two of them. But now that they were dating one another, they allowed their union to make each of them better students. When Constantine received an A on her math test and Tawkins had gotten a B, he congratulated her sincerely but he also reviewed her work, hoping to emulate her success.

At the end of the school day, for years now, Constantine and her girlfriends would huddle in the school yard to determine what they would be doing that weekend. When they were younger, they chatted about what they wished they could do. And now that they were young women, with more freedom and savvy, they talked about what they'd actually do. Gradually, Constantine stopped attending those weekly gatherings. She would say the same thing she had said the week before: she was spending time with Tawkins. She'd grown tired of politely declining and the friends, who were gradually becoming more and more like strangers, were tired of extending pointless invitations.

In her naivety, she didn't miss them. The things that she used to share with them, she now discussed with Tawkins, a feat she never thought possible with a boy or man. But as far as she was concerned, he was a different breed, nothing like her father or the other men who viewed their girlfriends and wives as sustenance to be expelled and discarded once they had gotten everything they needed. For weeks, months, and then years, Tawkins had proven that he saw more in her and would treat her accordingly.

Though she didn't share this with Tawkins, or anyone else, in the rare moments when she had the room to herself, she envisioned her wedding. She'd send off to England to have a dress made of lace. She saw the two of them making love, buying a house and then making a home together. She knew, in a marriage with him she wouldn't be ignored and disrespected. And after the two had set the standard for love in Jamaica, Grace Ann would have to admit that she had been wrong about this particular man.

On yet another evening spent thinking about Tawkins, Constantine was so swept up in her feelings that she subconsciously released a sweet, heavy sigh.

Olga, who was just five years older than Constantine, knew that sound. It was pregnant with a bittersweet longing. Olga, who had a boyfriend of her own, turned to Constantine with a wide, knowing grin on her face. "Wha yuh sigh for? Yuh thinkin bout Taaaaawkins, nuh?"

Constantine's body tingled at the mention of his name. She clenched her lips around her teeth trying to hide her guilty grin. "No, meh nah thinkin bout 'im."

Olga bust out laughing. "So yuh luhve 'im?"

It was a question Constantine had asked herself several times before. Though she wasn't necessarily ready to tell Tawkins, she knew the answer. "Yes, meh luhve 'im."

As the words fell from her lips, Olga sprang up from the spot on her bed and came over to sit next to her baby sister. She leaned in closer so their parents wouldn't overhear. "Yuh and Tawkins . . . unu do it yet?"

Exasperated, Constantine sighed and rolled her eyes. Naturally, it was something she'd thought about. And something Tawkins had mentioned once or twice. But she had her reservations. "No, we nah do it yet."

"Well, wha unu waitin fah?"

Constantine, feigning shock, turned abruptly to her sister, her mouth hanging open. "How ya mean? 'im ah wait pon me. Meh nah ready yet."

Olga kissed her teeth. "Yuh neva feel ready. Yuh mus' just do it."

Constantine's right eyebrow raised in piqued curiosity. Though she'd never considered this before, she realized Olga could help her with her questions. Her mother, who went to church every Sunday morning and was casting warnings and disappointment to her daughters every Sunday afternoon, would be of no practical help. "It did hurt yuh?"

Olga thought for a minute, her eyes darting upward as she recalled losing her own virginity. "It a likkle uncomfurtible at firs but den yuh bawdy relax and it nice, real nice." Olga swiveled her hips slightly as she remembered. She smiled to herself and then turned back to Constantine.

"Tawkins nah bodda yuh fah sex?"

"We talk bout it. Meh tell 'im meh let 'im know when meh ready."

Olga nodded, suddenly turning serious. "Take yuh time."

Constantine was confused by the contradiction. "Yuh did feel guilty when yuh and Ellis did it?"

"With Ellis no. But with Manning meh did feel turrible."

Constantine rolled her eyes recalling Manning. Despite objections from the entire family, Olga swore she was in love with Manning. So much so that she couldn't see he ran with the wrong crowd and away from any type of honest work. Constantine remembered how blind her sister had been to all this man's flaws until he was arrested for stabbing another man in the street. Then she saw who he really was. Recalling the nights she watched her sister crying over that no good man, Constantine vowed then, silently to herself, that no matter how much she loved Tawkins, she'd never be beyond logic.

**

Constantine thought perhaps her sister knew deep down, before she even slept with Manning, that he was the wrong one. Thankfully, she didn't have that feeling with Tawkins. She knew he wouldn't disappoint or embarrass her, the way Manning had with Olga when he was hauled off to jail. Not only was Tawkins different, he had known Constantine long enough not to humiliate her. And there was immense comfort in that. She didn't know exactly when or how the two would find themselves alone long enough for anything to happen but Olga had helped make her decision.

Not much had changed from the days she spent play teaching her little brother, Roy. Years ago, when her toes were just beginning to scrape the ground from her high wooden school chair, her classmates would tap her quickly and ask her to instruct them on their class work. She'd lean over or turn around and attempt to explain, but it wouldn't be long before a sister would scold or threaten to paddle her for what they presumed was cheating. Finally at thirteen, it had been Sister Marie who recognized that Constantine had the same gift the Sisters possessed.

And instead of punishing her, she asked her if she wanted to assist the other teachers in their classrooms with the younger students twice a week. Constantine observed them first, relearning the lessons from her earlier years. Then on her first day, she stood up in front of the classroom, mindful not to let the back of her uniform graze the chalkboard, feeling like she was merely imitating an adult. But after a week, looking in the students's eyes she was reminded of Roy. Now that her father was no longer paying Roy's school fees or supporting him in any other kind of way, his visits to the house had stopped completely. It had been years since he'd been around but she felt connected to him through these students. She liked the way their eyes glimmered and their backs and shoulders curved in comfort and familiarity when she entered the room. Now that she had been assisting for years, they'd come to learn that she didn't require the same posture the nuns felt was essential to learning.

In her last year of school, Sister Marie had spent many late nights and early morning prayer times thinking of about ways Constantine could continue nurturing her talent. She had already passed her secondary school exams and could very well continue her schooling instead of marrying off to stay at home and raise a bunch of children, as was the most common and respected life for a young, Black, Jamaican woman.

After weeks of searching, Sister Marie felt she'd finally stumbled across the right opportunity for Constantine. And the next day, after the students had been dismissed and Constantine was packing up her lesson plans to go home, she decided to share it with her. "Constantine, yuh know yuh have a great way wit de chirren dem?"

The corners of Constantine's lips immediately slid upward at the compliment. "Thank you, Sister Marie."

"Meh really feel like yuh could become a teacher if thas wha yuh want."

Constantine was paralyzed hearing her unutterable thoughts articulated by someone else.

And for the first time, in front of another person, Constantine was honest about what she wanted for her life. "Meh would love tuh become a teachah."

Encouraged by her willingness, Sister Marie explained the process. She told Constantine that she would have to continue her own schooling before she would be allowed to teach. She gave her two thin pamphlets detailing the courses she would have to take and their costs. Additional schooling meant additional money. But Constantine eagerly skimmed the glossy pages before placing them gently in her bag. She'd present the options to her father soon. He might fuss a bit, but she knew he had the money.

She practically skipped out of that room, her cheeks beginning to hurt from the smile she couldn't seem to remove from her face. As she glided out of the room, she passed the domestic work her sisters, with little education and children to raise, had been forced to do, despite their talents. She narrowly missed being at the mercy of a husband's every whim because without an income she didn't have a say. As she stepped into the sun, she walked into a life that would be more fulfilling than she had imagined.

She was just about to turn on the road that led to her street when she saw Tawkins walking several feet ahead of her, the dust obscuring the view of his dress shoes. Constantine, in her excitement, clutched her books and bags and took off in a short sprint to catch up with him.

"Hey!" Constantine shouted, playfully slamming her shoulder into his.

"Hey!" Tawkins returned, pleasantly surprised to see her. Immediately, he noticed the delight she had yet to express. "Whatchu skin yuh teeth fah?"

"Meh jus come from Sister Marie's class. She tell meh she tink meh mek a good teachah. And tell meh bout the schooling meh haffa complete to start workin. Meh been teachin for play for years wid mi brudda, Roy, but now she say dis, it mak me feel I might actually be good at it."

Tawkins nodded and smiled, the width of his grin broadening to match hers. "Of course yuh mek a good teachah. Meh coulda tell yuh dat long ago."

Constantine studied the genuine joy on Tawkins's face and felt a fluttering and then blossoming of gratitude and love. In the overflow of such emotion, she stepped toward him. Still clutching her books in one arm, she slipped her other one around his neck and kissed him hard right there in the middle of the road. He, following her lead, slowly slid his tongue in between her lips, rolling and pressing it against hers once it was inside of her mouth. Constantine pressed her body firmly up against his, trying to completely remove the space between them. With the slick gliding of their tongues and her breasts against his chest, Tawkins experienced a blossoming of his own.

Usually, this would have been the time she parted from him, whether slowly or abruptly, realizing that they had gone too far. But today she didn't pull away. Instead, she dropped the books she was still carrying and wrapped both of her arms around his neck. With no words, just the smacking of their lips and the grasping of her fingertips, she let him know she was ready. Tawkins picked her up swiftly, cradling her legs in his arms, and moved toward the field that lined the road. Leaving their books and belongings in the dirt, Tawkins walked her out several paces. Constantine chuckled at the thrill of the moment, thinking of the story she'd later make Olga beg for. Finally, when he had reached the place he deemed suitable, far enough from any possible onlookers, he knelt down to place her on her back. For a second, Constantine thought about soiling her clothes. The ground was still a little damp from the last rain and she didn't want to dirty her uniform shirt. But before she could protest and suggest another location, Tawkins was leaning over her again, searching and studying her face. Constantine forgot about the shirt. Soon after, the two were kissing again and Tawkins's hands were busy unbuttoning her blouse and then traveling up her thigh, leaving a trial of pleasant pangs in their path. Tawkins's thumb reached the band of Constantine's panties. She took notice of the way the muggy afternoon air hit parts of her that she thought she'd never expose to the daylight.

She'd been so focused on watching this whole scene unfold that it didn't even occur to her that it would be nice of her to help Tawkins get undressed. She reached up and pulled at his belt, unbuttoned his pants, and then unzipped his zipper. He pulled his pants and underwear down to the middle of his calves and straddled her. Just before he lowered himself, Constantine shifted herself slightly, curious to see exactly what he was going to put inside her body. After she found what she'd been looking for, she envisioned herself expanding to accommodate him. Tawkins had aligned himself up properly and just as the tip of him was inside of her Constantine tilted her hips upward to guide him the rest of the way. She waited for the pain so many of her girlfriends had told her she'd feel. But there was none. It took a couple of seconds before she found it enjoyable but it didn't hurt. And once she realized this wasn't going to be a traumatic experience, she lifted her legs to cradle Tawkins, stopped thinking, and started feeling.

Days after that afternoon in the field, Constantine couldn't stop replaying those stolen minutes in her mind. She fluctuated between a sense of sweet recollection, taking pride in what they'd done and shared and the shame she felt having deliberately gone against her mother's and

God's wishes. Though Grace Ann was too prudish to actually explain the details of sex to her daughter, Constantine assumed that her early warnings against the boys were rooted directly in what she and Tawkins had done that evening. So she felt guilty for having been what Grace Ann would have considered less than a lady, but was also thrilled about having become, in her limited understanding of the concept, a woman.

1938, Eighteen

Had Grace Ann known about the festivities her daughter enjoyed in the field, she might have warned her that since Tawkins had gotten what he wanted, she could be sure that he was on his way out of her life. But she would have been wrong. When Tawkins looked at Constantine, he saw the girl who competed with him for the best grades, and the young woman who had helped him improve them. Unlike anything Grace Ann or her daughters had ever seen, Constantine and Tawkins's relationship was fueled by both the sweet innocence of their past childhood and also hopes for the future life they wanted to build with one another. He noticed her hair, styled to perfection and knew he'd be the envy of men who'd wonder how he'd gotten her. He saw the clothes she crafted from her sewing machine and wondered what clothes she'd create for the children they'd certainly have. And on the nights when they went dancing, and he had to drag her off of the dance floor, her shoulders moving to the beat of the very last song, he knew life with her would never be dull.

Constantine looked at Tawkins and regarded him as an anomaly, the type of man a woman would be hard-pressed to find outside of the love songs her father played. But what made him even more magical, was that for all of his wonderment, he could appreciate someone like her. Observing her father's perpetual annoyance with her, Constantine assumed that other men would respond to her in kind. In the first months of her relationship with Tawkins, she diligently tried to hide herself, censoring her language and stifling her opinions so as not to scare off her new boyfriend. But her authentic self would only cower for so long before it came bounding forward. And when Tawkins chuckled instead of condemned her sharp tongue or relished instead of recoiled from the voicing of her opinions, Constantine knew that he was something to be treasured.

On the walk home from school one day, Tawkins told Constantine that he had decided to become a doctor. After her initial happiness subsided, Constantine felt a twinge of anxiety, assuming that once he became a big, fancy doctor, he'd leave and go work in London or America. Days later, unable to dismiss her concerns, she tried to bring it up jokingly. "Meh know once yuh become a doctuh yuh ah go leave meh here on dis island while yuh move away to London or America. Tawkins pulled away from her in shock and disappointment.

"Meh nevah practice outside ah Jamaica." He paused for a moment, weighing his words before continuing. "I don't wan' become a doctah jus tuh get rich or mek mi parents proud. Meh wan' be a doctah tuh help people—my people dem." Tawkins fell silent, casting his eyes toward his shoes.

Constantine searched for something to say to ease the tension she'd created, something that would take the place of an apology.

"Meh nevah know yuh feel so strong," She said softly, lightly touching his arm.

Tawkins looked up at her then, smiling weakly.

"And yuh know meh nevah leave yuh here alone Connie."

She reached out and grabbed his hand and the two continued their walk in silence, confident that all of their problems would be solved this easily.

But just as they were settling into the possibilities of their futures, both as individuals and a couple, there came a hurdle too high for either of them to clear.

Now at eighteen, it was time for Constantine to start the schooling that Sister Marie had talked to her about two years earlier. Before she could sign up for classes she would have to speak to Theophilus again about paying her school fees. She'd mentioned it when Sister Marie first told her, and he, without looking up, had only grunted and nodded. But now there was a greater sense of urgency in her delivery. Constantine didn't anticipate the conversation being a point of contention, she waited until both of her parents were seated at the dinner table to bring it up.

"Poppa, yuh know meh start school next year fi become a teachah and meh ah go need school fees."

Theophilus didn't raise his head from the plate of food in front of him. Constantine sat patiently for a few seconds thinking maybe he was working some figures out in his head. When another few seconds went by and he still hadn't said anything, she assumed he hadn't heard her. So she asked him, "Poppa, yuh nah hear meh? Meh askin yuh bout school fees fi 'elp meh become a teachah."

This time he looked up. "Meh hear yuh but meh nah pay no school fees."

If Theophilus had sent Constantine flying across the room with a stiff backhand, it would have paled in comparison to the pain she felt at his dismissive words. She swallowed down the tears that burned the back of her throat and steadied her voice just enough to utter one, desperate word.

"Why?"

"And waste mi hard earned muney? For wha'? So yuh end up droppin' out when dem fin' out yuh tun up pregnant? Yuh think meh nah know how yuh and Tawkins carry on? Is only a mattah of time before yuh end up like yuh sistah, whole heap of pickney widout a man in sight."

No one was more disappointed than Theophilus when Hilda got pregnant the first time. He was crushed when she had her second child and devastated with her third.

"Meh nah Hilda." Constantine's voice cracked. She willed herself not to blink. She didn't want the tears that had run anxiously to the base of her eye to jump, screaming of her pain as they fell.

"It nah matta. Yuh end up de same way, watch."

Constantine glanced over at Grace Ann, seated at the other end of the table. She seemed to be distancing herself from the room. She had turned away from her husband and his daughter, and was staring out the window. From the way her upper body was vibrating slightly, Constantine could tell her right leg was working feverishly underneath the tablecloth. Knowing that her mother couldn't and wouldn't come to her defense, Constantine couldn't look at her anymore.

As she sat finishing the last few bites of her food, Constantine kicked herself for giving her father so much credit. This was the same man who denied his only son a decent education. She snorted softly and then shook her head at his cruelty and the faith she'd put in him.

Instead of futilely trying to persuade him from his decision, Constantine stood, washed her plate in the sink and then spun on her heel, moving swiftly to her bedroom.

As Theophilus watched Constantine stride out of the room, he silently celebrated the victory over his biggest adversary in the house. For years, he suspected Constantine fancied herself his equal. He smirked to himself, thinking of all the times she had bucked his authority as her father and head of the household. Instead of listening and obeying silently, she had argued back, like a grown man. Admittedly, she had often done so wittily and even convincingly, so much that his only recourse was slapping or striking her to put an end to her noise. Those victories had been hollow; but today, using only his words and his power as a man, he felt vindicated. Just as she was beginning to step into her womanhood, he'd finally shown her that no matter how womanish she thought herself to be, she was nothing compared to a man.

Constantine received his message. But since she was powerless against her own father, she responded to the only other man in her life.

Tawkins was the first person she told about her father's dismissal of her dream and he sympathized with her, even suggesting ways that she could save up money and pay for the schooling herself. But she couldn't hear him over her own disappointment. Constantine knew that Tawkins would be the only one to see his dreams actualized. The friendly competition that had once existed between them had been perverted into a cruel and twisted game she could never win. She resented the fact that his parents were willing to pay for their son's schooling when his father didn't make any more money than hers. She resented *him*, though she knew it was foolish, for going on without her. And though these were things she would never consciously admit it to herself, it didn't make them any less true.

Instead of confiding in him any further, she shut down, attempting unsuccessfully, to pretend like her father's decision hadn't affected her. Tawkins watched as the passion he had once loved about Constantine drained from her face. And she felt the affection that she had for him succumb to the betrayal and anger she felt for her father. They saw each other less and less and when they did manage to spend time together, where she had once been doting, she was now distant.

After several dates, filled with strained conversations, Constantine decided to make an effort.

"Tawkins, meh ah go meet yuh afta yuh class on Monday. And maybe we can tek a walk aftaward."

That afternoon, she curled her hair in his favorite style and wore the paisley printed dress she knew he loved. When he walked out of the classroom, noticing immediately that she'd gone out of her way for him, his eyes creased into slits as he grinned in her direction. Though he appreciated the gesture, it didn't resolve the issue. And while they strolled as they always had, the words they so desperately needed to say, hung heavy over their heads.

Constantine was the first to puncture the silence."How yuh day did go?"

Tawkins nodded slowly in appreciation but responded shortly. "No special kind ah day."

Constantine nodded. The quiet that had once been comfortable and familiar now seemed to issue a warning.

With mannerly obligation, he asked her what she did today. Her face maintaining its lack of expression, Constantine told him that she did the same thing she had done last week around this time. Since Theophilus had dashed her dream of becoming a teacher, Constantine had fallen back on her other talents and started doing hair out of the home Olga shared with her husband Ellis.

Scrambling to make an effort of his own, Tawkins thought about something interesting that happened in class. "Mi teacher assign meh a new lab partnah today, Sheryl."

Tawkins continued telling his story but Constantine couldn't hear anything past the name. She felt her stomach tighten and her temperature rise. Sheryl. As Tawkins explained what they did in class, Constantine imagined that the girl must be fair skinned, with a narrow nose, long, straight hair, and delicate features. And with her looks, she was even more of a prize because she was educated.

The bile in her stomach rose as she thought about this Sheryl getting to spend the time she would have shared with Tawkins had she been allowed to continue her schooling. Constantine surmised that Sheryl must have been bright if her parents continued to pay for her education. And it was only a matter of time before Tawkins saw the value in her too. Soon, he'd be blindsiding her with his new choice.

The thoughts swirled, rushed, and clanged in Constantine's head until she burst, interrupting Tawkins's story. "If yuh wan break up wid me it's fine. But yuh nah haf fi throw anudda woman in meh face."

Tawkins was so stunned by her outburst that he stopped walking. "Constantine, wha' yuh a talk bout? She's jus mi lab partna. Meh nah know de girl."

Any rational woman would have seen Tawkins's reaction and known that she had taken things too far, letting her insecurities get the best of her. But Constantine was beyond rational in this moment. "Meh know is jus a mattah a time before yuh find one of those school girls fi sekkle down wit," she rolled her eyes, her nostrils flaring at the end of her sentence.

Watching the girl he'd grown up with spit words laced with anger and jealousy, when he'd done nothing wrong, Tawkins took a step away from her, watching her standing in front of him as if she were a stranger he'd rather not have met.

Tawkins saw Constantine's chest heaving as she waited for him to respond and wondered how he could escape her, if not this very instant, certainly in the future. That coming Friday, the two had plans to meet up and go to the Silver Slipper Club but if he couldn't even walk down the street with her without getting into an argument, he certainly didn't want to take her out, just so she could act like this in public.

"Uh, yuh know, Connie, meh know we suppose tuh go out Friday but mi fadda wan me help him wid some things aroun de house. So meh nah mek it to Silver Slipper. Meh sorry."

Constantine had been looking forward to Friday. Getting dressed up and dancing was the only time she felt like herself. And though her shoulders sank at the cancellation, she just mumbled a curt, "Fine," in response. At this point, she'd learned to numb herself to the feeling of men disappointing her.

It wasn't until three full days later that Constantine considered the possibility that Tawkins might have been lying about the plans he had with his father. She shrugged at the realization. She knew she had been getting on his nerves and he, understandably, just wanted a break from her. Admittedly, she had been getting on her own nerves lately. She figured the dancing would do her good so she decided to go with her sisters instead. She'd come back from the club rejuvenated and would try to be sweeter to Tawkins and share the feelings she had about the course her life was taking.

That Friday night, Constantine was dating herself. It had been months since she'd felt good and tonight she was going to look nice and dance hard. She hummed to herself as she ran a hot comb through her hair, parting it down the middle to create two barrel curls on the top of her head. She slicked the edges down with grease and a hard brush and then curled the back loosely around her ears. She arched the eyebrows she had been neglecting and put mascara on her lashes, hoping to make the eyes that had been looking drab and lifeless pop again. She carefully spread a berry-wine color on her thin, dark lips and rubbed them together, making sure the color covered every inch. And then, as she'd made a habit of doing, she curled her index and middle fingers at the knuckle, parted them with the bridge of her nose and slid them downward, pulling at the tip.

That night she was wearing a pale blue, chiffon party dress. It was one she had made herself for a special occasion. The dress was fitted on the bodice but had ruffled sleeves and a belled bottom. She'd made sure to include a modest V neck so she'd be able to show a little cleavage.

Constantine took a look at herself in the mirror and laughed, thinking about the days she'd needed to wear too-small shirts to highlight what were once developing breasts. Now, if she so much as sighed too heavily, an areola would pop out for the world to see.

At eighteen, Constantine considered herself a "big 'oman" but Grace Ann still insisted that she have a chaperone when she went out. So she enlisted Olga to go with her. It was all for the better—Ellis would be able to give them a ride in the back of his pickup truck.

When the three of them walked into the Silver Slipper, Constantine felt at home. The place was decorated particularly nicely this evening. It seemed that the chandelier had been polished and the marble floors had been buffed so furiously that they looked wet, and the band was playing her song. Constantine didn't have time to wait for a man to ask her to dance, so she grabbed Olga and pulled her into the center of the room.

As the two twirled and pulled each other, their shoes slipping and sliding across the dance floor, Constantine thought she recognized a familiar face, mid-spin. She steadied herself, feeling her smile fade and her eyes narrow as she identified him. Tawkins.

He wasn't alone.

Tawkins was standing next to the punch bowl looking bored while a woman, who she knew instantly was Sheryl, clasped his elbow trying to make small talk.

Constantine's intuition about Tawkins was right, just a little premature. He hadn't been cheating on her, merely enjoying conversations that didn't come with the headache Constantine had been giving him. After she falsely accused him, he figured, why shouldn't he? Sheryl seemed pleasant enough in lab. So when she suggested that Tawkins take her out dancing, he agreed. He didn't mean for anything to come of it. It was merely an opportunity to go out and have a good time with a woman who wasn't going to sully the evening.

For all his book smarts, Tawkins didn't think too hard about making sure to take Sheryl somewhere other than the Silver Slipper, the very club he and Constantine frequented. He assumed that Constantine was just going to mope around the house, pitying herself as she had been doing for the past few months.

But he was about to learn just how wrong he had been.

Once Constantine spotted Tawkins, she scurried off the dance floor, making sure she avoided his line of vision. In the bathroom, she thought for a second about how she wanted to do this. She could make a scene and dash punch on his clothes, scream and curse and slap the woman who had to be Sheryl. For a second, vengeance seemed appropriate. But breathing deeply for a few more seconds, she realized acting out in public would only make her look like a fool.

Constantine decided she wouldn't let her actions reveal that the blood coursing through her veins was boiling. She smoothed the strands of hair that had been lifted by sweat and checked her makeup. Looking in the mirror, she expected to see a woman who had been broken down. Instead, her anger gave her eyes an unusual fire, belying her devastation.

She walked briskly out of the restroom and across the dance floor, watching as Tawkins's face went from unamused to terrified. His reaction gave her the last bit of confidence she needed to confront him.

As Constantine stood face to face with Tawkins, she turned to size up the girl on his arm. She was cute but certainly no match for her. The girl's bobby pins had slid out of place, lying at strange angles in her head. Her dress hung limply over what appeared to be a decent shape, and though her body language read as if she were excited to be there with him, her eyelids had a natural, heavy droop that made it seem as she were perpetually sleepy.

Constantine dismissed the innocent stranger before turning her attention to the boy she'd known since they were in primary school. Even if Sheryl knew about her, this was his betrayal. And so, playing a role, she skinned her teeth and flashed the young lady a plastic smile. Then, with an icy expression, Constantine looked Tawkins dead in the face and said, "Unu haf a good evening."

Just as he parted his lips to utter her name and explain himself, she turned on her heel and walked away. The cool she maintained as she confronted him, suddenly vanished and she struggled to make it outside before anyone could see the tears beginning to stream down her face, smearing the makeup she'd applied just minutes earlier.

That evening, tears flowed again as she replayed all the times she'd spent with Tawkins. What were once fond memories felt like fantasies she had merely imagined. Tawkins had, despite her faith in him, fulfilled her mother's prophecy. And with reluctant acceptance and a stinging bitterness Constantine acknowledged the truth behind her mother's words: no man was to be trusted.

The next day Tawkins came to her house, a bouquet of flowers in hand, begging for her forgiveness.

Standing on the porch, Constantine loomed over him like God. And while she hoped he felt beneath her, in both position and character, she was also hoping he didn't notice her swollen eyes. She saw the slouch in his shoulders, the shame in his bowed head, the pain in his eyes. She saw it and took pity on him but her ego had been battered and pride had already showed up to lick the wounds.

So she dismissed him. As she watched Tawkins walk down the steps and away from her parents's home, Constantine had no idea she was sending away the first and only romantic love of her life.

By the end of that day, Constantine had sworn off men. Observation and experience had told her all she needed to know about them. She found herself uttering the same words of warning her mother had tried to issue to her all those years ago when she first made mention of her girlhood crush: *They couldn't be trusted.*

Grace Ann watched as her daughter, who had once been dazzled and dizzied by the love of a man, became sluggish and somber in her disappointment. The way she leapt about the house in anticipation of meeting Tawkins or the euphoria from just having seen him was replaced by a sloth-like shuffle as she came in from work every evening. And while a part of Grace Ann took a sick satisfaction in knowing her initial words to her daughter had been right, she also wanted her to return to herself and find another man. Though she had little faith the next one would be any better.

What she neglected to tell her daughter all those years ago in the kitchen was that men were a necessary evil. She had never seen one do right; but as a woman in this country, in this world, she knew her daughters would need them. Grace Ann worried that her daughter's despondent demeanor would repel any man who could potentially wind up being her husband. At eighteen, she knew her daughter would never be more attractive to men than she was now. Constantine couldn't afford and Grace Ann couldn't stand to watch her squander these prime years wallowing in anguish and wasting away in the house.

1941, Twenty-One

After the disappointment of her father and Tawkins, Constantine had concocted an entirely different plan for her life. At night, though her body was physically spent from working all day on her feet as a hairdresser, in the back room of her parents's house, her mind was overstimulated, running wild. Thoughts that would have been checked and dismissed in the daytime thrived and flourished in the night. It was then that she came to the conclusion that she would become a nun. More than dedicating herself to God, Constantine saw nunnery and the vow of celibacy as a way to honorably protect herself from men. The wild thought made so much sense in the night that the very next morning she went to a convent to investigate. Perhaps as a nun, not only could she evade men, she'd be able to become a teacher without her father's money.

Constantine passed the large, pink former hotel, now known as Immaculate Conception Convent, often as a child. But she'd never thought she'd have a reason to climb the cracked stone steps and go inside. Even though she went to a Catholic school, Grace Ann was very clear that she and her sisters were not to be baptized at any Catholic church. As Constantine crossed the threshold into the convent, feeling the coolness of the darkened vestibule, she heard her mother's words. *"We nah Catholic cuh dem place too much fait' in people. Dem a worship Mary and confess dem sins to a man who cyan forgive dem."*

It was only then that Constantine realized she hadn't given much thought to the religious practices. Still, she signaled the nearest Sister.

"Excuse me, Sister. Mi name is Constantine. Meh wondering if yuh could direck meh to someone who could ansah some questions about converting and becoming a nun?"

The Sister, just ten years older than Constantine, looked down at the skirt that stopped mid-calf, up at the makeup which appeared garish next to her own bare face, and up again at the delicately coiffed hairstyle, and rightfully doubted Constantine's commitment.

Still, they weren't in the business of turning people away. And after asking her a few questions, the Sister told Constantine to come back tomorrow when they'd set her up with a sister to shadow to see if she were really cut out for this type of service.

The next day, after a few hours of wearing a habit that seemed to want to distance itself from her head, Constantine began to think this hadn't been such a good idea. And by the end of the day, on their sixth prayer, when Constantine was sure there was nothing left to tell or ask God, she knew.

Constantine left the convent the next day and went right back to doing hair. Each day passed like the one before, long and uneventful as she listened to the predictable gossip from the handful of her regular clients. This one had seen so-and-so's man here. This one was talking about how the other had an odor. Another lamented the fact that she couldn't find a man. They all lobbed their stories at Constantine. Not for her to offer advice, though she did, or even sympathize with them. They just wanted to unload. And so she listened to those same stories for days, weeks, and then months on end.

It wasn't until a day in March that she got to hear a new one.

On this late afternoon, bustling around an unfinished head, Constantine heard Anita, one of her regulars outside the doorway. Ordinarily, she wouldn't have looked up, knowing that Anita didn't have trouble getting her attention once she arrived. But she heard her speaking to someone else, directing them into the salon. She dropped the hand that held the hot comb to her side and she waited with curiosity and alarm, wondering who Anita had brought with her. Constantine noticed the new woman's dress before anything else, the vibrant floral print over a bleached, white background. Had she not been so brown skinned, the woman would have looked like she'd been plucked straight from a Sears and Roebuck catalog.

"Connie, dis is Marie. Meh fin' 'ar on de road. And she tek notice of mi hair and wan know if you can give 'ar de same style."

It was only then that Constantine noticed that this woman was wearing a full hat, with every strand of hair tucked underneath. "Hi Marie," Constantine said flashing a quick smile. "Meh can do yuh hair next. Yuh haf time now? Me dun wid her hair in de nex' half 'our."

"That's fine. Tank you."

Marie took up the newspaper from a small table and looked around for a place to sit. Constantine kept her makeshift beauty shop spotless, but still she worried that lingering dust would ruin Miss Marie's pretty dress.

Once she'd finished with her first client, she directed Miss Marie to come to her chair. Anita, who had just gotten her hair done two days ago and always seemed to be running somewhere, sat still, in the corner of the small shop, her eyes trained on Miss Marie's every move.

Marie, who had seemed a bit put off by the shop's modesty when she first entered, walked toward Constantine with a thinly veiled look of shame and then desperation. "Meh haven't . . . um . . . no one nah look afta mi hair in a long time, yuh know."

Constantine nodded reassuringly, waiting for her to remove the hat. When she did, slowly, almost closing her eyes in anticipation of the judgment, Constantine pursed her lips to stifle the gasp.

Anita didn't take the same precaution. "Oh!"

Both Marie and Constantine shot a look toward her, one of embarrassment and the other scolding.

Miss Marie had just revealed a matted and tangled mess that would have stunned anybody with good sense. At one point the hair had been pressed but between the humidity and her propensity for slicking her coarse hair back into buns, without combing it, she was well on her way to achieving the Rastafari look.

"Meh can fix it," Constantine said quickly. Miss Marie sat down in the chair. Anxious to know more about this woman with the pretty dress and the untidy hair, Constantine struck a balance between asking Miss Marie questions but also volunteering information about herself so she wouldn't feel interrogated. It wasn't long before the two were having a pleasant conversation, with Anita breaking her intense concentration to chime in and comment every once in a while. While their chatter might have sounded trivial to someone else, it only helped Constantine to do better work. The more Marie talked, the better Constantine knew what to do with her hair. When she'd finished, she'd managed to create a sleek up-do with cascading curly tendrils to match the playfulness of Marie's floral dress. Looking at herself in the mirror, Marie took a moment to speak, running her fingers over the oiled and pressed strands.

"Well, wha yuh tink?" Constantine asked, unable to wait for her reaction any longer.

"Meh luhve it! Meh never see mi hair look so good!" Marie, shifting the mirror away from her face, stood up to hug her newfound miracle worker. Constantine returned her embrace, more satisfied with the day's events than she'd been in a long while.

Just as she and Marie were pulling away from each other, Constantine heard the door of her shop creak open again and the unfamiliar clack of a man's shoe sole on the tile and then the soft pinching sound of new leather.

"Oh, Constantine, dis meh brudda Evan," Marie said explaining the unsual presence of a man in this sacred space. "Meh did give him yuh address before meh come ovah here."

"Evan Andrews," the man said offering his hand to Constantine.

Constantine extended hers for the second time that day.

"Constantine Johnson. Pleasuh to meet you."

Constantine couldn't help but let her eyes scan the length and breadth of Evan's body. Like his sister, he was clean, with a suit that seemed to bear no wrinkles or sweat stains. Constantine was aware that Evan was watching her watch him but the euphoria from the day's accomplishment had erased the discretion she would have normally shown. Evan didn't seem put off by the attention.

"Evan, yuh see wha' Constantine did to meh hair?" Marie asked, still admiring herself, oblivious to the fact her brother was more interested in the stylist than the style.

"Meh see. It look nice." Evan answered looking at her only for a second. As casually and as discreetly as possible, given the surroundings, Evan, who towered over Constantine, bent down to whisper in her ear, "Wid de job yuh do here meh know my sistah a come back. But yuh would min' meh coming back . . . by miself sometime?"

Constantine, thrilled to be receiving this attention, felt the blood rush to her cheeks. She smiled sheepishly, her eyes directed to the hot comb on the table. Then, in an effort to express her certainty, she looked up, meeting Evan's eyes before nodding a bit more slowly than usual.

And just that easily, Constantine invited another man into her life.

On their first date, Evan showed up to her parents's doorstep in a long black car that must have just been polished. Constantine assumed it was for the occasion and was flattered. She didn't know yet that it was Evan's custom to have his car polished every Friday morning. From her room, in the back of the house, she watched him extend his long limbs, covered in tailored dress pants, out of his car before he made his way up to their doorstep. She wasn't the only one anticipating his arrival. Constantine had told both her mother and father that Evan was the son of Jamaica's only soap maker. Once Grace Ann learned that such a distinguished guest would cross the threshold into her home, she spent the entire day on her hands and knees cleaning and scrubbing the tiny house. Then, an hour before he arrived to introduce himself, she donned the dress she had starched and pressed for the evening, as if she were the one going on the date. It was she who flung the door open when he knocked, allowing Constantine to make an entrance and Theophilus to project an air of dignified aloofness as he sat in his chair, busying his hands by polishing his already-shiny cane.

Still, when Evan stepped in and introduced himself, Theophilus stood to shake his hand. Seconds after the two men were freed from the other's firm grasp, Theophilus excused himself from the living room, preferring to invest his time in something, anything else. So, Evan turned his attention to Grace Ann.

"Mrs. Johnson, nice tuh meet yuh. I'm Evan Andrews."

Constantine, who had come out of her room in the middle of this introduction, watched as her mother curtsied slightly before extending her hand to meet his.

"Pleasuh to mek yuh acquaintance. Would yuh like tuh siddown and have some tea before unu go?"

Evan looked at Constantine, deferring to her judgment. And though she was more than ready to leave this desperate scene at her house, Constantine nodded that it would be all right if they indulged her mother and had some tea for a few minutes. Once they were seated, Grace Ann started a polite probing.

"So, Evan, tell me what it is yuh do?"

Constantine restrained herself from rolling her eyes at her mother's attempt at perfect English and feigned ignorance about his family's wealth.

"Well, I work fa mi fadda's company. Andrews Soap."

"Oh, in the family business. Isn't dat nice."

The conversation stretched on painfully for everyone but Grace Ann. Finally, seeing no end in sight, Constantine interrupted. "Well, Mumah, meh tink is time we go now." She smiled knowingly at her. And Grace Ann nodded in agreement, realizing that she'd kept them too long.

As Evan opened Constantine's car door, Grace Ann waved from the doorway.

After pulling away from her mother's exaggerated grin, Evan drove for a few minutes to The Myrtle Bank Hotel where they had dinner. For years, Constantine had heard tales about this luxurious place, but she never imagined she'd been in a position to see the inside of it, unless she went to work there as a maid.

Once Constantine stopped gawking at the décor and the two ordered their entrees, Evan asked her all the questions one generally expects to hear on a first date. And though the conversation was pleasant enough, Constantine couldn't help but notice that as she was telling Evan about herself, he was scanning the room, as if he were waiting for a friend to join them. He didn't look around anxiously, nervously, or even compulsively. But it was noticeable.

Constantine assumed she was boring him and thought that perhaps he'd be more engaged if he were the one doing the talking. "Yuh did always want to go into business wid yuh fadda?"

A very fleeting and pained expression shot across Evan's face before he answered, with a stale smile. "Meh nevah really had a choice in da matta."

For a moment Evan's smile faded and he looked at Constantine expectantly, hoping that she'd ask the right question.

If Evan and his family were making less money, Constantine may have taken pity on him or even inquired about what it was that he'd like to do instead. But she didn't and Evan dropped his eyes slightly before scanning the room again.

Their dates continued in this fashion, with Evan seeming a bit disengaged and Constantine curiously trying to figure out why he seemed to distant. But despite their lack of chemistry, Evan's parents still wanted to know about the young lady he was spending his time with and their money on. And after weeks of dismissing their questions and putting them off, Evan finally told Constantine they were interested in meeting her. Looking for some insight into who Evan was, Constantine was sure meeting his parents would provide the answers.

She spent the whole week preparing for the dinner. Not only would this be the first time she'd get to meet Evan's parents, it would also be the first time she'd been invited to his house. Evan was a big man, with his own job but he still lived with his parents and would do so until he got married. If she were going to be the woman they would allow to remove him from their home, she would have to look presentable. In the days preceding the dinner, Constantine washed and pressed her hair, shaped and painted her nails, borrowed a dress Evan hadn't seen yet from Olga and even had her shoes polished.

By the time Evan picked her up, her right hand had begun to shake slightly. The two rode in silence as he wound his Cadillac farther and farther away from the city and up into the hills. The windows were down, letting the night breeze provide the soundtrack to their journey. Constantine needed the air to keep her from sweating in her sister's dress; but she worried that the wind, whipping in through the window, would ruffle the strands of hair she had so painstakingly placed and pinned to her head.

As they pulled up in front of his home, Constantine realized that no matter how much cleaning and scrubbing her mother had done, she couldn't have built an entirely new house. And that's what she would have had to do to compete with the size of Evan's home. With its circular driveway and tall, white columns, Constantine was sure he had made a mistake and taken her to another hotel.

When he parked his car, Evan sighed deeply before peeling, slowly, out of the car to open the door for Constantine. Evan let his fingers caress the back of her palm as the two walked up to the entrance. Just before Evan stuck his key into the lock, he turned to Constantine and smiled at her apologetically, rubbing her cheek with the outside of his index finger. Constantine's belly jumped. Evan pushed the door in. Before she could even get a chance to look around the foyer, she was greeted by the family's housekeeper.

"Gud evening, Mastuh Andrews . . . Ma'am."

The woman, who looked to be in her early forties with already-graying temples, gave Constantine a once-over before smiling sympathetically in her direction.

"Constantine, dis is Ms. Beverly." Evan smiled affectionately. As he said her name, she beamed back at him.

"Pleasuh tuh meet yuh," Constantine said, extending a well-manicured hand. It was then that she realized she'd forgotten her gloves.

Ms. Beverly seemed a bit taken aback by the gesture for a moment too long but eventually followed suit. Evan nodded slightly, still smiling.

Constantine had grown up with helpers herself but there had been several over the years. None of them had ever greeted company at the doorway or taken a sense of pride in the family's children and even ownership over the house the way Ms. Beverly seemed to. The helpers Constantine grew up with were always young women looking to make ends meet for a short period of time. They never stayed long and her father had never provided any of them with any type of uniform, much less the quality one Ms. Beverly was wearing.

"Mastuh Andrews, yuh parents waiting fah unu in de parlor."

Evan nodded, sighing again before placing his hand gently in the small of Constantine's back, leading her down the hall.

Constantine took in the room before she noticed the people in it. Her eyes were drawn to the chandelier hanging from the ceiling. As she followed it down, she took note of the lush cushions on all the seating. Then finally, she noticed the older couple, rising to their feet to greet her. It was Evan's father who reached her first. His hand fully engulfed her own. His skin was slack and damp, like yams that had been left to soak too long. She resisted the urge to wipe the sweat on her sister's dress as she took in the rest of Mr. Andrews. If he were standing erect, he would have towered over her but he'd bent so far down to shake her hand, she could see the thin coils of hair that framed a large, pecan-colored bald patch, glistening with sweat. When he stepped back, she saw he wore a vest that fit snugly around his protruding stomach. She could tell that there had once been a time when he had been in as good a shape as his son.

Mr. Andrews stepped to the side and gestured for his wife to come forward. Mrs. Andrews's coppery skin caught the light as she positioned herself to stand, her arms bent and her hands clasped daintily just above her waist. She corrected the slight snarl she had inadvertently allowed to cloud her captivatingly angular face. She replaced it with a disingenuous smirk and stood silently, not moving, not speaking.

Constantine, figuring it was she who needed their approval, obliged, extending her ungloved hand for the third time that evening. "Mrs. Andrews, pleasuh tuh meet yuh."

There was a pause before Mrs. Andrews lifted hers in return. If she had been a bit older, Constantine would have assumed the woman was hard of hearing. But not only had Mrs. Andrews heard her, she was fixated on her hand, hanging awkwardly in the air. Finally, she lightly placed her fingertips in the meeting of Constantine's index finger and thumb, forcing her to close the grip, as if she were a dignitary. Mrs. Andrews nodded silently in Constantine's direction.

"Well, unu come tek a seat." Mr. Andrews said, the first to break the silence. He sidestepped his way around the table, careful not to bump anything with his belly. Evan pulled out a chair for Constantine. She took her seat, bending down to adjust her dress. When she looked up, she saw Mrs. Andrews sitting directly across from her, taking in her every movement with a concerned expression.

As they got settled, the room was occupied by new faces, all with uniforms similar to the one Ms. Beverly had worn. Constantine made eye contact with each, smiling slightly. They nodded back, almost imperceptibly.

"So Evan, tell us how yuh did fin' such a beautiful 'oman like dis?" Mr. Andrews said with a wink in Constantine's direction. For what seemed like the first time that evening, Mrs. Andrews turned toward her son, her expression softening slightly.

"I met 'ar tru Marie," Evan said curtly.

"My Marie?" Mrs. Andrews asked, raising one eyebrow and one corner of her lip incredulously.

Constantine felt her own jaw tighten. "Yes, she was doing 'ar hair and meh went fi collect Marie from 'ar shop."

Mrs. Andrews opened her mouth to speak to Constantine for the first time that evening. "Yuh—Yuh have a shop?" Mrs. Andrews stammered a bit, stopping to temper some of the shock in her voice.

Constantine swallowed and said the first words that came to her mind. "No, ma'am, meh work out of meh sistah's house fah now."

Mrs. Andrews snorted.

Constantine heard the sound of her own voice before she realized she was speaking. "Mrs. Andrews, do yuh need some watah, yuh sound like yuh have something in yuh throat."

Mr. Andrews blinked nervously, while Evan's eyes bulged before shifting between Constantine and his mother. "No, my girl, meh fine, tank you." Mrs. Andrews said sternly.

Constantine nodded slowly, still holding eye contact with Mrs. Andrews.

Mr. Andrews tried to ease the palpable tension in the room. "So, Constantine, yuh did always have a knack fi doing hair?"

Constantine tore her eyes away from Mrs. Andrews's searing expression and softened her own as she responded. "Yuh know meh come from a family wid mostly women. Yuh haffa learn quick."

"Oh, yuh poor fadda, trapped in de house wid so many woman."

"Martin, you musn't assume de girl grow wid she fadda," Mrs. Andrews interrupted.

"Mudda." Evan's eyes bulged in horror at her insult.

Mrs. Andrews shrugged slightly, a sly, satisfied smirk spreading across her lips.

Constantine mirrored her expression. "Mrs. Andrews, I'll haf yuh know dat meh did grow wid meh fadda. Lucky for yuh de man teach me fi respeck my elders. If him hadn't me woulda lay yuh out right 'ere in front yuh husband and pickney."

With Mrs. Andrews mouth agape, Constantine smoothed her sister's dress before springing out of her chair. Just as she was about to step away from the table, she thought of something else to put the stush woman in her proper place.

"And yuh know, mi fadda did teach me something else." Constantine rested her palms on the table, leaning so her less-than-five-foot frame towered over Mrs. Andrews's stunned face. "And since it seem like a lesson yuh need fi learn, meh ah go share it wid yuh tunight, all de muney in de world nah buy nah class. Yuh 'memba dat the next time yuh wan sit up inna dis house and play Queen ah England."

With that, Constantine turned sharply and marched toward the door. She was so enraged, she didn't consider the fact that it was dark, late, that she didn't know how to get home from here, and that it was Evan who had driven her.

Luckily, when she did remember this at the front door, she turned to see him chasing after her. Before he could speak, Constantine looked into his eyes and said, "Tek me home."

Evan put his hands below each of her shoulders, grasping her upper arms. "Constantine, meh sorry for mi mudda's behavior. Yuh not de furst 'oman she disrespeck."

She knew Evan had offered this piece of information to make her feel better, but being reminded of his dating history and his mother's penchant for rudeness didn't help the situation. "Tek me home, please."

Evan nodded, exasperated, and opened the door.

On the drive home, neither one of them spoke. Evan didn't offer any more excuses and Constantine, with her blood still boiling, didn't apologize for practically threatening the woman in her own home. The wind that had threatened to ruffle her hair on the way up, had calmed. The air was stagnant and heavy now, pressing Constantine to acknowledge what she'd known from the moment Ms. Beverly answered the door, wearing a uniform more expensive than the dress she'd borrowed from her sister.

Still, when Evan pulled up in front of her parents's house, she lingered in the car longer than she had to, waiting to see if he felt differently. He turned off the engine, leaned forward onto the dashboard and placed his head in his hands. Constantine reached for the car door handle.

He moved toward her, touching her hand before she exited the car. "Meh really sorry fa de way meh mudda did carry on dis evening."

When he didn't say more, Constantine nodded in acceptance and farewell before closing the car door. Evan looked at her regretfully but started his engine. She stepped away from the vehicle quickly so she wouldn't sully her frock.

In the days and then weeks since that dinner in the hills, Constantine thought more about Evan's facety mother than she did about him. And each time she did, for months afterward, that same contempt would rise up in her belly. If she and Evan had worked out, either Constantine would have had to eventually fight the elderly woman, or Mrs. Andrews, with her red skin and smug expression, would have sent her to an early grave, while Evan kept living, sighing and shrugging off her pretension.

Once Constantine had stopped thinking about Evan and his mother entirely, she accepted an invitation from Hilda to go out dancing. The next evening, Hilda, with her daughter Daphne following behind her, came over to their parents's house to get dressed and made up. Daphne, a beautiful little girl with wide, knowing eyes and skin like her mother, considered herself peers to Hilda and Aunt Connie. She thought they were going over her grandparents's house to get ready to go out. It never occurred to her that she was only there so someone could watch her throughout the night. She was too young to go out dancing, but as a consolation, they allowed Daphne to press their dresses. And that night, they didn't dismiss her from the room during their adult conversation.

Dressed only in their slips, they took turns leaning into the room's mirror to apply makeup. While one extended her eyelashes or dusted blush onto her cheeks, the other talked about the night to come, laughing and joking about the characters they'd inevitably meet tonight. There would no doubt be a man, breath thick with liquor, who'd ask them to dance. Constantine stood up slowly to imitate the sloppy, clumsy way they moved. "Meh hate de ones who nah hold dem licka. Blowing dem breath, hot, hot, hot all ovah yuh face, beggin for a likkle dance. Yuh feel fah faint before he reach fah yuh han'." Hilda clutched her stomach, bowling over with laughter. The force of it caused her to pass gas.

"Oh! Excuse me," Hilda said, still laughing.

Constantine launched into her favorite motto. "Let it be free wherever yuh be, for dat was da death of poor Mary Lee."

Little Daphne frowned up, confused. "Wha yuh say Aunt Connie?"

"Meh say yuh haffa pass yuh gas as it come. Cuh holdin' it in caused Mary Lee tuh die, chil'!"

Daphne laughed at the first joke she could relate to that night.

Hilda saw Daphne's effort; and to make up for the disappointment she'd feel later, she decided to teach her a couple of moves she could practice while she waited to grow up big. Hilda stood over her daughter, seated on the floor, and rolled her slip down to show the midsection under her bra. "Daphne, roll ya shirt up so yuh can see yuh belly move."

Daphne, quickly getting to her feet, followed her mother's instructions.

"Now, stan' wid yuh legs apart. Get yuh stance. Den yuh roll ya belly." Hilda's face broke into a muted chuckle as she watched her daughter, with intense concentration, try her best to imitate her mother's signature move.

Constantine stood back watching her sister and her niece, the way the two seemed to mirror one another and the look of pure joy that radiated from Hilda's face. It wasn't a face she recognized from their childhood. Being nearly ten years younger than her sisters, she had never been particularly close to either one of them, but watching Hilda with her children, she found a new appreciation and fondness for her and wondered if she'd ever have a daughter she could teach to dance.

In a few short hours, it was Hilda and Constantine rolling their bellies and shuffling their shoes across the newly waxed dance floor at the Silver Slipper. Before they knew it, the DJ was announcing last call. And though Constantine knew she had stayed out too late, she decided that the consequences would be well worth it. Grace Ann would likely warn her about the uncouthness of a young woman being out at that time of night. She might even blame her partying for the reason she couldn't seem to find time to make it to church. Constantine would simply listen, apologize, and then fling herself into bed.

But when Hilda's boyfriend, who she was staying with that night, dropped her off at her parents's doorstep, Grace Ann wasn't the one up waiting for her. Instead when she turned the doorknob and stepped inside the house, it was the shadow of Theophilus's figure that greeted her in the darkness of the living room.

"Constantine, yuh tink it acceptable tuh come strollin inna meh house dis time a night?"

"Meh home, Poppa. Meh safe."

"Yuh know only whores an' murderahs roam de street dis time a night."

Drunk on the evening's fun, Constantine responded before she had time to consider the weight of her words. "Den why yuh home?"

Of all the years Constantine had been talking back to her father she had never said anything so bold. She couldn't see this in the darkness but Theophilus pursed his lips, his eyes bulging in fury.

He rose from the chair. "Wha yuh did say to me, gyal?" He walked slowly toward her, peering at Constantine through slanted eyes. The closer he got to her, the more Constantine was able to make out his face, contorted in anger.

She dare not risk her luck and repeat herself. Instead, she looked at him silently, bracing herself for the impact of his open hand or closed fist.

He got about an arm's length away from her and asked her again, repeating each word slowly. "Wha yuh did say?"

Constantine stared past him.

Theophilus raised his hand slowly. He meant for this blow to be delivered in the right position across her face, to erase that unaffected look. But before he could follow through and bring his arm down, Constantine's words caught him.

"Meh a big 'oman now, Poppa. De days ah yuh strikin' meh down done now."

Theophilus dropped his arm. Utterly shocked, he looked at Constantine, vacillating between confusion and intrigue.

She was right. If she no longer sought his approval or feared his hand, then he could no longer control her. The realization paralyzed him. Theophilus had thought that by denying Constantine her schooling that he would have tamed his youngest daughter just a bit. He assumed that him asserting his authority over her life would warrant the respect she seemed to lack for him from the time she came from her mother's womb. Instead, his decision had only made her bitter and emboldened. With nothing to lose, Theophilus no longer had any playing cards. The realization that his plan to stifle her had failed sunk him just a little bit that night. The girl child wouldn't be tamed. There was no reason for her to render the respect he was due as her father. She'd usurped him. And even though he didn't like the girl, he had to respect her.

The two stood there staring at each other for a few more seconds in silence before Constantine turned and went to her room. By the time she got there, she was shaking.

She couldn't take the chance of challenging Theophilus like that again and living to tell about it.

By the next week, Constantine had moved out of her parents's home and gone to live with Olga and Ellis. The two were young themselves so they didn't hassle Constantine if she kept late hours. But after months of watching her sit in the house without a date, they started to plot and scheme on ways to set her up.

Olga taunted her, "Connie, de men out 'ere nah good enough fah yuh?"

"Das right," she retorted. "Meh nah need a man fi bring stress inna mi life. Meh just keep tuh miself."

Olga and Ellis heard her and vowed to leave her alone. Until a suitor expressed his interest.

***

Right around the time Constantine moved in, Ellis had started a job at the Glass Bucket Club. Being the charismatic man that he was, he had quickly made friends at the place. One day, as he was sitting around talking to his coworkers, Olga came by the hotel to drop off his lunch. When she walked in all conversation ceased as the men needed complete silence to ogle her properly. As he stood up to meet her, Ellis swelled with pride, noting the shift in their demeanor. Once he'd reached Olga, he made a declaration by squeezing her tight.

Clifton, his closest work friend, was the first to speak. As they watched his wife walk away, he slid up to Ellis's side, whispering, "Dat yuh wife nah?"

"Yeah, man. Das 'ar. Yuh see she nice, right?"

"Yeah, meh see 'ar."

Ellis beamed. "Yuh nevah see ah 'oman like dat in de country, aye? De women up dere don even know how fi straighten dem hair," Ellis said, slapping Clifton's arm.

Clifton Reid had come from a small town called Tyre in Trelawny Parish, far away from the paved roads and the flashiness of Kingston. He had moved to the city to make money and was eager, almost desperate, to prove himself refined and cosmopolitan. "Say, Ellis, dere's more women like yuh wife dere?"

Ellis laughed at the game Clifton was playing. He'd seen the women he'd bedded. And though there were many, none of them would turn any heads in the street. Clifton would need the type of woman whose presence was met with wondering stares, whispered questions, and wanting. Olga wasn't the only woman in her family with that affect on men. And since Constantine had broken up with that rich, soap maker boy, perhaps she'd be open to taking a chance on someone with a little less.

"Yuh know she haf a sistuh. She nice too. But dis one, her name Constantine, she fiyah, man. She nah go easay."

Clifton, who knew quite a bit about taking risks, was sure that attempting to woo this woman would be another one; but he also knew that if it worked, if he succeeded, it would be worth it.

***

Before Ellis could set up a time for Clifton and Constantine to meet, Theophilus took ill. He stopped working at the bakery and spent most of his days in bed, staring at the ceiling, while Grace Ann waited on him hand and foot. But after two weeks of this, he started seizing and coughing up blood, and Grace Ann's nurturing spirit and home remedies were no longer a match for his condition. They checked him into the hospital, where his wife, daughters, and grandchildren visited him in shifts.

When she first learned that her father had been transferred to the hospital, Constantine expected to feel some type of remorse or guilt for the way she'd spoken to him during their last conversation. Instead, she was glad she had the nerve to say it to him then, as delivering the message to the man in this fragile state would have been too cruel. She replaced the vitriol that punctuated her last statement to him, with kindness. When it was her turn to visit him, she was respectful and helpful, tending to his every need when her mother or sisters couldn't be there. She reasoned that when he came home, he'd be back to his old, mean ways and she could go back to ignoring him again.

During the third week of her father's hospital stay, Constantine was walking home and noticed that the clouds in the sky had parted in such a way that the rays from the sun shone down in a stream of light, illuminating a distinct path leading up to the heavens. Somehow, she knew immediately that the way had been made for her father. Startled by the realization, she ran wildly, as if pulled, to the hospital.

When she got there, she found the room empty and her father lying on the bed looking even more emaciated and uncharacteristically tattered than she remembered from her last visit. Theophilus had become a fraction of the man who had patrolled the streets with an overcoat and cane. Today, as he slept, he resembled a boy whose face had aged decades ahead of the rest of his body.

Constantine walked slowly to his bedside, fearing that he might already be gone. When she saw his chest heave slightly, she pulled up a chair next to his bed and sat. She looked at him and chuckled slightly at the irony of this moment. She, his adversary, would be the one to see him off. Sensing someone's presence, Theophilus's eyelids fluttered and slowly peeled themselves open, then wider once he recognized his youngest daughter. He scanned the room to see if there were anyone else.

"Is just me, poppa."

He wasn't disappointed by the empty room, just surprised that Connie was the one who had known to come.

"Constantine." He called her name with the type of calm and accepting tone she could never remember him directing toward her. The gesture let her know he was grateful for her presence, so she moved her chair toward his bed, leaning in to him, closer than the two had been in years. She was seeing now, even in this dilapidated state, how much they favored each other. Theophilus reached out feebly for her, cupping the side of her face in his hand and then letting it slide down, unable to support the weight of his own limb. Instead, he let his hand rest on top of hers, squeezing her fingers as best he could. For a man who had never been overly affectionate with her or anyone else, the exchange felt a bit uncomfortable, yet seeing this once formidable man in such a position, Constantine sat still.

She watched his eyes shifting as he attempted to form his words. She held her breath, not knowing what to expect from him in this moment. Thoughts raced through her head, though she tried to remain still. Was he going to apologize, explain why they couldn't manage to get along all these years?

He cleared the phlegm from his throat, speaking slowly through the pain. "Meh wan tell yuh something. Yuh a bright girl. But if yuh evah go fin' a husband, yuh haf fi learn tuh min' yuh mout. Yuh tongue too sharp."

Constantine smiled at her father's stubbornness. Even as he was going to meet God, the man made time to remind her of her faults. And even though his delivery and timing always seemed to be off, she recognized that in this very backwards way, he was attempting to protect her, to impart the wisdom he felt she would need in order to live comfortably in this world as a woman. As a man, Theophilus was confident he could help.

And though Constantine had no intention of either changing or listening to her father's commands, she nodded and held his hand until he took his last breath.

***

Now that there was room for another man in her life, Clifton, as if on cue, made his way back around. He hadn't forgotten about Constantine and once he felt like a respectable amount of time had passed since her father's death, he approached Ellis again about setting him up with his sister-in-law.

Just as he had predicted, Constantine was resistant to the idea. For weeks, Ellis had been trying to convince Constantine to meet with Clifton. And for weeks, with the memories of both Evan and Tawkins fresh in her mind, she had been telling him no, reminding him that a man would bring nothing but trouble to her life. And she meant it.

Now that her father was gone, Constantine and her sisters made sure they were visiting their mother more frequently. Unlike Constantine or her siblings, Grace Ann was taking the loss hard. She couldn't differentiate the feelings of actually grieving her husband or the fate of she and her children, now that he was no longer around to provide. Grace Ann's daughters didn't have to be particularly perceptive to notice this. History had always shown their mother to be consumed with one worry or another. And while Theophilus's ways and whereabouts had been the cause of many of them, it wasn't long before she found something to take their place.

Her husband's passing had made her superstitious and irrationally fearful that death might strike their family in threes. But instead of living, Grace Ann succumbed to the idea, preferring to spend her days lying still in her bed. Constantine had witnessed this behavior one too many times and decided it would be best if she moved back in with her mother. And it seemed to help some. At least now, she was getting up out of bed and putting clothes on again.

In the past two weeks, she'd taken to smoking her cigarettes on the front porch again as she waited for Constantine to come home from work. And it was in this position Constantine expected to find her in as she made her way back from the shop. But she wasn't there. Spurred by her worst fear, Constantine bounded up the porch steps, flung the door open, scanned the living room, and screamed for her mother frantically.

"Constantine? Meh here, in de bedroom."

She felt her heart rate steady at the sound of her mother's voice. It wasn't until she walked in the room and saw her, still lying in her bed clothes, well into the afternoon, that Constantine's worry turned to irritation at her mother's regression. "Muma, wha yuh doing still lying in yuh bed? Yuh nah feel well?"

"Meh feel okay. Come, siddown 'ere."

Constantine, took a seat on the edge of the bed, inspecting the exposed parts of her mother's body for any signs of ailment.

"Meh wan tell yuh somethin'."

Grace Ann looked fine physically, but Constantine still braced herself for some bad news.

"Yuh know meh haf a hard time accepting yuh fadda gone. De marriage nah perfect but 'im always support his family, even meh chi'ren dem. God rest de man soul. And now dat him dead and gone, meh wondah how meh a go mek ends meet. The likkle bit ah pension dey give him..."

"Oh, Mumah, yuh know yuh nah wan' for nuthin when yuh haf yuh children fi help you."

"Mi pickney have dem own pickney now. Dey have their own responsibilities. But me wan talk to yuh cuz dese worries meh haf now, is not something meh wan see yuh deal wid as a young 'oman."

Constantine had heard this before; still, she was startled by the swiftness in the shift of conversation.

"Tomorrow nah promised tuh neither one ah us. We nevah know when de Lord go call us home."

Constantine resisted the urge to kiss her teeth at what was quickly becoming a dramatic monologue.

"So yuh mus promise meh dis. Yuh fin' a nice man who will be sure to tek care of yuh and yuh pickney dem."

Constantine couldn't stop the shock from appearing on her face. This same woman who had once correctly warned her about the dangers of boys was now telling her to find a man to take care of the children she didn't have. "Meh nah have chi'ren and me doing jus' fine wid meh likkle hair business."

"The likkle hair business nah feed pickney."

"What pickney?"

"Yuh mean fi tell me, yuh go die alone in dis world?"

Constantine bit her tongue to stop herself from crossing the line into disrespect. What came out next was the best she could manage. "Meh nah wan marry a man so 'im rule over me all mi life."

Grace Ann looked away from her daughter for a second, receiving the unblanketed insult. "De life of any 'oman is 'ard, Constantine. But it come easier if yuh haf a man fi help you. Meh ah tell yuh not to be so quick fi push people away."

For all of her earlier dramatics, Constantine heard her mother. And long after she left her mother's bedroom that day, Grace Ann's words kept replaying themselves in her mind. And against her better judgment and even her own conscience, she accepted them to be true.

Days later, when Ellis brought up his coworker's name again, with her mother's warning at the forefront of her mind, she agreed to see him.

A week later, Constantine was supposed to meet Clifton Reid on their blind date. Ellis had been tight-lipped about the details, but he did say that he had come from Trelawny to find work in the city. Constantine had balked at the idea of dating someone from the country but thought his move to Kingston showed a bit of ambition. So she agreed to go downtown to meet him for ice cream. Ellis would be there to make the official introduction.

On the day, Constantine dressed in a dark green, knee-length dress, with a thin, white belt cinched around her tiny waist. She found an empty bench in the midst of all of the hustling and bustling and took a seat, scanning the crowd for Ellis.

It was Clifton who spotted Constantine first. He watched her vacillate between trying to remain poised and looking around frantically, fearing she'd be stood up. Clifton patted himself on the back for his persistence. This woman looked better than her sister. Her hair, the darkest shade of brown, right before black, was sleek. And the rays of the sun made it shine. Her complexion was a smooth, dark acorn color that nearly matched his own. And with that belt, cinched at her waist, he saw that she was a dainty, little thing. A lady.

Clifton had been in Kingston, working at the Glass Bucket Club for about a year, and if his preliminary calculations were right this would have been the first time he'd stumbled across someone who might have more to offer than glistening legs parting eagerly to embrace him. Though, truth be told, he'd accept that too.

He put an extra jaunt in his step and made his way over to where Constantine was sitting on the bench, her back completely unbent.

"Miss Johnson, I presume." Clifton had decided on his way to Kingston that he would adopt a British accent, lest anyone would interpret his origins to mean that he was somehow less civilized. Though Mother England had been the one to enslave their ancestors and still exercised control over the island nation, the allegiance to their colonizer across the water ran deep. And though Clifton had only left the shores of Jamaica to swim, he thought the affectation made him sound well-traveled and refined.

Constantine noticed Clifton's phony accent immediately. And if it had been anyone else, she would have rolled her eyes at this pathetic attempt to seem cultured; but she had been so impressed by what she saw, she decided to ignore it. "Yes, I am. Are yuh Clifton?"

As Constantine took Clifton in, working her way from the top of his head to the shoes on his feet, she quickly realized that Ellis hadn't done this country boy justice.

Constantine had made a habit of looking at every suitor's grade of hair. She knew that she wanted her children to have a nice, wavy texture and the wrong mate could jeopardize those chances for them. Clifton's hair was thick. And coarser than Constantine would have liked, but she took comfort in seeing how he had parted it neatly on the side. His eyes were set deep in his face, the color of whole Jamaican allspice.

Clifton was shorter than your average man but being that Constantine was only four foot nine herself, it didn't make much difference. And he was clean. His shirt was stark white and pressed. The creases in his slacks looked as though they could have drawn blood and his shoes were shined so well, she could have parted her hair in them.

"Yes, meh Clifton Reid." When he stepped forward to shake her hand, Constantine caught a whiff of his cologne, a spicy and citrusy smell. "Meh was waiting fah Ellis but it look lik 'im nah show. Would yuh still allow me to buy yuh some ice cream?"

For a fleeting second, Constantine wondered if something had happened to Ellis. Then she surmised that the man had just been trying to play cupid, flinging his arrow and then disappearing. "That would be fine, thank yuh."

Constantine ordered grape nut ice cream and Clifton vanilla. The two continued walking around downtown, long after they had finished their cones. Clifton told her about his greatest accomplishment to date, leaving Tyre to make a life for himself in Kingston. He told her about his job at the Glass Bucket Club, and how he and Ellis had become friends. Constantine interjected herself into the conversation when she could, telling him about her work as a hairdresser. She held back any other identifying details of her life, not yet trusting him completely.

Seeing and talking to him now, Constantine felt she needed to explain why she had taken so long to agree to meet. "Meh sorry meh did take so long to agree fi meet you. But meh jus break it off wid someone."

Constantine wished that Clifton would ask her the man's name; but instead, his eyebrows raised slightly before he waited for her to continue.

"It nah work out because de family dem haf muney and tink dem bettah dan we."

That piqued Clifton's curiosity. "Wha dem people dem name?"

Constantine was relieved to have a prompt. "Andrews. Yuh know de family dat mek de soap."

In the short time he'd been in Kingston, Clifton had heard of them. Even if no one had spoken of the Andrews family, he couldn't have escaped their name plastered across the city's largest factory and stamped on packages in every grocery. His eyes shifted nervously for a second as he thought about the type of men Constantine was accustomed to. But just as quickly as the feeling emerged, a newer, stronger sensation took over. One that convinced him this woman could help him shed the sweat stench of field work and the shame of little education.

As the sun was beginning to set, Clifton offered to take Constantine home on his bike. He helped hoist her up on the handlebars and peddled, more cautiously than he usually did, to her mother's house. The ride on Clifton's handlebars was much more unstable and more uncomfortable than Evan's plush car seats. The only similarity was that the wind was still whipping through her hair. But this time, with Clifton, she didn't bother to try and smooth it back in place.

***

The next morning, in his own bed, Clifton woke early and went to the market. He walked up and down the bustling rows, looking at each type of produce. Once he'd found everything he needed, he bought a wicker basket and went down those same rows once more, picking the most brightly colored fruit, most perfectly shaped nuts, and the most neatly packaged chips and cookies.

Clifton held the basket in one hand and steered the handlebars of his bike with the other. When he made it to Grace Ann's house, he rearranged the items that had shifted, wiped the sweat that had collected on his brow on the way over, and made his way to her front door. He hadn't told anyone he was coming, so Grace Ann answered the door when he knocked. She wasn't happy to learn that Constantine had gotten rid of one of the richest men in town, still, she was eager to see how this new one would compare. And while she didn't curtsy when she saw Clifton on the other side of her door, she was still pleasant. From what Constantine had told her briefly from the night before, she'd had a good time.

"Yuh mus be Mrs. Johnson," Clifton said, bowing slightly in reverence.

"Yes. Yuh Mr. Reid?"

"Yes, ma'am. Meh jus' stop by tuh drop off a few things fah yah dawta." And then, thinking quickly, Clifton pulled out the single flower he had in the basket and handed it to Grace Ann.

She knew he was trying to make a good impression so he could get to her daughter; but that still didn't keep an involuntary smile from spreading across her thin lips, exaggerating the lines that had formed around her mouth from years of chain smoking. "Well, tank yuh, Mr. Reid. Meh nah remember the last time a man did bring me flowers. Come inside and siddown. Meh a go fetch Constantine."

Clifton came in and took a seat. He noticed the house's cleanliness. There were a few nice things sprinkled around here and there but it was a modest home. As Clifton sat there he rubbed his shoe against the tile, taking notice of the smoothness with which it glided across the floor. Though today his foot was bound first in thin socks and then in the pressing tightness of a dress shoe, Clifton recalled the feel of the wooden planks in his childhood home on his bare feet.

The paint on these walls didn't have any scratches. Their windows let in plenty of light and there were curtains in every one of them. As Clifton was taking in the scene, Constantine stood in the hallway, just outside her room watching him eye the house, wondering if he'd seen better.

Clifton heard her footsteps behind him, stood, and turned around to greet her. After yesterday's meeting, he had dropped the Miss Johnson title. He'd save that for her mother now that he'd met her.

"Good afternoon, Constantine. Meh stop by the market earlier today and pick up sum tings meh tink yuh would like."

Despite the voice in her head telling her not to let her guard down, Constantine felt a cracking of the shell with which she had attempted to defend herself. Still, she tempered her smile and took just a notch of excitement out of her voice. She wanted to express appreciation and not appear like she'd never been the recipient of such kindness.

"Tank yuh, Clifton. Dis is very sweet of yuh."

Constantine knew that if they stayed inside, Grace Ann would be just beyond eyesight but within perfect earshot of their conversation. So she invited Clifton outside to sit on the veranda where they stayed for the next two hours. Constantine asked Clifton what he thought of Kingston coming from Tyre. Once he'd gotten settled into the conversation, she could hear the struggling British accent fade as he spoke more authentically and wistfully about his childhood.

Clifton told her that even as a boy, working in his father's yam fields, with stalks of greenery towering over his head, he dreamed of being away from all of that, dressed in a suit and tie, with shiny shoes to cover his already calloused feet. At just five, a lawyer had left Kingston and journeyed to Tyre to settle some legal matters with his church, a mile or two away from his home. Clifton recalled how all the people in his small town hung on every word that fell from the lawyer's lips, how even the men who delivered the most soul-stirring and eloquent sermons on Sabbath morning suddenly became bumbling fools in his presence. He decided then and there he wanted to yield that type of power and command that type of respect. So he would become a lawyer.

Of everything Clifton had said on their first date and even here on the veranda today, this was by far the most interesting. "Why yuh nevah become a lawyer?" She asked him.

"Meh did learn that being a lawyer was about more than jus dressin' sharp an speakin wid big words."

That was the truth, partially. When Clifton learned of the schooling it would take to become a lawyer, he knew it was impossible. The school he'd missed working in the fields with his elderly father, supporting their family business, would keep him from it. But the desire to wear nice clothes and command respect when he walked into a room had never left him. And it wasn't long before Clifton discovered that what he lacked in book smarts he could make up for with charm and persistence. It was a revelation that had served him well.

"Yuh know, when meh did first come to dis town, meh was tuh work at de university. And meh tought I'd be in de building, near de classrooms. And meh was excited. I tought bein near de people dem meh coulda learn a few tings. But when meh reach and de woman tell meh about de position, meh see she only wan meh fi haul manure all over de campus. Meh jus' come from dat. Me nah leave home fi do de same ting. So even though I was set to start work de next day, I decide I going back tuh Trelawny."

Constantine watched as Clifton's eyes looked off into some distant memory and the timbre of his voice got lighter and more pensive. She knew he was speaking on a higher plane of truth than he had been earlier.

"On meh way back home I tought about how meh was gon tell mi family dem that I failed. And jus den, like yuh and meh sittin' 'ere talking now," Clifton snapped out of his trance to look Constantine in her eyes, "somethin' tell me to rap at de door ah one of de big houses dem."

Constantine felt her body shift toward him in anticipation of the story. "Wid de furs' house, meh could tell from she open de door she one ah dose women who love fi play White. And she take one look at meh wid the dust clouding up meh shoes and she start tun up 'ar nose. But before she mek de face, meh smile and start talk. I tell her mi name is Clifton Reid and I lookin a job as a helper, any type ah work de people dem might need around de house. Then she stan back and look me up an' down."

Clifton changed his voice to make it sound like a woman's as he repeated her words from that day. "'Oh I wish you woulda come yesterday. Meh did jus' hire a boy fi tend to the grounds. But looking at yuh, standing there, yuh would be just de type meh need.'" Clifton imitated the sound of her kissing her teeth . "'Shame. But I cyan tek back mi word. Yuh know we British people nevah tek back our word.'"

Clifton shook his head remembering the dejection he felt walking down that hill. Taking the risk to knock on her door had stemmed from the last bit of hope he had had that things would work in his favor.

"But before meh could even mek it all de way down, meh see a nex' house on top of a hill. It was one a dem big houses, wid de gate around the outside. Meh couldn't get to de door, so meh tek a stone an' t'row it at one of de windows dem. Meh musta threw tree stones when finally a man come outside. When him see meh, he say, 'Wha' yuh doin'?' Meh tell 'im jus' like I tell de British woman meh lookin' a job. Same as de 'oman, 'im look meh up an' down."

"Den 'im say, 'Where yuh from?' And meh tell him say Trelawny. Him eyes light up after I did say de name. Den him ask if meh know a man name Willington Miller. Meh nah believe it! I tell him say, 'Yes, das mi neighbor.' Well, from den on we was friends, real good friends. We stood out in the sun for a few minutes more before finally him ask meh, 'Will yuh abide wid me dis Sabbath morning?'"

Clifton paused, dropping his eyes to the floor. When he looked up and opened his mouth to start speaking again, his voice had softened and he couldn't bring himself to meet Constantine's gaze. "Yuh know dat was how meh know fah certain dat de Lord wan' me 'ere in Kingston. 'e made a way for me."

Clifton steadied himself, fearing that the threat of tears that had formed in his throat would be evident in his voice. Finally, he looked over at Constantine to see if she was still listening. He didn't know if she would be put off by him referencing God so quickly in their relationship. But if she was, it was better that he know now.

Her body still leaned toward him. From the time she was a preteen, Grace Ann had stopped forcing the girls to attend Sunday service with her. And Theophilus who had never set foot in anybody's church for as long as she'd known him, certainly hadn't objected to their decision to stay home on Sunday mornings. Even Tawkins never really had much to say about God.

On the rare occasions that Constantine thought about God, He seemed removed and certainly unconcerned with her own life. What would God care about a smart-mouthed little girlchild? But listening to Clifton, she wondered if she had been wrong.

The two talked a bit longer before the conversation faded and Clifton started looking away from her and down the road, as if he had somewhere to be. Before he could dismiss himself, Constantine spoke. "It's getting late nah?"

The two walked slowly toward the steps before Clifton doubled back, saying he'd forgotten something. He ran back into the house while Constantine waited outside on the front porch. Once he'd rejoined her outside, Clifton flashed her a big smile, lingering after he'd run out of words. Then he chuckled slightly before wishing Constantine a goodnight.

When she went back inside, Constantine spotted the real reason he'd run back into the house. Clifton had left a few crisp bills sitting on the end table next to the couch.

Constantine stood, paralyzed, looking at the money. They were glaringly out of place in her living room, tacky and unwanted. The corner of her top lip raised in disgust. The only women she'd ever known to receive money on tables, after being in the company of men, were prostitutes.

Even though she hadn't done anything to make Clifton believe that was who she was, the fact that he'd left the bills there seemed to suggest that's how he saw her. Or worse, he believed that she and her mother needed his charity. Either way, the money put a stain on a perfectly good evening.

***

The next morning, Constantine emphatically told her mother about Clifton's rudeness. Despite Grace Ann suggesting that Clifton was trying to do something nice for the both of them, Constantine told her not to touch the filthy money. "Only God knows how many bills 'im haf spread all over Kingston. Meh sure we not de furs' doorstep him darken wid his likkle piece of muny."

That night Constantine rehearsed what she would tell Clifton the next time she saw him.

When he stopped by her house a few days later, she greeted him with a scowl, forcing the smile Clifton had on his own face to fade. She opened the door not saying a word and Clifton cautiously stepped inside. Before he had a chance to take his hat off, Constantine pointed to the money she'd left in the exact position on the end table.

"Is dis yuh muny yuh leave 'ere?"

"Yes, meh leave it fah yuh," Clifton said, trying to read her face for clues.

"Mek mi ask you sumthin. What type of women yuh tek mi for?"

"How yuh mean?" Clifton stalled for time, certain that whatever he'd say wouldn't be satisfactory.

"Yuh think mi need dis muney from you?"

"No." Clifton smiled nervously. "Meh know yuh nah need muny from me but meh did tink it would be nice. Yuh know, tuh show mi appreciation fah you and yuh mudda being so kind tuh me."

Constantine paused, the tension in her shoulders evaporating away. "Well, mi tank yuh for de tought but tek up dis muny. We nah wan' it. Keep it fah yaself."

The truth wasn't that Constantine wanted Clifton to keep his money to himself. She just didn't want to see it. Money presented in this way was gauche. She preferred the materials and the experiences it could offer rather than the uncultured display of its mere presence.

Other men would have witnessed this type of attitude and fled. But it intrigued Clifton. The fact that he couldn't sway Constantine with money only made him more determined to find out what type of woman she was.

Weeks after his early misstep, Constantine continued to accept his invitations to go out. After several hints about missing the Silver Slipper and wanting a man to hold her in his arms on the dance floor, seemed to go over his head, Constantine finally told Clifton, bluntly, that she wanted him to take her dancing. The two agreed to meet the next Saturday.

Two hours before she was supposed to be ready to leave, Constantine pressed the dress she was going to wear that evening. As the iron smoothed the wrinkles, she thought about the way it would move across the floor as she and Clifton danced together. She assumed that with his muscular frame and sturdy hands that he would make a worthy dance partner.

Just as he had done nearly two years ago, Ellis drove Constantine and her date to the Silver Slipper Club in the back of his truck. Constantine brought along old towels to sit on, to be sure she and Clifton didn't soil the seat of their good clothes. It had been so long since she'd been at the Silver Slipper that she was ready to hit the dance floor immediately. When they walked into the building, the mento calypso band was already sweating, having been playing for a good hour already. She started snapping her fingers and rolling her shoulders, humming along to the words she would never memorize. She assumed that these signals would be enough to let her date know that she was ready to dance.

But Clifton seemed to have other plans in mind. He placed his hand in the small of her back, guiding her around the room, looking for people he might have known. After he'd spoken to the few people he'd met in the city and introduced himself to some strangers, he made small talk. After the song and three more had ended, Clifton suggested he and Constantine get some punch. He poured two cups, sipping from his slowly, still looking around the room, nodding his head slightly to the music. Abruptly, he placed his cup on the table before announcing that he had to use the restroom.

Constantine guessed that they had been there at the club for over an hour and they had yet to take a single step together. Huffing, she decided that when Clifton returned to the punch bowl, she'd let him know she hadn't put on her best dress and done up her face to stand around and drink punch.

She saw him leave the restroom and talk to a few more people on his way back over to her. He approached her grinning. Noticing that she only halfheartedly returned his smile, Clifton slid up next to her and asked if something was wrong.

"We musah been 'ere nearly tree 'ours and mi feet nah touch de dance floor." Constantine said intentionally exaggerating the severity of the situation.

"Oh, uh, okay . . . we ah go dance." Instead of his usual self-assured grin, Clifton's lips were pursed tightly in a straight line and his eyes shifted quickly, studying the other couples moving around them.

Constantine knew what this meant. She should have put the clues together sooner. The country, church boy, for all his charm, couldn't dance. She hoped for his sake that he was a fast learner because it was too late to get out of it. They were here now. She rested her hand on Clifton's forearm and waited for him to take a step. He pulled on the bottom of his suit jacket, straightening it, and then walked her to the dance floor.

What happened out there could only have been described as a near catastrophe. From the moment Clifton took his first step, Constantine knew that if she left with her toes still attached to her foot, she'd be a lucky woman. The man moved like he had cement in two left-footed shoes. She had to lead him in the steps because he didn't know any of them.

After four songs, when Constantine was sure one of her baby toes was bleeding, it was she who suggested they take a break and get some fresh air outside, where she could take her shoes off and tend to her wounds. Clifton went with her. As soon as they'd gotten away from the crowd and out of earshot, he knelt to help Constantine remove her shoe and inspect her toes. Any annoyance she felt inside the club quickly dissipated as she watched him humble himself to carefully and lightly rub his thick fingers over her feet. The sensation of her pantyhose rubbing against her skin under the weight of his fingers was lovely. Relishing the sensation, she realized how long it had been since a man touched her.

Far too soon, Clifton placed her foot back down on the ground and stood up beside her.

"Meh shoulda tell yuh mi nah dance much. Mi parents nevah allow us to listen tuh much music when we comin up. So meh never really learn. Meh hope meh nah embarrass yuh."

Had she been honest, Constantine would have told him that he had, immensely. She had a reputation at the Silver Slipper and since they hadn't seen her in a while, and even longer in the company of a man, she had something to prove tonight. She had had big, elaborate plans for how she was going to wow the crowd and prove to the world that Tawkins had not broken her. All of that proved futile when she emerged with Frankenstein. She knew she must have looked like a fool, grimacing every time Clifton's heavy feet came crashing down on her toes. But she didn't tell him any of this. Had he been rude as well as rhythmless, he might have gotten an earful, but his humility made her spare his feelings.

"No, meh nah embarrassed. Meh nah care what de people dem tink 'bout me."

It couldn't have been further from the truth but it worked. Clifton, with a newly restored confidence, gently but firmly grasped Constantine's chin and leaned in to kiss her. She waited and then parted her lips slightly to give him an opportunity to slide his tongue inside her mouth. But he didn't. When she realized it wasn't going to be that type of kiss, she too brought her lips together. Constantine figured that maybe kissing was something else Clifton hadn't learned to do either in his small town. After a few more seconds though, she realized he didn't need tongue. With lips just slightly thicker than her own, the puckering and pressing still caused her to shudder with pleasure.

1945, Twenty-five

After the dancing debacle, Clifton and Constantine avoided any type of outings that would call them to dance with each other. When Constantine got the urge to dance, she called her sisters. Instead, she and Clifton stuck to ice cream, walks, and dinner at Olga and Ellis's house. After months of this, Constantine noticed that she was putting more and more effort into perfecting her hair before she saw Clifton. She took great pains to ensure her dresses were still stark white and her makeup flattering. She was sure it wasn't love; but was grateful to be around a man who wasn't trying to stifle her in any way, someone who was focused on making something of himself, and who had a sense of morality.

But Constantine would quickly discover that Clifton's morality was a tricky thing. It served him well when it was used to gauge, measure, and critique the behavior of others; but when his own desires and impulses started talking to him, he could always find a way to rationalize or completely ignore the religious doctrine in which he professed to believe.

After months with little more than kisses that had gotten better over time, Clifton wanted more. First, there were subtle hints. He'd let his hands wander while they were kissing, groping and grabbing Constantine's breasts, sliding and lifting the hems of her skirts and dresses. She'd only let it go so far before she put her hand on top of his, reminding him that they weren't there yet, that she wasn't ready. And for a while he was patient. He'd remove his hands, swiftly at first as if he were shocked by his own actions. Then, as they continued seeing each other, his hands lingered longer even after she'd protested. The subtle signs that he was ready to move beyond kissing eventually turned into whiny pleas and then whispered promises.

"Meh nah hurt yuh."

"Just this once."

"Meh luve yuh."

Constantine knew better. She'd known love with Tawkins and that's not what she felt for Clifton. And though he was nice and treated her well, she knew he wasn't in love with her either. So she laughed his advances off, sending him home to cool down.

But as the weeks and then months passed, with Clifton ever persistent, it occurred to Constantine that she hardly remembered what sex felt like. And one afternoon, she let Clifton's hands continue wandering. As he was slowly removing items of her clothes she argued with herself. She wasn't in love with him. Still, she had been in love with Tawkins and look how that ended. She wasn't convinced there was a right way to do this. And since she had already excluded herself from the group of women that wait until marriage, she started assisting him with the undressing.

The same Clifton who had been so attentive to her toes when he'd nearly crushed them at the Silver Slipper paid very little attention to her body in bed. In fact, he seemed to look through her. She saw him, though. She noticed the strange contortions his face made, the way his nostrils flared as he expelled air out of his rounded nose into her face. And she felt the weight of his hands as he grabbed her breasts and then shoulders for leverage.

There was no kissing, so when she wasn't looking at Clifton laboring on top of her, she stared at the ceiling, noticing the cracks in the molding. The motion of her own body made it seem like the ceiling was jutting towards her only to be suctioned back into its rightful position a second later. She imagined that it was trying to tell her something. Perhaps, in between Clifton's grunts and thrusts, it was calling her name, issuing a warning. But before she could decipher the message, Clifton had collapsed on top of her and the ceiling fell silent.

Constantine had lain down feeling deliciously mischievous, sensual, and invigorated. But she got up from the bed feeling used.

She told herself that this was not something she would be doing again. And for the most part, she kept that promise. There were days when her curiosity, boredom, or hope for better got the best of her; but generally when he asked, she found some way to keep him off her.

***

At moments like those, Clifton felt fortunate to have his job at the Glass Bucket. Not only because it paid well, but because it exposed him to a hedonistic world. Watching those rich, White people jerk, sway, and stumble around, carefree, influenced him more than he'd admit to himself. Unlike those White folks, Clifton preferred to do his dancing horizontally and out of the public view. While he was waiting for Constantine to trust him enough to share herself with him again, he occupied himself with other women, both inside and outside of the club. Women weren't allowed to work at the club in the evening but during the day, a group of them washed the linens and cleaned the place up for the night-shift workers. Though they weren't privy to the nighttime scene, propelled by pleasure seekers, they were easily persuaded by the debonair waiters in their starched and pressed uniforms.

When Clifton considered all the women he was currently juggling, he assumed that it would be the ones in the club who would present the biggest headache if his relationships with them ever went sour. He would discover it was one woman outside his place of employment who posed the greatest threat.

Clifton walked into the Glass Bucket one evening, just as the sun was beginning to chase the horizon. He changed his shirt to complete the required uniform and went out to begin setting the tables before the first guests would start arriving. After he'd completed the task, he noticed that some of the other waiters, his friends, were going out back to smoke before the rush. Clifton didn't smoke but never missed out on an opportunity to chat.

The group stood in a semicircle puffing, laughing, talking, and enjoying the last few minutes of being their true selves before they'd have to transform for the tourists. Clifton walked up to them, relaxed and self-assured. "What lies unu tell tunight?"

They welcomed him with mock groans as they cleared a space for him in the semicircle. "Aye, Reid, yuh come fi watch us smoke again or yuh gon have a taste for yourself dis time?"

Clifton smiled sheepishly but before he could decline their invitation once again, he heard a voice he didn't recognize call his name from the darkness.

"Reid! Clifton Reid! Is dat yuh meh see stan up dere?"

Clifton tensed at the tone of the man's voice.

"Who dere?"

The man lingered in the shadows a bit longer. "Yuh nah know me. Is mi sister yuh look fi prey pon."

As his coworkers turned to him, their eyes questioning, Clifton ran through the list of women he was currently seeing, trying to recall if any of them had ever mentioned a brother. In this state of anxiety, he couldn't remember. So he waited, half frightened and half curious, for the man to reveal himself.
When he finally did step into the light, Clifton recognized him immediately. With that nearly flat face and doe-like eyes, he looked just like Lillian.

Lillian was a girl from his hometown. Though Clifton went from home, to work, to church and back home again, he somehow noticed Lillian, who'd never set foot in any of those places. She did live near the church though. And after Sabbath when service was let out, he'd see her, standing across the way, looking at the people dressed in their finest clothes leaving the modest building. Eventually, Clifton introduced himself. She was much younger than he was. But it wasn't long before he started sneaking up around Lillian's house on Saturday nights, to show her what made her a woman

Though Clifton was anxious to leave Tyre, he staged a production in his last meeting with Lillian, filling her head with all the ways he would miss her. He knew she believed him, still he was shocked to learn that a year later, she'd followed him to the city and found work as a helper in a local family's house. Though Clifton rarely thought about her in the year since he'd been gone, he saw no harm in picking up where they left off.

Lillian was so young, so infatuated with Clifton that she didn't ask much of him. She hadn't had enough experience with men to know that they were supposed to take her out to dinner, so she settled for seeing Clifton during the last or first hours of the day. She was content with the mere promise of one day being seen on his arm, no longer just the mother of his children, but his wife.

Clifton made sure to steady his voice before he spoke. "Wah yuh wan' wid me?"

"Meh wan meet de man who fadda two ah mi sister pickney den turn 'round and get 'ar pregnant wid a nex' child."

The men who were standing around him all shared a collective squirm. Those who were holding liquor took a swig. And Clifton felt his heart drop.
"Whaaa . . . how yuh . . . ? How yuh mean she did pregnant wid mi child?"

"Who else pickney it is? Yuh de only man roun like fi play wid girls too young fah yuh."

It was then Clifton figured his best course of action would be to deny any association with this man or his sister. "Mi nah mess wid no young girl. Any woman who give yuh mi name mus be a liar."

Before the word passed through his teeth, the brother lunged at Clifton, driving his fists into his abdomen. Clifton's coworkers tried to grab the man but despite his short and stocky stature, he was no match for them. He charged forward, sending the group of men tumbling through the door that led into the club's kitchen.

Recognizing that the men were doing more harm than good, Clifton, now enraged, shouted, "Let 'im go! Let 'im go."

The men stepped back and Clifton stared into the face of Lillian's brother before his fists connected to his jaw. The brother's eyes bulged at the shock of being struck. In an instant, he crouched and ran into Clifton's legs, bringing him to the ground. The two tussled on the floor, scraping and scrounging to pin the other one underneath him to gain the upper hand.

Clifton was leaner but he still managed to get on top of the brother. Once he realized his position, his movements became automatic as his thick hands rained down blow after blow with mechanical precision on the man's face.

Clifton's coworkers tried to pull him off him, sickened by the sound of blood and bone under his knuckles. But he couldn't sense or feel them behind him. Instead, he focused every ounce of his energy into his repeated movements. He would have still been beating the man today if the shrill, panicked sound of his own name being hollered by his boss had not returned him to the present.

"Reid, Reid! Stop it!"

He stopped midstrike, noticing for the first time the blood that had sprayed across the kitchen floor as well as on his uniform.

Still straddling the man's limp body, almost every part of him became paralyzed. The only part of himself that he could move were his eyes. They darted around the room, taking in each of his coworkers. The men, who had been jovial minutes before, stood back and watched him, shock and terror cloaking their faces. Then two of the men stepped forward pulled him off Lillian's brother and away from the heinous scene he had just created.

As Clifton stood, facing his boss, he attempted to hide his bloodied knuckles, placing his hands behind his back.

His boss, a balding White man whose clothes spoke of his prosperity, shook his head in disgust. "Go home, Clifton. Bring your uniform back once you've gotten it cleaned."

Clifton parted his lips to protest. Just as he was going to offer an explanation, his coworkers carried Lillian's brother, nearly unconscious, past the two of them. The sight of his face mangled into something unrecognizable, let both Clifton and his boss know that there was nothing left to say. And his boss walked through the kitchen doors. Before they swung closed behind him, Clifton caught a glimpse of the patrons in the dining area craning their necks to see what type of commotion was going on with the locals who were supposed to be preparing and serving their food.

Weeks passed before Clifton let the truth of his situation sink in. The fact that he had gotten a woman pregnant again, he could easily ignore. But his impatient landlord and the hunger pangs in his belly had to be addressed immediately.

So after nearly a month of eating sparingly and finally being evicted from his apartment, he had to humble himself and ask both Constantine and her mother if he could stay with them until he got back on his feet. He figured groveling in front of them would have been better than returning home to his family a philanderer and a failure.

After one of their evening walks, when the two returned to Constantine's house, Clifton asked her to bring her mother into the room. Immediately,

Constantine assumed that he was going to ask for her hand in marriage. As she went into the back of the house to get her mother, she pondered, for the first time, becoming Clifton's wife. The thought caused an oddly anxious feeling in the pit of her stomach. And though her body and even mind told her she shouldn't, she knew that if Clifton were indeed preparing to ask for her hand, there was a chance she'd say yes.

Grace Ann, who was still thin and spry in her greying stages, entered the room slowly and cautiously as if she were about to take part in a treasured and time-honored ceremony. Clifton looked from Grace Ann to Constantine and back again, pleading with his eyes.

Somehow Grace Ann caught the message. There would be no proposal today. Before Constantine could catch on, she turned to her daughter. "Wait for us pon de porch, nah."

When Grace Ann was sure that Constantine was far enough outside, she tilted her head slightly, suggesting that it was safe for him to speak now.

Clifton leaned in, the tip of his tie swinging forward, brushing the clasped palms he held in between his legs.

"Mudda Johnson. Meh did wan' talk to yuh 'bout something. Meh nah know if Constantine did evah tell you but meh from the country. Trelawny Parish. And meh came to Kingston fi bettah miself. But it nah easy. And meh haf fi work to finally mek it to de Glass Bucket Club. You did see meh took great pride in workin dere."

Clifton had learned as a little boy that the best way to get away with a lie was to pad it with truth. The truth is always easy to support and defend and folks would be likely to believe the lie if there was at least some merit around it.

"And up until just las week meh do mi best. But that nah stop de boss man from coming to tell me the club nah doing so well now and dem need fi let me go. The people dem tell me is nothing meh did wrong. Dey jus couldn't afford to pay meh any longer. Since meh was making one a de top salaries. It did mek de most sense fi send meh home."

Grace Ann let her upright posture relax a bit as she recognized he was here to take something besides her daughter from her.

"And Mudda Johnson as much as it pain me fi ask yuh dis, meh haf nowhere else fi look. And meh nah wan return home and look shame in front ah mi family dem. Meh would be most grateful an' obliged if yuh would allow me fi stay wid yuh and Constantine 'ere in de 'ouse."

Grace Ann drew breath quickly. The notion of her daughter's boyfriend living with them before they were married was appalling. She could not have yet another girlchild turn up pregnant before she was married off. But Grace Ann would have never force Clifton, or anyone else for that matter, to live in the street, begging for food. Still, she had her questions.

"Mr. Reid, before meh agree to yuh proposition, wha' yuh plans fi mi dawta?"

Though he should have prepared for this question, Clifton had never considered his true intentions for Constantine. He just needed a place to stay. But he knew Grace Ann wouldn't be satisfied with that answer. And while he was thinking frantically, he nodded his head solemnly to give the impression that it was something he'd spent hours pondering. Buying himself even more time, Clifton took Grace Ann's freckled hand into his own, and leaned closer. "I haf nothin' but de bes' intentions when it come to yuh dawta."

Clifton watched Mother Johnson blink, waiting to hear something more than what he'd just offered her.

"She is a beautiful yung lady and meh can see a strong future wid 'ar. But de only way fi do any a dem tings I see miself doing, meh need a place fi rest mi head and den a next job. Which is why meh here speaking tuh yuh today. Meh need some help fi mek dis happen fah yuh dawta."

Clifton nodded, reassuring her and congratulating himself on a lie well told.

And while she nodded, signaling that he had her permission to move in, she kept her arms folded as he moved to embrace her.

When Clifton left the house, he passed Constantine on the porch, throwing a few words over his shoulder. "Meh su come back. Mek yuh mudda tell yuh wha' happen."

By the time Constantine bounded into the living room, Grace Ann was long gone. She was at the back of the house, straightening the room where Clifton would house his belongings—Constantine's room. He could stay in the house, but sleeping in the same bed was inappropriate.

"Mumah, so wha Clifton come fi talk bout?"

Grace Ann kept moving, pulling the sheets taut on the already made bed.

"Mumah!" Constantine had been made to wait so long that the tone of her voice carried a hint of disrespect.

Grace Ann turned slowly, warning her daughter without words.

Constantine softened, "Mumah, wha Clifton ask yuh?"

"Him need a place fi stay and wid dere being no man 'ere, meh tought it would be a good idea. He left fi fetch 'im tings. He'll be back lata dis evening."

Constantine felt a sudden heat all over her body that produced a bead of sweat she could feel moving in the space between her flesh and the fabric of her dress. But more than her body's own forboding, Constantine was particularly surprised that her mother, with her beliefs, had made peace with the arrangement.

Grace Ann's decision to take Clifton in was two-pronged. In fact, it was the principles she'd learned in church that had helped her make her decision. Housing the poor man, in his hour of need, was the Christian, hospitable thing to do. But she also knew she was setting her daughter up for the marriage she'd always dreamed for her. If Clifton felt indebted to both her and her daughter, he'd be forced to marry Constantine.

So after less than a year of dating, Clifton brought the few clothes and items he had accumulated since he'd moved to Kingston to Mother Johnson's house. To keep things respectful, Grace Ann relegated Clifton to the couch, though he kept his belongings in Constantine's room. And in order not to appear shiftless and ungrateful, Clifton was up every morning before the two women, either looking for a job, tending to the yard, running errands for Grace Ann, or completing any other task, large or small, to prove he was grateful for their generosity.

Grace Ann told a comforting lie to herself, believing that nothing would go on between Clifton and Constantine. She reminded herself that they were never left on their own for too long and the two wouldn't disrespect both her and her home by having sex there. But truly, in the back of her mind, she remembered her own youth and how youth always found a way. It was just much easier to feign naivety. Still, if Constantine ended up pregnant, with Clifton under her roof and eye, there would be a ring and a wedding before her daughter gave birth.

The plan went into effect much sooner than she could have anticipated. One morning, before the sun had risen completely and the living room was bathed in a muted light, Clifton lay on the couch, thinking about Constantine alone in her bedroom. He stirred, and his body began moving toward her room as if without his permission. He paused for a moment, attempting to consider the consequences. But before he could process any type of thought, moved by another type of thinking, he crossed the threshold into Constantine's room.

Clifton tiptoed into the space. With only a small window in the back, it was darker than the living room he had just left. Constantine, who'd slept soundly the night before, sat up slowly in the bed as she felt the presence of someone else in her room. She eyed him groggily, assuming that he was coming into her room to get the clothes he needed for the day. Looking at him though, she knew instantly that he didn't come for clothes.

Pretending that she had no idea why he was standing there, Constantine stepped out of bed and walked to her dresser to actually retrieve the clothes she planned to wear that day.

On this morning, Clifton's face didn't break into his charismatic smile; instead he looked Constantine up and down, emitting a low "Good morning."

Constantine recognized the intent behind both his look and tone. They'd been here before, just never in her mother's home. And while this fact should have offended her sense of propriety as a lady, instead it presented just the right combination of thrill and risk that was almost overwhelmingly arousing.

With a new boldness, she deliberately stepped toward Clifton. And he, looking directly into her eyes, grabbed the fabric of the nightgown around her stomach. He bunched and gathered it until, in one motion, he lifted it over her head. Clifton looked at Constantine naked for a few long seconds before remembering that he was operating on limited time. He stepped into her, causing her to peddle backwards toward the bed. When she felt the mattress behind her legs, she sat down. Before she could even lie back, Clifton straddled her body, climbing on top of her. Constantine gladly spread her legs, anticipating.

Afterward, he thanked her breathlessly before lifting himself out her and her bed.

Constantine grabbed her nightgown and pulled it, almost violently, back over her head. The thrill that had preceded their early morning thrusting had seeped away and now, despite the physical satisfaction, she was left with a combination of guilt, shame, and resentment toward herself and her boyfriend-roommate.

But in the weeks that followed, Constantine and Clifton kept meeting in the morning. Most times Clifton would come into her room unannounced. Other times, Constantine extended an invitation.

When the sex became somewhat routine, Constantine started to take heed of the fact that Clifton still hadn't secured a job. Every morning he went out and claimed he was looking for something but every evening he came back and put his feet under her mother's dinner table, avoiding the conversation about his employment situation. It started off as a mere observation, a slight prick in her awareness. Then as the days passed, it became a question in her mind. Why hadn't he been able to find something—anything—by now? It wasn't until she asked herself that question that Constantine began to realize that perhaps Clifton had been working at the hotel not because it was the most prestigious club in the city but because he simply wasn't qualified to do much more.

Constantine couldn't come right out and ask Clifton if he knew how to read or write. But there were ways to glean this type of information.

She found her answer one night sitting at the table as her mother prepared their evening meal. Grace Ann, who had no formal education herself, made use of her daughters by having them read the paper to her. A small part of her wanted to be informed but an even larger part of her got a kick knowing her girls had learned to do something she could not.

This particular evening, Clifton, after living there for nearly two months, was home from yet another day of job searching. Constantine looked up from the words on the paper to focus on the leech that had invaded her home. She suddenly decided she would go into the kitchen, under the guise of giving her mother a hand with dinner. "Clifton," she said, "Finish de article fah me nah. Me wan' help mumah wid de dumplin."

Constantine saw the look of horror that arose on Clifton's face. And while this should have been confirmation enough, she persisted. "It's de one near de top right of de page."

Clifton relaxed a bit but made no moves toward grabbing the inked page.

"Is righ' dere. De one bout de prime minister."

He smirked uneasily, leaning back in his chair, trying to beguile his nervousness. "Connie, mek it stay til yuh come from de kitchen nah."

She could have stopped pressing, when she discovered what she'd set out to learn, but Constantine persisted. "It jus a few sentences more."

"Meh jus wan' relax for a minute," Clifton responded, wondering for the first time if she really wanted him to read the paper or not.

It could have gone on for hours; but Grace Ann, who had been distracted by the sound of water boiling and the sight of steam rising, stood still long enough to hear the two going back and forth. Instead of making an already hostile situation even more tense, she walked into the room and over to Constantine, standing shoulder to shoulder with her youngest girl. She turned her head slightly and said, in a small but stern voice, "Enough."

Constantine didn't bother Clifton anymore about his illiteracy. And though she never spoke to him about it, in her own mind, she scoffed at the predicament in which she found herself. She'd turned away a man who was on his way to becoming a doctor for a man who couldn't make it through the evening newspaper.

That night she knew she needed to get Clifton out of her mother's home and out of her social circle.

***

Anxious to get out of the house and away from Clifton, Constantine visited Olga and Ellis. The two were just beginning to catch up, talking about nothing in particular, when Olga stopped short to inquire about the reason she had assumed she'd come.

"So how de tree ah yuh gettin along, unda de same roof?" Olga asked stifling her giggle.
Constantine rolled her eyes, recalling his daily annoyances. "Yuh know it's hard fi look pon a man wid no job day in and day out."

Though she hadn't had any personal experience in the matter, Olga nodded knowingly. "Meh get de sense yuh neva like him all dat much anyway, job or not."

Constantine kicked herself again at those words. She hadn't. And she asked herself for the millionth time why she'd decided to see and sleep with him. In an effort to make herself feel better about her choices, she ridiculed his behavior in bed.

"Yuh should see how him face mash up and favor monkey, panting and breathing all in mi face."

Constantine concentrated on imitating the faces and noises she had plenty of opportunity to study in the months he had been living with her. And as she perfected her impersonation, Olga snorted and spit flew out of her mouth. And then, almost immediately afterward, she stopped short, her eyes darting upward as she quickly came to a realization.

"Wha's de mattah?" Constantine asked, puzzled by her quick shift in mood.

"Meh need fin' a restroom before meh mess up dis couch. Meh tink meh period jus' come down."

Constantine nodded in painful understanding. And then her own eyes shifted as she thought about the last time she'd seen her period. Usually, she started two weeks before her sister but there had been nothing. Once Olga returned from the bathroom, she went in to inspect herself. She checked her underwear to see if there was a trace of anything. There wasn't. She stuck her finger inside herself, hoping that the increased pressure might produce something.

Nothing.

Constantine didn't tell Olga or anyone else that she hadn't seen her period. She just quietly made an appointment to visit her doctor. Days later, she was sitting on the edge of the hard table, in her hospital gown, trying to warm herself with the paper-thin material. It was February and a breeze, cooler than usual chilled the room. Constantine had been so nervous, she hadn't been able to eat anything all day. As she waited, she began to feel the emptiness in her stomach. She prayed the doctor would come back and say the same thing about her womb. She couldn't be sure whether Clifton would make a decent father or not, but she twisted her face at thought of having to be involved with him for the rest of her life. She caught a glimpse of her sour expression in the mirror located across the examination room and was startled to see how much she looked like her father. Seeing his face looking back at her disapprovingly, she was reminded of his words. How he'd predicted that she would end up unmarried and pregnant. The words came back to her like an unwelcome message from beyond the grave and Constantine knew then, without confirmation from any doctor, that she was carrying Clifton's child.

Never in her wildest dreams had she seen herself in this predicament. And though she knew exactly which decisions had led her to this place, she wanted to, at least for a minute, blame her father for all of this. If he'd just allowed her to go to school, maybe she and Tawkins would still be together, probably married. In which case, she would have gladly welcomed a child.

Greater than the shock of having a child with a man she was sure she didn't love was the devastating notion that maybe her father had known her better than she thought.

Seconds later, Constantine heard the handle on the doorknob turn as her doctor walked in, looking down at the papers that detailed her fate. His unexpressive demeanor gave her a shred of hope that maybe she'd interpreted the message from her father incorrectly. Perhaps it was merely a warning. The seconds it took for him to take his eyes off the paper and make eye contact, seemed to expand for hours. Finally, he looked up with a judgmental glare, partially covered by an insincere smile.

"Miss Johnson . . ."
It could have been her imagination but Constantine swore she heard him place emphasis on the "Miss."

". . . you're pregnant, about three weeks."

Constantine was anything but happy at that moment and the tears that she had held back fell in streams while her shoulders shook in fear and shame. The doctor put a stiff hand on her back, mumbling words he'd had to deliver many times before. And then he left the room to allow her to collect herself and get dressed. As she was putting her underwear back on, she looked once more in vain to see if anything had come down. Again, they were clean.

She wondered how she'd take care of the baby growing inside of her. She made just enough money for one person doing hair and occasionally sewing but she didn't make enough to support a child, even if she was still living with her mother.

And then her stomach dropped, remembering that she'd have to tell Clifton.

Constantine suddenly felt like she needed her own mother more than ever before. So before she spoke to Clifton, she made her way home to inform her mother of her new grandchild.

Grace Ann was sitting on the porch smoking her usual cigarette when Constantine walked up to the house. She had relaxed significantly since Theophilus had passed away. Her movements were more fluid. Her nerves had settled. But when she saw Constantine walking sluggishly through the yard and up onto the porch, she immediately sensed something was troubling her daughter; and involuntarily, her leg, which had been steady for almost a year now, started to shake. Before Constantine had a chance to sit down or say hello, Grace Ann snuffed out the fire of her cigarette and sat up straight, ready to listen.

"Wha's de mattah?"

Constantine didn't have the words to communicate so she burst into tears, grateful to have a mother who knew her so well that she didn't have to speak to be understood. As much as she knew Grace Ann would never use her pregnancy as a way to embarrass her, her heart was breaking knowing that she was going to disappoint her mother.

"Meh jus come from de doctah…and 'im tell meh say…meh pregnant.".

Grace Ann sighed deeply. She fumbled, searching for another cigarette and then nodded knowingly. The first part of her plan had been set in motion. And then she asked what she considered to be an off-topic question. "Unu love each other?"

The word "no" got stuck in Constantine's throat amidst her guilt and embarrassment.

Since Constantine was born, Grace Ann had regarded her as different—her other, more ambitious and outgoing half, the girl and then woman she would have wanted to be if she could have been born at a different time. But today on the porch, for the first time, she was seeing the similarities between the two of them. And she thought it was time she share her story with her. It was the story she should have told Constantine when she first had come to her in the kitchen wanting to talk about boys. Instead, she was answering her question fifteen years later, when it was far too late.

"Yuh know Cissy and George dem? It was dem fadda meh was in love wid coming up."

Constantine knew very little about her older siblings. Much older than she and her sisters, Cissy and George were already grown and out of the house, with families of their own, before she came around. She'd seen them and their children often, but when she was growing up, her mother never talked about how they got here and somehow, Constantine knew not to ask.

"Dem fadda was somethin, handsome and meh was a wide-eyed likkle girl, amazed at everythin 'im say an' do. But it wasn't long after yuh brudda come dat meh learn mi love alone wasn't enuff, especially when 'im didn't feel it same like meh. Him disappear an' even doe meh was still just a baby miself, I stop living in a fantasy an' do wha' best for mi chi'rren dem. And teking care ah dem meant finding a man who would provide a decent life. And dats how meh come to marry yuh fadda. Meh nah love 'im and 'im nah love mi but meh and mi pickney nevah want fah nut'in."

Constantine shuddered listening to her mother's story, realizing how,

95

even despite their differences, it was becoming her own.

Grace Ann praised Theophilus for being a good provider because that was the only role he had mastered. As a child who needed her father's affection, Constantine wasn't quick to sing his praises. With the exception of a very few occasions, he always seemed to come up short. And she feared that Clifton might be the same way; or, as a man still without a job, even worse.

Constantine had never seen a serious future with him, so she'd never even asked herself what type of husband or father he'd make. She assumed he would be kind but when she really thought about it, she didn't even know what type of man he was. She clung to the image of him massaging her feet and bringing her fruit, hoping that illustrated his giving nature. But she also knew that men could wear masks for years. He could be the type of man who ran from the prospect of having children and she'd have to raise this one on her own. Her unborn child's fate rested in the hands of a man she didn't really know. She'd always imagined that she'd make a good mother, but here she was already putting her baby at a disadvantage.

But according to Grace Ann, there was no need to worry. "Meh personally see to it dat da man marry yuh."

Constantine sobbed again, picturing herself carrying on her parents's tradition, living as roommates in the same house with nothing but children to show for their union. She couldn't articulate her thoughts and nightmares through her tears. But even if she'd managed to speak, Grace Ann's course of action wouldn't have changed. She'd decided long ago that love and marriage didn't mix. It was a woman's job to take care of her children. And in Jamaica the only way to do so without backbreaking work and scraping coins together was to have a man around.

Sensing her daughter's pain and uncertainty, Grace Ann reached out and gently enveloped her in an embrace, pushing her head onto a chest that sagged from age and years of suckling children. She rocked Constantine as if she were still a child. As Grace Ann rocked, Constantine noted her mother's signature smell of cigarettes and khus khus. The familiarity and safety of the smell and the position comforted her. And as her sobs quieted, she could hear Grace Ann whispering, "Meh ah go fix it for yuh, baby, meh ah go fix it."

Constantine didn't say anything but she told herself that this was beyond fixing. Whether Clifton decided to marry her or abandoned all of his responsibilities and never saw their child ever again, her life would never be the same.

As the sun was beginning to set, Constantine sat upright, realizing that Clifton would be making his way up the porch steps soon. Grace Ann took note of the time too and stood. "Tell 'im tunight. And if 'im nah talk marriage, send 'im tuh me."

Constantine sat there on the porch, stunned. Though her mother had comforted her temporarily, she realized that her problems had only doubled since this morning. Earlier she was just pregnant, and now she was pregnant and in the process of begging a man she barely knew, and only half liked, to marry her.

Her doctor had told her that she was three weeks pregnant, just days shy of a month. And while she would have loved to put it off for a few more days, she couldn't look at Clifton day in and day out while he didn't know she was carrying his child.

She saw him coming down the road just a few minutes after she'd come to her conclusion. For the first time since he'd moved in, Constantine noticed the bend of dejection in his back. She saw the slump in his shoulders and the aimless shuffle of his feet. She took pity on him, sensing the weight he was carrying not having found another job. And she felt a tinge of guilt knowing she was about to add to it.

Clifton offered her a halfhearted smile out of nothing but obligation.

"Clifton, siddown a minute. Meh haffa talk tuh yuh."

He sighed heavily, believing that she and Mother Johnson had been conferencing behind his back and had decided that since he had yet to prove himself as a hard worker, it would be time for him to leave.

He took a seat in the spot Grace Ann had occupied an hour earlier as he thought about where he would sleep tonight.

The two sat in silence, each putting off a different inevitability

Finally, not wanting to prolong the moment any more than she already had, Constantine took a deep breath. "Clifton, meh went to de doctah earlier today and 'im tell meh say meh pregnant."

Clifton sighed, shifting his eyes toward God. Constantine thought he was asking the Lord how much more he was supposed to take. In reality, he was rolling his eyes in annoyance.

Constantine would learn in a year's time that this wasn't the first time Clifton had heard these words. In fact, this was the fourth time a woman had come to him and told him she was pregnant. And really, he was tired of it. Clifton, losing all sense of decency, threw his head into his hands and let out a muted yell into his palms.

All Clifton had were those empty hands he was facing and now here was another woman looking to take something out of them. It was out of this deep feeling of inadequacy and anger that he looked up from his emptiness and asked, "And how meh a fi know is my pickney dat?"

Constantine scoffed at his insolence, stunned. But she was rarely without a response, particularly when an interaction turned confrontational. "Meh wish it weren't."
Her response so matched his in the potency of its sting that it silenced him. Once he'd collected himself, he was able to respond more maturely. "How fah along yuh now?"

"Just tree weeks."

Clifton nodded, making a mental note to count the months from now until the baby arrived, to be sure that it was indeed his.

"Yuh plan fi be here fah ya pickney?" Constantine asked.

Clifton closed his eyes, resting his head dramatically on the back of the porch swing. It was all too much. He couldn't afford the children he had or the one who was on the way, and now here came another. When he imagined the new baby, all he could see was its mouth open waiting for food and Constantine's hand out waiting for money.

"If it meh child meh haffa be here fi help financially."

"Here again yuh a talk bout throwin muney," Constantine said, reminding him again how despicable the bills on the nightstand had been to her. "Meh wan know if yuh will be 'ere fi raise de child."

Clifton's eyes darted nervously. He knew where this was heading. This was very quickly beginning to sound like some sort of trap. For weeks Constantine had been more and more distant and now she wanted to know if he'd be around. Clifton pondered that word "around." Was she suggesting that he marry her so they could raise their child together? He tried to avoid the question, not wanting to commit himself to anything but a steady job.

"Yes, meh wan be 'ere fi help raise de child."

The words sounded strange coming out of his mouth though a part of him wished he could live up to them. Clifton knew he couldn't keep making babies all over Jamaica with no wife to speak of. Eventually, he wanted to be a husband, father, and provider, like his father had been to him. He just didn't want this particular situation.
"Yuh mek it soun like yuh suggesting marriage . . ." He left his thought unfinished, waiting for Constantine's reaction to tell him her true intention.

Constantine had to lock her jaw to keep it from dropping. The entire time they'd been seeing each other, she'd never seen Clifton angry, had never heard him raise his voice, or even frown up his face too hard. But here he was tonight in his true form, stomping his feet, calling her a liar, suggesting that the child might not be his. And while she didn't want to marry Clifton, she was appalled that he hadn't even hinted at marriage at this point. She told herself that the man must have no sense of decency.

"Yuh tink meh would evah haf fi beg a man fi marry meh? Meh nah propose marriage to a likkle piece of man like yuh. Is raising pickney meh ah talk bout. Will yuh be dere fi help?"

Clifton nodded solemnly, staring down the road he had just walked when his only problem had been lack of employment.

***

They say that trouble comes in threes. And these days, Clifton, who had always been too superstitious despite his religion, knew that to be true. Both Lillian and Constantine were pregnant and so were the silences that cloaked Mother Johnson's house. Before, Constantine had been the only woman perturbed by his constant presence. But now, with a new, innocent mouth to feed, Mother Johnson also would start to look at him expectantly. They weren't the only ones anticipating his next move. Lillian, the girl who was bearing their third child, in her naive mind, didn't want to know if Clifton would support she and her children: she wanted to know if Clifton would be with her as he'd promised.

In the days he had managed to sneak away from Mother Johnson's house, Clifton visited with Lillian. In the moments they lay still, atop of sweat-soaked sheets, Lillian would ask, with a meek urgency, whether or not Clifton planned to marry her. "Yuh know de baby be here before yuh know it."

He'd nod silently, not wanting to ruin the moment of release with thoughts of another child he'd have to feed with money he didn't have.

"Yuh ever did tink we should ah married before dis next one come. De people dem already talking, wid dis being meh third child widdout a husband."

Clifton could feel his temper rise. "Yuh know meh nah working now. How meh a go pay for ah wedding when meh can barely find muney fi buy miself piece ah food in de street."

He calmed himself, not wanting to upset Lillian or his unborn child. He lifted himself onto one elbow and with the other hand rubbed his thick index finger across Lillian's cheek. "In due time."

This baby would be the third child for Clifton and Lillian. And while he had never necessarily celebrated the announcement of any of his other children, this third pregnancy, along with Constantine's, seemed to only highlight not only his slipping moral standards but also, with no job or place to sleep, his inadequacies as a man.

In the midst of Jamaica's sunny skies and vibrant colors, the recesses of Clifton's own mind had become increasingly dark. He had left Tyre to become something. So far, the only thing he'd managed to do was lose a good job, his religion, and get two different women pregnant at the same time. Even if he wanted to run away from it all, he wouldn't have the money to get there. And if he did have the money to make the trip, he couldn't go home and tell his mother that not only had been fired from his job, he'd also fathered what would be his fourth child, just to send them back to be raised by his family in Tyre, like the other two.

Still, in spite of his despondency, he was out every morning looking for work. Every day, seeing the children poorly clothed begging desperately for food from strangers on the street, he was reminded of the stakes. He couldn't be there physically for his first two children but he always rationalized that by sending money for them, when he could. And for the past several months, "could" came far less and less often. There had been a few odd jobs here and there. But not only were they temporary, they only barely paid enough money to feed himself, let alone his children or put a few dollars in Mother Johnson's pockets for all that she'd done for him.

And though he was putting forth an effort, Constantine, with newfound priorities, resented him more and more with each passing day. Just as his charm had worn off and she was considering putting him out of her mother's house, she learned a piece of him was growing inside of her and she'd never be able to get rid of him.

In such a vulnerable position, Constantine would have liked to be able to confide in her sisters, to get their support and reassurance. But they were busy raising their own children, dealing with a husband or their fathers. So she turned to her mother. She walked into her bedroom one evening when Clifton was out working some temporary job and plopped down on her mother's bed. Her body bounced back up from the thin mattress. Aside from the absence of her period and an increased tenderness in her breasts, there was no sign Constantine was carrying a child. And while it was source of concern for her, Grace Ann was delighted to know that she wouldn't be showing for their wedding.

"Mumah, wha meh haffa do? Dis baby coming, Clifton cyan fin' steady work an' meh nah love 'im."

Grace Ann kissed her teeth slowly. "Love? It nah always bout love, Connie. Meh know Clifton is havin a 'ard time right now but tings will come aroun. And it's better to be wid de fadda of yuh children dem dan look for a next man to come and raise yuh pickney."

Constantine could feel tears spring to the corners of her eyes. She should have known that her mother wouldn't support the idea of her leaving Clifton. In the time he'd spent in their home, while Constantine was increasingly annoyed at the mere sight of him, Grace Ann was grateful for his presence. Constantine saw the uncharacteristic glee in her mother's eyes when Clifton put her on the handlebars of his bicycle and rode her to the doctor's office. She'd walk past the two of them, on occasion, in the living room discussing scriptures they'd both memorized, and it occurred to Constantine that this was the first time she'd ever seen her mother have a real conversation with a man. Though Grace Ann always told her she'd need a man around to take care of house and home, she could see that she enjoyed having Clifton around because, with her in the position of power, he had no choice but to respect her. Perhaps her mother assumed that Clifton would be forever indebted to Grace Ann and extend that same respect to her daughter.

Constantine wasn't convinced.

"Wha' mek yuh so certain dat 'im will be a good provider or even a good husban? 'Im nevah say nuthin' bout marrying me."

She paused, feeling the sting of truth behind her own words. Then, recovering quickly, "And meh thankful fah dat. A lifetime wid de man seem almost too much tuh bear."

Grace Ann stared at her daughter, her brow furrowed in confusion and her mouth slightly agape in shock. Somehow, even in her current state, with very little to her own name, aside from the house her father had left them, Constantine sat there high and mighty, too ambitious and unrealistic for her own good. She finally asked, "Yuh tink life easier wid ah child by yaself?"

Constantine sat quietly, knowing that the question had been a rhetorical one—an introduction to the wisdom her mother was about to impart.

"Yuh too proud fah ya own good. How yuh tink de world ah go treat yuh? A young woman, wid a likkle bit ah education, a chil' an no husban'? Yuh betta hope an pray de man wan' marry yuh."

Some part of Constantine knew that her mother was right. And still, a truer but less boisterous part of her understood she didn't have to do things the way they'd always been done just to live a stable life. Still, she recognized that her mother wasn't making this up, she was speaking from experience. So that tiny part of her fell silent, smoldering in her belly.

"Meh was about yuh same age when meh decide to be wid a man fah love. And look how him lef' me? Poor, raising two chil'ren. Yuh fadda . . . yuh tink meh nah know him have dis one and dat one on de side? Meh knew! But meh nah care. As long as da man tek care ah him chil'ren, let 'im have a woman on de side."

As much as Constantine wanted to buck from her mother's philosophy and proclamations, she was too close, too far gone, with one too many lives in her care to forge her own path. What opportunities did she have? Constantine was convinced now that her father's prediction over her life had actually been a curse.

103

⊁⊱ ⊁⊱ ⊁⊱

If Constantine knew Clifton's lack of intentions for her, perhaps she would have been less concerned about being trapped with him. Clifton hadn't envisioned himself marrying anyone any time soon. Even if he had, it wouldn't have been Constantine. The way she'd tried to embarrass him, with the newspaper, in front of her mother, had shown him all he needed to see. She'd spend her whole life trying to demean him, holding her little piece of education and city savvy over his head.

As the days dragged on, the three housemates found themselves sharing the same emotions of dread and fear. Clifton and Constantine, for their instability in work, life, and love. And Grace Ann with the prospect that her youngest daughter would be a mother before she was a wife.

While Constantine and Clifton were too content in their fears to speak up or change anything, Grace Ann knew she needed to take action.

One evening, when Constantine was out visiting Olga, Grace Ann called Clifton to the kitchen table for a chat. She was still putting the finishing touches on a meal of curry goat, cabbage, and yams to coat his stomach before she delivered the request that would surely upset it.

As he sat at the table, waiting, Clifton thought about how much he'd always liked Mother Johnson. With her head perpetually bowed, she had a quality of meekness that Clifton found appealing and even necessary in women of any age. Watching Grace Ann bustle about the kitchen, Clifton wondered how Constantine had failed to inherit this trait.

Today, as Grace Ann spoke to him from the kitchen, he noticed that she called him Mr. Reid. It was a tongue-in-cheek formality being that she was older than his own mother and he depended on her for shelter; but it made him feel at ease, as if he still had some control in the discussion he could sense they were about to have.

Making a man feel superior was a little trick Grace Ann had picked up dealing with Theophilus and virtually any other man over all these years. Like Theophilus, Clifton cared about reputation, perception, and prestige. And while Grace Ann was still nervous, as she always was, having seen and known Clifton, accurately sizing him up, she was sure that she'd be able to convince him to marry her daughter.

She grasped the plate, piled high with food, in both of her hands, careful not to let any of it spill.

"Yuh hungry?"

Clifton nodded, smiling in appreciation.

Grace Ann joined him at the table, without bringing a plate for herself. Instead, she sat opposite him and watched him intently as he ate, her hands folded to minimize their shaking.

"Yuh nah eating Mudda Johnson?" Clifton asked in between mouthfuls.

"No, yuh know when yuh cook a big meal, yuh nah haf a taste fah de food." That was a lie. Grace Ann's stomach was growling. But Clifton was chewing too loudly to hear it. She hadn't eaten all day—the anxiety wouldn't allow it. Her grandchild's future as well as Constantine's were hinged on her saying all the right things.

As Clifton was cleaning the last morsels of food from his plate, Grace Ann brought him some sorrel to drink. While he sipped, she sprang into action. "Yuh know, Mr. Reid, it nah long before Connie walk 'roun here wid 'ar belly poke out."
Clifton nodded, shoving the last forkful of goat into his mouth, completely unprepared for the direction this conversation and his life was about to take.

"Well, yuh know de people dem ah talk if mi daughter showing truh har wedding gown."

The food sat heavily on Clifton's tongue as he processed Mother Johnson's words. The juice from the cabbage began to trickle down his throat, burning slightly as it passed. But he dared not swallow, lest he choke himself.

Grace Ann took advantage of his silence. "Yuh look shock. Yuh neva t'ought bout marrying mi dawta?"

Having been asked a direct question, Clifton figured it was time that he clear his mouth so he could speak. As he did so, he thought carefully about his response. Since moving into her home, he'd developed a rapport with Grace Ann. And instead of dodging her question, as had been his first inclination, he decided to be honest.

Clifton sighed. "Mudda Johnson, yuh know meh love yuh like yuh mi own fam'ly. Yuh took me in when meh had nuttin and treated me like yuh son. And so meh feel meh mus tell yuh de trut'. Meh cyan see miself marrying yuh dawta."

Grace Ann gasped slightly, more for effect than in actual disbelief.

Clifton watched her for a second, waiting for her to pounce. When he saw that she was going to remain silent, he continued. "Meh really fond of Constantine and meh know she ah carry mi child. Meh know de right thing fi do would be tuh marry har. But me nah know what type a wife Connie will mek. Yuh know 'ar. Yuh know she mouf too slick. Seem like she live fi cut meh down."

Grace Ann had witnessed everything Clifton had said. She'd seen these qualities in her youngest daughter from the time she was a little girl. Her heart panged with guilt because she knew that in many ways, her fascination with her youngest girl child had enabled and even encouraged this behavior. But in all those years she'd spent admiring Constantine's feisty nature, it never occurred to her, like it had occurred to Theophilus, that her daughter's mouth might keep her from finding a husband. Tears sprang to Grace Ann's eyes.

Clifton made a sympathizing noise in the back of his throat then got up from his chair, walking over to Grace Ann, at the other end of the small table. He sat down, closer to her, reaching over to pat her arm, trying to soothe the pain that came with his truth-telling.

Now, that he was in the right position, Grace Ann lifted her head slowly but deliberately to stare directly into his eyes. "Mr. Reid, are yuh going to mek me look shame?"

Clifton's eyes widened, the question pricking his morality.

Grace Ann repeated, "Are yuh going to mek me look shame, after all we done for yuh?"

She hadn't expected to use the shame and guilt tactics so early in the conversation but time was of the essence and it was the truth. Or at least the truth as Grace Ann saw it. Like Clifton and her late husband, she too cared about what people thought, especially about her children and particularly Constantine. Grace Ann had been damningly silent when Theophilus tried to hold her back from becoming a teacher. She could not fail her again.

Clifton lowered his head. The weight of her words fell heavily on him, binding him to a life he would have never dreamt for himself.

"Is only yuh who can help save de family."

Grace Ann had painted him a picture in which he, the unrefined country boy, proves to be the only one who can save the relatively well-off city family by marrying their eligible, young daughter. Since he'd moved to Kingston, Clifton had spent significant time, energy, and money trying to impress these city folks, to prove that he belonged there. And now the tables had turned and they were coming to him for something only he could offer.

A mother's determination is a powerful force and so is a man's pride. The two came together that night to forever change the course of Constantine's life, without her even being in the room to see it happen.

With this decision having been made, there was no official proposal. No grand romantic gesture. Instead, a few weeks after his conversation with Mother Johnson, Clifton passed the news along to Constantine. "Meh an' yuh mudda did talk. And she did ask meh not to bring shame to de family. And after all she did fi me when meh lost mi job, it only right that meh do something for har."

Constantine held her face stone still. She had often envisioned the day a man would ask for her hand in marriage. She didn't need a white horse, but she certainly didn't want her future husband to be proposing to her mother rather than her. The least she expected was to have been asked rather than informed.

Constantine didn't have much time to be offended. Instead of worrying about her emotional state, Grace Ann was adamant about moving quickly with wedding planning before the baby started to show. Throughout the process, she consistently reminded both Clifton and Constantine that it would have been tactless to bring evidence of their fornication into the church. People would talk and the wedding she had worked so hard for would be a sham.

Grace Ann couldn't have known that there would be no reason for her to worry about Constantine looking too round in her wedding dress. She was already a thin woman and the pregnancy didn't agree with her body. For the first two months, she vomited every day. She seemed to be losing weight, instead of gaining it.

Still, Constantine took her mother's urgency and anxiety and transferred it onto Clifton, pressuring and questioning him about the money for the event. Not having had any say in the proposal, this was a means for Constantine to exercise the little bit of influence she still yielded in this situation. "How we ah go afford a wedding?"

"Meh figuh sometin out."

This was Clifton's first test as a husband and father and he was eager to prove to both Mother Johnson and Constantine that he could be an asset instead of a burden.

For months, the island had been plastered with signs advertising jobs in the United States. Clifton had once asked a friend to read the bill to him. Once he'd learned that they were looking for migrant workers, he turned up his nose at the offer. He wasn't doing farm work in Kingston, and he certainly wasn't going to leave the country to do the work he'd intentionally avoided.

But things had changed. These days Clifton found that he did a lot of scolding and reminding himself that he was no longer making decisions as a single man. And so with a mixture of excitement and dread, he signed up to go to America for a month to do the work he'd vowed to never do again.

The day Clifton was to board the boat to Miami, he dressed in a white, linen shirt and brown slacks. Constantine had ironed the pants and included a stiff front crease. He was going to America to cut sugar cane and pick fruit but he certainly didn't have to look like it.

After a boat ride that was much shorter than he had assumed, the captain announced that they had reached Florida. Though there were a few more paved roads, generally the state looked like the home he'd just left. It was the people who made the atmosphere unrecognizable. From the time the ship docked, Clifton and the other travelers were herded off the boat, into a line. Confused about whether this group was going to work, Clifton tapped one of the men in front of him, seeking clarification. "Excuse me," Clifton said, coating his voice with the unconvincing British accent, "is this the line for people who go work in the field?"

The man standing in front of him looked back with a scowl and turned to face forward again. Before Clifton could think to ask someone else, a pickup truck pulled up to the mass of people who'd just come from the ship. The group of one hundred men who had been virtually silent before, suddenly filled the thick, coastal air with clamoring noises as they pushed and shoved each other toward or away from the pickup. Luckily, Clifton found himself shoved toward the truck with the rest of group. After having to elbow a few people who tried to throw him off course, he was one of the thirty men who managed to climb into the back of the truck. As the pickup ambled unsteadily down the street, the men carved out the little bit of room for themselves in the back and the uncomfortable quiet returned.

As the thirty men rode, they collided into one another with each twist and turn the car took, until the truck came to a stop. Clifton followed the other men as they hopped out and made their way to a series of shacks that seemed as if they would collapse in the next rain. They stood around the most stable-looking structure in the middle of the others. As they were all coming to a halt, a man dressed in khakis came out of the shack carrying a clipboard, paper, and pencil. As he got closer, Clifton could see that the man was taking the names of the men and assigning them to the rickety shacks that surrounded them like gnarled, misshapen trees.

Clifton followed suit, as he had been doing all day. He gave his name and was assigned to one of the leaning wood houses. He stepped inside to find nothing but two beds, one of which was already occupied by a man sitting on it, resting. Clifton noticed his shoes were still tightly laced.

He tried to make conversation with the man who would be sharing his fate for the next few weeks. "How do you do? I'm Clifton Reid," he said, stepping toward the man cautiously with his hand extended.

The man looked up, slightly confused for a second, before standing, extending his own hand, and using the other to pat his heart as he said his own name. "Raul."

"Cuba?"

"Sí . . . yes." Raul said, offering a smile and a helpless shrug.

For the next few weeks, Clifton, Raul, and the other men in the circle of shacks worked from sunup to sundown, chopping cane, harvesting vegetables, and anything else that grew in the dense vegetation of the state. Though he'd avoided this work for years, Clifton knew it well; and while the other men would come back from their day's labor broken down and fatigued, he was able to remain hearty physically, though emotionally, he too was broken.

And alone. Many of the men there spoke Spanish. All of the English speakers were poor, White folks who banded together and wanted nothing to do with him. After the first week, Clifton learned that there weren't just men working. There were several women who took their money every weekend, offering minutes of distraction for those not too tired to socialize.

Clifton joined some of the men one evening. It would become his first and only time venturing away from the fields. The night he decided to go out, he found himself joining a group of men shooting dice. The game had been competitive, but still friendly, until one man accused another of cheating. Before too many words could be exchanged, the accuser had driven a knife through the palm of the other man's hand. The image of the man cradling his hand, staring down at his source of income bleeding out onto his clothes, remained with Clifton for days, acting as a bad omen foreshadowing a possible future. A pierced hand, like his Lord and savior, was a clear, terrifying message he couldn't ignore. He wouldn't participate in any more night time activities. If anything were to happen to him in Florida, it would be weeks before his soon-to-be-wife and Lillian would know about it. There were too many people he'd disappoint and possibly push into poverty if he didn't control himself for this month.

So for the first time since he'd left Tyre, Clifton did his work during the day and slept during the night, counting the money he'd made and the days before he'd be able to return home to Jamaica.

***

When he stepped off the boat back in Kingston, Clifton was amazed to see that after a full month, there still wasn't the slightest sign that Constantine was carrying a child. Lillian always showed early, her entire face becoming virtually unrecognizable as her nose spread wider with the passage of each month. But this child must have been trying to spare its mother from shame because Constantine, who was at the tail end of her first trimester, hadn't had to let out a single dress. Still, it was only a matter of time before her belly started to protrude and friends and family started counting the months after their wedding. So before Clifton could even enjoy the money he'd made toiling away in Florida, Mother Johnson and Constantine had already spent it. On his second night in town, after mother and daughter had prepared a feast for his arrival, Constantine sat down with him to speak of their plans.

"Me and Mumah been talkin bout de wedding and we wan it to be real classy, nice florals, a nice gown."

Constantine pursed her lips each time she said "nice," making a small, delighted kissing noise. The little quirk once intrigued Clifton but today, with her incessant chatter about his money, it didn't have the same effect. Though Clifton had spent virtually every day of his life in Kingston, trying to impress people, he resented the same behavior in his soon-to-be wife. There was no way he could have understood what this event meant for Mother Johnson. He assumed that in the month that he'd been away, this was the only topic that dominated their conversations

"We been planning dis pas' month, so mos' ah de details dem nailed down. We picked May 23 for de date."

"Dis May? Dat only two months away?"

Constantine nodded.

For a moment Constantine could feel sympathy seeping in. This was a lot of information to spring on him so suddenly. But then she remembered how she'd been denied an entire proposal and the guilt dissipated.

"We still need muney for de banquet hall, de flowers dem, mi gown from London," Constantine made that kissing noise again, smiling slightly. "Yuh can pick up the rings dem. And Mumah wan an orchestra for de reception."

With each item she named, Clifton subtracted its cost from the money he'd earned. If he'd thought about taking the money and disappearing, the plan was foiled when Constantine gave him a total before holding her hand out for the cash.

The only thing Clifton had any control over were the rings. A few days after he'd lost most of his money, he went to the jewelry store to spend even more of it. He picked out a thin band that bore the shiny, yellow hue synonymous with Caribbean gold. Her band featured carefully drilled indentions as decoration. Clifton purchased a simpler, slightly thicker band for himself.

Always with a flair for something extra, Clifton told the salesman that he wanted an engraving. "Hers should read, *C.R. to C.J. 23-5-45.*"

The salesman took down the inscription silently.

***

Months later, just days before the wedding, when he came to pick up the rings, suddenly the jeweler was ready to chat. Jokingly, he smiled at Clifton, playfully holding the box away from his grasp. "Yuh sure bout dis nah?"

Clifton smiled back, nodding slightly. The man handed him the box and Clifton took Constantine's ring out to inspect it. He checked the inscription, then double and triple-checked it, lest he be blamed for any errors. As he rolled the ring between his heavy index finger and thumb, he heard the words of the salesman echo in the background.

"Yuh know dis forevah. The ring cyan be broken. De same is true fi de union."

Clifton nodded weakly.
On the day of her wedding Constantine was numb. In fact, she seemed to be a spectator at the event. She watched herself step into the wedding dress, watched herself walk down the aisle to a virtual stranger, watched herself promise to God and the congregation that she would love a man she didn't know if she liked. The only time Constantine felt present in her body was when the minister asked the people assembled if there was anyone who objected to Clifton and Constantine being united together as husband and wife. Constantine was zapped back into her body at that moment because it was then that she felt the child growing in her womb kick her for the first time.

Later, during the reception, the orchestra played and the couple shared their first dance. Spinning around the dance floor with her new husband, there was no way she could have understood how hard Clifton had labored in Florida. She did know that the man had broken tradition and paid for the whole affair himself, making her mother beam with pride in the face of those who she swore questioned the morals of her family. And in that moment, more than the uncertainty, she was grateful. For the first time since they'd started seeing each other, Constantine wasn't irritated by the fact that Clifton kept stepping on her toes.

But while most wives spend the first couple months of their marriage celebrating the new lives they're building with their husbands, Constantine was too busy trying to control her constant nausea. After the wedding, the vomiting continued. As much as it was a nuisance for her, the problems of her pregnancy distracted her from her new life as a wife. She still cooked and cleaned and opened her legs for her husband in the evening, but the pangs and preoccupation of bringing a life into the world took priority in her mind over the fear she felt in her new union.

When she wanted a respite from both pregnancy and thoughts of motherhood, she had to imagine an escape. During the days when Clifton went to work and her mother was taking her daily nap, she liked to stare out of the window and pretend. When it rained, she imagined herself in London. Having just finished teaching her students, she would have a cup of tea and grade papers. But it wouldn't be long before her daydream would be interrupted by a lurch in her stomach and she had to run outside to the bathroom.

After she finished expelling the contents of her stomach, she returned to the kitchen to pick up where she left off with her daydream. It was still raining and she decided to open the window to smell the air. But it wasn't the air that attracted her. It was the dirt made pungent by the rain that had softened it. Constantine hadn't played in dirt since she was a child but suddenly, the smell propelled her outside to be near to it.

Once she stepped outside, she found a spot where grass refused to grow and knelt down, placing her hand there. She pinched a mound of it in between her fingers and rubbed them together, feeling the grains of moist dirt that were not quite mud on the tips of her fingers. She put her hand back on the ground, this time digging and clawing at the soil. Collecting the dirt under her fingernails, she brought her hand to her mouth and inhaled. Seeing the filth under her nails, she used her teeth to clean the soil out from underneath them.

Even as a child Constantine had never eaten dirt. But tasting it today, in the rain, it was ambrosia, salty green and strong. She could hear the particles being ground on the top of her molars at the back of her mouth. And the dirt, though moist, left her mouth feeling dry. Still, it satisfied a nagging craving she didn't even know she had until she ate it. And satisfying this craving produced the first blissful feeling she'd felt since she'd gotten married.

Once she'd had her fill and went back inside, her clothes dampened and sticking to the body that had finally begun to swell, she told herself that the first time was the last time. If anyone ever caught her out there squatting and kneeling in the dirt like some kind of animal, they'd think she'd lost her mind. But the craving the dirt satisfied and the way her body relaxed as the soil touched her tongue was too good to go without. And she found herself eating it again and again, particularly after it rained, when the smell beckoned her.

Despite her efforts to keep her new habit hidden, it wasn't long before her niece Daphne caught her out in the yard at her grandmother's house, digging and putting the earth in her mouth.
Constantine had been anticipating the day someone would catch her in the act. She imagined she'd be mortified before trying to come up with the perfect excuse to rationalize her behavior. Instead, what she felt was overwhelming relief in the fact that she no longer had to hide. Of course, her mother and sisters tried to dissuade her from doing it, all to no avail.

Three months later, in October she gave birth. Alton came so fast that the doctors didn't have time to clear Clifton from the room. And the sight of their son emerging bloody and wailing from Constantine's bared body was too much for him to stomach and he fainted right then and there at the foot of the hospital bed. Constantine couldn't help but laugh at the man. In the midst of her and her son laboring to get him into the world, he'd managed to make the moment about himself. The doctors treated him with smelling salts and assisted him out of the room after he'd regained consciousness.

Once Alton's legs slipped out of her body, the doctor smacked him to produce air. The thin, slippery baby let out his first sound. The nurses whisked him away to wipe some of the blood and fluid off his already silken skin. They returned minutes later, placing him in the crook of Constantine's arms.

She took in this child, her child, for the first time. With eyes wide, black, and shiny, he was already curious, looking around the room as if searching for adventure. A mass of thick black hair coiled into perfect c's at the top of his head. Ebony skin seemed to glisten over his infant frame. Constantine thought she had already learned to love her son as she was carrying him; but the love she felt for him now, holding him in her arms, was frightening. It almost stifled her it was so overwhelming. She and Alton stared at each other and she vowed never to hurt him, to always protect him from all harm and danger and to make his happiness her number one priority. These were promises no mother could ever keep, but still she meant all of them.

The doctors assured her that both she and her son were perfectly healthy. And the two of them were released after six days. But within the first month, things began to change. Alton's skin which had glistened when he was born, was now ashen and cracked. With nearly every breath he was wheezing and he'd lost his appetite, refusing to nurse from his mother's breasts. They went back to the hospital; and though the doctors could see that he wasn't healthy, they didn't have a diagnosis and sent the two of them home, telling her to keep an eye on him and bring him back if his condition worsened. Her family never told her directly, but they all believed the dirt she'd ingested during her pregnancy had poisoned him. Constantine didn't have time to wallow in her own guilt for what might have caused his sickness; she was too busy looking for answers.

One afternoon, she sat at her mother's table crying as she described

Alton's condition. "'im haf so much trouble breathing from 'im mout' that 'im nah eat. Both a we scared 'im ah choke trying fi breathe an eat at de same time."

Grace Ann listened carefully, weighing her words. Once Constantine had stopped talking, she told her she had a friend who might be able to help.

"Get yuhself together. And covah yuh pickney, we going tuh run into town."

They walked through the market past the fruit carts and fish stands, Grace Ann with a quickened, determined gait. The women stepped carefully over puddles of pooled rain water and dodged the cats who were employed as pest control. Finally, when they had maneuvered through the dirt pathways to the back of the market, they found a woman who sat in the doorway of her shop in a folding chair, asleep.

Constantine studied the woman's face. She was a toffee color with blackened lips and cheeks that never seemed to settle, like she was smiling even when her face was at rest. Grace Ann leaned forward and gently rubbed the woman's shoulder, trying to wake her. "Mattie."

The woman opened her eyelids slowly but she woke up instantly alert and unsurprised to see two women and a baby in front of her. "Grace Ann, how yuh doing?"

Grace Ann shook her head, the concern showing on her face. She wasn't going to waste time with pleasantries.

"Yuh see mi grandson 'ere? 'im nah doing so well. 'is coluh lef 'im and 'im wheeze every time 'e tek breath. Dis him mudda 'ere, mi dawta. She did tek 'im to the doctor but dey cyan do nuthin. Yuh haf something fi help 'im?"

Mattie stood up, her face mirroring Grace Ann's. She gathered the front of her house coat, wiping her hands on the excess fabric, exposing even more of her thick legs. She walked towards the bundle Constantine was holding in her arms and gave a quick smile, simultaneously acknowledging his mother and asking permission to examine him. Constantine, feeling a sense of comfort with this stranger, nodded her approval and adjusted Alton in her arms so the woman could get a better look.

"Hmph," was the first sound that escaped Mattie's mouth as she pursed her lips staring down at Alton. She stepped back and touched Constantine's arm sympathetically. "Yuh pickney sick sick."

Constantine nodded, tears springing to her eyes. But before they had time to drop, Mattie continued. "Meh haf somethin fi cure 'im."

Constantine breathed in relief, trusting Mattie's abilities instantly. She leaned in closer in anticipation, listening for her next instruction.

"Wha' meh a give yuh de doctors dem nah wan yuh fi see it. Dey say it's harmful. But meh been meking dese teas for a long time and meh pickney who look like yuh son com back, jump up, and run outside."

Mattie chuckled to herself, confident in the memory of her own success stories. "Is ganja tea. It's cut up. Yuh jus add two tablespoons of butter, boil de leaves and stems dem in tree cups of water. Fuh de next seven days, when yuh feed yuh son, give 'im a likkle of dis tea wid 'im milk. After de seventh day, he'll be much bettah."

Constantine hesitated. She'd heard of mothers giving their children ganja tea. But mostly older women, mothers who had come from the country or the rastas, who thought the herb was a panacea. They all extolled the virtues of the natural medicine, but still she didn't know if Alton could handle its potency.

"Miss Mattie, yuh sure dis ganja tea nah too strong for mi son? 'im just now tu'n two months old."

"Right. Mi nah give yuh a lot, just enough fi piece out over de seven days. When yuh boil de ganja it tek out sum a de potency. It's nah de same as smoking it. Dere's a reason God gave us this plant nah and it not just fi get high. It heal."

Her words comforted Constantine and with no other options, she agreed to follow Miss Mattie's instructions.

Mattie disappeared into the back of her store and came back carrying a small bottle of dried marijuana leaf. After she'd handed it over, Constantine thanked Mattie for her help while Grace Ann slipped her a few bills. As they were headed back down those same muddy alleyways, Mattie called after them and told Constantine to come back and see her once Alton was well again.

When they got home, Constantine started giving Alton the tea. She had to force him to suckle just a little bit, using a dropper to put some of the tea in his mouth along with her milk. She watched his little face scrunch up in disgust as he tasted the herb for the first time.

With each passing day, Constantine watched first as Alton's appetite increased. His eyes regained some of their clearness as he started showing signs of his earlier curiosity. By day four, his skin shone with the newness it possessed rather than the ashen color it had developed as of late. Within a week's time, the wheezing was gone as well and there were no signs that he'd ever been sick. Constantine thanked God that her child was back and healthy. After another two weeks, watching him to make sure he didn't regress after she'd stopped giving him the tea, Constantine dressed Alton up in his best outfit and took him to see Miss Mattie again.
"Meh almost don't recognize de boy," Miss Mattie said when she saw Alton this second time.

Constantine beamed with gratitude. She kissed Miss Mattie, thanking her for saving her child.

After Constantine was sure that Alton had been cured, with the little bit of money they had left over from Clifton's work in Florida, the new family was able to get their own small house, not too far from Mother Johnson. After that, Clifton found himself in another employment slump. In the past, Constantine would have had idle time to shoot daggers of disgust in his direction, but now she was so devoted to the baby's health and progress that Clifton was given a reprieve. And though she was easier on him, with a newborn son and Lillian's on the way, Clifton was, once again, made to feel like he wasn't living up to the man he could be.

Every day when he went out looking for a job, again Clifton began to romance the idea of abandoning everything and everyone. He thought about leaving Kingston and going somewhere else, someplace new to try his luck. But every day around dinner time, he decided, after much self-convincing, that he was better off going home. He couldn't keep running.

One day when he came home, Constantine, greeting him nonchalantly, gave him the best news he'd heard since his son was born: "Some guys stopped by de house today. Dey left something fah yuh dere on the dressah."

Clifton walked back into the bedroom and recognized the logo from the employment bureau. He grabbed it and came out immediately to tell Constantine the good news.

"Dis card about a job!" Clifton held the card tightly, lest he lose his opportunity.

Constantine raised her eyebrows before nodding distractedly. She was working on getting Clifton's dinner on the table, tending to Alton, and most of all she doubted whether this particular opportunity was going to turn into anything permanent.

"Could . . . could yuh read it fah me, yuh know to mek sure meh understand everything?"

Constantine turned abruptly to lock eyes with him, irritated once again by his helplessness. She kissed her teeth before putting the plate down and holding her hand out for Clifton to give the card to her.

"It says dey wan yuh ta come to the bureau tomorrow at nine a.m. bout a job. But it nah say nuttin else."

Clifton took the card back from her, looking over it, hoping to glean any additional information she may have left out. It was just after six o'clock, still, Clifton felt it was better to go by the bureau now, just in case the job couldn't wait. He changed quickly into a fresh shirt and walked the twenty minutes to the office.

Just as he was walking up, he recognized a familiar face, locking the front door to the building.

"Reid! How yuh doing, man?"

The man was one of the young boys that used to visit the club, looking for extra food the kitchen staff might be able to spare at night. Clifton made a habit of feeding them once and it became a bit of a tradition for as long as he worked there.

"Ah, meh doing alright. Meh jus come 'ere because I see someone left this card wid mi wife about a job. Meh figah de office close already but just in case . . ."

The man nodded sympathetically, noting his old friend's desperation.

"Yeah, man. Meh and some of de fellas went by the Glass Bucket Club de other night looking fa you. And when we nah see yuh, we ask fa you. 'Reid. Where is Reid? What 'appen to 'im?' De men dere tell us say yuh nah work dere in a long time."
He averted his eyes a bit to save Clifton some of his dignity.

"Well, me and de fellas we remember how yuh always did tek care ah we. We'd come over to de club hungry, hungry man. Wanting hamburger, cheeseburger, Slim Jim, ice cream, juice whatever, and couldn't afford nuthin.' And ya know yuh was de only one who would give de food to us."

Clifton smiled, proud of himself for having shown such generosity.

"We nevah fahgit dat. So, when we hear yuh nah working for Glass Bucket, we looks yuh up. And it was meh who left the card wid yuh wife."

Clifton was overcome. He felt the threat of tears so he steadied his voice before extending his hand to the man. "Tank you."

The man began speaking quickly, giving Clifton an opportunity to get himself together.

"Yuh welcome, man. So fa de job tomorrow be here at nine a.m. Dey looking for twenty English-speakin' men from Jamaica to go and work at de U.S. Naval base in Cuba. Yuh tink yuh could do that?"

Clifton took the news as another sign. God was rewarding him for honoring the vows he made to his wife by coming home on those days he only wanted to run away. It was just the escape he was looking for, masquerading as an employment opportunity.

"Oh sure! Meh be back 'ere tomorrow mawnin."

The two men shook hands again. And this time, just hours after he'd made the trip the first time, Clifton was returning home with hope.

The next morning before eight o'clock, Clifton was back at the employment bureau. He quickly learned that he wasn't the only one who'd heard about the position because there was a line of men outside, wearing a desperate look that matched his own.

After more than an hour on line, he stepped into a room with two naval officers sitting behind a desk. Though the room was cooler than most he'd been in, with two fans humming, the officers's faces were a blotchy crimson, dotted by beads of sweat that seemed to sit on top of their tight, almost suffocating collars.

Clifton adjusted his own tie and smoothed his jacket before he stepped forward.

The soldiers, still looking down writing, asked him to state his name.

"My name is Clifton Reid, officers."

Hearing his shoddy British accent, the men glanced upward, amused.

"Mr. Reid," said one of the officers, "We're looking for men to travel to our naval base in Cuba and be of service to our officers there. Does that sound like something you'd be able to do?"

"Oh, yes, sir."

Another officer, doubtful, asked him if he'd ever worked in hospitality before.

"Yes sir, I did work at de famous Glass Bucket Club, waiting on the wealthy tourists dem, while they dined. If you was to go dere today, dem would tell yuh bout Clifton Reid." He knew what exactly they'd tell the officers was debateable, but he had only said it because he assumed the officers wouldn't have time to inquire about him or the reason he had to leave the club.

"Mr. Reid. We're looking for someone who has some culinary experience. A lot of our soldiers come from the United States and will, naturally, want American food while they're away from home. Are you familiar with American cuisine? Do you know how to make, for instance, hamburgers?"

Clifton had never made a hamburger a day in his life. But he'd seen the cooks at the Glass Bucket accomplish this feat many times. "Yes sir, I do."

Assuming that it would be to his benefit to describe the process, Clifton recounted what he'd only observed. "It's simple. First, yuh haf ta season the meat. But we keep it simple with salt, pepper, a little onion powder, garlic. Then you flatten the ground beef into a patty and put it on the grill, till it brown up on one side and then yuh flip it to the other."

One of the officers nodded.

"We'll just get straight to the point. It seems you have all of the qualifications we're looking for. We'd love to offer you the job in Cuba. Do you accept?"

Clifton's lips cracked into the first sincere smile he'd given in weeks. "Meh gratefully accept, sir." He stepped forward to shake the officer's hands. "Tank you very much."

"You're a very lucky man, Mr. Reid. You just secured the last position."

Clifton's heart fluttered slightly, recognizing his blessing. After he'd gotten the offer letter from the officers, he strode out of the room, restraining himself from skipping out the door.

***

The day he set sail for Cuba, Clifton stood on the deck, the wind whipping his customary travel outfit, a white bush jacket and brown pants. Men all over the Caribbean were fans of the two pleated cotton shirt. They all had different names for it but a clean, starched guayabera, as it was called in Cuba, sent the same message. It told anyone who saw this man that he had somewhere to be, something to do. That he was to be respected. Clifton had become accustomed to wearing them on his seemingly endless job searches, but this morning when Constantine presented the shirt to him, after she'd pressed it, he wore it with a different sense of pride. Today it told the truth.

With each push away from Jamaica's shore, Clifton breathed easier. For far too long Kingston had tested the limits of his manhood. In the past year, he felt the city was trying, despite his best efforts, to expose his inferiorities. His lack of learning, character and ability to provide were in a consistent battle to be showcased. And he was slowly losing his mind trying to hide what he considered the worst parts of himself from the public eye. This job in Cuba represented not just an end to that soul-stifling game but also an escape from the people, young and old, who watched him with wide, expectant, disappointed eyes, waiting for him to prove he could be the man he pretended to be.

It wasn't long before Clifton saw his blessing from God as a tool to live the life that had been snatched from him. During the daylight hours, Clifton wore his ring, selling himself as a friendly, dutiful family man. And in the evenings, he removed the semblance of his commitment and picked up a few Spanish words to speak to the Cuban women. Every other week, when he wasn't strengthening Jamaican-Cuban relations, Clifton returned to Kingston, alternating between visiting his girlfriend and wife.

He managed this maneuvering seamlessly. If he planned on seeing Lillian, he'd tell Constantine that he was arriving the day afterward, so she wouldn't be looking for him.

In the last month of the year, when Alton was just three months old, Clifton returned to Jamaica to the news that Lillian had welcomed a girlchild into the world. Telling Constantine that he wouldn't be able to make it back into town that weekend, he went to see the infant and her mother. Clifton held the girl Lillian had told him she'd named Mavis. With a round, protruding nose much like his own, and eyes set deeply in her face, Mavis slept peacefully in her father's arms. Clifton looked down at her, envying that type of peace. He knew, studying her tiny features, that, like his first two children who'd been sent to Trelawny, to be raised by his family, there wouldn't be any more of this.

Clifton reasoned that as long as the baby was snuggled in his arms, Lillian wouldn't try to attack him. Now was the time to tell her. As he shifted in the chair, getting ready to deliver the blow, Mavis stirred and began crying. Lillian swooped in from the kitchen, where she had been preparing Clifton something to eat, to come nurse her. She scooped Mavis out of his arms, and in what seemed like one, swift motion, freed her left breast to feed the child.

Clifton sighed, his strategy having been thwarted. "Lillian," he said softly.

She looked up from Mavis's face and into his.

"Yuh know meh did marry a 'oman, " Clifton said, unable to look directly into her face.

She cast her eyes downward again, nodding. "Meh hear."

"And she jus give meh a son," Clifton said, a smile inadvertently springing to his lips.

Lillian's posture tightened suddenly and her nipple slipped out of her child's mouth. Mavis let out a whimper and Lillian, readjusting herself, wondered if she were crying because the milk had stopped flowing or because she knew that her father was making his exit.

Once Mavis had latched again, Lillian turned to Clifton and said softly, "And meh just give yuh a dawta."

Clifton's mouth hung open. Just as Constantine was always ready to slice you with her words, Lillian had always been silent and accepting. In all the years he'd known her, she'd only spoken up to answer a direct question. Clifton looked at her puzzled; and after a second or two, she averted her eyes.

"I know. And I see she gon be a beautiful girlchild. But yuh know meh haf an obligation to mi wife now."

He paused, waiting for another reaction. Lillian stared at the wall across the small room, while Mavis suckled loudly.

"Meh haf a good job in Cuba now. So yuh nah haf fi worry bout muney. Meh send de muney but outta respeck fah mi wife, meh nah come 'round 'ere no more."

Lillian would have been better off looking at Clifton's face. If she had, she might have seen a bit of the shame and guilt he felt. Instead, the words darted through the air and stung the side of her face, causing a single tear to fall. It left a trail, as if attempting to soothe the cheek that had been struck. Lillian knew that if she spoke anymore her voice would crack, the tears would continue, shaking her body, and Mavis, who had drifted back to sleep, would wake. So she sat there, silent.

Clifton stepped closer to her. "Meh . . . do . . .wan yuh fi know meh care about yuh. And I tank yuh for mi chirren dem. But me wan de right thing for mi son and mi wife."

Lillian had always respected the sanctity of marriage. And in her mind she knew that Clifton was right for wanting to be there for his wife. Still, she couldn't understand why she, the woman who had borne three of his children, the woman he had known first, wasn't the one given the title. Another tear rolled down the right cheek.

Quickly, before she crumpled completely, Lillian turned to Clifton, allowing him to see the trails the tears had left, and asked him, "She does know bout me and de pickney dem?"

Clifton hesitated, trying to decide the best course of action. If he told her the truth and said no, Lillian might try to find Constantine and introduce herself. And though it was a possibility, Clifton knew that this type of confrontation wasn't in her nature. So he decided to be honest.

"No. She nah know about unu."

Lillian winced slightly before she locked eyes with Clifton and said, "Yuh leave here."

He nodded. As he walked past Lillian, he reached past the breast that he knew so well and stroked the coils on Mavis's head. At the doorway, Clifton left some crisp bills on an end table before closing the door behind him.

1946, Twenty-six

Now that Alton was older and healthier, Clifton invited his family to visit his new family and their new house. Clifton's family members only spoke briefly to Constantine during their wedding. The hustle and bustle pulled her in different directions that day, and they couldn't get a good sense of who she was. They hadn't even known she was pregnant at her wedding. It wasn't until they heard of Alton's birth that they all counted backwards and raised their eyebrows. She had proven herself less than pious in that regard. So when they received Clifton's invitation, they made plans as soon as possible to travel the hour to Kingston, anxious to learn more about the fast, city woman.

Constantine spent the whole week prior to their arrival cleaning and scrubbing the house. With Alton bouncing on her hip, she went to the market at least three times that week to buy new, white tablecloths and sheets. When Alton took his nap, she took the time to polish the flatware, before wrapping it up and placing it back in the drawer. She checked on it daily to make sure she hadn't missed any spots.

Clifton had nine brothers and sisters, but only four of them and their mother were traveling into the city. Constantine breathed a sigh of relief when Clifton told her it was only going to be four of them. Still, if she said or did anything they didn't like, four people was more than enough to spread the word to the rest of the family.

Clifton and Constantine didn't have enough money to prepare a big meal for all those people so she cooked ackee and saltfish with yam, green bananas, and dumplings.

By the time Clifton, who'd picked them up from the bus station, knocked at the door to announce their arrival, Constantine had just turned down the eyes on the stove, letting the contents of the pot cool before she placed the brightly colored food on the white plates, over the white tablecloth.

Leaving the kitchen, Constantine made her way to the door, studying each of Clifton's family members as they filed into her home. She noticed first that neither of Clifton's two sisters, Evelyn and Iris, had her hair pressed nor wore makeup. Their hair thick, coarse, and braided into a crown on each of their heads. They each inherited the same thick nose Clifton had. The sisters dressed very simply, like Grace Ann would have, with shirts buttoned up to their neck and skirts that covered their ankles. Constantine, with her knee-length hems and penchant for displaying her cleavage, realized they probably regarded her as a harlot.

Behind the sisters came their mother, Jane Reid. She wore a broad hat and had a small, soft voice, similar to the one Grace Ann would have had if it had not been hardened and hollowed by years of cigarette smoking. Constantine hugged her when she came in and Jane returned the embrace, warmly. Looking at her now up close, Constantine could see that Clifton was the spitting image of his mother. All of them looked like they belonged to each other with that distinctive peek of pink on their bottom lips.

After the two sisters and Jane came the brothers. The first, Bawzie, entered the home, his face fixed in disgust as if he smelled something rancid. Constantine panicked, thinking that she had neglected to clean something.

"Hey Bawzie…is everything alright?"

He smiled politely but his face still managed to look displeased. "Everything is jus fine. Tank you." Had he not leaned over and kissed her on the cheek, she might have doubted his sincerity. She came to the conclusion that the scowl was just his default expression.

The other brother, Durrell, who looked pleasant enough, paid little attention to Constantine when he walked in. Instead, he seemed to be inspecting the house, making sure it was to his liking. The rest of the family had come in and sat down in the living room; but before Constantine could even offer him something to drink, Durrell had walked off to explore the bedroom, kitchen, and bathroom, making quiet, grunting noises as he went along.

After they were satisfied with their tour, they all sat around the table. Listening to his family, Constantine could see that perhaps Clifton was the least conservative of the bunch. Nearly every other word from the sisters was about the Sabbath and Constantine wondered if they were trying to convert her. Perhaps they felt that she'd led their brother away from his faith and were trying to save his soul before he was too far gone. She wondered how much Clifton had told them about her and her family and whether or not he'd mentioned the fact that they didn't go to church often. And while it might have been assumed, she hoped that at the very least he'd made sure they knew that she had converted to become an Adventist. As they lectured, Constantine smiled graciously. And when they stopped talking, she assured them that she had every intention of making sure their son grew up in the church.

After the religious talk died down, Clifton's siblings showed a different, more relatable side of themselves. It wasn't long before the group was reminiscing about their childhood, laughing over plates that had been scraped clean. Had Constantine not stood to clear their dishes, drawing attention to herself, perhaps the mood would have stayed like this. But as she stood, Durrell leaned back in his chair at the table and looked around the house from his seat and then directly at his brother. He wasted no time before he fired away.

"Clifton, meh woulda t'ought yuh done bettah dan dis. Yuh been in Kingston almost tree years now an' dis all yuh have fi show fi yourself. For dis yuh coulda stayed in Trelawny."

Though the rest of the family members fell silent, their eyes darting between Durrell and Clifton, Constantine watched the scene unfazed. It was clear from the way that Durrell walked in the house, that he had something to say. If she were surprised about anything, it was the fact that it had taken him so long.

Clifton sighed heavily before responding. "Yuh sit pon de bus fah hours just fi come an insult meh and mi wife?"

Durrell scoffed. "Meh a wonder why yuh left yuh children. Yuh say yuh wan give dem a bettah life wid de muney yuh making in Kingston but it seem like it nah much."

Constantine froze. What children? The voice in her head was screaming so loudly, she thought her husband and guests had heard her. And then realizing they hadn't, she spoke her desperate inquiry aloud. "Clifton, wha' chil'ren him ah talk bout?"

The rage welling up in Clifton prevented him from hearing his wife beg for answers. Instead, he glared at Durrell, contemplating which utensil would cause the most damage when he shoved it into his brother's throat. The only thing preventing Clifton from lunging at him was their mother sitting in the middle of the two of them.

While Clifton was ready to fight, Constantine's eyes darted from Clifton to Durrell to Jane in search of an answer. No one spoke up to refute the claim. Constantine leaned back fully in her chair, her arms folded across her chest. Clifton perceived it as some type of battle stance but it was really her feeble attempt to stop herself from shaking in ire. Clifton turned to her to deliver a silent eye message that said, "Quiet, we'll talk about this later." Constantine bit her tongue, wanting to follow her husband's direction. But in the silence that fell over the table, Constantine reminded herself that this was her home and she wasn't going to be the only one who didn't know what was going on in it. And if Clifton were lying about something as big as having children, she deserved to get the answers right now.

"How many pickney yuh have, Clifton?"

He turned to her, his head bowed. "Meh haf tree chi'ren. A boy an' two girls."

Durrell was next to speak. "Oweee, is tree yuh have now! Das news tuh me! Last meh check, it was only de two pickney yuh haf." Durrell chuckled to himself at the theater show he'd unwittingly directed.
Constantine looked at Jane to see if she was going to reprimand her sons, one for speaking so out of turn at what was supposed to be a family dinner and the other for lying to his new wife about the children he seemed to have all over the island nation. But Jane didn't. She sat with her head bowed, occasionally looking up to sip the last bit of sorrel from her glass. His sisters took their cues from her while the other brother turned his nose up even further in genuine disgust this time.

Seeing that everyone was determined to ignore the situation, Constantine excused herself from the table, claiming she needed to take care of Alton. In reality, as her son was the only person she could stand to look at, Alton was the one who needed to take care of her. Walking back to him, Constantine wondered if Clifton's family had known he hadn't told her about the three other children and had come specifically to embarrass her. As rude and abrasive as he was, Constantine appreciated Durrell telling the truth about the existence of his nieces and nephew.

Minutes later, the family was packing up their belongings to head back to Trelawny. Constantine emerged from the room to say good-bye and wish them safe travels. Everyone but Durrell hugged her. Instead he gave her an exaggerated, patronizing bow as he backed out of their humble home. Constantine held her face deadpan until he dropped the sinister grin on his own face.

When Clifton came back from dropping his family off at the bus station, he tiptoed back into their room, hoping Constantine would have fallen asleep with the baby. Not only was she still awake, Constantine had been listening for his key to turn the lock for the past twenty minutes, jumping at every noise in the house. She walked into the living room to find him seated, his head in his hands.

"So, when yuh did tink yuh should tell me 'bout de tree chi'ren dem? If yuh brother nevah come inna mi house and mek a scene, when yuh a go tell me seh yuh son haf a brudda an' two sistahs?"

Clifton felt as if he had been bowed since Durrell made his announcement. Several thoughts had zipped in and out of his cradled head. But now, listening to the muffled sound of his wife's voice, he asked himself why he hadn't told her about his children before. He had had every intention of being honest. But certainly not when they first began dating. And as their relationship progressed, proving more and more hostile with each passing day, he knew that if he ever told her before they were married, she would have dismissed him. As much as he hadn't wanted to marry Constantine, he didn't want her to be the one to dump him. He certainly couldn't admit that he was seeing Lillian the same time he was seeing her. And then, after he'd moved in with her mother, he could no longer afford to tell her and risk being kicked out onto the street. So he kept it from her. It hadn't been all that hard to do. In many ways, Clifton had convinced even himself that he was free and single. Like Alton, the children who came before him weren't planned. And like Alton, he did love them but his youth, his selfishness and his inadequacies kept him from being the father they all needed. As Durrell said, Clifton had told their mother and his family that he was leaving Trelawny and his children because he wanted to work in Kingston where he'd be able to make more money for them. And that was true, he *had* been able to make more money in the city. But there was another reason which he rarely allowed himself to consider.

Clifton remembered it had been a full week after Lillian had given birth to their first child before he finally went to go see her and the child. He bought a fresh white shirt for the occasion and paired it with a tie, then stopped by the market to present Lillian with some flowers. He didn't know which color or type was her favorite but eventually settled on some white orchids. By the time he got to Lillian's door, the new shirt was clinging to his skin, more from nervousness than the island heat. She opened the door, and despite his tardiness, grinned before inviting him to step inside.

Clifton thrust the flowers in Lillian's direction. She took them and disappeared into the kitchen and he took a seat in the living room. When she returned to the front room, she was carrying their son. He was covered so thoroughly, Clifton craned himself out of his seat to see the boy's face. Lillian, seeing his curiosity, placed the infant in Clifton's arms and smiled, waiting for his approval.

Clifton's arms barely registered the weight of the tiny baby and he feared it would be all to easy too harm this tiny boy. When he looked into his son's eyes, wide and probing, seeming to see an invisible part of himself, Clifton knew for certain that he would.

"Lillian, come tek de boy," he said trying to keep the tears that were pooling in his eyes from falling.

"Whas de mattah, yuh don't wan hold 'im any longer dan dat?" She asked softly, wondering if Clifton had noticed something wrong with the boy she had missed.

"Nothing nah wrong. He's a good lookin' boy. Meh jus cyan stay long. I jus come to see unu and mek sure everybody doing ok."

Lillian nodded, a confused frown creeping across her face.

The very day he held his son in his arms for that brief moment, he knew he had to leave Trelawny. He knew he had to make money for the boy. And he also knew he couldn't stand to be seen anymore by those eyes. It wouldn't be long before those probing eyes would be followed by legs that ran after him, hands that sought to grab him and a mouth the called out his name and questioned his absences.

"What Durrell say is true, dere was no muney in Trelawny fi support chi'ren. And it was embarrassin' me as a man to nah give mi chi'ren dem de things they need. Den when meh furst come here, de same woman, she follow behind me. Before meh met yuh, she tun up pregnant again."

He knew even as he said it that his lie would fly back in his face if ever Constantine met Lillian and their children. But he assumed that Constantine, as his wife, would be in no rush to do that. As she sat quietly listening to Clifton's side. She held her lip in a perfect curl of contempt, occasionally releasing grunts of disapproval.

He lied and said it was hard for him to leave them, when he knew he had been looking for an escape. "But mi mother, the same 'oman who raise me and mi brothers and sisters dem, she would be de bes person to raise dem up, teach dem about de Lard. Meh trust 'ar."
She knew Clifton was full of shit. But she didn't know him well enough to see the truth behind his story and so she reduced him to just another whorish man who was in the habit of making babies and then leaving them as he went on about his life, exploring and repeating the cycle. She knew then that he had the capacity to be cruel and callous. He was a man who would leave behind his own flesh and blood if he felt they were going to slow him down. And though she was sure she had pinpointed his vile nature, she still had one question.

"Why yuh nah tell me?"

She couldn't understand how a person could pretend their children didn't exist. Clifton didn't have to dig to know that in the beginning Constantine would have never even looked at him if he told her he had two children living with his mother. And in this instance, tired of spinning lie after lie, he decided to tell the truth.

"In de start meh knew yuh woulda judge meh and nevah see me. Den aftah de time pass, meh nevah knew how fi bring it up. Yuh woulda dismiss meh no mattah when meh did tell yuh."

Constantine had a headache. She threw her hands up in the air, exclaiming, "Why meh haffa go and marry a liar, Lord Jesus?"

Turning back to Clifton she said, "Meh hope yuh at least tek care a dem. Dat Bible yuh profess to live by say a man who nah tek care of him family is no bettah den an unbelievah. Meh hope yuh at least doing dat."

Clifton nodded slowly, thinking about the weeks he hadn't been of help to anybody when he was unemployed.

Then speaking to anyone who might be listening, Constantine offered up a prayer. "Fadda God, meh hope de man nah plan fi leave meh here tah care fa de pickney by miself. Give me strenth, Papa Jesus, fah 'im jus run up and down breedin' up Jamaica."

The prayer didn't soothe her. She paced around the house fussing, calling Clifton everything but a child of God. The anger was directed at him but at herself too. She had put herself in this position. She thought about Hilda. She'd had five children by this point and had never married. Constantine had always pitied Hilda and even resented her for putting their mother through so much pain. But standing here, in the home she shared with a man who would lie about his own flesh and blood, she wondered if her sister were better off.

Then Constantine interrupted her own thoughts. "Yuh really send muney fi yuh mudda tuh tek care a yuh pickney dem?" She asked for his children but she also asked for Alton. There was no telling how long this odd marriage was going to last and she wanted to know what would become of her and her son should Clifton ever decide not to return from one of his stints in Cuba.

"Yes, meh send dem a likkle muney every munt' or so."

She scoffed at his foolishness. "Yuh mek sure yuh send muney every munt', enough for dem to live and eat good on."

Repulsed by her husband and exhausted of this conversation, she walked out of the room to go nurse her son. Sitting in the chair, distracted by Alton's suckling, she let her mind wander.

Constantine knew money alone wouldn't make a difference to those children when they needed their father. Having just had a child, she couldn't imagine leaving him to be raised by someone else. But the fact that she had married a man who had done so rocked her. Had she known Clifton was in the habit of leaving his children, she would have never even entertained the idea of being seen out in the street with such a man. It wasn't so much that he'd had other children. Both her father and her mother had had other children when they married. It was that he pretended he didn't.

She thought back on their first awkward interactions, when he was just an eager boy from the country. She wondered why she never picked up on the signs that he was a meandering Casanova. Maybe it was all a part of his game, to convince women that he was sweet and harmless until they found themselves, legs cocked up in a bed, giving birth to his children. She and the son in her arms were living proof that it had worked.

Then, for the first time since she'd heard the news, Constantine thought about the other woman. Did she know about her? Surely word had spread that Clifton had gotten married. There was a good chance that Clifton was still seeing her, that they took turns laughing and joking about his poor, stupid wife at home. Or did this woman envy her for having been the one to receive his last name? There was a good chance she'd wanted to marry Clifton herself. And if she carried children for the man she must have been expecting some type of commitment. Constantine wondered what lies Clifton had told her. What type of promises had he made? And, more importantly, what was he telling her now that he was married?

She tried to imagine this woman. She might wear her hair unstraightened like his sisters. If he'd met her in the church, she might wear long skirts—that no doubt had been lifted up at least three times. She wondered if this woman knew her husband any better than she did. For a second, the thought that someone might have more insight into Clifton produced a feeling in the pit of her stomach that surprised her. Here she sat nursing her baby, jealous of a woman whom she'd never met. And then, in some type of sick pacification, Constantine comforted herself with the fact that she'd won. Though Constantine knew her mother had forced his hand, she hadn't put a gun to his head. Clifton had chosen her over the woman who had given him three children.

She should have been more careful with her thoughts when she was nursing her son. As Constantine sat there thinking about who had won, when neither woman had much of a prize to begin with, she was unknowingly nourishing her son with milk that had been laced with envy, betrayal, and fear.

1947, Twenty-seven

In the two years since she'd married Clifton, Constantine had never felt more trapped. She dreamed about taking Alton, packing a few things, and leaving. She wouldn't even bother with a divorce. She told her mother of her half cocked plan one day, hoping that she'd find an ally.

But Grace Ann issued her daughter a warning instead. "Oh, child, yuh nevah know bout it? Yuh tink yuh can do bettah wid a next man? Dem all de same. Yuh might leave dis one tuh find de new one carry more fleas. Yuh a married 'oman, girl. Do yuh best fi accept yuh husband."

So she stayed. Reminding herself, almost daily, that she was sacrificing herself and her happiness for her child.

Months after the conversation with her mother, Constantine was still trying her best to work with what she had. She'd "tried" so well that she and Clifton were expecting their second child. As she lay in bed next to her husband, she thought about the unborn child, hoping it would be a girl. It was early in her pregnancy, just two months along, and though she was throwing up nearly every morning, she was excited nonetheless. She and Clifton lay there in bed talking about nothing in particular when she remembered that she needed to ask him about some new shoes for Alton. The boy was toddling around now and couldn't stand for his mother to hold him, so Constantine knew it was time for him to get some shoes, the good, sturdy kind that would set his feet the right way.

"Listen, could yuh giv meh ah few dollars fi buy Alton some shoes?"

Clifton sighed. He thought they had been having such a nice conversation and now here she was begging for money. The entire month had been a strain and he really didn't have it.

"Mi nah haf it dis munt', Connie."

Constantine rolled her eyes. She found it hard to believe that he didn't have it. In fact there were a few reasons why he probably didn't. "Maybe if yuh would stop wasting yuh muney up gambling then yuh son could get 'im first pair ah shoes."

Before the words even had time to settle in the air, Clifton kicked her.

The force from his foot landing in her abdomen was so strong that it sent her sailing out of bed. She lay there paralyzed, partially in shock but still able to marvel at how far she'd fallen. Clifton jumped down off the bed, not to help her back up but instead to loom over her chastising her in this subservient position.

"Don't yuh evah question meh bout wha meh ah do wid mi muney. Yuh nah bring no muney inna dis house fi raise up Alton. Alla wha' yuh see 'roun dis house, is my job dat pay for it. And meh nah haf no 'oman fi tell me how fi run mi house."

Spittle hit Constantine's face as he continued scolding: "Mi nah hafta be 'ere, yuh know? If meh woulda never married yuh, where would unu be? Is ah favor mi did yuh mudda. Don' fuhgit dat."

His expression was drastically different from any she'd ever seen from him. His eyes were narrowed to daggers, his nostrils flared, and he almost snarled as he glared down at her. Constantine was terrified and, even worse, after the way he'd looked at her, she felt like a piece of trash he'd meant to discard long ago.

She prayed that the kick and lecture would be the last of it. Once Clifton realized she wasn't going to argue anymore, that he had won, he turned and walked out of the room. She heard their front door slam on his way out. When he was gone and Constantine was sure that he wasn't coming back for a while, she allowed a few stifled sniffles and sobs to escape from her body, hoping not to wake Alton. Crumbled in the corner crying, she was transported back to her childhood home, reliving the worthlessness she felt after her father beat her. He had been the last man to put his hands on her. And she was sure when she stood up to him in the living room, that it would be the last time any man would. But here she was, with a child of her own in the next room, sobbing next to the bed she shared with her husband. The way he had kicked her, so brutally, she knew there would be no negotiation with him. This was no way to live but she was so bound to this man and his resources that she knew, even as she sat there, feeling the soreness in her belly, that she wasn't going to leave him and risk struggling with her son and unborn child.

As her body shook from her sobs, she felt a bursting release of fluid from between her legs. Just as she had done that night on the porch when she first started her period, Constantine put her hands down in between her legs and brought her fingertips to her face. They were covered in blood. The faint sobs immediately turned into loud, sorrowful wails as she wept for the baby she knew she had just lost.

Constantine lay back down rubbing her womb for what felt like hours. And when the tears stopped flowing, she stared up at the ceiling from her position on the floor, replaying all the interactions she'd had with Clifton, wondering if she had missed some sign, some clue that he was the type of man to hit a woman. But now that she was the one who was indebted to him, she was learning, every day, about the real man she'd married and not the representative she'd dated. Though she had never considered herself and her husband a team, she could have never anticipated this type of betrayal. She had foolishly believed that after watching her give birth, he would have more respect for her, if not as a wife, certainly as one of the mothers of his children.

With blood slowly seeping from between her legs, Constantine felt rage swell up inside of her. Made up of a stomach-churning mixture of betrayal, disappointment, and pain, it shook her whole body and she was weakened from it.

Her only comfort was that she wasn't bringing another child into what was shaping up to be a dysfunctional household. From the time she was a little girl, Constantine had known she hadn't wanted to have a marriage like her parents's. Now it seemed she had something far worse.

Eventually, she got up. Painfully, she passed the underdeveloped embryo in the bathroom, into her hand. Constantine thought it might have been a good idea not to look at the child that would never live. But feeling it, slippery in her hand, she couldn't resist. She peered down and saw, inside a bloody sac, a tiny, abnormally shaped head, legs that would never kick and arms that would never reach for her. Seeing how far along the child was, she wondered if it had suffered before it was expelled from her body before its time. The thought troubled her. So she did the only thing she could, prayed for the child's soul before burying it, like a seedling in the ground, at the back of their house.

When she came back inside, Constantine washed herself, put on her sanitary belt to catch the blood that was still flowing, and returned to bed. By the time she was finished, Clifton still hadn't made it back home yet. She was glad for that and eventually she fell into a fitful sleep. When she woke up the next morning, She was surprised to see Clifton was lying next to her peacefully, as if nothing had happened.

They never acknowledged what he'd done that night. Neither one of them could speak about it, but they each told themselves a different lie for comfort. Clifton firmly believed that it was his duty as the head of the household to train her, and instead of admitting to himself that it was his actions that caused them to lose their child, he reasoned that

Constantine had put herself in that dangerous position by talking back to him, out of turn and out of order. And every morning as Constantine wiped the blood from in between her legs, she pretended as if it were just another menstrual cycle. Having to acknowledge that this blood once nourished her child, recalling what the embryo looked like in her hand, and the swift, calculated motion that placed it there, was too much. She had never had something so precious snatched from her and rather than relive the loss over and over again, for the sake of both her son and herself, she thought it better to focus on the son who had already made it into this world.

Constantine would have never spoken of this lost child again but she'd already told her mother and sisters that she was pregnant. And when they asked her how she was feeling, expecting for the second time, she had to share this news too.

"Meh los' de baby. Meh held it in de palm of mi han' before I bury it in de backyard."

Everyone was full of sympathetic looks and gentle touches. It was Grace Ann, who sat at the head of the dining room table, a position she'd claimed ever since Theophilus passed, who asked the most pertinent question. "Wha happened, nah?"

Constantine locked eyes with her mother, shocked by the fact she'd known, immediately, that she was omitting a detail. She hung her head in shame for the abuse she endured and also so the women who crowded the room wouldn't witness her tears. "Clifton kicked me in mi belly. Meh feel somethin burst and meh lose de child." Constantine forced the words through a burning throat.

The room reached a weighted silence as the women leaned in, listening for more details.

"Meh an Clifton was on de bed arguing about muney an' I guess meh say somethin he nah like cuz 'im tear up 'im face and kick me right in mi belly and I fell outta de bed. Meh felt da blood. And when I look up ta see if 'im notice what 'im done, the dawg have his back turn ta me, walkin outta de room."

Constantine had re-imagined the scene so clearly in her mind that she hadn't noticed her current surroundings and the way her family was processing the story. Once she'd stopped speaking and looked around, she saw that Grace Ann sat at the table silent, shaking as she reached desperately for the cigarette between her thin lips.

Daphne, who was too young to be listening to the conversation, was crying without sound, tears tumbling down her round face. Olga shook her head in disbelief. Aside from Grace Ann, who'd sponsored Clifton for months, Olga knew him the best. He'd worked with her husband and had eaten food she prepared from her table on several occasions. Even though men hitting and even beating their wives wasn't an anomaly in Jamaica, she had no indication that Clifton, with his dashing smile and the constant talk about his faith, would be one of them.

Hilda felt the betrayal, the shock and the sadness of the rest of them. But she wasn't content to sit in the room and cry with her mother and sisters. The lines in her face contracted as she mulled the situation over in her mind. She came to a solution and slowly started gathering her things and her daughter and she motioned for Constantine to meet her in the kitchen. When they got there, Hilda, who towered over Constantine, leaned in to her. "When Clifton ah come 'ome next?"
"'im due back dis weekend."

"Okay." Hilda nodded her head slowly, sliding her tongue over her front teeth. "Meh comin to unu house de night before 'im due tuh come in and meh will tell 'im de next time 'im wan fi kick somebody, he can try him luck wid me."

***

In two days time, Clifton was making his way back to Kingston. This particular day, Constantine's weekend, he was looking forward to seeing his wife and son in the home he made enough money to keep over their heads. He'd come a long way since he was jobless, roaming the streets, practically begging for work. Now that he had a good, steady check,

Jamaica seemed to resemble the island paradise people swore it was. Clifton chuckled to himself on the walk home, thinking how he'd really started to resemble a family man. By the time he got to his front porch, he was almost whistling he was so happy; but when he opened the door the song disappeared from his heart and his lips.

Experience had taught him that any time Constantine's sisters visited their home, it usually meant trouble for him. They'd be there talking all night, in tones so hushed, Clifton could only assume they were chatting about him. Whenever they were there Constantine practically ignored him. And days after they'd left, she'd be even more headstrong than usual. She fed off them in ways that only made his life more inconvenient.

Clifton saw Hilda's face contort as he walked inside. She was sitting, her arms splayed, in what had been designated as his chair. "Hello, Hilda," Clifton said, greeting her cautiously. He was certain that once again they had been discussing him in his own home. Before he could even get in good and take his shoes off, it began.

She scoffed. "No need for nah pleasantry, Mr. Reid. Meh come 'ere to get one ting straight."

Clifton started scanning his brain, thinking of all the things she could possibly want to address.
"What dat is?" he asked, trying to make his voice portray innocence.

"Meh hear say yuh kicked meh sistah," She stressed the ed on kicked, so Clifton could hear how barbaric even the word sounded. "Dat's why she did lose de baby." Hilda's eyes bore into his and she inched closer to the doorway where he was still standing.

Before he could feign the shock necessary for such an accusation, Clifton felt the blood rush to the top of his skin in a surge of panic. Despite the perspiration beading on the back of his neck, he tried to speak as if he were appalled and offended.

"Hilda, where yuh hear dat? Meh would nevah do nuthin like dat!"

Hilda shook her head, kissed her teeth, and brought her right leg up into her lap so she could remove the shoe from her foot. "'ow yuh think meh did 'ear bout it? Yuh nah remember Connie mi sistah?"

Constantine looked back between Clifton and Hilda, wondering how this was all going to end. She knew Hilda believed her without a shadow of a doubt and Clifton would never admit to doing such a thing. The conversation could only go so far.

Still, he said nothing else. To deny it again would insinuate that Constantine was a liar and judging by the disgust on Hilda's face, it was best he say nothing further.

Hilda took Clifton's silence as an admission. And she took her other shoe off before rising from the chair. "De next time yuh feel fi kick someone, yuh mek sure yuh call me."

The last word of her sentence had just reached Clifton's ears before Hilda lunged at him. Clifton, reacting quickly, pulled open the door he'd just closed and ran. Hilda, who was much taller than Clifton, extended her limbs and was right behind him, shouting obscenities and threats that only a fool would dismiss as idle. He ran down the porch steps, stopping briefly to unlatch the gate at the front of the yard. Hilda's face had morphed into something unrecognizable in her rage.

While Clifton ran through the gate, Hilda, who ran track as a young girl, cleared it like a hurdle, still with enough air in her lungs to call out to him down the street. "Mek meh catch yuh, yuh goat-faced mongrel, meh box yuh into next week."

Hilda chased Clifton for twenty minutes until she got tired and went back to Constantine's house. Clifton, fearful that she might be there waiting for him, slept, restlessly, at Lillian's that evening and traveled back to Cuba the next morning.

1948, Twenty-eight

With Constantine's family so close and heavily involved in their marriage, Clifton knew that if he ever put his hands on her again, he'd be dead. And so he restrained himself. Still, the damage had already been done. Constantine knew Hilda couldn't monitor Clifton's every move. So she tiptoed around her husband, careful not to trigger his temper.

After months of no incident though, she let her guard down. And it wasn't long before their family expanded. Three years after Alton, Constantine gave birth to their second son, who they named Winston. He arrived screaming healthily. Unlike his brother, Winston was fair-skinned, the color of butterscotch, like his grandmother. If Grace Ann had been younger, people would have sworn Winston had come from her. Constantine was delighted. Never had she imagined that she and her husband would be able to have a child this fair.

While Constantine took pride in the new baby's skin color, Clifton wasn't pleased. In fact, he took Winston's complexion as a sign that he wasn't his. After all, he was spending weeks away from home. It would have been more than possible. He didn't understand genetics or realize that a child could resemble his grandparents more than his parents. And he didn't keep his ignorance to himself.

He peered down into the hospital bed, at the baby in her arms and asked almost nonchalantly, "Connie, yuh nah tink dis boy too light fi belong tuh me? Him don look nuthin like me."

For months Constantine had a sneaking suspicion that Clifton hadn't been faithful to her. But there was no proof, no confirmation, until she heard him say those words.

It could have been anyone. In this country or the next. Now that Clifton was married, he'd suddenly become that much more appealing to women who weren't his wife. Constantine was sure they were all over him and he them. But she wasn't going to make a big scene about it. She wasn't going to leave him over it. Picturing her husband with another woman wasn't pleasant but Clifton wasn't the first man to have another woman and he wouldn't be the last. In fact, a part of her wanted to thank these women for wearing her husband out a little bit before he came home and jumped on her. After Clifton was finished with her, the only energy she would have had to cheat would have been depleted. She only strayed from her marriage in the recesses of her mind, imagining the ways in which her relationship would have been different if she'd forgiven Tawkins. Constantine had no illusions about being in love with Clifton. She wasn't. In fact, she hadn't known anyone who'd married for love. And so infidelity was to be expected and even excused. It wasn't the stepping out that was the issue. It was being accused of breaking her vows when *he* was the one who was dishonoring both of them. She couldn't let this foolish remark go unchecked.

"Is a shame yuh nah see de boy look jus like yuh people dem wid mi mudda complexion."

She spoke calmly, willing herself not to upset the sleeping boy in her arms. She felt Clifton puff up, frustrated, so she set Winston down in the bassinet next to her hospital bed. Once she had him settled, she chuckled smugly. "Don' come in 'ere an' accuse meh of sleeping wid ah nex man. Is meh who lay dere while yuh pumpin, pumpin, pumpin on top. Is a good ting de pickney come from mi womb, cus de way yuh walk de streets like a whoremonger, we woulda never know who 'im belong to."

Maybe it was the adrenaline that lingered in her system after having just given birth or maybe it was the fact that Clifton hadn't struck her since Hilda threatened him that made her feel so emboldened. Whatever it was, Clifton took none of it into account. By the time Constantine had closed her mouth, she felt the sting of his palm across her face. The pain grew and rippled through her cheek, into her eye socket and then her forehead. Propped up in her hospital bed, Constantine clasped her cheek. Despite her intention to appear strong and unfazed, she cowered, shrinking.

Clifton softened, seeing her fear. He stormed from the room repeating Constantine's word to himself: "whoremonger." It was that single word, with its threat of religious condemnation that set him off. Constantine couldn't have known what type of vulnerability she'd struck. Clifton believed in the fire and brimstone preaching and teaching of his youth and was certainly concerned for his eternal soul; not enough to change his behavior, but concerned nonetheless. After each encounter with a woman he washed himself clean, praying for forgiveness and now his wife was the one to throw his filth back into his face.

Clifton told himself that if Constantine knew the severity of the word, the origin, and the consequences, she would understand why she had been punished. It was vulgar and she herself had appeared vulgar using it. He had merely reminded her of her rightful position.

After she was released from the hospital, Constantine spent the following days at her mother's house. She offered no explanation to her husband but told her mother she needed her help. Grace Ann didn't ask any questions.

Though Grace Ann knew she had interfered in bringing the two together, now that they were married, she felt it best to stay out of their business. After nearly a month away from her house and husband, it was Grace Ann who suggested Constantine go home.

She went back grudgingly. When Clifton came home from Cuba, she cooked his meals and washed his clothes, but at night she slept with her back to him, daring him to touch her.
In their waking moments, it was her duty and devotion to her sons that kept her distracted enough to get out of bed each day.

Where Alton was wide-eyed and adventurous, exploring, climbing in and out of cabinets and running around with his older cousins, Winston was more reserved and skeptical. By the time he turned one, he didn't trust many people and wouldn't go to just anyone. He clung to his mother. And in the few moments when they weren't together, he watched her from below his thick, dark eyebrows. Winston was such a pretty child people often mistook him for a girl, a fact in which Constantine took great pride. If nothing else, she was thankful to Clifton for giving her attractive children. Looking at Winston day in and day out, she couldn't see how her husband had ever denied the boy. And as Winston got older and Clifton saw more of himself and his family in his son's features, Clifton, though he never said so, was convinced. Having struggled to get Alton healthy and having lost a child before Winston, she understood, now more than she had before, how precious they both were.

Perhaps Winston also sensed the danger that had preceded his arrival. He needed his mother more than his brother. Winston trailed Constantine, holding on to the bottom of his mother's skirts for protection from anyone who would try to take her away from him.

Clifton, when he came home, was particularly tickled by the dependency. "De boy musah tink yuh Jesus de way he ah touch de hem of yuh garment."

Winston always became especially anxious when his father was home. Not only was Clifton never around long enough for him to feel comfortable, he sensed the change in his mother's disposition. While it might have been best to wait for the boy to warm up to him, Clifton would grab him up, trying to force a playful, rough-and-tumble relationship when no familiarity or trust had been established. As such, Winston regarded Clifton carefully. He was simultaneously fascinated with him and hesitant of ever getting too close. When Clifton reached for him, Winston recoiled in fear.

1950, Thirty

Winston, like his brother before him, had been privy to his parents's arguments, but he internalized them differently. By the time he was two and Alton five, they were both accustomed to their parents's raised voices and snarling faces. But while Winston attempted to hide from these interactions, Alton studied them. He'd memorized the cycle. His mother would often be the one to say something she knew his father wouldn't like. The two would go back and forth, their voices rising. Finally, Constantine, standing bold in Clifton's face, would turn up her face in disdain and deliver a quiet, barely audible verbal jab that would be followed by his father's physical one.

In a strange way, Alton was relieved when that moment finally came. He didn't take pleasure in seeing his mother crumple; but once that happened, the house would return to its natural quiet, his father usually left, and he could go back to playing.

Constantine assumed, incorrectly, that her sons weren't processing the fullness of the dysfunction in their home. But in the moments when they locked eyes with her, in that deflated and defeated state, she hoped that they would eventually come to see her sacrifice to them and love her more for it.

***

Meanwhile in Cuba, Clifton had developed a reputation for himself. He wasn't satisfied back in the kitchen flipping burgers, a skill he had mastered since his interview. He wanted to interact with people. So every day, he found some way to leave the kitchen and introduce himself to the guests. He dodged popping oil and placed a napkin under his chin when he taste-tested anything, to keep his chef's uniform as clean as possible so that when he appeared in the dining room, he wasn't an eyesore. He emerged, armed with that charming smile of his and an exaggerated chef's hat that he removed once he reached an officer's table. Most times, Clifton would bow slightly, asking the naval officers, in his faux accent, if they liked the food. And the conversation usually flowed from there.

"Where are you from?" He'd ask the men. They'd tell him some place he'd never heard of in the United States, though he'd nod and pretend he was familiar with it. And then they'd ask him the same question. Clifton would chuckle, telling them it was a small town in Jamaica they'd never heard of.

Occasionally, one of the overly confident men would say, "Try me." And Clifton would tell them about the little town of Tyre. And just as he'd suspected, it would be too obscure. And they'd all chuckle again.

It wasn't long before the officers were requesting Clifton as their server. And not long after that before they began telling him that he could do more than be a chef and server in Cuba.

"You know, Clifton, we would love to take you to the States."

At first, he didn't think much of it. He'd been to the United States before and wasn't all that impressed. Not wanting to be rude and insult their country, he'd offer a gracious smile as a thank-you for the compliment and go on with his day. But each week, the offers started to hold more and more weight.

"You could really do well for yourself in the U.S.—much more money than you make here in Cuba."

Clifton thought about the first time he'd come to America. Like every other person from an island nation, he'd heard the myths about the gold-paved streets. But when he was in Miami, cutting cane and picking fruit, he found that, with the exception of more paved roads and taller buildings, it was just like Jamaica. But over there, he had only been good enough to do the work from which he'd fled. He wasn't looking forward to repeating that lonely and agonizing experience.

"Yuh know, officer, meh been tuh to de States before. And it wasn't what meh tought it would be."

The men frowned, not understanding how a foreigner could come to America and not immediately fall in love with it. They had been nonchalant in their attempts to convince Clifton to come over before; but now, out of a sense of defensive patriotism, they were all the more determined to persuade him to return.

"Ah, no. They had you in the field with the Mexicans. A nice man like you could do so much more in America. I'm sure you could find something where you wouldn't have to break your back."

"Yuh serious, sir?"

"Sure. I know there are plenty of opportunities over there. Half the boys here could use someone like you working for them when they go back home. I'll ask around for you."

"Tank yuh, sir."

Clifton didn't get his hopes up too high; but if the officer's words were true and he wouldn't have to spend his time in the bush, under a blistering sun, swatting off mosquitos, he certainly wouldn't mind making good, decent money in America.

Two weeks passed and the officer came back with one of his subordinates, a man named Elgin Nyehart.

"Private, this is the man I was telling you about, Clifton Reid. Mr. Reid, this is Private Nyehart. He's newly married and almost finished with his service. He could use someone like you to help he and his wife once he gets back home."

"Pleasure to meet yuh, Private Nyehart."

As Private Nyehart smiled, extending his hand, Clifton sized him up. The man was at least five years his junior. The thought that someone this young had already established himself enough to need domestic help was a sobering one. Even if Nyehart had inherited this money from his family, Clifton figured that if he could work his way to even a third of the prosperity this man had, it would be better than staying in Jamaica—or any other part of the Caribbean—for the rest of his life.

"I've heard some really good things about you, Clifton. Do you think you could be comfortable in America this time around?"

Contemplating his response, more than the delivery, his standard patois started to seep out. "Of course meh would love to move to the United States. But meh a married man now. Meh nah know if mi wife would wan me tuh go."

The superior officer spoke first. "Oh, I'll go and speak to her. It's a great opportunity. I'm sure we'll be able to convince her to see it that way. And in a few months's time, she'll be able to join you."

Clifton wasn't sure what Constantine would say about uprooting their entire lives, leaving their families and moving their children to a new country. He knew if he presented the option to her over the phone, she'd shut him down before he even had a chance to finish his sentence. So Clifton decided he'd just show up with the officer and let him do all the talking.

The next time the boat docked in Jamaica, Clifton brought a uniformed U.S. naval officer home to Kingston.

It didn't occur to Clifton until he and the officer were walking up to his house that Constantine might be so irritated by this unexpected guest that she'd shut down any type of request, from any type of stranger, uniform or not. He exhaled loudly, hoping that at the very least, Constantine would keep any anger or resentment off of her face until the man left.

When they reached his house, Clifton told the officer to wait in the yard while he prepped his wife. The officer took off his hat and held it between his hands expectantly while Clifton ran up the porch steps and in through the door.

"Connie, Connie! We haf a visitah. One ah de officers from de naval base come fi speak tuh yuh."

Constantine stepped out in an old but presentable dress, Winston hanging from her hip.

"Yuh nah tell me we fi haf company."

"Meh know. Meh couldn't get word to yuh before we arrive. But de man waiting downstairs. Jus put yuhself togetha likkle bit while meh bring him up."

Clifton dashed back outside, while Constantine stood frozen, wondering what she could fix quickly. She turned on her heel, back toward the bedroom. She freed herself from Winston's grasp and he immediately started whimpering. She stripped quickly and put on a nicer, newer dress, running her hand over it to smooth out any wrinkles. Now that Clifton was away so often, she found that she could appreciate him in smaller doses. So the night before, she'd pressed and curled her hair. With this White man coming to her house, she was thanking God that she had done so.

She heard the door open once more and Clifton telling the man to have a seat. He called for Constantine again. She took one last look at herself in the mirror before grabbing the still-crying Winston and walking out into the living room.

"Ah, dere she is. Officer, dis meh wife, Constantine," Clifton's mouth was smiling but his eyes darted between the officer and his wife to see if he approved.

"Mrs. Reid, nice to meet you. I'm sorry to stop by like this but it was important that I speak to you today."

Constantine smiled politely. "It's no inconvenience. Would yuh like somethin tuh drink?"

"I would love a glass of water if it's not too much trouble."

As Constantine started toward the kitchen, Clifton, playing the role of the gentleman and dutiful husband, gestured for Constantine to sit down and whispered, "Don't worry, sweetie, I'll get it."

Constantine and the officer made small talk while Clifton brought him the water. When Clifton returned to the table, the officer got down to the purpose of this unexpected house call.

"Mrs. Reid, I'm here today to talk to you about a great opportunity your husband has. All the officers have been so impressed with his professionalism and service at the naval base that we've recommended that he come work in the United States."

Constantine raised her eyebrows, surprised. She hadn't time to think what the officer might want to discuss with her; but even if she had, she would never have anticipated this.

"I know this may come as a bit of a shock and surprise but we believe your husband could make much more money in America. That would mean more money for you and your children. And in a few months, you all would be able to join him."

Constantine nodded but sat silently, attempting to process all he was saying.

"Mrs. Reid, Jamaica is a beautiful country. But America is a growing nation, with plenty of opportunities for young immigrants like yourselves. Clifton's told me you have another son too. In the U.S., both boys would be able to get a top notch education."

As the officer spoke, Constantine thought about what American citizenship would mean for her boys. But also about leaving her family, her country, and her home behind.

Though it hurt her to acknowledge it, she knew that Jamaica couldn't compete with the life they'd be able to have in America. She'd witnessed firsthand how Clifton had had to pull himself up from nothing on more than one occasion. She'd watched his spirit sink when he came home after spending the day fruitlessly looking for a job. And she expected that if they stayed on the island, it wouldn't be the last time their family would have to endure that hardship. It wasn't something she wanted to live through again or ever want her sons to know. So, with them and their future in mind, she responded to the officer, her heart aching but her mind resolute.

"Yes, dat's fine with me. As long as we're able to join him soon, that should be good. Tank yuh for comin all dis way tuh come and talk tuh me bout it."

Within a month after the officer's visit, Clifton and Constantine were packing and preparing for him to travel to the States. Their move was made less painful by the fact that Clifton was leaving before the rest of them. Since he was already usually gone for days on end, it was as if he were just sailing to Cuba again: Alton, Constantine, and even Winston had become accustomed to saying good-bye to him. Clifton, having taken on extra shifts at the naval base and cutting out his extracurricular spending and gambling, had saved up the equivalent of sixty American dollars to cover the additional cost of the plane ticket instead of taking the boat, like the first time. Clifton counted and recounted it before sticking it in his sock for safekeeping during his travel.

The night before he left, after Alton and Winston fell asleep and while Constantine was packing him a lunch for the plane, he ducked away into the boys's bedroom to say a prayer, placing his heavy hands on their heads as they slept.

All of his life Clifton had heard the preachers and even his father pray as if it were a very formal and auspicious conversation. Since he didn't speak to God candidly and not as often as he should, he did the same this evening.

"Fadda God in heaven, grant mi travelin mercies as I journey to de States. Be wid the pilots of de plane, Lawd, and help us ta land safely. Righteous Fadda bless me in de States. Help mi, mi wife, and de churren dem fi prosper in dis new lan. Help us to rememba yuh always, Lawd, and we'll be sure fi give your name, de praise, de glory, and de honor. In de precious name of yuh son Jesus de Christ, I pray. Amen."

Clifton wiped away the tears that had formed in his eyes. He composed himself quickly before removing his fingers from the tops of their heads.

After Constantine finished his lunch for the next day and pressed his shirt and slacks, the two said good-bye to one another with an ebb and flow of movements before drifting into a light sleep.

Early the next morning, Ellis was there to pick Clifton up and take him to the airport. Clifton threw his luggage into the back of the car before kissing Constantine and the boys good-bye. He waved from the front seat as the car pulled away from the house. Just as he started to let his mind drift to what he would do and have in America with a more comfortable job, Ellis was pulling up to the airport.

Neither one of them had been there before. But even without instruction, it wasn't hard for the two men to locate the front desk. A friendly woman with breasts that seemed to almost burst through her foliage-green uniform greeted them with a smile.

"Good mawning, gentlemen, 'ow may I help unuh dis mawning?"

Ellis, looking for an excuse to talk to the woman, spoke first through skinned teeth. "Mi frien 'ere travelin' to America and 'im need a ticket."

The woman lifted her eyebrow in slight annoyance toward Ellis before turning completely away from him, facing Clifton. "What's yuh name, sir?"

"Clifton Reid."

"All right, Mr. Reid, which state yuh traveling to today?"

"Meh heading to Indianapolis."

"Wha? Me nevah heard ah Indianapolis. It's in the United States?"

Clifton nodded, a bit unsure himself. He was hoping he hadn't given up his job in Cuba just to be taken for a fool.

"It may very well be, Mr. Reid. We can get yuh to Florida and from dere you can fin' ya way to . . . Indianapolis."

Clifton looked once again at the sponsor book Private Nyehart had left for him to travel with. He read the word "Indianapolis" once again, remembering the way Nyehart had taught him to pronounce it. Since he wasn't a citizen, he'd have to present that sponsorship booklet at every juncture.

"Do yuh haf a passport, Mr. Reid?"

He didn't. Instead, he presented the sponsorship booklet for the first time to the woman.

"Okay, this will do. So, the total for your ticket to West Palm Beach is sixty Jamaican pounds even."

Clifton felt a tinge of panic. He took a minute to do the calculation in his head. Sixty pounds was about forty-eight dollars of the sixty dollars he had for the trip. He had allocated sixty dollars with the assumption that he would be able to travel with change left in his pocket to support himself for a while before his first pay date. The receptionist, with her less than sincere smile, had just dashed those dreams. But in order to keep up appearances in front of the big-breasted receptionist and his brother-in-law, Clifton gingerly handed over much of the money he had worked so hard to save.

Clifton didn't know if he'd be able to get from Florida to Indianapolis with the less than twelve dollars he had left. But he also remembered his prayer from last night and figured the Lord was going to work something out for him. He just had to get onto American soil. Ellis wished him farewell and Clifton boarded a plane for the first time.

Though he had been exceedingly nervous, after eating the meal Constantine had prepared for him, Clifton eventually dozed during the forty-five-minute flight. He was jolted back to wakefulness when the plane landed shakily on the tarmac. A stewardess announced that they'd arrived safely in West Palm Beach and they would be able to disembark shortly.

Clifton knew he needed to find a phone so he could call the Nyeharts and tell them about his predicament. Not wanting to waste another cent on something else, he asked one of the receptionists, this time a thin, younger White woman, if he could use her phone. She smiled at him, tickled by his accent.

Clifton smiled coyly, happy to see that even in the midst of his misfortune, his charm worked on White women too.

The phone rang three full times before a woman with a thick Swiss accent picked up.

" 'ello, Nyehart residence . . ."

"Hello, dis is Clifton Reid, from the naval base in Cuba. I supposed to be meeting Mr. Nyehart. Is 'e in right now?"

"Oh, Clifton. Nice to be speaking to you. I've heard great things about you. This is his wife, Freida Nyehart. "

"Oh, hello, Mrs. Nyehart."

Clifton informed her of his location and financial situation.

"Listen, Clifton, you have to find a Traveler's Aid office. Ask around for it. Once you get there and show them your sponsorship booklet—you still have yours, right?"

"Yes, ma'am, meh still haf it."

"Show them that sponsorship booklet and they'll house you for as long as you need it."

"All right, Mrs. Nyehart, ma'am. Traveler's Aid. Tank you. I'll let you know if meh need yuh help again. But meh will see yuh soon in Indianapolis."

Clifton found a Traveler's Aid office and just as Mrs. Nyehart promised the people at the government office not only put him up in one of the finest hotels in West Palm Beach for the night, they also paid for his train ticket to Indiana.

A day and a half later, in mid-afternoon, after transferring from a train to a bus, a disheveled Clifton arrived in a place that was marked with a sign that read Holliday Park. From there he called the Nyehart residence and told them he was ready to be picked up. While he waited for his ride to arrive, Clifton strolled around the park. The trees were different than the ones in Jamaica and even Florida. They had rough and robust trunks and the branches on some of the larger ones seemed to extend upward forever. Clifton bent back to take it all in, grateful to be inhaling clean, fresh air after traveling for so long. He noticed there was a measure of crisp coolness in it, though it was summer, unlike the thick, damp Caribbean humidity he had known all his life.

As he was admiring the newness of Indianapolis, he was startled by the sound of a car horn. Nyehart, whom Clifton was seeing for the first time out of his military uniform, looked like his youth. Still, Clifton extended his hand and greeted him as if they were still on the base.

"Good afternoon, Private Nyehart."

"Good afternoon, Clifton. Now, that we're off the base, you can just call me Mr. Nyehart."

Clifton nodded. Nyehart opened the back door and Clifton placed his bags inside the car. He was going to climb in the backseat behind them but Nyehart told him to sit up front. Working at the Glass Bucket Club, and going out after hours with his coworkers, Clifton had had some experience driving people's cars. But none of the cars he'd driven in Jamaica looked like this or rode as smoothly. Clifton watched, engrossed, as the scenery along the tree-lined roads played like a movie on the hood of the car.

Nyehart broke his concentration.

"Oh, so do you have that sponsorship booklet?"

"Yes, 'ere in mi pocket," he said tapping the pocket at the top of his shirt.

"There's some very valuable information in here. I would hate for it to end up in the wrong hands," Nyehart said smiling nervously.

That's when Clifton remembered that the Nyehart's salary had been listed in there. He had been guarding the booklet for so long, he didn't realize that Nyehart wasn't asking to make small talk. He was asking because he wanted it back.

Clifton remembered the number in the book: $18,000 a year. It was more money than he ever imagined making but he wasn't sure if most of America lived like this too. Judging by Nyehart's fierce protectiveness over the information, it was either a number to be ashamed of or one to hide so as to not leave himself vulnerable. Clifton was guessing it was the latter.

The two men arrived at the home and Clifton could immediately see just what $18,000 a year could do for someone. The two-story white house, with blue shutters and a short winding driveway might have been considered quaint by most American standards, but it was high class to Clifton. Nyehart parked the car and escorted Clifton in through the large front door.

The two men stood in the foyer, Nyehart throwing his keys down on the table in the center of the short entryway. Clifton felt honored to know that he would be living in the home.

Again, Nyehart interrupted his thoughts. "Let me go find my wife. We'll take you to your sleeping quarters and then I'll show you the rest of the house."

"Okay, sir." When Nyehart disappeared from the entry, Clifton held himself still so as not to disturb any of the decorations in the entrance. It didn't occur to Clifton that perhaps, since they had hired him, taken him away from a good job and his family, and since he was standing there alone in their home now, they trusted him enough already.

After what seemed like too many minutes to Clifton, Nyehart returned with his wife. Mrs. Nyehart had a movie-star frame, voluptuous with a small waist. But her face didn't match. She had large droopy eyes and lips so thin that if she had applied lipstick, it would have been virtually invisible to the naked eye.

She greeted Clifton warmly. "Hello, Mr. Reid. How do you do, sir?"

Clifton beamed. "Oh, I do fine, Mrs. Nyehart. Glad tuh finally be 'ere in yuh lovely home."

"Thank you! Let's show you around."

As Mrs. Nyehart took Clifton on a tour of the home, she explained what he would be expected to do in each room of the house they passed. When she opened the double doors to the couple's bedroom, she said that she would just like for him to tidy it up a little in there, make the beds in the morning, picking up any clothes one of them may have strewn across the floor. When they left the various rooms, Mrs. Nyehart pointed out furniture that needed frequent dusting. Somewhere during the tour Mr. Nyehart had slipped away. Mrs. Nyehart seemed not only unfazed by her husband's departure but also unafraid of being left alone with a virtual stranger.

Finally, she led him to a small door in a hallway that wasn't easily visible to company.

"This is where you'll be staying, Mr. Reid."

Clifton looked around the small room that was sufficient for his needs. He had a clean bed and a table, and the room even came with a window.

"We hope you'll be comfortable here. All the other housekeepers in this neighborhood live in quarters not attached to the house." She leaned in closer to Clifton, whispering, "It might be best to tell people that you live outside the house as well." She paused again, her eyes relaxing in reflection. "It's probably just better that way."

Clifton nodded, not exactly sure what she was trying to communicate through her hushed tones and knowing eyes.

After months living and working with the Nyeharts, making their beds after Elgin left for work, straightening up the common space areas, Clifton got a feel for the couple and his duties. Getting a paycheck for the groundskeeping and tidying up around the house seemed like robbery compared the fruit-picking he had done in the Florida sun. When he'd leave the confines of the house to cut the grass or take a walk after all of his duties had been completed, he met other housekeepers in the neighborhood. Clifton learned that not only did all of the Black housekeepers sleep outside of the house, social custom almost made it mandatory. And while Clifton had heard whispers of the mistreatment of Blacks in America, the Nyeharts had been nothing but kind to him. A wiry, thin woman from the neighboring state of Kentucky, who also worked as a domestic, told Clifton that it was because he was not American.

In an accent more Southern than the one he'd become accustomed to in Indiana, she said, "Never try to pass as American. That's where the 'mm'grants go wrong! I been Black all my life. And my people born in this country for as far back as I can remember and we ain' never got no respect. But if you speak with an accent, like the one you got, watch these White folks fall all over themselves treating you like you different from the rest of us when we all know we're the same. You might not have noticed it yet because you new to the country, but you living it. You the only one get to live inside the house. Just keep your eyes peeled, you'll see what I'm talkin bout."

It wasn't long before Clifton did notice the preferential treatment. During one of his weekends off, he decided to treat himself to a movie in Broad Ripple, an area not too far from the Nyehart's house. Not familiar with the segregation laws at the time, Clifton went through the front door of the Vogue Theatre, like everyone else. What he hadn't noticed was that he was the only one like himself going through that front door.

"Boy, whatta you think you're doing going through this front door wit the White folks? The Colored entrance is around back."

It took Clifton a second to process the words coming from the man's mouth. Colored? Still, he hadn't come out to start trouble.

"Oh meh sorry, sir. Meh new tuh dis country. Where's de back entrance?"

The man, shocked to hear that accent come from a man who looked like all the rest of the Black folk he'd ever seen in his life, cocked his head to the side, puzzled.

"Where you from?"

Seeing that the man's tone had softened, Clifton smiled slightly before answering.

"Meh come from Jamaica."

"Oh, ok…well you wouldn't know then. Alright. You can go through this door here. But just this once, the next time, you'll have to go through the back."

"Ok. Tank yuh."

Clifton watched the movie but vowed never to go there again.

Being in America, just a few months, he'd learned the accepted pathos when it came to Negroes, as they called themselves. In the extremely rare instances when he saw Black Americans depicted on the Nyehart's television or in the instances when he heard White people talk about them flippantly in the street, the characterizations were always the same: loud, lazy, lawless, and lascivious.

And as an immigrant, anxious to ingratiate himself into the American culture, he internalized those messages and, in his own mind, attributing the treatment of the Negroes born in this country to the mere fact that immigrants like him were willing to work harder. And so he distanced himself from the Negroes, the men and women whose ancestors had been on slave ships with his, but had traveled the extra distance to North America instead of docking in the Caribbean. While one woman was suggesting he cling to his Caribbean roots, another was advising him to let them go.

One day as he was straightening up the living room, humming a hymn he used to sing as a little boy in church, Mrs. Nyehart came in and sat down, wanting to get a better listen to the off-key sounds that came from Clifton's mouth.

Once he noticed that she was in the room, she smiled as she asked, "Clifton, do you ever miss Jamaica?"

He chuckled at her sudden interest. "Oh sure, every now and den. It's mi home. But meh lookin' for bettahment and it's 'ard fi fin' dere. More dan anything is mi wife and chi'ren, is dem meh miss."

In the months he'd been working there, Mrs Nyehart had failed to notice the wedding band on Clifton's left hand. And now, hearing that he was married, came as a shock and a bit of a disappointment to her. "So, you're planning to leave us and go back to Jamaica eventually?"

"Oh, no. Meh was savin up mi muney tuh bring mi wife and sons up 'ere to de states."

Mrs. Nyehart's face dropped before she asked her next question, "Clifton, you love this woman back home?"

"Sure!" He said, furrowing his brow, not understanding where this line of questioning was going.

"I think it would be best for you to just divorce that woman in Jamaica and get another one here in America. You know, start over fresh. We just really can't accommodate a whole family here, in the house. By the time you find a new wife here in the city, you'll have saved up enough money to maybe get your own place."

Mrs. Nyehart delivered her words as if they were a hard, uncomfortable, yet inevitable truth, rather than a selfish request to help her save face in the neighborhood. Clifton staying in her home was one thing, but she didn't know how she'd explain a whole family of Black people moving in, especially with her own children in the house.

Clifton was silent as he continued cleaning the living room. Mrs. Nyehart continued. "I know this is a lot to think about, but I think it would be best for you in the long run. You don't want to be tied down when you're just establishing yourself in a new country."

Clifton nodded distantly, wondering how the woman had suddenly turned so cold. Mrs. Nyehart took Clifton's silence for acceptance, stopped talking, and dashed out of the room. In the next minute she was back, carrying a beer in her hand. "Here, Clifton, drink this. It'll make you feel better."

Clifton had never had a beer in his life. But curiosity got the best of him and he drank a few sips before putting it back down on the table. Mrs. Nyehart had been wrong. It didn't make him feel any better. But he did realize that if he were ever going to be reunited with his wife again, he'd have to leave her house.

But he had to do it quietly and carefully. Both the Nyeharts and their young children had become very attached to him, in different ways; if they found out he was trying to leave, they could make life very difficult for him as someone who had yet to earn his U.S. citizenship.

So he used the people he had met. Clifton talked to the Black housekeepers who worked near him, asking if any of them had heard of work. He was careful to mention that he was looking for a friend so that if word ever got back, he'd have an excuse.

Clifton was pleasantly surprised to learn that the Nyeharts had often mentioned the quality of his work and character to their friends. So it didn't take long for him to find another position, this time with the Brown family. But after a few months that job wasn't panning out either. They too weren't interested in helping Clifton bring his wife and children to the States.

Maybe it was the fact that people kept trying to keep him from his wife or that he yearned to speak to someone like him, who knew where he came from, or maybe it was seeing so many portrayals of families in America, from the television shows to the people around him. Whatever it was, Clifton was surprised at how restless he'd become in the months he'd spent without Constantine and their children.

Once he left the Browns, he ended up with another military family, this time, a captain in the Navy, by the name of John McWurther. Before he even hired him, Clifton told McWurther that it was important that his wife be able to join him in the United States. McWurther promised Clifton that he would do his best to make sure that happened.

The man kept his word. Within the first two weeks Clifton worked at his home, once McWurther saw how professional and efficient he was, he got to work on getting Constantine to Indiana. One night, after Clifton had finished his work for the day and was on his way to the domestic quarters, located outside of the house, McWurther invited him into the living room. He had something to tell him. Recalling his last living room conversation, Clifton was apprehensive but he put on a genial, unassuming face anyway.

"Yes, sir."

"Clifton, I've been very impressed with the work you've done here. And I want to keep my word about making sure your wife makes it over. I happen to be friends with Senator Capeheart. He owes me a favor so he'll be working personally to make sure your wife is able to travel to America."

Clifton smiled and extended his arm to shake the hand of his new employer. "Tank yuh, sir. I appreciate it. It been a long time waiting."

In the eleven months Clifton had spent in Indianapolis, he'd experienced the hot and humid summer and seen snow for the first time in the bitter, bone-chilling and spirit-trying winter. And while he wanted to believe that McWurther was being truthful, he had worked with enough families to know that talking and doing didn't always go hand in hand. Still, he smiled on the off chance that the man was able to deliver on his word.

In two weeks's time, Senator Capeheart stopped by the McWurther house to meet with Clifton and interview him. He was a busy, no-

nonsense man and wasted little time with pleasantries.

"All right, first question. Name of the family member you're requesting to bring into the country."

"Constantine Reid."

"Her current address?"

The questions went on like this for twenty minutes. Clifton answered them all while Senator Capeheart took notes. He left that evening and came back two weeks later with more paperwork and more questions. Then, after another two weeks had passed, Clifton walked into the living room to find McWurther standing there reading a letter.

"Clifton, this is for you from Homer—Senator Capeheart."

Clifton stepped toward the letter, expecting that it contained bad news. He extended his hand and looked down at the short, handwritten note.

"Meh eyes not so good at reading other people's handwriting. Yuh min' reading it fah me?"

He directed the paper back to Mr. McWurther.

McWurther paused for a second, nodding slowly in solemn understanding before taking the paper back and reading what he had already scanned at least twice already.

"It says: *Clifton, all the necessary paperwork to bring your wife to Indiana has been filed and submitted on my part. If she should have any trouble entering the country it will be the fault of the Jamaican government and none of my own. If they approve everything, your wife should receive immigration clearance within the next week or so and should be on her way soon. Good luck to you both. Senator Capeheart.*"

"'im say he work everythin' out?"

"That's what he said," McWurther said, a hint of a smile starting to spread across his lips.

"Meh family tanks you, Mr. McWurther," Clifton said stepping forward to vigorously shake the man's hand. "Meh cyan tank you enough. It seem like de day never come where meh would see mi wife again. Now, I jus hope and pray the Jamaican govament do dere part."

They did. And a month later, Constantine wrote to tell Clifton she was on her way to Indiana.

***

As Constantine packed and prepared herself for the trip to Indianapolis, she was filled with anxiety. She replayed one of many phone conversations she and Clifton had had while she waited for him to tell her it was time for her and the boys to join him in the states.

"We cyan bring the boys dem right away. The sponsorship is only fah yuh and me. We'll be able tuh bring de boys dem over once we establish ourselves.."

Constantine's heart dropped. "How long it go tek?"

Clifton had never immigrated to another country and had no concept of the required time frame. But he reassured himself that this was America, a just nation. Certainly a country like that wouldn't keep people away from their children longer than they had to. He knew he needed to say something to reassure Constantine of the plan so he made up a number, something that seemed reasonable but not too long to discourage her entirely.

"'bout ah year."

Constantine's knees buckled. Up until now, all of the validation she'd ever known in her life came from being a mother to those two little boys. How could she manage without them? Immediately, she thought about the day that she'd learned Clifton had those two children in Trelawny and how she'd despised him in that very instant for abandoning his own flesh and blood. Now, she was doing the same thing, except on an even grander scale. Whereas Clifton just moved a few hours away, to a different parish, Constantine was relocating to an entirely different country, a place you couldn't reach in a day's bus ride.

She hoped that Alton would take her leaving relatively well; but she knew it would devastate Winston. Thinking about saying good-bye to the both of them and how it would forever change the three of them, she dropped her face into her hands, her body rocked by the strength of her sobs.

Even over the phone, Clifton was softened by this sudden display of emotion. He went silent for a moment, thinking of the right words to comfort her. "De boys dem haf plenty ah family dere fi occupy dem. By de time dem look up tuh miss us, we ah send fah dem in America."

Constantine wailed. Both she and Clifton were shocked by the foreign sounds coming out of her body. Her shoulders shook as she thought of her children loving her family members in the way they should have only been able to love her.

Clifton tried again. "As soon as we get de citizenship we a send fah dem. The boys dem still young, when dem get big dem probably won't even remembah."

Constantine quieted, not because his words had calmed her but because a numbness was spreading throughout her body. Before it had a chance to soften her mind, she thought back to the day the officer visited the house and how quickly she had agreed to his offer, not knowing the actual cost.

Clifton, seeing that he was losing her, kept talking. "De chil'ren dem will haf a bettah life 'ere in de States den in Jamaica. Yuh know dat. Meh nevah haf a chance to get schooling like mi should. 'ere, everybody get educated."

Just then, Constantine saw her father sitting smugly at the dining room table, telling her, without an ounce of remorse, that he wasn't going to pay for her to go to school. She visualized her face in the place of his and saw her boys, young as they were, standing at her feet begging her to let them come to America. They didn't have dreams yet but she wouldn't be the one to stand in the way of them once they did. With tears and heartache, she made her decision.

But because she and Clifton did very little without strife, the two argued over who should keep the boys while they got themselves settled. Naturally, Grace Ann, her sisters and Daphne wanted the boys to stay with them. They had grown up closest to them and knew them better. But Clifton's family was vying to get the children to live with them in the country.

"De boys dem already know dis side of dem family," Clifton said. "Dey could benahfit being wid mi sistah. She would tek dem to church. Dey nah git dat wid yuh fam'ly, Connie."

Constantine snapped back, "Is nah church dat mek a person righteous." She paused, letting the implication behind her words sink in.

Clifton sighed, swallowing the jab, and moved forward with logic. "If dey live in Tyre, dem could haf a chance tuh meet and know dem brudda and sistahs."

Constantine fell silent, accepting the good intent behind his suggestion and the loss of this battle.

That conversation had taken place months ago. And today, after more than a year of being away from her husband, Constantine was set to leave Jamaica. Clifton had been right about it taking a year for her, so Constantine assumed that it would be the same for her children. And while a year was far too long to be away from young children, Constantine comforted herself with the knowledge that she and Clifton would be able to work to ensure that they had something when the boys finally got to America. And while Constantine herself didn't have anything just yet, she wanted to at least look the part. Clifton had been sending money home for her and the children and she took a portion of it to buy fabric to make a beige skirt suit with large cream buttons. She didn't want the people on the plane to know she was going to America to clean somebody's house. She styled her hair in pin curls in the front and let the back hang down.

Once she was dressed, she walked the boys over to their grandmother's house. The morning had been filled with hugs and kisses—and tears that Constantine turned her head to wipe away. She stared at her sons, making sure she had a clear imprint of their faces in her memory. It would be a whole year before she'd see them again and she knew they would change drastically in that time. Winston must have sensed something was wrong because he was particularly clingy, toddling behind her as he held on to the hem of her skirt. Normally, that would have hampered her movement and irritated her. But today, though it still slowed her down, she relished these last minutes. As she gathered her bags and grabbed hold of the boys, she turned to see her first home stripped of most of its possessions. In the years that came, she would look back on that house and see it for the meager structure that it was. But today, she felt like she was saying good-bye to the best, or close to it. Her children had been born, nursed, and nurtured within these four walls and now she was leaving it for some other family to occupy.

Constantine's eyes misted for what must have been the fortieth time that day before she forced herself from the doorway and walked the boys to her mother's house. They would be spending a few days there until Clifton's sister could come get them and take them back to Trelawny with her.

The whole family had gathered at Grace Ann's waiting to greet the children and send her off. At the sight of everyone in that house, Winston clung even closer to his mother while Alton skirted off to play with his older cousins. At five, he understood that his mother was leaving but didn't know how long a year was or understand the gravity of her relocating to another country. To him, it was more time to stay at his grandmother's house and play with his cousins.

Though Winston often imitated his older brother, he didn't share the same sentiment. The hem of his mother's skirt had completely crumpled inside his tiny fist.

After Constantine had said her good-byes to all of her nieces, nephews, and her sisters, she went to Grace Ann. As she took the first step toward her mother, seated at the table, the tears that were pooled in her eyes quickly ran down her cheeks. Constantine kneeled, placing her head in her mother's lap. Grace Ann held her daughter's face in her soft, wrinkly hands.

"No, nah cry, Constantine. Dis will be a great ting for you. Yuh ah go to America not just for yuh chil'ren but fah yuhself too. Yuh can make somethin ah yuhself dere. Dere's nuthin lef fah yuh in Jamaica. Go."

Constantine nodded, believing the promise of her mother's words. She stood up to briskly pull her mother in close for a hug, taking in her familiar and comforting scent one last time. "Tek care of mi boys dem, Mumah."

Grace Ann nodded, solemnly accepting the duty. It went without saying. But as a mother, she understood why Constantine had to say it.

Finally, it was time for Constantine to say good-bye to her sons. She wiped her tears before she spoke to them. Winston was still right next to her, even more alarmed having seen his mother weep for the first time. She had to call for Alton. He and his cousins came bounding into the front room.

Constantine dropped slowly to her knees, eye level with the both of them. She pushed them both close to one another and squeezed them tightly for the tenth time that day. She felt their arms attempt to reach around her back. Constantine pulled away from them so she could look back and forth between Alton and Winston.

"Meh haffi go now. Meh nah see unu for a while but yuh nah fuhgit me, right?"

Alton, staring back into his mother's eyes, shook his head no and Winston, following his older brother, did the same.

"The next time unu see me, we'll be in America! Won't dat be nice?"

"Yes, Mommy," Alton said, nodding slightly, a look of concern growing on a face that had been carefree just seconds earlier.

As she went to take a step, she was halted by Winston's tug. She looked down slowly, knowing she'd torture herself by looking in her baby boy's sad and pleading eyes. She didn't want to remove his hand, to pry the short, fleshy fingers open and slide him away from her. She couldn't bear their last interaction to be her pushing him even further away.

Before she could look up, scan the room, and silently beg someone to help her, she saw her mother rise quickly for a woman of her age and stride swiftly but softly over to Winston. Her mother bent down to pick him up.

"Come, baby."

Constantine kissed him one more time in her mother's arms, rubbing his cheek.

With a look, Grace Ann stole her daughter's attention away from her son's and whispered, "Go."

She waved good-bye to everyone and blew one last kiss to Alton, who had yet to resume playing with his cousins. Instead, he stood watching his mother's lingering departure.
It wasn't until she got to the veranda that she heard the smack of the screen door trigger Winston's wailing.

***

Like her husband before her, this was also the first time Constantine had ever flown in a plane. She had the fortune of sitting next to a window so she watched as the island country, her family, and her life, blurred by her tears, got smaller and smaller in the distance. She kept chanting to herself that she was leaving for a better life, for more opportunities, for an education for her children. And as devastated as she was, knowing she wasn't coming back to Jamaica any time soon, she was also hopeful. She didn't feel any apprehension about moving and trusting that Clifton would be able to survive in this new country. He'd already proven himself by sending for her so soon. Constantine chuckled, thinking about the doubts she had had. When she waved good-bye to Clifton in front of the house they shared, a part of her thought it could very well have been the last time she saw him. He had history to prove the concept wasn't so novel. And she had grown up with countless stories of men leaving their wives and girlfriends to take up with a new love in Canada, England, or the United States. She would never know that he'd been advised to do just that.

Constantine wept off and on throughout the short flight. But once the plane landed roughly with bumps and skids, she scolded herself to get it together. She applied pressure underneath her eyes to reduce some of the puffiness. Then she retouched her makeup, repositioned hair that had fallen during the ride, and smoothed out her skirt, with the exception of the wrinkles Winston had made. Afterward, she stood up, walked off the plane, and into the next chapter of her life.

Though it was spring time, immediately she noticed there was a coolness in the air and a coolness in the way people looked at her too, if they acknowledged her presence at all. She was the only Jamaican woman on the plane, amidst the tourists returning home. They'd seen plenty people who looked like her during their vacations, so no one paid her much attention. But now that she was on the ground, in America, aside from the shoe shiners, she was the only other person with skin like hers in the airport. And the looks either lingered curiously, menacingly, or past her entirely.

Constantine cut her eyes at the people, searching for Clifton in the crowd. The eagerness and anticipation she felt waiting for him surprised her. She must have looked particularly uneasy because a woman walked up to her and asked if she needed any help.

Constantine smiled at the friendly faced, portly White woman. She appreciated the kindness. As she told the woman that she was looking for her husband, she watched as the woman's face twisted, her nose scrunched, and she leaned in closer trying to decipher her accent.

"I'm sorry, say it again, honey," the woman said.

Constantine thought she was speaking the way she'd heard Americans do it in the movies, shortening her vowels and adding a nasally twang to certain words. After several attempts, the woman finally understood what she meant and stood with Constantine, helping her look. After a full minute, Constantine spotted Clifton and tapped the woman, pointing him out. Constantine noticed he was craning his neck looking for her too. She stood back for another second admiring the sight before she waved a gloved hand to let him know she was here. He strode quickly over to her, that same charming smile he'd worn on their first date brightening his face. Once he reached them, the friendly woman smiled and said hello before patting Constantine on the back and wishing her good luck. Clifton embraced her tightly and she felt him exhale, relieved. She couldn't remember a time they'd ever hugged like that and it made her wonder about his own adjustment to this new place.

He stepped back from their embrace, still squeezing her arms. "Is good tuh see yuh, Connie."

"Good tuh see yuh too, Clifton. Yuh lookin' well."

For a second Constantine thought about those people who had been staring at her earlier. She thought that to them she and Clifton must look like the most picture-perfect couple, happy and smiling, hugging each other intensely. She wanted to keep the charade going and she hooked her arm around his. "How yuh been here? Yuh like it yet?"

Clifton talked first about the cold. He told her before they'd have to be sure to get her a proper coat before the winter came back around. He told her the weather had just broken and was finally becoming bearable again. Constantine remembered the coolness she'd felt stepping off the plane; according to Clifton, it was going to get far worse.

"But wait till yuh see de snowflakes dem. Buh-u-ti-ful."

Clifton talked a mile a minute as he collected her luggage. She listened as he waxed poetic about the people, the food, some of which he liked. He told her he'd noticed how it was so hard to get good fruit here. He described the huge houses that lined the streets, the fancy cars people drove, the skyscrapers he'd seen downtown, and what he knew must have been the world's tallest Christmas tree, which was really a monument draped in Christmas lights. He told her about the movies Americans had and the Seventh Day Adventist church he'd found for them to attend. He told her that there were other Jamaicans that attended the church and they'd helped to make him feel at home. He said he was sure they'd do the same for her and eventually their sons too.

By the time he had run down the highlights, they were on their way outside. She watched as Clifton walked up to a black car that looked as huge as a limousine. She knew it didn't belong to him. She could see her reflection in the car's rounded edges. Constantine didn't know much about cars, had never even learned to drive one. But it looked nothing like the rusted, beatup pickup trucks she'd ridden in back home. This car, the way it shone without a speck or blemish, must have been expensive.

"It's ah Cadillac," Clifton said beaming.

She thought she'd heard that name before. And if she'd heard the name, it must be nice. There was no way he'd done that well in just a year. He rested her bags on the curb and leaned against the car, grinning.

"Clifton, get off de people dem car before 'im come back and see yuh."

"Yuh nah see this our car." Clifton reached into his pants pocket and dangled a set of keys from his index finger. Constantine frowned, still doubtful. Noticing her skepticism, Clifton turned and stuck the key in the door, popping it open.

Constantine gasped before getting in the front seat. As she sat on the leather seat, inspecting the car, Clifton busied himself putting her luggage in the trunk. When he got to the driver's seat, that smile was still on his face.

"Dis really de car nuh?" she asked.

"No, it's not," Clifton said, his smile fading a little bit. "But de McWurthers dem allow meh tuh drive it. Yuh get ah ride into de city wid style, Mrs. Reid."

Constantine smiled, feeling almost giddy. She couldn't be entirely sure but she thought Clifton was flirting with her. After the day she had, saying good-bye to her children it was a welcome distraction.

As he was driving he explained that the family he'd been working for— the same family she was would work for—had sent him with this car to pick her up. Riding in it, Constantine had nearly forgotten that it would be the last bit of luxury she'd experience for a while. This chariot was transporting her to domestic work. She sneered slightly to herself at the thought. Clifton would tend to the outdoor grounds while Constantine would take care of the inside of the couple's home, sweeping, dusting, making beds, mopping, and straightening up.

Just as Constantine was starting to imagine herself in a uniform cleaning these people's house, Clifton drove up in front of black cast-iron gate, with swirls and loops that looked as though they could have gone on forever if it weren't for the stone pillars that blocked their endless spiral. She stared speechless at the opulence. Clifton jumped out, leaving the door open, and stuck a large key into the center of the gate, swinging both doors open. He returned to the driver's seat and slid the car smoothly through. The first thing Constantine noticed were tall, impeccably dark green trees with leaves that attempted to kiss the ground. She couldn't even see the house yet but it looked like they were going to be working in a palace. As Clifton kept driving, slowly so she could take it all in, a three-story mansion sprang into view. It was all brick, with Roman columns at the door. It was beautiful, something completely out of a movie set.

"But Jesus, de people dem rich!" Constantine said, no longer able to contain her amazement. Clifton laughed heartily at the comment, happy to be the one to introduce her to this type of grandeur, even if it wasn't theirs to fully enjoy.

Clifton pulled the car around to what Constantine thought was a much smaller house to the right. The car rolled over a paved lane. He parked it and hopped out, going around the back to grab Constantine's things.

She sat there, straightening herself up before she got out of the car. Constantine told herself, you never know who could be watching. For all she knew the lady of the house could be staring out one of those windows looking to see what type of woman was coming into her home and she wanted to make a good impression. Clifton, with her suitcase, under his arms, came around and opened her car door. Constantine stepped out, breathing the coolish air and taking in the smell of all those trees. In Jamaica the air held the smell of the sea but here in Indianapolis, in the middle of spring, it smelled like wet earth.

Constantine thought they'd be walking into the building right in front of them but Clifton, laughing at her, told her this was just for the cars. She shook her head in disbelief once again. Entire families could live in homes the size of that garage.

Clifton walked her over to the place where they'd be staying. More than just the spare room she was expecting, it was a small cottage. In addition to the bedroom, their space included a little kitchen with a stove. Seeing all of this laid out for them, Constantine had to ask what type of people these were.

"Clifton, how des people dem make dem muney?"
"Mi nah sure but mi tink Mr. McWurther is a lawyer. De wife nah work."

Constantine nodded.

After she put her few belongings away, it was time to meet the man who had helped her get to America. As Clifton walked her from their little house to the big mansion, Constantine tried to think of something pleasant and polite to say.

Clifton walked her into the home from a back door that led directly to the kitchen. With white and black linoleum floors and appliances that looked as if they had been plucked straight from the pages of a catalog, the space was breathtaking. And this was just the kitchen. Clifton led Constantine through a series of hallways, left turns, and right turns, then they passed a living room, an entryway, a guest bedroom, and at least two indoor bathrooms. When they came to a heavy, mahogany door,

Clifton stopped short, causing Constantine to stumble into him as she was still gawking at her surroundings.

He leaned in close to her, whispering, "Here suh is the office where Mr. McWurther do his work." And then reading the tenseness in her body, Clifton said, "No bodda worry bout making a good impression. He's ah nice man."

Constantine, an even five foot in three-inch heels, straightened her back and tugged at the bottom of her suit jacket as Clifton knocked at the door.

From inside, Constantine heard a muffled and very twangy country-sounding voice telling them to come in. Clifton plastered an even bigger smile on his face as he turned the doorknob. Before she could see the man, Constantine heard, "Ahh, Clifton. How are ya?"

In his accent, Clifton said, "I'm doing well today, Mr. McWurther. I brought someone for you to meet."

It wasn't until then that Clifton stepped out of her view that she got a chance to take a good look at the man. Even seated, she could tell he was tall, with thick, pale skin that rippled and dimpled instead of lying flat and smooth over his heavy bones. At fifty, he was twenty years their senior, but his closely cropped, full beard aged his face ten years. His hair was a graying blond that he had parted on the right side and swooped over the very top of his square forehead. He wasn't Constantine's definition of attractive but his eyes, a hazel-green color, were warm. Clifton stepped aside to reveal his wife, and Mr. McWurther flashed her a welcoming smile and stood to give her a firm handshake.

"Nice to finally meet you, Mrs. Reid. Your husband here went through a lot of trouble to get you up this way."

Constantine nodded, plastering an exaggerated smile on her lips before touching Clifton's arm.

"Yes, and meh very grateful tuh him fah dat. And yuh too sir." Constantine beamed.

Mr. McWurther nodded at her, acknowledging his contribution. "Well, I'm sure Clifton won't have any problems giving you the tour and explaining how things go around here. I'll leave him to it."

"Tank yuh, sir." Clifton tipped his head before ushering Constantine out of the room and closing the door behind him.

After more rooms and hallways, Clifton took Constantine to meet Mrs. McWurther. She didn't leave as much of an impression on Constantine as her husband had but Constantine didn't hold it against her.

Mrs. McWurther shook her hand firmly too but as she did so, she looked Constantine up and down, as if trying to determine her predilection for theft. Constantine had seen that look before. She'd watched her mother give it to the women who came to work in their home. Back in Jamaica, Constantine had always regarded the practice as mostly innocuous, a precautionary measure. Back home, there weren't worlds of difference between the helpers and the families who employed them. Neither had too much. But Mrs. McWurther, with her grand house and her college-educated husband, was different from her. And more than her trying to sniff out any criminal activity, with that look, Constantine sensed the distance between them.

***

As the first couple of months went on, Constantine found that she didn't mind the cottage too much. It wasn't home but the living arrangements were far more comfortable than what she had expected. And once the weather broke the summer was quite pleasant. The only thing that bothered her was the work. She had cleaned as a girl, completing the chores Grace Ann had assigned her. For a time she'd earned her keep cleaning Olga and Ellis's house too. And she was good at it. Every Jamaican woman knows the importance of keeping a tidy house. But it was the taking of orders that was an adjustment. Clifton and Constantine were just a few years older than their son Elliot. So while the McWurthers treated them kindly, still they were reminded daily, in small ways, of their position of servitude and at times, inferiority. It was in the way the McWurthers ignored both Clifton and Constantine when other White people were in the room until they needed something. Only then would they signal them with a snap or a wave, never making eye contact. It was in the comments they made about Black Americans when conversation moved from pleasant and cordial to fear-filled and angry.

"This is why we made sure to get our help from the islands. The nigras over there are just different. They don't feel entitled to everything like the colored folk over here," Mrs. McWurther said one night at a dinner party, unmoved by the fact that both Clifton and Constantine were standing in the room.

Later, when Constantine asked Clifton if he'd heard her comments, he brushed them off, choosing to regard them as praise. "Meh tek it as a compliment, Connie. De 'oman say we nah like dem. And from de way she chat, seem she don care fah the American Blacks all dat much."

Constantine kissed her teeth. "Bes' believe if anything in dis house go missin' or get bruk up, weh start to look jus as Black as de Americans dem."

When she wasn't learning the ways of White folks, Constantine found her days were long and monotonous. She scrubbed the floors daydreaming about what her sons were doing. Playing? Eating? How much had they grown since she'd left? Were they getting along with their brother and sisters? Were they being treated well by Clifton's people? She had enlisted Daphne to send her letters of her sons's progress, but at just twice a month, there was still so much more she wanted to know.

She wondered if in the few weeks she'd been gone if the boys stopped looking for her to come and get them. It pained her to consider the possibility that Alton might have resolved that she was never coming back and Winston might have forgotten her completely.

At night when she and Clifton lay in bed, they talked about their children: what they wanted them to have in this country, and making sure they were as informed as possible about what was going on back at home. Since the boys were staying with Clifton's family in Trelawny, Constantine wrote to his sister as well. She asked for updates and she encouraged her family to go check on her boys as often as possible to make sure things really were all right. Clifton took note of how often she was writing and it made him a little uncomfortable. He couldn't read those letters, not the ones Constantine sent nor the ones she was receiving.

After watching her write what must have been her fourth letter that month, Clifton decided to speak up. "Why yuh mus write dem so often nuh?" Then hearing how ridiculous he sounded, he softened his tone. "Yuh mek me tink somethin wrong."

Sitting at the little table in their quarters, her back facing Clifton, she rolled her eyes. The man wouldn't let her do anything in peace. "If meh cyan see mi pickney dem, how meh mus know if meh nah ask? If anything come up, yuh be de furst tuh know."

Clifton nodded, still unconvinced. "Promise yuh nah mek decisions about de boys dem widout me."

Constantine, hearing the desperation in his voice, turned around to face him, looking in his eyes before nodding her head in agreement.

Not even three weeks after they'd made this arrangement, Clifton brought the mail in. Constantine eyed the stack in his hand, recognizing Daphne's signature scrawl. Constantine grabbed it and sat on the edge of the bed as she read. As much as she enjoyed getting these letters, a part of her always feared that she would open one of them and learn the worst. Clifton was hovering over her as she read it, thinking the same thing, hoping to interpret something or gauge her reaction in the event that it was something serious. The first line of the letter wouldn't allow that though.

Dear Aunt Connie, please do not share this letter with Mr. Reid.

"What it say nuh?" Clifton asked desperately.

Constantine thought briefly of shielding the text from him. But even if he couldn't read the letter, he surely knew how to read her. She had to be careful.

"Nuttin' much yet. She just tell me de boys dem doing well in Trelawny."

It couldn't have been further from the truth. Daphne, who was a teenager now, wrote that her little cousins weren't comfortable with their paternal aunt. Clifton's sister was too strict on the boys. When she went to visit with her mother, Alton told Daphne that the woman beat them for the tiniest infractions, thought they spent too much time playing, and was absolutely adamant about them being in church all day on the Sabbath, every Sabbath.

Daphne said that they thought it would be best if she were to go and get them so they could be with family they already knew and were comfortable with.

Constantine didn't need much convincing; the thought of someone beating her children, the way Clifton told her he'd been beaten as a child, nearly everyday, made her nauseated. For a split second, Constantine considered being a woman of her word and consulting her husband about moving the boys back to Kingston. But she could almost hear his voice now: he would tell her that discipline was good for the boys, that he was raised the same way and had turned out well. Naturally, that was debatable. More than anything, Constantine couldn't imagine her boys suffering more than they already were with their parents away. So she told Clifton everything was fine at home, made up a believable story about what the boys were up to, and said that Olga and Ellis were getting ready to have a child, which was true. And she left it at that.

Once she was sure that Clifton had believed her, her thoughts returned to her sons. What they must have thought of their parents. Alton and Winston probably assumed the worst, that she and Clifton were living it up in the finest clothes, attending the most lavish parties, and driving around in an expensive car, happy to have escaped their children, leaving them in the hands of an overly cruel aunt. She wrote to her cousins, her sisters, and her mother begging them to let the boys know that they were here working and saving every little bit of money they earned. Working to make it better for them, so they could eventually join them.

Constantine would rest a bit easier knowing that her sons were being raised as she had been. She wrote back to Daphne telling her to get the children. She told her to tell Evelyn, Clifton's sister, that both she and Clifton wanted them to return to Kingston. She instructed Daphne to show her the letter if she put up a fight. It wasn't a sustainable lie; but she told herself that when Clifton eventually learned of the news, she'd deal with the consequences then.

The only reason Constantine had agreed to let the boys see that side of their family was because she wanted them to be raised in the church and know their siblings, but not at this price. Clifton could take them to church once they got here. Plus, since her father had passed, Grace Ann had been going to church more often now. Maybe she'd be able to convince the boys to go with her.

Constantine scoffed at the lie she'd just told herself. Grace Ann had tried fighting that church battle with her and now even Daphne and her siblings. They never went and she never forced them. Today, in Indiana, disconnected from everything and everyone she knew, Constantine had a different appreciation and respect for the church.

The McWurthers didn't require Clifton and Constantine to work on Saturdays. So they were able to go to Circle Center, the Seventh Day Adventist church he'd found in the city. The people there, some of them Jamaican born, seemed decent enough.

Constantine, always wary of new people, could take or leave the congregants at Circle Center. She really went for the music they sang, what she learned about God, and the uplift she felt as she and Clifton rode back home. It was the highlight of her week. And though she was sure it might not have meant the same to her as a child, Constantine wished she had been raised in somebody's church. She wondered how her life would have played out differently had she grown up a church girl. She imagined herself in churchgoers's staples: dresses with collars so tight it was hard to swallow, hems that skirted the dusty ground, and wide-brimmed hats that attempted to blot out the unrelenting sun. She chuckled at the thought. She was too flashy to be a church girl, with entirely too much lip.

At first, Constantine found the Adventist rules restricting and odd. And though she wasn't a fan of staying in on Friday nights and waking up early on their day off to attend services, she couldn't deny that her husband and their relationship was better for it. There hadn't been too many violent outbursts and his kind moments were more frequent. The cooler weather seemed to have the same chilling effect on his boiling temper. And he was more serious about his spirituality these days, along with his reputation. Even though they had their own quarters, the McWurthers saw Clifton and Constantine every day. If she were walking around with bruises or moving slower than usual, they'd know it was Clifton who had caused them—not that they would have felt inclined to do anything about it. The people at church made up nearly all of Clifton and Constantine's social circle. It was harder for him to act hellish in the street and at home with his wife and then smile in the faces of these people as if nothing had happened.

1952, Thirty-two

In the day in and day out of working for the McWurthers, Clifton had forgotten that the year which he had promised they would be reunited with their sons, was quickly approaching. But Constantine had not. And on a year to the day that she had come to Indianapolis, she started pelting him with questions.

"Clifton. Yuh know it been a year now and meh nah hear yuh mek one mention about de boys dem coming up 'ere to live?"

Clifton was appreciative to both Senator Capeheart and Mr. McWurther for helping him get Constantine into the States, but he didn't want to push his luck. He wasn't sure they'd be willing to help him again, so soon after they'd just extended themselves. Still, throughout the course of his own life Clifton had learned, over and again, that sometimes the first step in obtaining anything was to be bold enough to ask for it

"Ok, Connie. Meh ah ask Mr. McWurther about de boys dem tomorrow.

The next day after his shift, Clifton found Mr. McWurther in his study.

"Yuh know, sir, meh hate tuh come trubble yuh again after yuh and Senator Capeheart work so hard to reunite me and mi wife but I haf fi ask anudda favah. You know now that she's 'ere, meh and mi wife want our sons to be 'ere wid us too. Can Senator Capeheart start working on that fah us?"

McWurther said he understood but didn't know how Senator Capeheart would respond to the second favor. He told Clifton that he would ask him about it.

Three days later, McWurther came back and told Clifton that he'd spoken with Senator Capeheart. "He said that while he would love to be able to help you, you'll have to become a citizen of the United States before you're able to bring your children over into the country."

Clifton had considered the prospect of becoming a citizen but didn't necessarily know what it meant to attain it. "What we haf fi do to get citizenship? Is more papahwork?"

McWurther's shoulders dropped slowly and he pursed his lips. "No. It's more than paperwork. You have to be interviewed and then take and pass a test . . . an oral test."

Clifton's mouth dried as he struggled to keep his jaw and his heart from dropping. How was he supposed to study for a test when he barely had gone to school? It would take him forever.

Despondent and discouraged, Clifton told Constantine the news and the two went about learning about the government, history, geography, and Constitution of the country they hoped their sons would one day call home.

Even though things seemed to be going better between her and her husband, Constantine wasn't in any hurry to bring more children into an unstable situation, especially when she felt she couldn't be a mother to the children she already had. Clifton and Constantine were just beginning to establish themselves, saving virtually all of the money they'd earned, with the exception of what they sent home to their sons. She had been so concerned about coming to the States that she didn't even think about the possibility of getting pregnant. It wasn't until a period arrived later than usual, that she was reminded the she needed to take something to keep that from happening.

Constantine scolded herself for being so irresponsible. None of her children had been planned, so she should have known better than to take this type of chance. A week later, a doctor fitted her for a diaphragm and then Clifton told her how to get to the pharmacy by bus.

The next Sunday, Constantine spent twenty minutes on the city bus to reach the place. It wasn't her first time there but today, by herself, knowing what she had come to get, she felt a bit anxious. She approached the pharmacist standing behind an counter. Constantine watched the men in white coats, studying labels and searching for prescriptions. She rang the bell to get his attention. A young man with an orb of sandy brown curls walked up and smiled at her, asking how he could help.

"Meh lookin . . . tuh pick up mi de . . . de . . . diaframe." Constantine said, trying to speak in hushed tones.

The pharmacist nodded in understanding, his curls tumbling over his forehead as he did so. He asked for her name before turning suddenly to go search for the device.

When he returned, Constantine paid for it at the cash register and left the store, relieved. She took the apparatus home and practiced inserting it until she could do so with ease.

She had every intention of using it. Every intention. But one night, when Clifton came back to their room after working all day, she couldn't convince him to stay off her long enough to say good evening, more less insert a diaphragm. He was too quick, too persistent. Constantine told herself that this one time wouldn't take—she'd simply have to will herself not to get pregnant.

Nine months later, she gave birth to another son. Luckily by the time he was born, in late September, she and Clifton had saved up enough money to move off the McWurtheres's property.

Though this child couldn't replace her first two, Constantine was happy to have another baby in her arms. It had been almost three years since she'd arrived in Indianapolis and still their family wasn't complete.

Now that Clifton finally felt he had made something of himself, having saved up enough money to buy a home of their own in America, he was honored to give his name to his son, this American-born boy, in the hopes that one day he'd grow to be proud to carry it.

While Constantine knew having three children in the house would make her life more difficult, having Clifton Jr. only reminded her of the time when Alton and Winston were that small. And she wondered which other fleeting changes she was missing with them in Jamaica.

1953, Thirty-three

Studying for their citizenship took up much of the couple's spare time. But it wasn't all consuming. In the months after Clifton Jr. was born, Clifton Sr. joined the usher board at Circle Center. Though Constantine initially scoffed at Clifton's decision, convinced that it was just a way for him to showboat in the church, she learned there was a benefit for her in all of this. She loved the way Clifton looked walking down those aisles, in his uniformed suit jacket and pants.

She personally starched and pressed them to perfection. The jacket and the pants, with the crisp seams, laid perfectly over his body, still toned from all the manual labor he'd done throughout his life. But what really got her were his gloved hands. Rocking her sleeping son in her arms, Constantine studied her husband and his hands intently from the pews, admiring his sharp movements. Right there in church, she thought about what was underneath those pants. She thought about how his thick, strong hands felt against her body and found it impossible to concentrate throughout the rest of service. By the time it had concluded, she was ready to jump out of her skin. Usually, Clifton stood around the church long after the message, socializing with his fellow congregants. But today, as soon as service was over, she signaled for him to come over to her and told him they needed to get home immediately, for the baby's sake.

Typically, Clifton was the one who initiated sex while Constantine almost always obliged, occasionally she enjoyed their closeness and was able to lose herself in the experience. Other times, his approach was so abrupt and uncaring that she just lay there, staring at the ceiling, waiting for it to be over. This Sabbath afternoon was different. After she'd put Clifton Jr. down for a nap, she was the one who offered to help Clifton out of his church clothes. Clifton, who had been completely oblivious to his wife's desires, got the picture as he listened to her deep, loud breathing and watched the quickness with which she was removing his clothing. More than arousing, the whole scene was strange and curious and he found himself stunned into near paralyzation, watching it all unfold. Constantine removed his gloves and looked at the hands that bore calluses from picking fruit in Florida to pay for their wedding. She unbuttoned his shirt, exposing the chest that had cradled all three of their sons when they were born. She took in the legs that had pedaled her mother to and from her doctor's appointments.

She stepped away from him now, staring in admiration. Clifton lowered his head, not able to be on the receiving end of such intimacy. And just then, for the first time since she'd known him, she got the inkling that maybe she did love her husband.

So, with the love she felt for him in this moment and the ones that had led up to it, Constantine made love to her husband and conceived her fourth child.

***

This pregnancy felt different than all the others before it, more agreeable and kind to her body and Constantine knew she was carrying a girl, a kindred spirit.

Shortly after she perceived this exciting bit of information, the life of the girlchild she had been waiting for was jeopardized.

During her eighth month, Constantine opened a letter from the electric company to discover a past-due notice. All throughout this pregnancy, Clifton had been discussing the prospect of buying his own truck and working for himself instead of always being at the whim of rich, White folks. Constantine admired his efforts and his entrepreneurial spirit but she'd also noticed that his laser-like focus had caused him to neglect some of his current responsibilities. With four children between them, and the three he had on his own, it was an insecure road they couldn't afford to travel right now.

That evening when he came home from work and sat down to the plate of food she'd prepared for him, Constantine shared her thoughts. "Clifton, yuh know we receive dis letter today bout de electric bill bein' late."

She watched his body tense. He cleared his throat but his voice still came out sounding dry and worn. "Okay, meh a go tek care of it. Meh jus try fi get de business movin and it mus ah slip mi mind."

Clifton assumed that this would be the end of the conversation. But Constantine proceeded. "Meh know yuh trying fi get your business off de ground but meh and de pickney dem cyan freeze inna dis house while yuh do it. Yuh mus put de tings dem in dem propah ordah."

Clifton sighed deeply, wondering why the woman couldn't ever just let things go. "Mi hear yuh, Connie. Yuh nah hear meh say mi a go tek care of it?"

By this time, Constantine felt her own temper start to swell. She thought she had come to him calmly and here he was getting upset. Suddenly, she had much more to say. "Why yuh vex? If meh nah read de letters dem and come tell yuh what dey say how yuh would know we and de chil'ren dem on our way to de street?"

She let the question suspend in the air for a few seconds. Realizing she'd won this battle, Constantine turned her back and walked into the living room. She had just crossed the threshold from one room to the next when she heard him slide away from the dining room table. Constantine turned around, thinking Clifton had followed her with something else to say. Before she could even focus her eyes on his figure lunging toward her, his fist connected with her cheekbone, right beneath her eye socket. She sailed over one of the arms of the couch and landed in its seat. Gravity with the added weight of her belly caused her to roll off. She managed to grab her stomach before she hit the ground, face forward. With her face against the wood floor, she figured this would be the end of it; but no sooner had she started to collect herself and stand up, Clifton came charging at her. He straddled her while she was on the ground, slapping her in the face. Constantine drew her legs to her chest and put her arms up trying to shield herself from the blows. But Clifton just worked around them, punching her in the side, all the while screaming and scolding her like a child.

"Meh ah go teach yuh to watch yuh mout!"

Constantine wasn't hearing any of his words. Instead, she was absorbing the blows, waiting for it to be over, praying desperately that she wouldn't lose another child. Had there not been a knock on the door, she might have.

The knock and then the pounding snapped Clifton out of his rage. He didn't want his wife thinking she was higher or mightier than he; but more than that, he wanted the people outside of his home to regard him as a gentleman, the friendly, righteous man he could be sometimes. So, still panting and breathing hard, sweat dripping from his brow, he tucked his shirt in, wiped his forehead, and went to answer the door.

He meant to just leave it ajar, exchange a few pleasantries, and return to his dinner. But as he turned the knob, their neighbor, Mr. Lewis, burst into their home. He'd heard the noises from outside and knew exactly what was going on within those walls. Seeing for himself the horror that had just taken place, he brushed past Clifton and ran to Constantine's battered body, crumpled on the ground. He cupped her bloodied face in his hands before lifting and carrying her into his own house next door. Clifton didn't protest. Instead, he sat on the couch, cradling his own head while a man carried his wife out of their home.

Once he'd gotten Constantine to his house, Mrs. Lewis helped clean the blood on her face with a cool, wet washcloth. As they were attempting to remove the blood, tears of shame and humiliation started to stream down her face. It was one thing to endure this type of beating in the privacy of her home but having the neighbors know about the volatile nature of their relationship was almost too much to bear. Mr. Lewis interrupted her thoughts, suggesting she go to the hospital.

"Tank you for yuh help, Mr. Lewis, but meh nah wan anyone else fi see me like dis. De swelling ah go down in a few days."

Mr Lewis shook his head, breathing deeply. "Constantine, you need to go to make sure your baby's all right."

She had been so consumed with her own shame that she hadn't thought about the baby since she had protected her stomach in the living room. She thoughtfully nodded her acceptance. Constantine borrowed a scarf and some sunglasses from Mrs. Lewis and the three of them all got in the car together.

At the hospital, even before the doctor attempted to check the baby's heartbeat, he instructed her to remove her scarf and sunglasses. The sight of her injuries gave him pause. And just as Constantine had been dreading, he asked her how she'd sustained them.

"Meh tripped and fell down de stairs in mi house."

The doctor, who had been looking down, detailing the nature of her injuries, looked up over the top of his glasses. It was a lie he'd heard time and again.

"Mrs. Reid, are you sure that's how you sustained these injuries? The bruising on your face and side indicate that something—or someone—struck you several times repeatedly," he said, raising his eyebrows knowingly. "It would be almost impossible to exhibit this kind of bruising from a fall down the stairs. And if you fell face forward, as your bruising shows, your baby would be in danger."

Constantine just looked at him, blinking. "Doctor, is meh baby okay?" She finally asked, frustrated by this line of questioning.

The doctor sighed, slid his pen in his white coat pocket, placed Constantine's chart on a nearby table, and asked her to lie down so he could see if the fetus was in any type of distress. He spent a few minutes pushing and poking her abdomen, asking if certain movements hurt. When she responded no, he placed the stethoscope to her stomach and moved it around slowly before stopping, squinting his eyebrows in concentration.

As she waited, Constantine filled the silent seconds with her own fears. For the first time tonight, she winced from the terror in her mind rather than the soreness of her body.

The doctor's smile shook Constantine out of her nightmarish musings. He told her he'd found a strong heartbeat.
Later that night, after the hospital had treated the injuries and released her, Mr. Lewis took her back to his home. His wife fixed her some food, which she forced herself to eat despite her lack of appetite, and they allowed her to sleep in their guest room for the night.

The next morning, Constantine woke up to the smell of eggs, toast, and sausage. Though Seventh Day Adventists didn't eat pork, she indulged in all three that morning in silent, passive protest. As she ate her breakfast, the Lewises kept the conversation light for as long as they possibly could.

After having sat quietly at the hospital, Mrs. Lewis shifted uncomfortably before asking sympathetically, "Sweetie, do you have any family in the city?"

"Meh nah haf family in dis country, more less de city."

Mrs. Lewis's eyes welled up as she questioned her, "So where will you go?"

Constantine let out an embittered gust of air before answering her. "Where else would meh go except back home to mi son?"

Clifton Jr. was still at the house with his father. And though she was sure Clifton would have been able to fend for himself and take care of their one-year-old for a night, that was all the time she needed to get herself together.

That afternoon, after she had showered and scrubbed the droplets of blood out of her dress, Constantine stepped out of the shelter of the Lewises's home and back into the war zone that was her own.

The next month, on December 9th, she gave birth to her first daughter. Constantine hadn't thought about a name for this child until she heard the candy-stripe volunteers singing Christmas carols outside her hospital room. She named her daughter Noel and decided to honor her mother by making her middle name Grace Ann. Constantine looked down at the baby girl in her arms and saw hope. Before this girlchild had even entered the world, she'd proven herself a survivor. Constantine vowed to nurture that innate fight so that when life's challenges arose, as they inevitably would, she'd always emerge victorious.

After Noel, Constantine knew she couldn't risk bringing another child into the world on a wing and a prayer. She spoke to her doctor once again, telling him that she needed something that she wouldn't have to fool around with.

"When mi husband come fi me, 'im ready. Meh nah haf time to put in a diaphragm or nothin' else."

"From what you're telling me, it sounds like the best option for you would be an intrauterine device or an IUD for short. We'd insert it into your uterus. The device releases hormones which will keep you from

getting pregnant. It stays in place and will work for up to five years."
Constantine listened to the doctor in disbelief. The thought of pregnancy-preventing chemicals being released into her body was far from comforting. But it seemed like the best option. She couldn't undergo that type of scare again. And the diaphragm had proven unrealistic and ineffective. Thankfully, it was the perfect solution.

1954, Thirty-four

A year after Noel was born, Clifton ran into their bedroom with news from the immigration office. "Read dis for me nah, Connie."

Constantine, seeing the government seal on the outside of the envelope, knew it was something important. Since they'd moved into their new house, Constantine had stopped working outside of the home. When she wasn't tending to the children, cooking for her husband, or cleaning the house, she helped Clifton study for the citizenship test. She read and learned the information and then taught it to him until it became a part of his memory. With all of her efforts, they both passed the test and then set about filling out the paperwork to get Alton and Winston to Indianapolis. This letter had to be about the boys.

She tore the envelope open fiercely, careful not to rip the actual letter itself. Since they'd first gotten to this country, Constantine had made a habit of pretending to be a slow reader. She'd read everything silently to herself, processing the information before sharing it with Clifton. After reading the first two sentences, tears sprang to her eyes. Both the U.S. and Jamaican government had approved her sons's immigration into America.

Constantine read the letter aloud to Clifton, watching his eyes mist. After she'd finished reading the entire thing, in her excitement, Constantine sprang up from the bed and held her husband in a rare embrace, sneakily wiping her falling tears over his shoulder.

Clifton, taken aback, held her too, trying, unsuccessfully, to blink back the tears of his own.

The next week, the couple returned to the airport for the first time since Constantine had flown in, three years ago. In the truck Clifton had managed to buy, she wore a dress she'd reserved for church and Clifton a suit and tie. On the way, he alternated between chatter and heavy silence while Constantine fidgeted nervously. But as they rode, Constantine couldn't ignore the unpleasant thoughts that taunted her. Though she thought of him daily, there was no way Winston would remember her. He was too young to recall the day she left or recognize her as his mother. Alton might remember. But she thought Alton might look at his new brother and sister as replacements. The thought caused an uncomfortable feeling to rest in the pit of her stomach.

Both she and Clifton had been working to build a home for them but she wondered if her children would ever feel like they belonged there. She had made the decisions she did out of love for them; but in the darkest corners of her mind, she wondered if it'd be possible for them to love her back.

The concept being too painful to consider, Constantine shifted her mind to a more pleasant train of thought. Alton was nine-years-old now, and little Winston, who had just turned two when she left, was six. Over the past four years, as she had gone about keeping the McWurtheres's and her own home, she often tried to imagine what her children would look like. They'd had their picture taken shortly before Constantine left but it felt like a lifetime had passed since they'd sat for that photograph. She wondered if Winston still had his father's thick features and hoped that Alton's hair was still wavy, like it was when she left. She wondered if she'd be able to pick them out in the crowded airport. Furthermore, would her children recognize their own parents?

She and Clifton arrived at the airport an hour before their flight was supposed to get in, just in case it was early. The four had been separated from one another for so long that the last thing she wanted was for her sons to step off the airplane in a strange country and not immediately see their parents. They waited next to the gate beside a sign reading that the plane was coming in from Jamaica. The moment was quickly approaching, and neither one of them spoke, each lost in their own fear, excitement, and insecurity.

Finally, Clifton noticed that people were starting to exit the gate. Constantine collected her bag, filled with candy she had brought for the boys, and both of them walked as close to the door as possible. In their minds, the plane seemed to be filled with thousands of people; every face that didn't belong to a chid was a disappointment. After nearly fifty people had exited the plane, Constantine saw a leggy, blonde stewardess holding the hands of two sharply dressed boys. The smaller one was sniffling away tears from what Constantine assumed was a long and scary flight. And the other, was wide-eyed, searching expectantly.

Constantine looked quickly over at Clifton, beaming at him before moving toward their sons. She clutched her purse around her arm and nearly skipped over to the stewardess who had taken care of them. Once she reached the three, a bit nervous and unsure of how to proceed, Constantine flashed the stewardess a quick smile and a thank-you before identifying herself as their mother. The stewardess nodded and unleashed the boys's hands. Constantine knelt down so she could be eye level with Winston, who was still wiping stray tears. She reached out slowly to touch his face. He stiffened, gasped, and drew closer to his older brother.

Tears immediately sprang to her eyes. She took a minute to compose herself before she spoke. "Meh know yuh nah remember me, Winston, but I'm yuh mother."

Winston stared at her, weighing her words carefully. His grandmother, the only mother he'd ever known, told him often that he and his brother were going to go live with their parents, and later, their brother and sister in America. But in his six-year-old mind, the story seemed more like an oft-told fairy tale than this unpleasant reality. He didn't know he would be leaving Jamaica forever until his grandmother placed him on a plane and waved good-bye. What he did sense first and know later was that this was the last time he'd ever see his grandmother. And he mourned her absence throughout the entire flight and for the weeks, months, and years that would follow in Indianapolis, with his new family.

Not wanting to frighten Winston any more, Constantine turned her attention to her firstborn. At nine years old, in a navy-and-green plaid blazer and khaki pants that matched his younger brother's, Alton was cautious and reserved but not frightened. Unlike his baby brother, he remembered Constantine. Most of the time he'd spent with her had been lost. The only clear memory he had of her was the day she left. At the time, he knew his mother was leaving but none of them knew how long they'd be away from each other. In the years that followed, Alton had, at first, asked for his mother every day, then once a week, every other month, and then not at all.

Constantine hugged both of her boys, kissing them on their cheeks. When she pulled away, she offered her hands for them to grab like they'd done the stewardess's. But Clifton stepped in. He bent down slightly, talking to his sons with an obnoxiously loud voice and a huge smile, that revealed his nervousness, pride, and love. "Look at mi boys dem. Yuh looks good."

Both Alton and Winston looked up at their father, confused but intrigued. Living with their grandmother, aunts and cousins, there had been very few men around. His face was a particularly unfamiliar one. As Clifton had worked in Cuba before he moved to the U.S., Alton hardly remembered him and Winston not at all.
"Did unu have a nice trip?" Clifton asked placing his hand on Alton's shoulder as a gesture of affection and to also indicate he was expecting an answer from him.

Alton, who still hadn't broken his gaze, nodded his head slightly, telling the first lie to his parents. The flight had been long and terrifying to young children traveling alone. But seeing that his father was expecting more, Alton let a weak, "yes" escape from between his lips. Clifton heard him and instead of extending this uncomfortable exchange, he told the boys they were going to pick up their luggage and then they were going to see their new home. Now that Winston's tears had dried, Clifton's own happiness and excitement shielded him from noticing the sadness in their sons's eyes.

As they rode back to their home, all four of them squeezed into the front seat of Clifton's new truck. Clifton pointed out the different sights they were passing. He talked about all of the things they would enjoy doing

in America. He kept saying, "Dis place is nuthin like what unu used to."
And Constantine would cringe every time. Of course it was nothing like
what they were used to—they could already sense that their worlds had
been shaken. While she understood that Clifton was just trying to get
them excited about the move, she wished he would find something else
to talk about. So in an attempt to change the subject and give them just
a little bit of home, Constantine fell back on food.

"Unu hungry?"

Alton turned away from the window and nodded. Winston followed.

"Good, cuz mi made unu stew chicken, rice and peas and dumpling.
As she listed each food, Constantine smacked her lips, as if she were
already eating. "Dat soun' good?"

Alton nodded again and turned to look out the window. Winston kept
staring at her. Something about the look made Constantine shudder
inside. She imagined Winston trying to remember her from somewhere
in his mind. His eyes seemed to probe her, asking questions he wouldn't
be able to articulate for years to come.
In actuality, Winston did find a similarity in Constantine's face and the
ones belonging to his cousins and aunts. But more than anything he was
confused. Though he wasn't ready to speak to them yet, he wondered
why, if they were his mother and father, they lived in a place so far
away that he and his brother had to fly to get to it. His whole life he had
thought Grace Ann, with her wrinkled skin, shaky movements, and her
ever-present housecoat, was his mother. He and everyone else around
him—his cousins, aunts, and brother—had all called her "Mumah." He
had no reason to question the moniker. He was seeing now that maybe
mothers were supposed to be young and pretty with husbands and
uncertain smiles.

When they got home, Clifton Jr. and Noel, who had stayed home with
Mrs. Lewis, came bounding and toddling toward the door. Constantine
watched as all four of them froze. Clifton Jr. and Noel, who were dressed
casually in their house clothes, looked at Alton and Winston in their
finery and wondered who they were. Clifton was the first to speak.

"Unu see yuh bruddas dem?" He turned to Alton and Winston. "Here, come introduce yuhselves."

Clifton walked over to the older boys, nudging them toward their brother and sister. Alton, stepping into his role as the oldest, waved cautiously. Clifton Jr. smiled while Noel stared wide-eyed. The rest of the night went on like that with awkward, forced interactions, questioning faces, and extended silences.

It would take months, with the six of them living under one roof, before Constantine would just begin to see, firsthand, what the separation between the four of them had done. She'd often catch Winston crying silently or sobbing loudly when he thought no one was around to hear him. Alton, who had been the man of the house in Jamaica, and was used to being treated like one, tried to continue to play that role here in America. He shielded his tears from his younger brother, choosing girls at church and a social circle as his coping mechanisms.

Constantine watched them both, adjusting in their own ways, and wondered if the theories and ideas she'd allowed to pacify her over the years were really worth all the pain and turmoil she and Clifton had caused their sons. In her longing to see them, she hadn't considered that not only would they not want to see their parents but they preferred not to think about them at all. She didn't realize that her nine-and six-year-olds wouldn't view America as the land of opportunity, but rather a foreign, cold place that took them away from everything and everyone they loved.

Seeing them now, it was undeniably clear that she'd missed their formative years. Things most parents knew about their children, she had to learn about hers. She had not only been unable to protect them from hurt as their mother, but her actions had caused this pain. Logically, Constantine knew that bringing them to America prematurely, when they hadn't received their citizenship, would have been irresponsible. They ran the risk of being deported if they were caught. Still, emotionally, it didn't help her to feel any better about her decision to leave them. Looking in their sad eyes and hearing Winston's sobs day after day, she wasn't even sure if the opportunities they'd have in this country were worth not knowing these despondent children of hers.

Clifton also noticed Winston's tears. But instead of allowing him to grieve in his own time, he took a different approach than his wife. He walked into the living room one day to find Alton sitting with his arm around Winston, who was trying, unsuccessfully, to stifle his cries.
"A big man lik yuh still cry?" Clifton asked, trying to shame his son into silence.

Winston's arm shot up to his face to wipe the tears as he tried even harder to steady his breath.

Alton looked up at this stranger, his father, and frowned, resenting the comment. Still, Alton, like his younger brother, wanted this man who claimed him as his own to approve; so, tightening his grip around his brother's shoulders, he said nothing.

"Tell me what unu want?" Clifton asked them, desperate to stop the tears and get rid of that look in their eyes.

For the first time since they'd landed in Indianapolis, Winston spoke to his father: "We wan go back to our mother. We wan go back home, to Jamaica."

Clifton was crushed. But the hurt quickly morphed into irritation. Years of backbreaking work and his sons didn't want to leave their grandmother. "Unu cyan go back to Jamaica. Yuh nah see yuh family 'ere now?"

Before he could even finish the sentence, Winston started wailing. Clifton panicked.

"All right, all right. Shut up ya noise, boy! Unu can go back to Jamaica. Yuh mus do what yuh mother tell yuh and if unu behave meh ah send yuh back."

It was a lie from the pit of hell. And the moment he said it, he knew he had taken it too far but he couldn't bear to break their hearts again. So

Clifton let them enjoy a bit of temporary happiness.

"Now, be sure unu keep dis conversation between de tree of us. Don't tell yuh mudda."

Alton and Winston nodded their obedience. The lie was enough to pacify them for a time. It wasn't until they enrolled in school that it failed to be enough.

The children in Indianapolis, many of whom had never even seen a river much less crossed a sea, didn't know how to respond to the boys from Jamaica, with their strange names and funny way of talking. Alton and Winston learned quickly that they'd be ridiculed for speaking, so they remained silent. Their classmates regarded their silence as a way of expressing superiority, and their teachers believed it was a lack of intellect. And since neither the students nor the teachers knew anything about Jamaica and didn't care to learn, the students, and eventually even the teachers, dismissed them as inferior. After the newness of their presence had subsided, they weren't regarded at all.

Initially, the boys tried to soothe themselves with the fact that they weren't going to be there much longer. It didn't matter that these kids didn't know what they were saying or refused to talk to them because they'd be going back to Jamaica where they already had friends and family who spoke just like they did. It wouldn't matter that people thought they were dumb here. When they got back to Jamaica people would know better.

After about six months of waiting and inquiring, Alton was the first to realize that perhaps their father hadn't been truthful. Maybe they weren't ever going back to Jamaica; maybe this was their new, permanent home. And to confirm, he decided to ask his mother. In the short time since they'd been living with their parents, Alton had noticed a distinct difference between Clifton and Constantine. Their father didn't like to deal with any unpleasantness. He'd much rather pretend like everything was okay or like nothing had happened. But their new mother, no matter how ugly the truth was, was willing to tell it. And so Alton went to Constantine.

"M...mommy?"

He was still having trouble picking a name that fit his mother. "Mumah" had been reserved for his grandmother and he couldn't remember what he'd called Constantine when they were all living in Jamaica. Eventually, he decided on—or he was told—to call her "Mommy." But it didn't flow off his tongue easily just yet.

"Yes, Alton, wah yuh want?" Constantine was running around the kitchen, feeding Noel, trying to fix dinner, and listening to make sure Little Clifton wasn't getting into something, as he always seemed to do.

"Meh wan know when meh and mi brudda can go home, back to Jamaica." Alton spoke firmly and stood flat-footed. He thought he and Winston had been patient enough. And if he was going to have to wait some more, he at least wanted an idea of when it would happen.

Constantine froze. She didn't know where Alton had come up with the idea that he and Winston were going back to Jamaica but she felt a prick in her heart knowing she'd now have to dismantle it.

"Who tell yuh, unu going back Jamaica?"

"Daddy tell us, long time now, dat if we good, stop cry, we can go back to Jamaica fi live."

"Lawd Jeezus have his mercy," Constantine hissed under her breath. She thought it was a good thing Clifton wasn't home because if he were she would have dropped everything to wring his neck. Instead, she calmed herself and talked to her small-framed son with his resolute eyes.

"Alton, it nah true. Unu live 'ere now wid us, in Indianapolis. Meh know yuh miss Jamaica. Meh miss it too, very much. But dis place nah bad. It jus tek some gettin used to. But yuh must give it a chance. Try and mek de bess of it and I promise likkle by likkle it'll get bettah. Den maybe one day when unu older we can visit back home. But unu mus know meh and yuh fadda work hard fi bring de two a you come live wid us."

Alton knew his mother was going to tell him this before he even fixed his mouth to ask her; still, hearing the finality of the words shattered the last shred of hope to which he'd been clinging.

"'e lie tuh us?"

"Don't say lie Alton."

Constantine saw him look up at her confused. Lie was exactly what their father had done. With his feelings so deeply hurt, she broke custom and offered him an explanation for one of her commands.

"Lie is too vulgah for a likkle boy. Yuh mus' say 'tell a story.' It jus sound nicer."

Alton could care less about word choice at this particular moment. Instead, he was envisioning himself dealing with those cruel children at school for the rest of his life. He saw their faces turned up in laughter and mocking as they pointed at him, making fun of his accent. He imagined himself drifting through life in this strange place, completely overlooked and misunderstood by everyone except his younger brother. And he cried. Right there in the kitchen, with the pots boiling and his baby sister banging on the tray of her high chair.

Constantine took two swift steps across the kitchen, wrapping him up forcefully in her arms. Her heart broke for her child but she also relished the fact that she was just now allowed to act like his mother. She held him while he cried, rubbing his shoulders and telling him it would be okay. His tears fell for just a few seconds before he stepped away from her, composing himself.

Alton and Winston, with no other choice, did what children do, they adapted. Not devoid of scars, they each charted out their own course of survival. Alton's saving grace was that, even at ten years old, he had a way with the ladies. Had Clifton's sister not been so strict, it might have been better for Alton to stay with her in Trelawny, where someone could have kept an eye on him. In Kingston, there were predators disguised as caring, concerned authority figures, waiting to expose him to thoughts and behaviors a boy his age should know nothing about. Though his cousin Daphne had eventually come to his rescue, fighting a woman off him, a weed had already taken root in the garden of his mind, snuffing out his innocence long before his time. Society would eventually deem what Alton had experienced as sexual assault. But in his ten-year-old mind, he had been acting as a man. He had started studying the men he saw pass through his grandmother's house. They were mostly the boyfriends of his aunt and cousins. He'd sneak around paying close attention to how they spoke to his relatives, noting which words and phrases elicited the strongest reactions. And he'd put his studying to good use with other girls his age. By the time he left Jamaica, he had an arsenal of what he regarded as tricks and techniques. And though he had lost interest in the academic part of school, he was anxious to see if the American girls would respond to his miniature, manufactured manhood. He discovered, all too soon, that they did.

Winston had a harder time. He was much more sensitive and far less sure of himself than his older brother. He couldn't distract or impress the bullies with all the girls who wanted to get to know him. He chose not to shock the teachers with the knowledge he possessed. It wouldn't have made any difference. He was reminded every day, during virtually every minute of the day, that he didn't belong. Not in this country, in this school, not even in his home.

Where Alton tried to make the best of the situation, Winston couldn't stop reflecting on how his parents had betrayed him. Now that he knew, he wasn't going back to Jamaica, the tears he had stopped shedding returned again. Now, they came at night when he was lying in his too-comfortable bed, thinking about the thin pallet he'd had in Kingston. Before he was even ten years old, Winston harbored a pain so deep that it would seemingly disappear, only to reemerge again with a vengeance. Where Alton used his differences, his Jamaican-ness, to stand out, Winston found it easier to assimilate. He practiced speaking like the Americans did, with a twang. After two years of practicing in the bathroom, Winston felt like he'd perfected it, just in time for the class to deliver their oral report on a book of their choosing.

Winston was mortified from the moment his teacher said the word "present." And though he was dreading having to get up in front of the class, he wanted to do a good job, to prove that he wasn't some ignorant, island boy. Winston poured himself first into reading and understanding the book he'd chosen, *The Black Stallion*. Aside from wanting to do well during his presentation and impress his teachers and classmates, Winston enjoyed the book, even identifying with one of the main characters. Black, the horse, had been stolen from the country he knew and loved and was taken to America, where he had to become a racehorse.

After he'd completed the book and written his report, he'd have to share what he learned with his classmates. As he took his position at the front of the classroom, he steadied his hand to keep from shaking. He told himself to just tell the story he'd come to love. That's all he had to do. Surprisingly, the words came to him. Winston split himself into three parts. With one part, he listened to his voice as if he too were a part of the classroom. The other part took note of how the audience sat engaged, listening intently. And finally, the third recounted the story. Winston felt like he was beginning to soar, until one word sent him crashing back down.

"Alec feeds Black veg-eh-tehbles . . ."

Before he could finish the sentence he heard his classmates, who had once been attentive, giggling behind their palms. Roger Wilson, the boy who was always ready with an insult, was the first to speak coherently through his laughter. "You mean vegetables? What are veg-eh-tebles?" The class erupted again.

The two years of practice were dashed with a single slip in pronunciation. Winston couldn't get past their laughter. He stopped his presentation and scanned the room, taking in the faces of his peers cackling and pointing at him. Finally, the teacher, a stocky and patient woman who always wore her hair in a high bun, spoke up. "Don't worry about them, Winston, continue on with your report."

Roger spoke again, this time mumbling beneath his breath but still loud enough for all to hear. "Yeah, Winston, finish telling us about the vegch-tcb-lcs."

He looked around the classroom for his classmates to appreciate the joke. They did. The sniggering continued. The teacher, not fully recognizing the severity of the situation, pretended not to hear Roger Wilson and instead instructed the class to quiet down and Winston to continue.

Winston shifted the papers and tried again to find his place on the page. But he couldn't see the words. They were hidden behind the film of his own tears. He refused to cry in front of his classmates so he took a different course of action. In a moment that seemed to pass in slow motion, Winston dropped his stack of papers and charged down the desk aisles, leaping into the air in Roger's direction. Right before he made contact, Winston noticed the look of terror on Roger's face. It was too late for sympathy though. And Winston landed on top of Roger's body causing him to fall out of his chair and onto the ground. This alone would have been enough to prove his point; but after all Winston had been through in the past two years, leaving his home and his family, being lied to by his father, being teased and taunted at school, and trying to master their country-hick way of speaking, it just wasn't enough.

Winston laid into Roger, his fists connecting with the heckler's face a good three times before his teacher, with the help of some of the other students, was able to pull the two away from one another. As they stood separated, glaring into each other's eyes, his teacher, suddenly concerned with her students's behavior, started hollering. "Winston Reid! Get to the principal's office right now!" Winston looked around the classroom and saw that his classmates, for once, weren't regarding him as inferior or dumb or different. There was fear, shock, and, most importantly, respect in their eyes.

Winston swelled, witnessing their terror. For the first time since he'd made it to Indianapolis, he felt seen. He'd discovered the way to make it in America and the feeling was euphoric. The classmates who weren't too intimidated to look him in the face noticed that he wore a thin, satisfied smile. Even his teacher, who was known for her brutal paddlings, flinched a little as he passed her on his way out the door.

Walking through the halls, he wasn't concerned about confronting the principal or even dealing with his parents when he got home. He'd found a way to survive. That was more important than any punishment he'd have to endure once he got home.

Principal Miller was busy when he first walked into his office. And his secretary told him to sit in the chairs in the lobby and wait for him. When Principal Miller finally called him in, Winston sat down, attempting to explain himself.

"Mr. Reid, tell me what happened today."

"I just finally had enough today, Principal Miller. I've been here for two years now and the other students *still* make fun of my name, my accent, my whole country. I worked so hard on my book report today and Roger Wilson ruined all of that trying to tell a joke."

Principal Miller nodded. He'd only asked Winston what happened because it was proper protocol. He hadn't been listening. And even if he had been, he didn't really care about what happened in that room.

The principal gave Winston a serious tongue lashing about the importance of learning to control his anger. He told him Roger Wilson didn't deserve his abuse and then asked how he planned to fit in and make friends at this school if he went around fighting people. As he spoke, Winston replayed the whole incident in his head. Roger's joke, his own quick reaction, being pulled apart by their teacher, and lastly, and most memorably, those looks. He only rejoined Principal Miller in the room when he announced that he would have to call his parents.

"One or both of your parents are going to have to come up here and escort you off the premises because they need to know you won't be back here for the next three days."

For the first time, Winston felt his own twinge of fear. His father was out of town until tomorrow and it would be a hassle for his mother to ride the bus to get to the school when she was at home taking care of his little brother and sister and completely unable to drive. He wouldn't be allowed to leave the premises until an adult came and got him.

The principal pulled up Winston's file and dialed the number that had been listed for his parents's new home on Washington Avenue.

"Hello, may I please speak to Mrs. Reid?" The principal's tone softened significantly as he was preparing to speak to Constantine.

Winston could hear his mother's voice faintly in the background acknowledge that it was indeed she on the other line.

"Hello, Mrs. Reid. This is Principal Miller and I'm calling to inform you that your son Winston has found himself in a bit of trouble." Principal Miller frowned briefly in Winston's direction. "He was fighting in class and was sent to me. And school policy dictates that he'll be suspended, out of school, for the next three days."

Winston watched Principal Miller's brow furrow in concentration as he tried to decipher Constantine's accent, which had become even more pronounced through her anger and disappointment. She was still speaking when Principal Miller cut her off.

"Yes, I understand, Mrs. Reid. Will you be able to pick Winston up from school?"

Principal Miller soon learned that Winston wasn't lying about his mother's inability to pick him up. Winston shook his head at yet another person who didn't take him seriously. Just as Winston thought Principal Miller was going to hang up the phone, he heard him say, "Oh, Winston is right here. Would you like to speak with him?"

Winston's body tensed. He saw Mr. Miller handing him the phone. He watched as his own fingers grasped the slick, black plastic of the receiver. He felt the weight of the phone in his hand and then slowly brought it to his mouth. "Hello."

"Winston?" He heard the shrill tone of his mother's voice and prepared himself for a lecture.

If Winston had only been able to hear his mother's voice faintly when she was talking to Principal Miller, he was sure Principal Miller could make out every single word she was saying.

"How dare yuh haf des people dem call an' embarrass me at mi home all cuh yuh wan fight at school like yuh haf no 'ome trainin'? Den I haf fi tell de man all mi business, dat meh nah drive and him haf tuh tek mi pickney come bring home." Constantine paused for a moment, then asked, "Why yuh was fighting?"

Winston opened his mouth to answer, to tell his mother how the children had been taunting and teasing him since he had first gotten to school. Today had been the last day he was going to take it.

But none of that came out. And Constantine got tired of waiting for his response.

"Nah bodda answer. We'll talk when yuh get home. Ya teacher say fah punishment yuh muss spend the next tree days at home. Meh a tell yuh right now Winston, dis won' be no vacation. Yuh gon work while yuh here wid me. Yuh hear?"

"Yes, Mommy."

Winston heard his mother slam down the receiver on the other end of the line.

Winston passed the phone back to Principal Miller.

Minutes later, after Principal Miller silently gathered his belongings from his office, clearly irritated, the two rode in the car to Winston's house. When Principal Miller dropped him off, Winston hopped out of the car, grabbed his things, and mumbled a good-bye before he heard Principal Miller's tires screech away from the curb.

As Winston made his way up the cement walkway, he thought about what his mother would say to him and what he would say to her. He'd try to explain that he had been having a hard time at school and that he had lashed out before he really knew what he was doing. He'd tell her that he hadn't planned to fight that day. Winston had been scolded for doing little things around the house but for the most part, this was the first time he'd been in serious trouble in his life. When he got to the door, he turned the knob, knowing it would be unlocked.

It wasn't. He sighed, trying to muster up some courage before having to knock, like a stranger, at what they told him was his own home. He was shocked to see his father answer the door.

Winston soon learned there no explaining with Clifton. When he saw his son standing there, he looked past him briefly to see if Principal Miller was going to come in and speak to them. When he saw that he'd already pulled away, Clifton snatched Winston's stocky eight-year-old frame into the house. Winston hadn't noticed the belt in his father's hand but the sting he felt through his clothes confirmed its presence. As Winston tried to shield himself, he felt the belt replaced with a shoe and then his father's open hand.

As Winston tried to duck and dodge the blows, he could faintly hear his father's spitting disgust. "Yuh tink we bring yuh 'ere so yuh can embarrass mi and yuh mudda? Meh a learn yuh tonight. De 'oman dem in Jamaica ruin yuh but meh ah go mek yuh undastand . . . Yuh wan fight like a man at the people dem school? Yuh mus fight meh too when yuh get home."

The sense of accomplishment that Winston had felt earlier that day began to disintegrate with each lash. Instead of tears, Winston shed layers of trust and innocence, confidence and kindness. It was true the women in Jamaica, his grandmother, aunts, and cousins, had been more patient and understanding. They'd recognized his sensitivity and they were sympathetic to the fact that he was growing up without his parents. They'd done nothing to ruin him; they'd nurtured him. And his parents took him away from that. As Winston waited for the beating to be over, he wondered if anyone would ever treat him with such kindness again.

When Clifton was finished, Winston was left with hot tears of humiliation and anger. Though she hadn't defended him against his father's blows, Constantine came to sit and talk with him now.

"Why yuh fighting at de people dem school?" She asked, embarrassed that she hadn't gotten an answer before Clifton attacked him and he had a chance to explain himself.

Winston sat, his heaving chest his only response. He wanted to speak, to tell her what he'd been going through; but each time he opened his mouth, sobs threatened to escape.

Constantine waited, rubbing his back, trying to coax the words out.

When he steadied his breathing, Winston blurted simply, reverting back to his native patois, "De chi'ren dem mek fun of me."

Constantine sighed. Having bypassed the cruel-children phase in her immigration journey, she couldn't fully empathize. With other children to tend to and a shortage of time on her hands, she offered a piece of shallow advice. "Winston, yuh mus pay de pickney dem no mind. If dey touch yuh, den sure yuh mus defend yuhself. But yuh cyan walk around ready fi box up everyone who haf an unkind word." With that, Constantine slowly lifted herself off the couch to go serve dinner.

In the kitchen she thought about all she'd learned of this country in the time she'd been here. It wasn't the utopia they'd made it seem in Jamaica. She'd been in America long enough to know how Negroes were regarded here. She and Clifton had been turned away from clubs because they were presumed Negro. They'd been forced to use certain back-alley entries, drink from certain fountains, and use the restroom in unkempt structures. They both knew what it felt like to have people think that all you could do was serve and clean. The schools had just this year been desegregated and Clifton and Constantine knew that White folks, who were still very much embittered, were looking for any reason to get Black children out of them, looking to highlight and amplify any fault to prove what they vehemently believed. Clifton and Constantine had never considered themselves Negro. And they still didn't. They were Jamaican. But they weren't naive. They understood how they were viewed in this society. Before they opened their mouths and people heard their accents, they saw their skin color. And in this country, that was enough to be presumed inferior. It was her job to teach Winston and all of her children that any bad behavior on their part, no matter what the White kids were doing, only confirmed the White man's prejudices.

Later, sitting at the table, reflecting on his beating and his mother's subsequent words, Winston scoffed at her hypocrisy. She'd stood there, watching the same violence she'd condemned in him. Winston surmised that while she said one thing, her actions had shown that physical brawn was the best way to get a point across and to demand respect. Winston, who had felt real fear and real terror looking into his father's face as he beat him, changed for the worst. He'd recognized his power and respected him simply because, at eight-years-old, he was no match for his strength. He vowed then, sitting in the midst of his newfound family, that he'd work to command that same type of fear and respect from as many people as he could.

That night after the children and Clifton had fallen asleep, Constantine thought again about the day's events. She realized that this might have been the first time Winston had been beaten. Grace Ann never really had the temperament for that when she was growing up, so Constantine knew she had spared her poor grandsons. She didn't have that luxury here in the States. It was better for his father to beat him instead of being beaten by the White man, so she finally fell asleep, having made peace with her husband's actions.

1956, Thirty-six

It seemed to Constantine that the minute she had her IUD removed, she was pregnant again. She told herself that she needed to give her body a break from the device and presumed the pregnancy-preventing hormones were still lingering in her system. She was wrong. Shortly after she learned of the news, she wrote to her mother, informing her of the pending, new grandchild.

Constantine had to laugh at Grace Ann's response, penned by Daphne: *"How yuh let de man breed yuh up so?"*

It wasn't that Grace Ann was unhappy about the prospect of a new grandchild. She would love any child her daughter birthed. She just knew from experience how children, five of them, limited a woman's mobility, especially a woman who didn't work. Since Clifton had started his trucking business, Constantine told her mother that she didn't have to do the domestic work she'd done when they first moved to this country. She could stay at home and clean her own house and raise her own children. Grace Ann wrote that she was happy that her daughter wouldn't have to grind her life away, cleaning people's houses. But she also issued a warning to her daughter: *"Meh nah wan yuh live a life like mine. Meh spent much a mi life sit and wait pon a man fi tell meh when tuh shit and sleep."*

Grace Ann rarely cursed. She employed the device here to prove a point. In her old age, she was enjoying freedom, for the first time unattached and unfazed by the attention of any man. She assumed when she sent her daughter to America that the opportunities wouldn't just be for Clifton and the children, but for Constantine as well. Her daughter was smart and had been properly educated and Grace Ann wanted her, if she could, to change her plight before it was too late. And if it were possible anywhere, America was the place to do it.

Reading the words from her mother haunted her. Constantine wondered if her warning had come too late and she'd missed her window of opportunity. All throughout her childhood she'd promised herself that she would never live like her mother. Sadly, the similarities between the generations were terrifying.

Just last year, shortly after Noel turned two, Constantine started to think more seriously about her life. Having a daughter, someone who would be watching and mirroring her actions, forced her to look at herself in a different light. She didn't want to just point to the domestic work she'd done. Instead, she thought she'd capitalize on the skills she already had.

She recalled a day at the grocery store. A woman had been staring at her from across the aisle for too long. In Constantine's mind, it seemed like she was studying her, sizing her up. Finally, the woman started walking toward her. And with her son's hand in hers and her daughter on her hip, Constantine braced herself for the potential threat. As the woman got

213

closer to her, she could see that she wore a look of curiosity, not malice.

"Excuse me, I'm sorry to stare," the woman said, her brow still furrowed. "I was just admiring your hair and I wanted to know who did it."

Constantine relaxed a bit at the compliment but she looked the woman over quickly to see if she seemed decent. Her clothes were neat and her eyes kind. So she obliged her. "I did mi hair miself."

The woman gasped, "Oh, it's very nice! So, do you do hair for a living?"

Constantine snorted quietly, thinking of her past life in Jamaica, long before she'd met Clifton and her children were even a thought. But instead of reminiscing, she smiled and told her she didn't.

"You seem really talented. Like you have a knack for this. I don't know if you'd be interested but there's a new cosmetology school opening up on this side of town. I just saw the sign for it. If you're interested you should look into it."

Constantine raised her eyebrows, her interest piqued. Before she left, the woman wrote down the name and number of the school on a slip of paper. Once she'd gone, Constantine thought about the opportunity to have her own salon. It would be lovely, not to have to rely on Clifton for everything she needed. She thought if she started doing hair again, she could have her own pocket change and she could buy odds and ends for the house without having to argue with him about it. She could just see herself, hustling and bustling about in a proper shop with hair dryers, sinks, and chairs you had to pump to elevate.

As soon as she got home and put the groceries away, she put little Clifton down for a nap and bounced Noel on her hip as she called the cosmetology school. When she got the receptionist, she asked a few questions about the school first, just to seem polite, and then she inquired about the cost of enrolling. The receptionist told her it was seventy-five dollars.

Seventy-five dollars was steep, especially for a woman who wasn't working. It certainly wasn't an amount she had in her back pocket right that instant. But it wasn't completely out of reach. Constantine knew that if she went back to the very domestic work she had left behind, she could have the money in several weeks. She decided she wouldn't even tell Clifton what she planned to do. Once he saw how serious she was, he'd support the endeavor, especially if he didn't have to pay for it.

Scrubbing the floors, sweeping, and dusting had been next to torture when she first moved to Indianapolis. But now, with all of her children under the same roof and with a goal of betterment in mind, the time slipped by. Constantine enlisted the help of her neighbor to watch the two younger children while she worked during the day.

These days as she moved about on her hands and knees, Constantine smirked at all of the money she would make. What woman didn't need her hair done? If her past in Kingston was any indication of her future success, it wouldn't be long before her house would look more and more like the ones she cleaned for these White folks.

In nearly three months time, she was able to save up the seventy-five dollars she needed. She took the bus to the school and paid the money to register. When she put the money down, a woman gave her a receipt stating that the fee was nonrefundable. Constantine shrugged, knowing that she had every intention of putting it to good use. Classes would start in the fall. She smiled the whole way back home thinking about how she would tell the families's she had started cleaning for that she was quitting because she was going to school.

And then one evening two weeks later, after Clifton had come home from one of his trips, she told him about the cosmetology classes. She presented it like a win-win situation for both of them, because that's what it was: more money coming into the house.

"Meh tink meh foun' ah way where yuh nah haf fi work so hard."

Clifton perked up, curious to hear her plan. "How yuh figuh dat?"

"Meh enrolled in cosmetology school." Constantinc couldn't contain her excitement and a smile broke out across her face. Clifton's reaction was the exact opposite. His body tensed as he gripped the fork in his hand more tightly.

"Why yuh wan go to cosmetology school?"

"Yuh know fi help round de house, tuh be able to buy what meh wan' widout having tuh run tuh yuh for it. Yuh know meh used tuh do hair back in Jamaica. Meh good at it. And I was thinking once meh graduate from this school I could open mi own beauty shop. Then we'd really be set up nice."

Clifton simply shook his head no.

"What problem yuh have wid meh going to da cosmetology school?"

Clifton's real reason was buried beneath shame, pride, jealousy and control; but acknowledging that would be too painful, make him appear too vulnerable. So instead, he deflected and tried to guilt her, reminding her of her responsibilities as a mother.

"And wha de children dem gon do while yuh away at de school? Who 'ere fi watch dem during the day?" Clifton looked around the room in dramatic flourish. "If yuh wan make a likkle extra muney, go back to de domestic work for the Walters dem. Dat way yuh can work in de days and be ready fah de kids dem when dey come home from school. If yuh go tuh cosmetology school, yuh nevah be home fah dem."

"So yuh de only one who can leave de house and haf a likkle piece of somethin fah yuhself?"

She watched Clifton swell.

"Yuh tink meh like wake up 'fore de sun come up in de dead ah wintah fi try start de truck? Meh do it fah yuh and de kids dem. So yuh can be 'ere fah dem. Now yuh a tell me is more yuh want? De baby still on yuh hip and yuh ready fi leave." Clifton stopped short.

In a last-ditch effort, Constantine softened her approach, trying to reason with him. "But Clifton meh already put down de muney for the classes dem. Dey cyan refund it."

The argument only made him more resolute as he wondered how she'd managed to save up money without asking him. "Den yuh shouldn't ah paid de muney widdout talkin' tuh me furst. Dat muney wasted." His answer was final.

Constantine watched the doomed moments after he'd made his decision stretch on like the months she'd spent scrubbing and wiping, sweeping and cleaning—all to save up for a goal that she knew, at that very moment, she would never realize. In a matter of minutes, her husband, who feared that her independence would empower her to leave him, successfully squashed the life out of her. He'd convinced her that perhaps her past success wouldn't translate over here. He made it seem that she was behaving like a child when she was far too old to be thinking up new career goals, especially when she had so many children still to raise. She was a mother now and that was her job, along with being his wife.

Her mother's letter had brought all of that to the forefront of her mind. And instead of smiling as she refolded the letter and placed it on her nightstand, as she usually did, she casually let it fall out of her hand and into the trash can.

1957, Thirty-seven

Having spent almost half of her life pregnant, Constantine thought that her body would one day acclimate to the condition. But with each child, she was surprised to learn that her body rebelled instead of embraced the condition. She was always vomiting. During her first two pregnancies, back in Jamaica, she had been able to soothe her stomach with the dirt. She was sure now that it was the dirt that cured her nausea. But she also knew that the behavior that had been frowned upon in Jamaica could have gotten her committed in America. And now, worrying about two older children, chasing after a five and six-year-old, all while pregnant, the last thing she needed was for any of them to judge her, or worse, pick up any of her bad habits. More than any of her other children, Constantine was counting the days until this child's arrival.

And right at the top of the year, her second daughter was born. Feeling overcome as she had with all of her children, Constantine named her Pearl Joy Reid. As the months passed, Constantine couldn't help but notice that her second daughter favored her second son in complexion. She found great joy in seeing how they'd reached back and grabbed their grandmother's skin tone with her own petite facial features. Constantine chuckled to herself at that thought. Her features were the only thing that was petite about her these days. She was no longer the skinny island girl. And it wasn't just because she had just given birth; the true sign that they had made it in this country were her and Clifton's expanding waistlines.

1960, Forty

Constantine jokingly told anyone who would listen that Pearl came at the top of the year because she couldn't wait to get here and meet her mother. As soon as Alton, Little Clifton, and Noel learned to walk and talk they ventured off to find adventure of their own, together. But Pearl was more dependent and clingy, mimicking everything she did from the very start. As she got older, Constantine saw that her second girl was like her second son in more than just complexion. She too was always underfoot. Even at three years old, Pearl had a strong desire to please her mother. And she wondered if this was how Winston would have remained if she hadn't removed his hand from the hem of her skirt all those years ago.

The same year Pearl turned three, Clifton and Constantine saved up enough money to take the children back to Jamaica to visit their grandmother—or at least some of the children. Alton and Winston had made it very clear that they didn't want to visit. When she asked them why, they, entering the age of angst, interpreted the invitation as a continuation of the betrayal they had felt from childhood. They opted to stay and spend time with their friends. If the boys had said this when they first came to the country, she would have accepted this as a victory.

But knowing them better, Constantine sensed that the opportunity had passed. Now it would be too painful to return to the place they'd been stripped from. Having been in America all the years, spoiled by the nation's wealth, they knew their childhood home would have lost much of its enchantment and instead would be only a marker of their humble beginnings. Winston didn't tell his mother this but as a young boy, first coming into this country, he'd vowed never to get on another airplane as long as he lived. The experience had been too traumatic. And it wasn't one he wanted to duplicate even now that he'd aged. While she knew her mother would have loved to see them, Constantine didn't press the issue. Clifton would stay home with them while she took Little Clifton, Noel, and Pearl.

Constantine passed a mirror as she was packing her suitcase and for the first time, wondered if her family would recognize her when she stepped off the plane. Whether they saw the same girl or not, she knew she'd be regarded as a success story, even if they teased her about the extra pounds. Constantine stuffed each child's suitcase with clothes, shoes, and beauty products for her mother, sisters, nieces and nephews. As much as the gifts were for them, she was repaying a debt. After all they'd done, it would have been a disgrace for her to return with empty hands.

Constantine was anxious for her mother to see and touch her grandchildren. When life in America lost its luster, especially in the winter, she lamented the fact her American-born children wouldn't have the same close relationship with their grandmother that their cousins and older brothers got to experience.

True to their nature, Clifton Jr. and Noel were excited from the moment they stepped on the plane. A bit older, they had a better grasp of what was going on. They were traveling to the place where their mother was born and they were going to meet the grandmother they'd heard so much about and even spoke to on the phone occasionally. Pearl who was troubled by the uncertainty of all the newness, only took comfort in being forever by her mother's side.

When they arrived at their grandmother's house, where all their cousins were waiting for them, Noel and Little Clifton seemed right at home, bounding up to meet their new family members. The minute they got to her mother's house, Grace Ann took one look at Little Clifton and decided the adult name didn't suit a child like him.

"How yuh ah call dis sweet faced likkle boy a big name like Clifton? Meh ah go call him Boysie. It fit bettah." The name stuck for the rest of the trip and the rest of his life.

Pearl didn't take well to all of her family looking at her, touching her, and trying, unsuccessfully, to pull her away from her mother. When her aunts reached down to pick her up, trying to loosen her from her mother's leg, she wailed. They could barely look at her before she started to scrunch her face up, forcing tears to stream down. But as long as she was next to Constantine, she was happy to observe her relatives from within her the confines of her mother's grasp.
After three days of their two-week trip had passed, Beverly, one of Constantine's few friends, came by the house to catch up with her. "Connie, how yuh been? Yuh looking plump. America mus be treating yuh and yuh husban real nice."

Constantine smiled at the backhanded compliment, nodding at the cleverness and in acceptance of the slight jab.

"Yuh a big 'oman now eh?" Beverly continued. "Yuh sekkle down wid a whole heap of pickney. Yuh does haf fun in de States like we used tuh do here? Clifton tek yuh dancing nah?"

"Fun, wha?" Constantine said, kissing her teeth. "All meh do is tek care of mi kids dem, mek more pickney, cook, an' keep up mi house."

"Ooo. Well, den yuh must come out wid us dis evening. A bunch of us ah go tuh Silver Slipper like we used tuh bak in de days. Yuh still know how fi dance nuh?"

Constantine wondered if she really could keep up. These days, the only dancing she did was a little bop or two-step she might have done when she hummed to herself as she straightened up the house. They didn't have a stereo system at home and the only music Clifton was interested in listening to was the hymnals they sang at church. Constantine wasn't sure whether she would be able manage. But there was no way she was going to pass up the opportunity to dance like she was a teenager. "Meh tink meh could hold up."

"Well, good den. Meh pick yuh up round nine tirty."

It wasn't until after Beverly left that Constantine started to have reservations. She hadn't packed anything to wear to go out dancing and she knew Pearl wouldn't do well being left alone, but she figured she'd be asleep before she left and she could sneak out and return in the early morning before she woke up. A part of her felt a twinge of guilt but a stronger whisper from her former self reminded her that she deserved it. Being in her hometown, with "no husband," Constantine couldn't help but jump at the chance to relive part of her youth. She shook her head, chuckling at the memory of the way Clifton had stomped and clumped around the dance floor, nearly crushing her toes. The thought of the two of them going out today was laughable.

At around seven thirty, Constantine started getting ready. Pearl, following behind her mother like a shadow, rubbed her tired eyes, sensing that she was leaving without her. Sitting on the bed, after being fed, bathed and dressed in her pajamas, she watched as her mother pressed and styled her hair to perfection, tucking and pinning the loose, freshly straightened ends into intricate swirls about her head. Constantine moved Pearl further away from her as she used the edge of the bed to press the dress she was going to wear that evening. It wasn't like the chiffon numbers she wore back in her twenties. It was more sophisticated. There was a square cut out that exposed a bit of cleavage but the hem of it would rest tightly just above her knees.

Still in her slip and brassiere, Constantine stood in the mirror in her room applying makeup; no foundation but a bit of power to smooth her skin, blush for her cheeks, and her signature wine-colored lipstick. It had been so long since she'd dressed up to go anywhere but church and she was enjoying this process. By the time she finished it was nine o'clock and Pearl still hadn't shown the slightest sign that she'd be going to sleep anytime soon. She was lying down, but every time Constantine took a step, Pearl would sit up, trying to see if her mother was leaving her as she suspected.

Finally, at nine fifteen, Constantine put on her dress and sprayed on her favorite Estée Lauder perfume. And fifteen minutes later, just as she had promised, Beverly showed up in the passenger seat of an old Chevy to take her to the club. Olga and her niece Daphne were going that night too and they hurried her along, trying to reassure her that Pearl would be all right with her grandmother. Constantine kissed her screaming daughter good night, leaving a wine-colored lip print on her already blushed cheeks, then scurried out the door to meet Beverly.

For the first five minutes, as the car peeled away from her house, Constantine felt guilty having left her daughter traumatized. But she settled herself with the fact that this time, she knew she was coming back.

With Beverly talking and joking with her sister and niece, Constantine relaxed into the possibilities of the night. There was no way she couldn't enjoy herself. Just a little respite from her children would do her good.

By the time they arrived at the Silver Slipper and stepped inside, Constantine sighed in nostalgic bliss. It was just as she remembered it, like stepping back into time. The decor was a bit dated now, but it had been maintained well and now it had an old glam about it that was charming. The music had changed and Constantine didn't know much of it. She had no idea what people in Jamaica, or, for that matter, people in America, were listening to nowadays. But that didn't stop her. She fed off Olga and Daphne's energy as they pulled her to the dance floor singing, stepping, and rolling their hips and bellies to the rhythms.

Out on that dance floor, shuffling her feet, Constantine hadn't felt this alive since she'd left Jamaica. She marveled at the movement of her limbs, the sound of her heels on the floor and the width of her smile. She was in the midst of a deep gut-and-shoulder-shaking laugh when she saw Tawkins from across the room.

She stopped dancing and the smile morphed into a concentrated gaze. She squinted in an attempt to confirm. Tawkins must have been watching her for some time because his eyes were locked on hers. It had been nearly twenty years and three lifetimes since she'd seen him last. And though her years and experiences should have given her the tools to handle this moment gracefully, she still wasn't sure how to be around him. Really, there was no bad blood between them so she smiled and waved before she got back to dancing again, waiting for him to make his way over to her, as she was sure he would. Though she never stopped moving, Olga hadn't missed a beat.

"Is Tawkins dat?" She asked Constantine.

"Yeah, das 'im."

"Yuh ah go speak?"

"Meh will talk if him come ovah. Meh nah walk cross de room fi speak tuh de man after more dan twenty years."

Constantine, much to her embarrassment, found that she couldn't stop grinning. She made a conscious effort to close her lips; but every time she caught a glimpse of him, the grin returned. It had taken twenty years, a troubled marriage, and five children, but the resentment she'd once harbored for the man who had ruined her happy ending, had faded.

As the song ended, another slow one replaced it. One by one men came to dance with Daphne, Olga, and Beverly until Constantine found herself standing alone. She turned to get a drink of water. But she hadn't taken two steps when she saw Tawkins making his way toward her. Before she could collect her thoughts and come up with some clever, ice-breaking line, her first love was standing directly in front of her.

"Constantine. Yuh lookin good still after alla dese 'ears."

Constantine snorted, barely audible. She knew she was still foxy but she didn't look anything like the little girl Tawkins had known. And just as she was going to return the compliment, she decided to take a good look at him and see if time had been equally kind to this man. It had. He too was a little wider around the waist. His hair was cut closer to his head to disguise the thinning. But his eyes held the same light they had even when he was a boy.

"Yuh lookin' good too, Tawkins."

He grinned, his eyes darting toward the floor. The look gave Constantine a bit of comfort. She was glad to see she wasn't the only nervous one. And then, almost as quickly, his face straightened into a curious, yet stern expression.

"So meh hear yuh married ah long time now. Yuh husband treat yuh well?"

Constantine smirked, trying to keep her eyes from revealing the reality of the situation. For a moment she thought about telling him the truth, giving him the opportunity to rescue her from her marriage. She scolded herself immediately. What was the man going to do, rescue her and her five children too? She settled for a measure of the truth.

"We do all right. Yuh know how de men dem stay, Tawkins." Constantine looked at him accusingly, taking the opportunity to take a jab after a couple of decades.

Tawkins looked embarrassed for a moment before shaking his head. "Meh see yuh nah change. Yuh still haf dat sharp tongue."

Constantine couldn't help but laugh, thinking about her father's warning on his deathbed. Since he'd said it, all the men in her life had said the same thing in one way or another. She didn't allow the thought to get her down. Instead, she turned the conversation to him. "So, yuh married, Tawkins?"

She knew the answer before he opened his mouth. She'd seen the ring on his left hand. She really wanted to know who he had married. "Yes, meh married Sheryl not too long after yuh married."

Constantine flinched internally at the mention of the woman's name, just as she'd done the first time he had spoken about his lab partner. Tawkins went on to explain that he had come out with his buddies to get a couple of drinks. Constantine barely heard him. She was concentrating on looking unfazed by the news that he'd married Sheryl. But her eyes darted quickly and she wondered if Tawkins had noticed her disappointment. She'd hoped that it would have been anyone else but Sheryl. She didn't know how to proceed with the conversation and instead of asking the obligatory follow-up questions, she fell silent.

Luckily, Tawkins interjected, "Yuh mean fi tell me yuh husband let you come out 'ere on yuh own tonight?"

Constantine snapped out of her funk. "'im back home in the States with our two eldest boys."

"Oh, meh see. Any udda chil'ren?"
Constantine beamed, thinking about the five bright spots in her otherwise gray existence. "Yes, five pickney. Tree boys and two girls."

"Whoa! So yuh been busy."

She shrugged and smirked in mock innocence and asked if he had any children of his own.

"Yes, two. A boy and a girl."

Constantine nodded approvingly. And before either one of them could say anything else, the DJ played The Drifters's "This Magic Moment." And Constantine lit up, squealing subconsciously before she began to sway to the music. She hadn't started moving to solicit an invitation, but her reaction was too strong for Tawkins to ignore.

"Yuh wan dance?"

Constantine hesitated, wondering if she were disrespecting her husband by dancing with a man she'd once loved. But then she thought about what her husband was probably doing out in the streets, particularly now that she wasn't home, and she decided a little dance wouldn't hurt. "Yes, meh love to."

As Ben E. King and The Drifters crooned, Constantine leaned into Tawkins's sturdy frame, closing her eyes as she took in his scent. Her fingers hadn't forgotten his back and they gripped it instinctively. She noticed the tingling sensation Tawkins's hand on her lower back sent up her spine and relished it, recognizing its sweet but fleeting nature. Constantine was more than aware of the impossibility of a reunion; still, tonight, at least for the duration of this song, she wanted to pretend they were dancing together in a different reality. She breathed deeply, thinking about the life they would have shared if he'd never stepped out with someone else or if she'd been able to forgive him for it.

In the ideal world she'd be on the dance floor as his wife, on one of the many times they went out dancing as a seasoned married couple. They would have had their arguments, like all married couples, but on the dance floor all of that would melt away. People in their town would look at them and marvel at the beauty of their story: childhood sweethearts who had somehow managed to stay in love all these years.

Tawkins would have been the type of husband to push her to go back to school, insisting that she complete her dream of becoming a teacher. He'd know that her intelligence and schooling didn't make him any less a man. She'd never spend a day on her knees cleaning and shining floors. In fact, they'd employee their own helpers. She wouldn't know cold winters or the dirty looks White folks gave her in the streets. She'd never have to look into the eyes of children she'd birthed but didn't know. She'd never know the feeling of her skin stinging from his blow, no matter what smart things she'd say. And his lying in order to take Sheryl out would be a distant memory they occasionally laughed at. It would represent a fluke, a snag in the fabric of a decent and faithful boyfriend, husband, and then father.

Just as Constantine was getting settled into her fantasy life, she heard the last chords of the song play and she was saddened to feel Tawkins's hands sliding off her back, his body stepping, cautiously, away from hers. For a few seconds afterward, there was silence as he stared down

at her and she up at him, thinking, remembering, wondering.
Tawkins broke the silence again. "Yuh wan step outside for a bit and get some air?"

Constantine nodded. "Mek meh tell mi sister. One second."

She walked quickly over to Olga. "Meh ah go tek ah walk wid Tawkins for a bit. We nah be gone long."

Olga pursed her lips and cut her eyes suggestively in Constantine's direction. "Umm-hmm. Nah gone long, eh?" She flashed Constantine a grin full of devilment. Constantine shook her head, trying to mask a smile of her own. She looked over at Tawkins standing by the door waiting for her but turned back to her older sister, halfway scolding her.

"Nuthin ah go happen. Both ah we married people. Meh cyan be like de men dem and spread miself all over de place. Meh come back in a likkle bit."

Constantine tried to contain her excitement as she crossed the dance floor walk over to Tawkins. She picked a suitable pace, trying not to appear too eager or disinterested, and once she got to him she nodded signifying that she was ready to go.

Walking outside in the night air with Tawkins was something straight out of her memories and she couldn't help but smile at all the sweetness her life held in those days. Today, Tawkins was standing a little bit farther from her than he would have in the past but the comfort and even the giddiness she felt was still the same. A part of her couldn't believe that she, a grown woman at forty years old with a whole heap of kids and a husband, was feeling so much like her teenage self.

As they walked along outside, Tawkins asked her what she did in the States. Constantine had to weigh every response carefully before she answered. She didn't want him to believe that her life had completely gone to hell since she'd dumped him. Surprisingly, she found herself bragging on her husband just a bit.

"'im jus start a likkle trucking business which not doing too bad. We haf a house now but it nah come easy. In the beginning we both haf fi do domestic work to get sekkled in. Den we bring meh eldest boys dem up. Now meh spend mi days dem looking after mi chi'ren and keeping mi house clean."

After Tawkins had digested the information, Constantine inquired about his life. "What about yuh wife?" She couldn't bear to call her name.

Tawkins told Constantine that with the exception of domestic work, they had led similar lives to her and her husband's. "She mek a good wife and mudda. She work as a nurse at de hospital."

Eager to change the subject, Constantine asked about him specifically.

"So yuh did become a doctor like yuh wan?"

"Meh did." Tawkins said. He smiled contently at having accomplished the goal and being able to share this with the woman, who in many ways, had been there to help him do it.

And then he talked about his children, how he was in the hospital when they were born, and the pleasure he took in watching them grow, healthily. "Yuh know dem attend St. Mary's school. All de sisters dem still dere teaching and swatting the chi'ren dem 'ands or bottoms when dem ah ack up. Nothing nah change."

Tawkins and Constantine chuckled at the overly strict nuns, grateful for their dedication, no matter how problematic. And then Tawkins stopped short.

"Yuh know, Constantine. After yuh dump me, meh waited for yuh. Meh always did hope me an yuh would be together."

Constantine gasped at his admission. While she was flattered by this revelation, it also annoyed her. Twenty years later, what good did it do to know he'd waited for her?

"Das why yuh marry yuh lab patnah?"

Tawkins shook his head at her stubbornness. "Ah woman, if nothin' else yuh stay consistent."

Constantine pursed her lips and snorted slightly. It was true she hadn't changed. She was still stubborn and occasionally unyielding. But that didn't dismiss the validity of her question.

"Meh wasn't the first tuh marry, yuh memba?" Tawkins offered.

Constantine nodded pensively, thinking back to the day she learned she was pregnant, wondering if she, knowing what she did at this very moment, could have made a different decision.

"Meh was pregnant, yuh know? Das the only reason meh marry 'im. Mi mudda begged 'im fi marry me and nah shame de family. Trut is, before meh fin' out meh pregnant, we wasn't on good terms. Mi and Clifton was never supposed tuh be tuhgedda."

Tawkins sighed, wondering if he should have tried harder to get her back. He took Constantine's hand, staring and studying her intently, silently extending an invitation, asking if they should abandon their pride, correct their mistakes, and make another decision, at least for this evening.

Constantine felt like her insides had been bathed in light. Her temperature rose and her skin prickled, anticipating his touch in places other than her hand.

As she considered Tawkins's silent proposition, Constantine reasoned that she would have been well within her rights to spend just one evening with him. Clifton had made a mockery of their marriage vows who knows how many times over. She could go with him this once and return home to the States, with no one the wiser except for her, her sisters, Tawkins, and Father God in heaven. It sounded like a great plan and there was no doubt in her mind that she deserved it. Alton and Winston had known of the dysfunction in their home long before they could identify it. And now the same was true for Boysie and Noel. It wouldn't be long before all of them recognized the true nature of their parents's relationship.

But then Constantine thought about Tawkins's children and their mother. She didn't know whether Sheryl loved him or not but there was a strong possibility she did. Tawkins was a decent man and probably good to his wife. Sheryl probably couldn't help but love him. Even if she didn't, if she'd only settled into a fondness for the man, Constantine knew she herself would have wished another woman would take her feelings and her children's feelings into account before they spread their legs. If the women who'd entertained her father had behaved that way, maybe then her mother wouldn't have been so finicky and jumpy all the time and Hilda wouldn't have spent her adolescence trailing her father in the street.

Constantine was a woman, grown with more children than she ever thought she'd have, but standing there, holding Tawkins's hand and gazing into his eyes she hadn't realized she'd missed so much over the years, she wasn't thinking about her womanliness or fairness or even revenge. If she had yielded to any of those forces, she would have gone, unashamedly. But instead she thought about his children and then herself. His children wouldn't understand that their father had loved her first, that she and Tawkins, in a kind and just world, were supposed to be together. Their only concern would have been for their mother. Their heartbreak and disgust would have been hurled at their father for hurting her and disappointing them. And she couldn't bear to be responsible for Tawkins's children resenting him the way she had resented her father.

And then she did think about herself. However the story with she and Clifton would play out, she wanted to be the one to present herself blameless in the pending calamity. If her children had any questions about their parents's marriage, she wanted to tell the truth, to be the martyr in the story. She took solace and pride in one day being able to say that she had endured in the face of adversity and temptation. And she would want them to know that she had done it not for herself but for them, to ensure that they had a better life with two parents in the home. That would be the greatest revenge. Forcing herself into near sainthood while her husband was the rogue in the family legacy. That—and not a romp in the island heat with her first love when she'd only have to return home and keep the secret—would leave the greatest mark. And so with herself and her legacy in mind, Constantine declined Tawkins's invitation. She gently rubbed the back of the hand that grasped hers. "We bedda get back inside. Meh tell Olga meh would only be gone ah few minutes."

Walking back inside, with Tawkins having just propositioned her, the corners of Constantine's lips turned up into a slight smirk. After two decades and good fifty pounds heavier, she was still desirable.

Two days after the dance, Constantine and her children were heading back to Indianapolis. Her brother, Roy, whom the kids called Uncle Son, was going to be the one to drive them to the airport. Roy, a DJ, had done well for himself in Jamaica and he pulled up in front of Grace Ann's house in a shiny, candy-apple-red corvette. Seeing him pull up in that car, Constantine smiled, remembering how he'd told her the story of his decision to change his name from Johnson to Johnston: "De people dem drag de name out suh till it soun vulgah. Jaaaaawwwnnson."

Roy had told her that the "T" made them cut the word, plus he thought "Johnston" sounded more distinguished. That was the reason he gave her. But Constantine suspected that it was also because he had no real allegiance to the name anyway. Aside from allowing him to get to know his sisters, that was all Theophilus had really given him. It was humorous. All those years her father complained about being in a house full of women, how he longed for a son. And when he finally got one, the boy wanted nothing more than to drop his surname, ending the lineage right with Theophilus when he died.

Earlier in the week, Pearl had shied away from Roy, just like everyone else. She had made a particular effort to avoid him, who, at over six feet tall and with a booming voice, frightened Pearl even more. When Constantine stepped outside, Pearl, still in her mother's arms, was so taken with the car, she reached and squirmed before whining, "Down." Constantine was so intrigued by this command that she had no choice but place the girl on the ground, wondering why all of a sudden she wanted to be independent.

Pearl, barely a foot tall, walked right up to her uncle and stood in front of him. Everyone watched in silent amazement at her sudden bravery. She looked up at Uncle Son, considering him a giant from her three-year-old vantage point, then raised both arms, fingers spread, and issued a request: "Up?"

Roy burst with laughter at his niece's sudden boldness. "Oh, now yuh wan come tuh me!" He chided.

Still, he bent down to lift her, so as not to disobey the three-year-old. As soon as she was in his arms, she craned her neck to see the red car and pointed to it, requesting to get in. Uncle Son went around to the driver seat and got in, letting her stand in his lap, pretending to turn the steering wheel. Through his laughter, he called back to his sister, "Connie, yuh bedda come now 'fore me and dis girlchild leave unu right 'ere on de porch."

***

A few months after she returned from Jamaica, Constantine jumped back into her normal routine. She had gotten back to cleaning her house, running after the kids, and tending to her husband. But she often recalled that most recent visit to Jamaica, holding the time she'd spent with her family close to her heart and the moment she'd had with Tawkins ever on her mind.

She thought about Tawkins's eyes and his touch on the days when Clifton or the children got on her nerves. The memories lifted her on many days until something so disturbing happened, that even her daydreaming wasn't enough to escape her predicament.

One morning, Constantine found herself up and alert before her usual hour. Instead of laying in bed and relishing the moment, she decided to take a shower and start cooking before the kids woke up. She stepped into the bathroom and undressed in front of the mirror, inspecting her body, as she frequently did. Her breasts sagged from having nursed five children; the skin on her stomach looked as if it had been clawed by the babies that had inhabited her body. And her belly hung slightly over her hips. Constantine slid her hands around her stomach lifting and rubbing it gently. She dropped it suddenly and then, sighing, turned the water on and stepped into the shower. She lathered up her washcloth and wiped down her arms, scrubbed her armpits. She moved to the nape of her neck, squeezing the rag to let soap run down her back. Then she turned around and let the water rinse the suds away. She washed her legs and then put some more soap on the cloth to clean her vagina.

Constantine had made a habit out of washing her vagina last because she wanted it to stay fresh the longest. She took her time with this part, first cleansing the hair that might carry any odor, then she spread her legs slightly so she could thoroughly cleanse the skin. Constantine was rubbing her washcloth across the inside of her lips when she suddenly felt a burning, stinging sensation. Instantly she knew that the skin had been punctured. She rested her washcloth on the faucet as she used her fingers to find the source of the problem. It wasn't long before her index finger dipped slightly into an inflamed and sensitive bit of skin that was raised and swollen in some parts and scooped out in the middle.

Normally, she would have dismissed this as an impurity bump, something she got during the time of her period. But a voice whispered, "Take this seriously. Go to the doctor."

Two days later, she arranged for Alton and Winston to stay home with the younger children for a couple of hours after they'd gotten home from school while she went to her gynecologist. She described the sore she'd found on her body. And in an attempt to calm her own fears, Constantine added quickly, "Is probably just an impurity bump i'n it? Meh jus wan get yuh opinion tuh be sure."

"Well, lay back, let me take a look."

Constantine abhorred this part of the visit. Lying back and having some man stick his face in between her legs made her severely uncomfortable and she counted the seconds until it was over. Constantine watched as his gloved hands swabbed around the raised area with a Q-Tip and then placed it in a plastic container. Once he was done, she snapped her legs closed and pulled the gown down past her knees, trying to pretend that

233

her doctor hadn't just, seconds before, been examining a strange bump in her vagina.

He looked puzzled, disturbed even, contemplating. Finally, remembering Constantine was in the room, he looked up. "Um, okay. I'm going to examine this sample quickly and see if there are any, um . . . distinguishing bacteria present. Unfortunately, the results won't be in until tomorrow. I'll set you up with an appointment for the same time as this one. Does this same time work?"

Constantine nodded.

Minutes later she watched the tail of the doctor's white coat whip out of the room. As he closed the door behind him, she knew something was wrong. The timbre in his voice had betrayed his efforts to hide his concerns.

The next day, she found herself in the same, thin gown, sitting on the same table, waiting for her doctor to return. After what seemed like no time at all, he came into the room, flashing her a quick and unconvincing smile. Constantine searched his face trying to guess the answer as he spoke, a little too slowly.

"Um, Mrs. Reid, based on the appearance of that rash, it seems you have syphilis."

She blinked.

Constantine had always heard stories about women, particularly British women, who fainted at the sound of bad news. She had always considered those stories preposterous until she found herself nearly experiencing the same thing. She was instantly lightheaded, the room started spinning, and the rest of the doctor's words faded to silence as she tried to maintain her composure. In the middle of her haze, she felt the doctor step toward her and place his hand firmly behind her shoulders.

That helped. With the weight of his hand on her back, Constantine recentered herself in that moment, in that room. She looked up to the doctor, her eyes pleading. "Meh goin' tuh die?" Constantine's voice cracked as she uttered the last word. She could feel the water collecting behind her eyes.

The doctor smiled reassuringly. "No, luckily you caught it very early. Syphilis can be treated and completely cured with antibiotics after just a couple of weeks. You're going to be fine."

His words finally broke her. Forgetting all sense of pride or propriety, Constantine leaned her head into the doctor's chest and sobbed. She cried for the life she thought she was going to lose, the children she would have to leave—some for the second time—and the life that had led her to this cold and sterile room. It took her a full five minutes to collect herself. While she cried, the doctor gently rubbed her back, assuring her that they'd get rid of the disease and she'd be fine.

As her final sobs faded away, the doctor stepped away from her, cautiously making sure she was ready to be left alone. He quickly took two steps across the small room to take a seat on the thickly cushioned swivel stool. He grabbed Constantine's chart and scanned it quickly before looking up at her again, sighing sympathetically. Behind the wire-rimmed glasses Constantine could see that he was contemplating his next words carefully.

"And um . . . unfortunately I'll have to ask you some, uh, pretty invasive questions. Please don't be offended or take any of these questions personally; we need to have this, uh, information so we can prevent this, as best as possible, from spreading to other people."

Constantine nodded.

"Mrs. Reid, can you tell me the names of your recent sexual partners?"

Constantine rolled her eyes. It was one thing to know that her husband had been unfaithful. It was an entirely different thing having to speak about that unfaithfulness with a stranger. In her day to day life she could pretend that Clifton was always working when he said he was. In many ways, she had come to accept it. But in this moment though, with this White man questioning her morality, her husband's indiscretions were too much to bear. Constantine fluctuated between fiery rage and sinking shame.

The doctor, sensing her tension, explained carefully. "Well, I, uh, ask because we're trying to figure out where you may have gotten this from."

Constantine scoffed. Shaking with rage, she said, "Doctuh, de only man meh sleep wid for de past fifteen 'ears has been mi 'usban'. Now, where 'im been and who 'im ah screw meh cyan tell yuh. Yuh'd haf to tek dat up wid 'im."

Blushing a little, the doctor said, "Uh, okay, well, it's very important, Mrs. Reid, that you go home and tell your husband about your test results. You'll need to tell him that he *must* come in and get tested so we can determine if he has the disease and give him the proper medicine to get rid of it."

Constantine kissed her teeth. For a moment she considered not saying anything to Clifton and letting him suffer in ignorance for his own scandalous ways.

The doctor must have read her mind. "Uh, Mrs. Reid, I cannot stress enough the importance of relaying this message to your husband. Like I told you, it's good that you noticed your symptoms early and you came in to get diagnosed. We shouldn't have any problems curing it. But you need to understand that if, for some reason, the illness goes untreated in, uh . . . in either one of you, it could lead to a host of other nasty symptoms, insanity, and eventually death. It's very important that you tell him."

The thought of Clifton going insane was enough to convince her that she did indeed need to tell him. Today, in his sane state, he was already too much to handle. Plus, it was likely that she wouldn't be able to keep him off her and he'd just reinfect her. She had to tell him.

"Yes, meh ah go tell 'im. 'e should be stoppin' in tuh see yuh widin de nex few days."

The doctor nodded his approval. "Great. I'm glad to hear that. Now, let me write you this prescription." And then he said it again for good measure: "Mrs. Reid, please don't assume that you and your husband can take the same antibiotics. We'll need him to come in, tell us about his, um, other sexual partners, and then we'll test him to see if the disease has advanced."

Clifton was back in town the very next day. Constantine waited until the kids had eaten, bathed, and gone to bed before she broached the subject of their shared STD. And as was his custom the night he came back into town, Clifton looked longingly at Constantine, expecting to be welcomed home.

Knowing that tonight he wouldn't have his way made the prospect of breaking the news to him that much easier. "Nah bodda look pon mi. Meh haf fi talk to yuh."

"Connie . . ." Clifton said charmingly, lightly stroking her shoulder. "It cyan wait til de morning nah?"

"Meh went tuh de doctor dis week. And 'im give meh some news. Him tell mi say mi haf syphilis."

Clifton froze. He'd heard about syphilis when he was in Florida the first time. Someone had warned him to stay away from the women who came by the farm because they all carried it.

With those stories in mind and feeling so uncomfortable being confronted with his own dirt, he wondered, momentarily, if Constantine had been stepping out, seeking revenge only to catch a venereal disease. He tried to hold off the inevitable moment where he would have to accept and acknowledge that it was he who'd brought a disease into the home he shared with his wife and children.

"Did de doctah tell yuh where yuh did get it from?"

At the suggestion that it could have been anyone but him, Constantine's outrage nearly boiled over; but instead of screaming, a dark, twisted laughter erupted from her mouth while her eyes remained locked on her husband.

"Yuh mus tek meh fuh dunce. Yuh tink meh nah know yuh love fi run round playin wid women all over de city? De women in de church dem is no bettah dan de whores dem on de street. I bet yuh any likkle bit of muney dat is one of dem give yuh dis. Den here yuh come and pass it on to me." Spitting her words, she continued, "Mi belly ah jump just tinking 'bout de filthy, frowsy puss women yuh ah play wid. Yuh tink meh nah know bout dem? Meh know. But mi would at least tink yuh would haf de good sense fi pick women who know how fi keep demselves clean. Nah, instead yuh come home, come bring mi syphilis."

Clifton sat there silent, his head hung in undeniable shame. Usually, the arguments between him and Constantine were an even exchange of insults, culminated by the occasional strike. If she ever hinted that he had stepped out or spent his money on some other woman, he vehemently denied it, calling her sanity into question or suggesting that being in the house all day had caused her mind to create stories where she was always the victim. But now, with proof of his infidelity brewing within both their bodies, there was no sense in attempting to lie or deny what he had done and would continue to do. The shame was too great. And as a Christian, Clifton believed he deserved this condemnation. So he sat silently and took his punishment.

Constantine paced the room, seething. "And yuh know what mek it worse? Yuh know meh haf tuh sit up inna de doctor's office while 'im ask *meh* bout de men I sleep wid. Him figga is meh who spread mi legs to every Tom, Dick, and Harry and catch dis ting. But meh haf fi tell 'im say is mi husband who run around sticking 'im ting in anythin dat haf a hole."

Constantine kissed her teeth, drawing out the sucking sound as long as she could.

Clifton focused his gaze on the floor, his face vacant.

"But yuh know yuh lucky, ya see? If meh naw come home and tell yuh dis, de doctor say yuh could get off yuh head and den die. Yuh come home and give me dis and meh *still* haf tuh come home, cook yuh dinner, lay in dis bed wid yuh, and give yuh de news to save ya life."

Clifton only rubbed the top of his head.

"Yuh tink God only look pon yuh on de Sabbath? Yuh tink Him nah see yuh de rest a de week? Cha!"

Clifton lifted his head and softly spoke for the first time since they'd gone into the bedroom, away from their children. "It mi fault, Connie." That was all he could offer her at the moment. He wanted to say that he was going to do better or be more careful and use a condom but it would have been yet another lie, an insult added to injury. Clifton knew he might calm down for a while but as many times as he'd vowed to do better and prayed to God for forgiveness, he knew in the front and back of his mind that once he was cured from this, he'd be right back to his old ways.

Constantine scoffed. Finding him despicable and pathetic, she walked out the room.

The next day, Clifton and Constantine went and visited the same doctor. He shared the results from Constantine's blood test, confirming that it was syphilis. He recommended that Clifton take the results immediately to his own doctor so he could be examined and treated.

Clifton's doctor confirmed that he had the disease and had most likely given it to his wife. Luckily, he was still in the early stages too and the both of them would be able to share the same prescription.

The syphilis slowed Clifton down a little bit. Years of listening to sermons and heeding the threats of his parents about fire and brimstone made him afraid of death. He terrified himself with thoughts of dying young and having to answer and atone for his many sins. Plus, his doctor told him that neither one of them was supposed to have sex until the sores had healed and they were able to come back for another blood test in a

239

couple of months. In the following weeks, Clifton had never been home so often. Constantine couldn't stand the sight of him around the house but she knew it was good that the children got to spend this extra time with their father. Despite their personal issues, she wanted her children to have respect for Clifton. She wanted them to know that he had indeed sacrificed for them and for that he should be honored. Someone should revere him because she surely didn't. And she was happy now to have a right to express her disgust without fear of reprimand or punishment. At night she could sleep soundly, knowing that he wouldn't dare ask her for as much as a Kleenex, let alone sex.

If the word "syphilis" didn't come with such the sting of shame, Constantine might have told someone the truth about her husband, the upstanding man. But even if she were able to reveal her misfortune, there would have been no one to listen. Constantine was, with the exception of a few neighbors and one or two women at church, alone. Most of the people she knew were Clifton's friends, people he'd known before she even came to the country. Their loyalties would always be to him. There was certainly no one she could trust with this information. If she told even one woman at church, she might as well put it in the church bulletin. She thought to write to her mother, but she felt a bit betrayed by her, remembering how she'd fought so hard for the two of them to marry. Constantine had to constantly remind herself that there was no way any of them could have predicted how diabolical Clifton would be as a husband. Plus, knowing all that her mother had been through with her father, she might have dismissed everything Constantine said, excusing Clifton's foulness with some adage like, "Das 'ow de men dem stay."

She decided to write Daphne. She'd had time to speak with her the last time she was in Jamaica. She was a "big 'oman" now, who'd had boyfriends of her own. Constantine didn't want to dissuade her from socializing with men but she did want to warn her what could happen with them, tell her how they could deceive and trap you with charm and children. It was important that she knew what lay out there, even though her youth and eagerness wouldn't allow her to comprehend until years later. But more than issuing a warning, Constantine wanted to be able to tell somebody what was going on with her. She had to get all of it out on paper because the thoughts of infidelity, their diseased bodies, and his volcanic temper were too much for her to carry alone. If she didn't tell someone—someone who was young enough not to accept this as status quo—those thoughts would rot her from the inside out.

She kept it light for the first couple of letters, telling Daphne about the subtle details of her life, informing her of the children, mentioning Clifton in passing, if at all. After Daphne proved to be a good, listening ear, Constantine told her about the syphilis as well as the shame of having to sit in church with women who knew her husband as only she should and having the doctor inquire about her sexual partners as if she was the irresponsible one. She warned her niece that whatever she was doing with her boyfriends in Jamaica, she should be sure not to get pregnant because then she'd be stuck.

Though Daphne was her outlet, still there were times when she'd burst before she had time to get to pen and paper. Constantine preached to her children about respecting their father but she didn't exactly model the behavior. There were several times when she went out of her way to speak ill of him, not really for the benefit of her children but because, despite her troublesome mouth, she still had so many unexpressed thoughts and feelings that made her bitter.

That bile got the best of her one day when Clifton received a picture of his brother and sister posed together in front of their house in Jamaica. He wanted to frame and hang it in the house somewhere but before he could do so, he left it lying out on their dining room table. The next day as Constantine was dusting, she stumbled across the image, in the way of her housework. She picked it up, studying it. And then kissing her teeth, she said out loud to no one in particular, "Dem ah favor monkey." She dashed the picture back down carelessly on the table.

It wasn't the first time she'd insulted Clifton or his family. She said the words flippantly, temporarily soothing her own pain with insults Clifton had never heard. They were spoken so quickly and out of such anger, she had often forgot that she'd uttered them at all.

Months later, Boysie was getting dressed to go to school and, looking him over, Constantine remarked, innocently, that he looked like his father's side of the family. It didn't occur to her that her son had been listening to her bash his father's side for years. And so he assumed she was doing the same to him. Her words left a lasting impact, reappearing as taunting whispers from the crevices of Boysie's mind for far too many years. Though Constantine reminded herself daily that she was staying with Clifton for the sake of her children, the pain she so carefully tried to store and conceal had the tendency, despite her best efforts, to seep out, slicing and stinging the very people she was trying to protect.

1962, Forty-two

After the syphilis scare, she was able to keep Clifton off her for almost a full year. He had been so ashamed and they both had been so frightened that it became easy to just leave one another alone. Since she wasn't sleeping with her husband, when Constantine had the IUD removed, she opted not to replace it with a new one. With five children at forty-two, she assumed her body had had enough by this time, and her baby days were over. In fact, with the recent stunt Alton was trying to pull, she was willing herself not to bear another child to stress her any further.

Just after Thanksgiving, a seventeen-year-old Alton had announced to the family that he was getting married and though everyone from his parents to his friends and even his younger brother Winston tried to dissuade him, it was something he decided he had to do.

After his father forbid it, making it legally impossible, he came to Constantine with his petition. "Mommy, I have to marry this girl."

Constantine saw him standing there, his eyes desperate and pleading, and all she could think about was the boy who'd stepped off the plane, trying to put up a strong front when he was so tragically sad. Those eyes had watched her, wide and wary, when she said good-bye to him in Jamaica. And even as an infant, those very same eyes looked up at her desperate, struggling and pleading with her to help him live. Now, that same child stood up in front of her, convinced of his manhood, ready to marry a girl and start a family of his own.

She sighed before answering him.

"Alton, 'ow many times yuh fadda haf fi tell yuh, yuh too young fi marry. Yuh fresh out a high school and now yuh wan rush fi start a family? Why? Yuh see meh and yuh fadda? Yuh wan dis so soon? Why won' yuh tek yuh time and enjoy yuhself nah? Why yuh mus stress me?"

Alton narrowly missed rolling his eyes at his mother as he thought about her ignorance. What he and Katrina had was nothing like she and his father. "Mommy, I love her! Our marriage won' be like you and Daddy's. But I need your permission to do it. You have to help me."

"Wha mek yuh tink meh ah go sign a paper fi watch meh son t'row 'im life away. Meh nah dew it!"

Alton paused for a while, hoping the conversation wouldn't have to come to this. "Mom, if I cyan marry Katrina, meh kill myself." The emotion in Alton's plea caused him to slip, momentarily, back into his patois.

Constantine gasped, clutching her chest. "Whachu did say?" she asked, narrowing her eyes into small slits.

"If I cyan marry Katrina, meh kill mehself."

Nothing could have compared to the shame that would have been brought upon the family if Alton had taken his own life. A decision like that would have consequences in this life and the next. "Alton! Yuh mussn't say dat!"

"I mean it."

Constantine looked at her eldest's face, attempting to gauge the seriousness behind his declaration. Never in her wildest dreams had she even considered suicide as a threat for any of her children. In reality, it wasn't even an option for Alton. Still his words were delivered so powerfully, Constantine couldn't be sure. And in the off chance he was serious, she didn't want his blood on her hands.

243

"Bring de papah come."

Alton leapt to his mother, enveloping her in the most heartfelt embrace he'd given her since they were living in Jamaica. And though Constantine knew she was helping him spoil his young life with this silly girl, she relished the joy of being able to make her firstborn happy.

The two teenagers married in the courthouse and Alton moved out of his parents's house. Dealing with her son's marriage in addition to having to go back to work, Constantine couldn't find the time or the energy to take a trip to Jamaica that year as she had originally intended. This holiday season would be different with Alton out of the house. And her heart broke because of it. The time she had with her son had been shortened once again, this time by his own doing.

The thought of his falling into the same trap she and Clifton had plagued her. Though she and her husband had never pretended to be in love with one another, the possibility that Alton might wake up one day and resent his wife for the decision they'd made as children festered in her mind. Still, she couldn't allow it to distract her from all that needed to be done in her home with the other four.

***

The holidays were always a good time in the Reid household. The spirit of the season was strong enough to infiltrate the home and the children found that their parents were civil, even jovial to one another. With three boys and a husband, Constantine cooked plenty of food every day; but for Thanksgiving, she spent days shopping, chopping, and prepping. Clifton would flit around the kitchen, bantering and pretending to help her prepare the meal. A month later, at Christmas they were even more festive. Constantine decorated the house in poinsettias and ribbons. Clifton took the children to see Santa Claus at the mall. And once they returned home he'd have them write lists detailing what they wanted. He instructed them to set milk and cookies out for the fat, White man who would slide down their nonexistent chimney and leave them presents. Clifton got a kick out of telling them these stories. And for the most part the kids liked playing along too.

Except for Noel. Something about the idea of Santa Claus terrified her and she'd spend Christmas Eve in her bed, with the covers pulled over her head, sweating and panting as she listened out for the stranger who would stomp across her roof and then enter her living room.

For New Year's Eve, Constantine adopted the Black American tradition of eating black-eyed peas on the day for good luck for the rest of the year. New Year's Day was Clifton's birthday and he was big on celebrating it. So she would try to be sweet, letting him have at least a day without dramatics. The night before, they'd allow the kids to stay up and count down to midnight, watching the ball drop on the television and drinking sparkling grape juice. The next day, the kids would make him some type of card or present to give him, Constantine would cook his favorite meal, and the day would be peaceful.

This year, riding on the high from all of the holiday celebrations, Clifton and Constantine were acting as husband and wife again. It started on his birthday, with Constantine graciously obliging his requests and the late-night meetings continued.

By March, Constantine noticed that she had missed her period again. This was the seventh time this had happened. But still she didn't assume it was another pregnancy. Instead, she thought this was one of the first signs of menopause and she went about her business. It wasn't until she started throwing up everything she ate that she knew the truth. She made a doctor's appointment. She went in hoping the doctor would tell her she had some type of stomach virus. But he didn't.

"Congratulations, Mrs. Reid! You're about six weeks pregnant."

Before she felt anything else there was shock. She was too old for this! Then there was frustration. Pearl had just turned four and though she still clung to her, she was increasingly independent and self-sufficient. Now, she'd have to start all over again with a child who would need her undivided attention. And more than the weight of having to raise another baby, Constantine thought about what this would mean for her married life. After the syphilis incident, she started fantasizing about possibly leaving Clifton after Pearl got a little older. Now that she was having another, that day was looking like it would never come.

She went home and thought about how she was going to tell Clifton that they were having another child. With his trucking business thriving in the way that it was, they could afford to raise another child, but she didn't know if he was going to feel as she did. They were creating yet another tie that bound them together when it was so clear that they needed to find a way to part.

She walked into the house, preoccupied with the news she needed to deliver. It was dinner time but Constantine didn't want to be in the kitchen all day, so she prepared a simple American dish, beans and wieners over rice. She cooked some corn to go along with it, taking care that her children were eating some kind of vegetable.

By the time her husband got home at eight o'clock, she had been out of the kitchen for nearly three hours. He came in and threw himself down at the table, exhausted from driving his truck all over the state. Looking at him, beat and worn down, Constantine took no pleasure in adding this to his plate. She figured maybe she should wait until after he was finished eating, just in case he started choking on his food.

Afterward, in the living room, the two sat across from one another, both wondering why the other was there. Usually after dinner, Constantine went to take care of the kids and then busy herself in their bedroom, anything to minimize their time together. For some reason, today, she'd deviated from the script and he noticed. Before his wife opened her mouth to say anything, he braced himself for the blow.

"Clifton, meh haf fi tell yuh somethin."

Thinking about the last time she'd uttered similar words, Clifton sighed, not ready for any more shameful announcements.

Sensing his tension, Constantine couldn't help but scare him a little bit, just for a second. "Meh went bak tuh de doctor today . . ." She watched as his body tensed then continued, "Yuh know de same one who tell me, meh haf syphilis?"

Clifton nodded begrudgingly, frustrated and embarrassed at the mention of this particular doctor. He'd never forgotten the day he learned he was sick. In addition to the own shame he felt, the doctor questioning him outright about his behavior as if he were a child, felt like Judgment Day come early.

"Well, him tell me dat meh pregnant again."

Constantine blurted the words so she could take in Clifton's reaction. She watched as his pained face relaxed in relief. She had mentioned the syphilis solely to scare him. But her attempt at teasing helped to open him to the pleasant possibilities of having another child. Clifton knew that it would mean less money in his pockets, but another child, for all their troubles, brought him joy.

Nodding and smiling slightly, he said, "Well, muney ah be a likkle tight wid a nex baby comin but we ah go mek it work."

They did make it work. As with all of her children, Constantine stopped taking the little side jobs she had become accustomed to to supplement their income. She stayed home during the day teaching Pearl, whom she had decided to homeschool for the first two years of elementary school. She had heard and seen with Alton and Winston what the school system could do to children who were different in any way. And being that Pearl was so attached to her, she wanted to shield her from that cruelty for as long as she could.

As Pearl got older, she followed her mother around less and less and instead did more investigating, trying to determine who she was. Any time she wasn't right up under her, Constantine would walk into her room to find the girl standing in her closet, her face buried in her hanging dresses. When Constantine asked Pearl what she was doing, she responded matter-of-factly, "Smelling you."

As she got older and taller, Pearl decided to take some of those clothes off the hanger. One day, Constantine looked up from the light housework she'd been doing, noticing that Pearl wasn't anywhere to be found. At six months pregnant, she waddled to the stairs in search of her. Before she could make it up to the top, she saw her second daughter, her head swimming in the excess fabric of one of her dresses.

Constantine's growing belly shook with laughter and she reached down to still it, wondering what this next child would do to tickle her.

***

As she progressed in her pregnancy, Pearl became more and more concerned for her mother's health and safety. She could tell something was happening.

Not understanding what was going on with her mother's body, she assumed that Constantine was carrying a balloon. She had experience with balloons and it almost never ended well. They either popped or flew away. And she didn't want either of those things to happen to her mother. So she continued following her. But these days it was more out of fear and protection rather than the intrigue that had once motivated her.

Watching her mother grunt and struggle to perform the tasks she had been doing for as long as she'd known her, Pearl insisted on helping Constantine around the house. She was there to greet her at the side of her bed every morning. Constantine almost tripped over her in the kitchen and Pearl ran behind her as she straightened up the already neat house every day.

As Constantine was preparing to vacuum one day, she bent down to plug the cord in the socket and felt a strain in her back. She grabbed it immediately, groaning slightly. Pearl, seeing her mother in pain, burst into tears. Constantine, who still hadn't managed to plug the cord in, was distracted by her daughter's distress and rushed over to her as fast as her changing body would carry her.

"Pearl, wha trubble yuh? Why yuh cry?"

Through tears and sniffles, Pearl told her what had been bothering her for months now. "You're getting so big, like a balloon. I'm afraid you're going to burst."

If Pearl hadn't been so genuinely worried Constantine would have laughed. The notion was so preposterous yet logical that it could have only come from a five-year-old. Constantine pulled Pearl in close to her. "Nothing nah happen to Mummy. Meh nah carry a balloon that burst. Memba how meh tell yuh, yuh soo haf a new brudda or sister? Is de baby growing inside of me das meking meh swell up so."

Pearl had been listening to her talk about a baby for months now; and while she trusted her mother, she doubted this story. Her balloon theory sounded much more plausible. "So, you won't blow away?"

A couple of weeks later, Pearl woke up to the sound of her parents shuffling around the house in the middle of the night. Her father was moving quickly, collecting a bag and buzzing around Constantine, who wore a strained grimace. Pearl ran out of her room to follow them.

"Go back tuh bed," Clifton told her. He spoke more sternly than necessary. Even after five children with this woman, his anxiety about birth never went away.

Clifton quickly told Alton and Winston to watch after their siblings until he returned. And Pearl went back to her room and cried herself to sleep, certain that her mother wasn't returning.

The next day her fears were realized: a slow-moving Clifton entered the house without Constantine. Although the rest of the children seemed unfazed, tears met at the corners of her eyes as she spoke her next words, "Daddy, where is Mommy? Did she burst?"

"No, she nah burst. She 'ad a baby. Unu have a new sister. We name 'ar Lavinia Maxine Reid."

Pearl heard him. But until she saw her mother, she wouldn't feel comfortable.

Four days later, she would get all the confirmation she needed. Clifton left the older boys in charge while he went to go pick up Constantine from the hospital. Before he left, he told Pearl that he was bringing her mother back to her so she could see for herself that she was alive and well. Pearl, perching in front of the living room window, waited anxiously as the couple of hours he was away seemed to stretch on for weeks. She watched each car drive by, wondering if her father was telling her the truth. After almost three hours, Pearl, who hadn't been sleeping well for the past week, fell asleep on the couch in front of the window.

But it was a light sleep. The tumble of the lock woke her and she darted up to see if her father had brought her mother back as he promised her. When she glimpsed Constantine's face coming through the threshold, she looked at her mother's stomach to see what had happened to the balloon. It had deflated.

Then, looking at her mother's arms, Pearl noticed that she was holding a bundle of blankets. She and her siblings followed behind as Clifton led her up the stairs and into their bedroom.

When she reached her parents's bedroom, Pearl and her older siblings crowded around their mother, peering down into the blankets. Pearl pushed her way between Noel's and Boysie's legs, straining to see.

Seeing Pearl for the first time since she'd given birth, Constantine smiled, remembering how her daughter had been so worried about her weight gain and her limited mobility. "See, Pearl. This is who meh was carrying." Constantine lowered her arms to reveal the little girl. "This is yuh sister, Lavinia. Isn't she cute?"

Pearl nodded, falling in love with the little girl that instant.

1966, Forty-six

The passing of Maxine's fourth birthday, in December, reminded Constantine that she needed to take her youngest daughter to see her grandmother in Jamaica. But with the birth of Alton's first child and the end of his brief marriage, she had been particularly preoccupied this year.

Later that month, less than three weeks before Christmas, Constantine was decorating the tree when the phone rang. She hung the last golden ornament on the limb of the plastic evergreen before she turned to answer it. By the time she heard the first syllable out of Olga's mouth, she knew something was wrong. She sounded burdened. Grace Ann, in her early eighties, had been living with Olga and her husband once she proved she could no longer take care of herself. Hearing her sister's voice, Constantine knew that it was their mother she was calling about. Constantine waited with raging anxiety as Olga tried to speak through sobs.

"Connie. Mumah . . . she's . . . she's gone."

Constantine dropped the phone.

She heard the clang of the receiver as it hit the table. Her eyes scanned the room around her. She looked at the half-decorated tree, at Boysie, Noel, and Pearl sitting in front of the television, not having heard a thing. And then she spotted her husband. He was sitting at the dining room table, holding Maxine in his lap and chatting with her about her four-year-old life as the two of them shared a snack. He must have sensed her staring at him because he looked up to meet her eyes.

He saw the overcast look on her face, the slack of her lips, the unspeakable pain in her eyes, and he gently placed Maxine on the floor and tossed the cookie he was eating on the table before he went to her. Once he'd crossed the room, Constantine didn't even speak. She just fell into his arms, nearly collapsing to the floor as she sobbed.

Boysie, Noel, and Pearl had only met their grandmother once. And now

Maxine would never get a chance to. For most of her children, Grace Ann was the sweet and soft-spoken woman they'd heard about often. But for Alton and Winston, she was their mother. And Constantine knew the news of her passing would be especially painful for them.

The two brothers came home that evening to an unusual scene. Constantine was sobbing into Clifton's chest as he stroked her back, saying nothing.

They stood there silently, waiting for someone to explain.
Ever since he'd broken the habit himself, the sight of people crying deeply troubled Winston. Having never seen his mother like this, he took a step away from his parents, frowning, feeling as powerless as he had been as a child.

Alton was the first to speak. "What happened?"

Clifton looked up at the two, remembering his false promise, and his heart broke for them. Fighting back tears of his own, his voice cracked as he spoke.

"Mudda Johnson . . . Yuh grandmutha passed last night."

Alton's hand flew to the top of his head and he grabbed a clump of his hair. When he was able to speak, he managed to moan a pained, "What?"

Winston stood next to him, statue still. His tears flowing freely.

Constantine lifted her head from Clifton's chest to see her sons. No one could empathize with her pain like they could. They'd all lost their mother today.

Constantine spent exactly one day in bed, mourning. She cursed herself for having postponed her trip that year. The guilt in combination with the loss felt like someone had placed a weight on her chest, she was too weak to remove. But after that one day, Constantine could no longer afford to wallow at home. There were arrangements to be made, tickets to be purchased, and so much more. That year the Christmas tree remained only partially decorated as she made plans to return to Jamaica to bury her mother.

Constantine and her sisters decided that all the women in the family were going to wear matching hats and gloves to the service and since she was the best seamstress out of the three, she volunteered to make them. She didn't want her mother's body to be above ground longer than it had to, so she rushed to complete the items. She and Clifton couldn't afford to take all of the children to Jamaica with her. But out of respect to their relationship with Grace Ann, Constantine asked Alton and Winston if they wanted to fly back with her. Winston, her most sensitive child, despite his exterior, said he'd rather not attend.

"I just want to remember her the way she was." He spoke softly, tears threatening to cloud his voice at the mere thought of seeing his grandmother being lowered into the ground.

Alton, who had his child and divorce proceedings to comfort and distract him, said that he too would stay behind. It was Noel, sensing that her mother might need support on this trip, who volunteered to go with her.

Shortly, after they arrived in Kingston, her brother-in-law Ellis took her to the funeral home where Grace Ann's body had been embalmed and was waiting to be dressed for the ceremony the next day. Constantine wanted to make sure that her mother looked perfect, so she went to see her, to make sure her hair and outfit were up to par. The funeral director asked if she'd like someone to stay in there with her. She told them no, not knowing quite how she was going to react. She reasoned that should she have a breakdown, she didn't want anyone to witness it.

Looking at her mother on the table, Constantine had the feeling that she'd wake up any minute, surprised and excited to see that she'd returned home, at least temporarily. As she stepped closer, still not ready to touch her, Constantine could see how the formaldehyde had already transformed her mother's looks. The skin had been stretched, making her face look freakishly younger than she actually was. She could see that they hadn't used any makeup yet and that she would have to restyle her mother's hair.

Finally, unable to waste any more time just looking, she reached out, placing her fingers on her mother's hand. Feeling how hard and dry her body had now become, Constantine snatched her hand back immediately, covered her mouth, and started sobbing. This wasn't her mother. And if this wasn't her mother, where was she? Just then, she heard a voice say, as clear as if the person were standing in the room with her, "To be absent from the body is to be present with the Lord." She recalled the day she'd heard that line for the first time. Sitting next to Clifton, in the church pew, the dress she'd worn that day had been soaked through with both her sweat and that of the sleeping child she rocked in her arms. Whether it was the distraction of the heat, the movement of the baby, or lack of experience, the words had meant nothing to her. But today, they were comforting and rang true. Constantine imagined her mother in good hands and moved to the top of her head to begin working on her hair.

She reached for the tools she had in the bag she'd brought with her on the plane and started combing through what was left of Grace Ann's cottony soft, almost white tresses. She brushed the sides so the edges laid down smooth and gathered the ends at the top of her head, pinning the strands to make an elegant design at the crown. Grace Ann never wore much makeup, and so Constantine used a pencil to shape her eyebrows, put a tiny bit of mascara on the lashes that managed to hang on in her old age. She used Vaseline to add some sheen to her lips. Hilda and Olga had already left the outfit she was to wear at the funeral home. Constantine thought to dress her mother too but that would require lifting and bending. The thought of fighting against her mother's now rigid bones made her stomach turn. Instead, knowing this was the last time she'd see her before the funeral, Constantine stood back and admired her work. She'd accepted that while Grace Ann didn't look entirely like herself, it would do. And her mother would be pleased that someone had taken the time to care for her so lovingly during her final appearance.

The next day came quickly. Constantine awoke cloaked in grief. Underneath that, though was a modicum of comfort, knowing she'd be able to say good-bye today. Meditating on those thoughts, she was calm, which surprised her. After she'd done her hair and made up her face, she slipped on the gloves and hat she had made for the occasion. Shortly after all of the sisters and grandchildren were dressed and ready to go, Constantine looked Noel over one more time to make sure everything was sitting and laying right.

The car ride to the service was silent. Usually, when Grace Ann's children and grandchildren got together there was loud, animated talking accompanied by shoulder-shaking laughter. But today their faces hung. Their eyes wore the film of a week's worth of tears with the promise of more to come. All of them avoided eye contact—looking into each other's faces, they might see hints of Grace Ann. When they so yearned for her, these traces would only produce disappointment and more grief. So they looked out the windows, trying not to upset the temporary silence.

When the women got to the church where the service was to be held, they all filed in, taking time to graciously greet the people who had showed up to honor their mother and grandmother. There were friends whom Constantine remembered stopping by the house to chat when she was a girl growing up. The faces she didn't recognize she assumed were members from the church her mother attended. Constantine continued searching the room and saw Mattie, who had saved Alton all those years ago. Sitting a bit away from everyone else, dressed in long, dark, flowing robes, Mattie's eyes held the telltale signs that she'd been crying. For the first time since she'd met Mattie, Constantine wondered how well her mother and this peculiar woman had known each other and what they'd meant to one another. Constantine was suddenly struck by the fact that she wouldn't be able to ask her mother anymore. She wondered how many stories and how many pieces of wisdom had died with her.

As they took their seats and the service began, Constantine felt waves of numbness. In her more alert moments, she felt like she was watching the service take place removed from her own body but still keenly aware of the weight continuing to press down on her heart, making it almost impossible to breathe. She watched people she'd never seen in her life, people from her mother's church, take the podium and speak more for the glorification of themselves than her mother. Then there were those who had truly loved Grace Ann. When they stood to sing deep, slow and mournful songs, she sat twitching in her seat, making sure she was still breathing. The sounds of her sisters and nieces wailing caused a stream of seemingly never-ending tears to fall from her eyes. Unlike them, she tried her best to keep the carnal sounds inside of herself.

She was the picture of poise. The lady her mother had admonished her to be all her life. After the service was over, Constantine stood and followed the rest of the family outside to bury the body.

As everyone stood around the coffin in a semicircle, looking distractedly down into the pit that had been dug to house Grace Ann's shell, Constantine felt her heart swelling. She felt her face melting, her eyes slowly squinting, her lips turning in uncontrollable angles and then she heard it. It was a sound so wracked with pain, so desperate and infantile that a part of her mind wondered where it came from. She tried to stifle the noise, her chest heaving as she tried to contain it. But all to no avail. She felt her face break and heard the sound come forth again. This time, she yielded to it.

Noel, who had been standing beside Constantine, froze, frightened by the display. All of the very trying and heartbreaking experiences she had been enduring at home paled in comparison to this moment. Having only met her grandmother when she was very young, Noel could only relate by proxy. Though she heard her mother talk about Grace Ann all the time, she didn't know her kindness and nurturing firsthand. She was only able to empathize as she imagined losing her own mother. Still, Noel didn't know quite how to respond. She reached out, rubbing her mother's back gently, hoping the gesture would soothe her.

The feel of her daughter's hand on her back only reminded Constantine that she'd never be able to touch her mother again. Constantine heaved. Death is never easy for those left behind and it was even worse for Constantine because she hadn't said everything she needed to Grace Ann. She wasn't in the habit of saying the words "I love you" to her mother, or even her children. It was just something that was supposed to be understood. Constantine knew her mother loved her and she thought Grace Ann knew she loved her too. But the fact that the words hadn't been exchanged and there would never be another opportunity to do so made the weight on her chest feel even heavier.

Standing in front of her mother's grave site, Constantine realized that they were burying the one person who thought the highest of her. Grace Ann hadn't had to tell Constantine that she was her favorite; it was something she felt. She knew beyond a shadow of a doubt not only that her mother liked her more but that there was something she possessed that Grace Ann admired. Grace Ann had expected her to become something. And standing at the grave wearing the hat and gloves she had so expertly sewn, Constantine didn't know if she had done that. It seemed that all she had done was have children. Constantine loved her children more than anything; they were the reason she was able to endure what she had. But she always wondered if she had used them as an excuse to become complacent and stagnant. Standing there above the hole designated for her mother, she was struck with the feeling that she'd squandered her talents.

At the thought, her knees buckled. Just as they were lowering the casket into the ground, Constantine wobbled away from her daughter's unsure hands and walked, shakily swaying, toward the hole.

Noel looked around at her family members and the people assembled there, waiting for someone to grab her mother and carry her back to her seat and away from that depth. No one moved. Instead they watched silently, unmoving, seeming to accept this as a necessary part of the service.

At the edge of the pit, Constantine, dressed in her finest clothes, fell down next to it.

Noel instinctively ran toward her mother, kneeling to speak to her. As Constantine's body writhed with each sob, Noel attempted to get her back on her feet.

The hat Constantine was wearing slid and rested, cockeyed, on the side of her head. The gloves became sullied by the dirt. As her daughter struggled with her, Constantine spoke audibly for the first time that day. "Mi wan go wid 'ar! Mi cyan live widout mi mudda!"

Noel frowned, personally insulted by the statement. She understood that her mother was suffering a great loss but she had too many people, too many children, counting on her. Noel didn't know if her mother was being dramatic or she really felt like she wanted to die. But either way, she knew she had gone too far.

"Mom!" She hollered to break through the force of grief that had overtaken her.

Constantine hadn't felt like a mother at any point during this day. She was a child with no parents. But hearing the name being yelled in her direction, she turned, remembering that Noel was with her.

"Get up!"

Noel had never spoken to her mother this way before. Under normal circumstances this tone would have warranted at least a slap in the face; but this day, at this moment, the power had shifted. Constantine was the one who needed mothering. And it was only fitting that she lean on her eldest daughter. Constantine obeyed her and stood up slowly, still sobbing quietly.

Once she'd returned to her seat, the men continued lowering the casket. Noel held her mother, rocking her back and forth as they both watched Grace Ann's body being lowered into the ground. When Constantine's sobs got louder, Noel tightened her grip. Once Grace Ann was in the ground and the harnesses had been removed, the family members walked up to the open grave to throw flowers on top of the casket. Constantine looked at her daughter for permission to join them. Before she let her go, Noel grabbed her mother by the shoulders and looked her dead in the eyes.

"You have got to get yourself together. I didn't know my grandmother well but if she was all that you say that she was, she would not want you acting like this. She's gone but she wouldn't want you to go with her. You have children at home and too much to live for. She would want you to live your life."

Constantine nodded, marveling at this thirteen-year-old's wisdom. She was right. It was agony saying good-bye to her mother but throwing herself into the ground with her wasn't going to bring her back. She'd just be inflicting that same sorrow onto her own children, and having to experience this grief wasn't something she wanted for any of them right now

Wanting something living to take back with her, Constantine grabbed a small piece of the plant that was displayed so beautifully during the service. She wrapped the plant in a wet paper towel at the roots and placed it in her brassiere. The whole plane ride, she could feel the tension from the stalk pressing against her breasts. As Noel slept in the seat next to her, Constantine thought about what she'd said to her at the grave site and the maturity in that statement. It was so wise and so well-timed that it was almost as if it had come from someone else. She chuckled, remembering that Noel carried her mother's name. She took it as a sign and knew that her mother, wherever she was, was still looking out for her, even in death. And since her mother was so clearly instructing her to live, Constantine reflected on the concept, asking herself what it would mean to truly do that. She didn't know exactly when or how but she knew that a part of that change would be leaving her husband.

1967, Forty-seven

When Constantine took the Christmas tree down at the beginning of the next year, noticing the areas where it remained undecorated, she knew that the holidays would never be the same for her again. It took her longer to remember that Grace Ann wouldn't be in Jamaica for her to visit, wouldn't answer her long distance phone calls, and wouldn't be sending any more letters through her niece. And while the loss was too great to speak, too much to comprehend, Constantine had heard her mother's message and knew now that it was her responsibility to be for her children what her mother had been to her.

Feeling like it was time for Pearl to become a little more independent, she enrolled her in a nearby elementary school. And it wasn't long before she came home pulling a flyer excitedly out of an oversized but mostly empty schoolbag. The school was hosting a Valentine's Day dance for the parents. Constantine immediately wanted to go. The idea sounded romantic and was probably far more than what she could expect Clifton to do for her. He hadn't always been so nonchalant. While he hadn't taken her dancing since that date at the Silver Slipper, it was his sweet, thoughtful, and unexpected gestures that influenced her to give him a chance. Now, between six children and their constant arguing, those moments were few and far between. Constantine imagined if she and Clifton had married under difference circumstances, perhaps out of desire instead of duty, he might have remained that way. But that wasn't the life they led; even still, it would be fun to pretend for a night. It would be an opportunity for her dress up, do her hair, and dance, even if just a little bit. After Grace Ann's passing, Constantine longed for an opportunity to feel anything other than grief and emptiness. What Clifton might think of the event was an afterthought. The man could be so unpredictable; it really just depended on his mood. She at least had to give it a try when he came home that evening.

After the family had finished eating and the children were in their rooms, the couple sat in the living room, watching the local news before they went to bed for the evening. Clifton seemed relaxed and content, so Constantine decided it was a good time to broach the subject.

"Did yuh haf plans for us on Valentine's Day?"

Clifton, who had been slouched on the couch, sat up abruptly, wondering if he'd heard his wife correctly. They'd never made a big deal of celebrating Valentine's Day. It didn't make much sense to pretend and he wondered why she suddenly felt plans were appropriate. He thought maybe this was her way of testing him. So he lied.

"Nothin' majah . . . mi did haf some plans, yes. Why yuh ask?"

Constantine ignored the white lie. At least he was trying. She put a bit more lilt in her voice to show that she was trying too.

"Pearl come bring dis flyer from school 'bout a dance dem ah host for de parents. Mi tink it would be a good way to meet her teachers dem. Yuh wan go?

Clifton chuckled loudly. Constantine tensed assuming he was going to reject her and the offer.

"Yuh know mi nevah learn fi dance. But mi ah go tek you so yuh can get out de house come Valentine's Day."

Constantine should have known he would say yes to any opportunity to peacock in front of Pearl's teachers and the other parents. If nothing else, Constantine and Clifton were never more in sync than when they stepped out of the house together, cleanly dressed. It was an opportunity to project a different picture about their lives. In the right clothes, Clifton knew that people assumed things about him and his family that he would likely never refute. And whether they twirled or stumbled across the dance floor on Valentine's Day, he was eager to keep them talking and wondering.

Usually, Constantine would have made her own dress; but she was pressed for time and wanted to go and buy something nice for herself and just step right into it. Though it was Valentine's Day, she regarded red as a color a woman of her complexion should never wear. So she bought a long-sleeved, pale pink, satin pencil dress.

She spent almost the entire day of the dance preparing and pampering herself. In between cooking dinner for the kids, who were just starting to trickle back into the house after school, she set her hair in rollers, put a coat of clear polish on her nails, arched her eyebrows, plucked the annoying hairs that had started sprouting from her chin, and soaked in a long bath. By the time Clifton got home, the two of them had an hour to get ready.

Seeing Constantine in her slip, Clifton couldn't help but admire his wife and the great effort she took in putting herself together. Even with the extra pounds, occasionally, he'd glimpse the glamour and allure of the girl he'd met in Kingston. It was moments like these that Clifton knew Constantine deserved better, that he just could never be the man to give it to her. Tonight though, he would try. So he showered quickly after work and dressed in his nicest suit and tie.

As the two of them were looking themselves over one final time before they stepped out, the children, from Winston to Maxine, all stopped and marveled at their parents, each for a different reason. The girls noticed how stunning and timeless their mother looked in that dress, with her hair perfectly coiffed. The boys, who had seen their father's suit several times when he wore it to church, took note of how he was doting on their mother this evening. They noticed the difference in the way he looked at her and the particular care he took in guiding her around, making sure she didn't stumble in the heels she wore. And all of them were shocked and surprised to see them going out together. Pearl, who took full credit for orchestrating the outing, was beaming.

Later, when they stepped into the school's gymnasium, Constantine felt all eyes on her. Some admired her hair and outfit. Others stared at her in curiosity. Pearl, who had been homeschooled during the beginning of her academic career, was different from the rest of the children. She spoke with her mother's accent; and like her brothers before her, it presented a problem. Like Winston, Pearl spent time practicing all the words she had been mocked for mispronouncing. But when the children still made fun of her speech, she just stopped speaking in class all together. She faded into the background. And while it was easier for her peers and her teacher to overlook her, her parents would not to be ignored.

Parents of fellow students came up to Clifton and Constantine all night, introducing themselves so they could find out who they were in return. And as they spoke, exchanging pleasantries, the mothers and fathers whose children made fun of Pearl were the same ones who found Clifton and Constantine's accent exotic and delightful.

During all the chatter, Constantine failed to notice the school's assistant principal eyeing her from across the room. He had been watching and waiting for her husband to step away so he could swoop in. The moment came toward the middle of the dance when Clifton found himself engrossed in conversation with one of the other parents. He'd left Constantine standing alone sipping punch. And seizing this opportunity, the principal pounced.

"Hello, I'm Joseph Roberts, the assistant principal here at Crispus

Attucks." The man, who was tall but with a stomach that was beginning to peek over his waistband, held out his fleshy hand for Constantine to shake. She did so reluctantly, getting an odd energy from him immediately.

"I'm Constantine Reid."

"Very nice to meet you, Miss Reid." Roberts flashed her a smile. Constantine sensed the slithery flirtation to come, and was put off.

"It's Mrs. Reid, actually." For once, she was happy to throw that title around. She looked around the room for her husband, "That's mi 'usban', Clifton, over dere speakin to dat gentleman."

Mr. Roberts feigned embarrassment. "Oh, forgive me, Mrs. Reid. I just assumed that no husband would leave a wife as beautiful as you by herself for even a single second."

Constantine's stomach dropped. So as not to cause a scene at Pearl's school, she stepped closer to him so he could hear every syllable in her lowered voice

"Mr. Roberts, I am a grown woman. Mi husband know meh can tek care of miself," Constantine said sharply. In mixed company, at what was a bit of a formal affair, Constantine had attempted to curb her accent and speak like the Americans. But in her irritation, the patois crept in.

Sensing that he was losing the favor of his audience, Mr. Roberts tried a different approach. "So you have a student who attends Attucks?"

Happy to be shifting gears, Constantine nodded solemnly and stepped back again. With the remnants of disdain fading from her face, she said, "Yes, Pearl Reid."

Like most principals, Mr. Roberts was only familiar with the students who were sent to his office frequently. And Pearl, in her quest to be accepted, was not one of them. He didn't know her.

"Oh, yes! Little Pearl. Bright, sweet girl. Her teacher never has any problems with her."

Constantine knew he wouldn't know Pearl if she came and stepped on his shoe. Still smiling faintly, she said, "Well, that's good to hear."
Then Mr. Roberts, continuing to misread the situation, tried one more time.
"I know you're married, Mrs. Reid. But I would just never be able to forgive myself if I went home tonight without asking you to dance."

Constantine having run out of all patience and pleasantries, sneered slightly. Luckily, before she had to embarrass him, Clifton slid up next to her, resting his hand lightly in the crease of her back.

"Mr. Roberts. I see yuh met my wife." He smiled briefly before pursing his lips and raising his eyebrows, his eyes stern. He had been watching the exchange from across the room, wondering how it would play out. He only decided to step in after seeing the look of disgust on Constantine's face, knowing that there was a good chance she'd make a scene.

"Oh, um, yes, I have." Mr. Roberts smiled nervously.

"Well, if you don't mind I'm going to steal her away for a moment and have this dance." As Constantine had done seconds earlier, Clifton was speaking in his best English.

"Yes, of course. Enjoy the rest of your evening." Mr. Roberts nodded, stepping back and finally acknowledging his defeat.

As Clifton walked her out onto the dance floor, Constantine looked over her shoulder at the creepy assistant principal, smiling smugly as she grasped her husband's arm.

It wasn't until they made it to the dance floor that they both remembered that Clifton couldn't dance. But tonight, it didn't matter. In one of his former chivalrous gestures he'd saved her. And she was appreciative.

"De man 'im facety, yuh see? Mi husband just a few feet away and 'im up in mi face like we born and bred in de same place." Constantine punctuated her statement by kissing her teeth.

As he stepped awkwardly around the dance floor, Clifton leaned back just slightly so he could get a good look at Constantine's face. He was amused by this reaction. She hadn't said the words "thank you" and she never would but Clifton could sense her gratitude.
"Meh saw 'im from 'cross de room. The man mus be dunce, 'im nevah notice yuh face tun up like yuh smell someting dead." Clifton laughed heartily, replaying the scene in his head. And then suddenly he stopped.

"But when meh look pon yuh dis evening meh see why 'im was so eager fi tempt you. Yuh hair, dis dress, yuh looks nice, Connie."

Constantine felt blood rush to her face and she dropped her eyes to her shoes. After all she and Clifton had shared together, from babies and immigration, to disease, and even the death of a woman they had both loved, it was this flirtatious side that was too much to handle. She couldn't look him in the eye as a smile spread across her lips. She was surprised to feel the smile coming on, even if she knew why it was there. Though she often told herself otherwise, she knew she cared for Clifton deeply, might have even loved him in some way. And since he was complimenting her like a man in love, Constantine decided to bend a little and reciprocate.

"Tank you. Yuh luk nice too."

Clifton relished the look on Constantine's face and took great pride in having been the one to put it there. The other couples had lost interest in the foreign-born parents but it didn't matter. In this moment they weren't putting on a show for anyone.

That night, after the dance, Clifton didn't have to beg his wife or tackle her in the bedroom,. She invited him. And for the first time in a while, she felt like her husband, recognizing that she had options just like him, was more attentive and considerate that night.

Clifton didn't have to leave for work that week and so he was still home when Monday rolled around. That morning, he told Pearl that instead of taking the bus, like she normally did, he and her mother would drive her to school. The change of pace and the chance for her classmates to see her parents was thrilling. There was nothing her peers found more intriguing than discovering what one of their classmates's parents looked like. There was something about seeing a classmates's parents, where they came from, who they favored, and having proof that someone loved and valued them, that made these sightings so engrossing. The student who revealed something about their life outside of school was bound to get more attention that day. And Pearl could use the attention.

As the three rode in a comfortable silence, each of their minds were filled with thoughts and predictions about the day to come. Pearl sat in the backseat, watching her parents with baited breath, wondering if they would receive the approval she so desperately craved.

Just before they got to the school, they paused at a stoplight. Pearl turned to look out her window. Staring out, she noticed that the car had been still for too long, longer than the average stoplight. Not wanting to be delayed, she turned, exasperated, toward the driver's seat. Just as she did so, she saw her father lean over and give her mother a quick peck on the lips.

Pearl gasped before covering her mouth, giving the two some privacy. Never in her life had she seen her parents hold hands or look at each other lovingly and she didn't want to be the one to disrupt the mood. She had since forgotten about rushing to get to school or what her classmates would think. More than any of her other siblings, Pearl yearned for peace, but living with Clifton and Constantine, it was hard to come by. But this morning, watching them engage in this type of affection, Pearl felt full, seeing this tiny glimpse into the life she'd always wanted. Pearl watched them kiss one another and fantasized about her parents ending the loud talking and arguing that disrupted the tranquility of the home they'd worked so hard to create for themselves. She yearned for them to be like the White families she'd seen on television whose biggest problem was about a dog who'd run away. Not knowing the full story of her parents's sordid history together, she couldn't understand why their problems couldn't be solved in thirty minutes like everyone else's. But this kiss gave her hope for normalcy. And she clung to it, not only in the immediate days after, but for years to come.

But the pleasantries of that morning didn't last long.

Two weeks later, the kids were home from school and doing their homework in the kitchen and living room. It was after eight o'clock and though Clifton was in town, he still hadn't returned home yet. Constantine started pacing the floor. He should have been home by now and she was starting to think that something had happened to him out in the street. Just then the phone rang. Constantine moved to answer it, still unsettled. It was her one friend from church, Gladys. Unlike the other women in the church, Constantine believed Gladys acted like she had some sense. She was neither too holy to be honest about her shortcomings nor too high and mighty to be kind to people. Constantine trusted Gladys and was grateful to have a friend who hadn't come from her womb or lived in a different country. And though she appreciated Gladys, in the years to come, Constantine would wish that she hadn't made this particular phone call.

"Hey, Gladys. 'ow yuh doing?"

"Oh, um . . . I'm doing fine, Connie. How are you?"

"Meh holding up. Meh just waiting pon Clifton tuh get 'ome."

"Umph," Gladys interjected into the receiver. "That's why I'm calling you now." Gladys, a Mississippi native who'd migrated to Indianapolis, had a Southern accent that, to Constantine's ear, weighted her words. Each of them dripped with a sweetness and sorrow only the American South could birth.

"What's going on, Gladys?"

"Connie, girl, you know I take no pleasure in telling you this . . ."

Before she had finished her sentence, Constantine's heart dropped. She knew from Gladys's tone that her husband wasn't dead on the side of the road or injured or in some type of trouble that left him immobile.

"Yuh say yuh did see mi husband nuh? Where yuh see 'im?"

"He was over near Capitol."

Constantine didn't know any woman who lived over there. But it was probably for the better. "Okay, Gladys. Tank yuh for de information."

"Yeah. You know I'm sorry. I'll call and check up on you later."

Constantine snorted. "Yuh ah go check pon meh tuh see if mi ah kill mi husban' nuh?" Constantine laughed ruefully before looking for a way to end this conversation. "Okay, haf a good night."

They both hung up the phone. Constantine paced the house a few times before sitting herself down in the living room. It was all to no avail. She was still fuming. Just when she'd let her guard down and was opening herself up to his charms, he proved, once again, to be the man he'd always been, slapping her in the face in the process. More than feeling angry toward him, she was furious with herself for falling for his charms, for believing that he could change after all these years. She popped up from the chair and went to the closet to grab her coat. She was going to find him this time, catch him in the act. She wouldn't even require that he explain himself. She just wanted undeniable proof so that at least now he wouldn't be able to lie to her face as he'd done every single time she accused him of stepping out and spending money, trying to impress women all over the city when he had a wife and a house full of children.

Noel, who was doing her homework in the kitchen, had heard and seen enough of the phone conversation to know that her mother's ire was going to be directed at her father, whenever she caught up with him. And the way she stomped off to grab her coat, Noel assumed that this would happen pretty soon. She put her pencil down.

"Mom, it's nine o'clock. The buses have stopped running. Where are you going this time of night?"

"Meh ah look for de place yuh fadda lay 'im head dis evening," Constantine shot back.

If it was just her words alone, Noel would have ignored her mother. But her crazed look let her know that Constantine had every intention of confronting her father tonight.

Noel panicked. Her mother still couldn't drive, so she'd be stomping up and down the city streets, so furious she wouldn't be able to see straight. She'd be in the dark with no type of protection.

"Mom, I'm sure he'll be home soon. You can speak to him once he gets in the house. But it's too late and too dark for you to be out in the streets hollering for your husband."

Constantine, in her enraged state, couldn't hear the logic behind her argument. It didn't occur to her that she didn't have an address. Instead, she snatched her keys off the table and marched toward the door. Just as she stepped out, she looked over her shoulder at Noel.

"Look out for yuh sistas nuh?"

Before Noel could answer her, Constantine had closed the door, heading out into the brisk, March night air.

When Constantine got out into the street, she was still so angry that she didn't feel the forty-degree-wind smacking her in the face. She was running on pure adrenaline, not knowing exactly where she was going. All she had was the street name and at nearly ten o'clock, she marched toward it, determined to find her husband. Constantine breezed past the smokers and users and those who'd made it their profession to hang on the corners all times of year. If they thought about violating or harassing anyone this night, they knew from the bounce in her step that she shouldn't be the one. There was too much fight in her. In fact, they felt sorry for the man she was looking for. They all knew it was a man. Only a man could inspire this type of step and that crazed look.

As she got farther away from her home, Constantine saw scantily clad women beginning to peek out of alleyways and down the sidewalk, preparing themselves for the long night ahead. Just as she was beginning to wonder if any of them knew her husband, she reasoned that perhaps he wouldn't go that far. Constantine sneered at them, thinking of the husbands they had seduced away from their homes. Looking in their direction, she threw her nose up in the air, thinking herself better than them, though they were all out in the street together.

For all the years they'd been married and all the years Constantine suspected, and then knew, that her husband had been stepping out on her, he had never admitted it. When people in the church started to look at her funny and she asked him about it, he said that she was looking for a reason to fuss at him. When women who wanted to inform or embarrass her told her about seeing him in the street, just like Gladys had done tonight, he said they were jealous. The only time he didn't try to assert his innocence was when they both were infected with syphilis. Silence was as close as he'd get to admission. It was no secret to anyone that Clifton had been unfaithful but she wanted him to acknowledge his sins. Not that she had any intention of forgiving him.

Constantine hadn't planned what she was going to say when she reached the woman's house. She would just be happy to have caught him and tell him, to his face, once and for all that she knew what he was doing; and that for all the time he spent in church, playing holy, he was living foul.

Her daughter's pleading or the presence of prostitutes on the street hadn't swayed her from her late night search. But there was someone who could. Constantine was walking past a gas station when she noticed a group of boys, standing around their car, smoking, talking loudly, and laughing at nothing in particular. They were trying to intimidate passersby, asserting what they believed to be manhood. Constantine glanced at them as she had glanced at everyone else she passed that evening. And just as she was going to keep moving on her quest, she noticed one of those boys looked quite a bit like Winston.

The anger that had fueled her started to dissipate and was replaced with concern. She inched closer to the boys on the street, trying to stay out of view. As she closed in, she confirmed that it was Winston. She could see, much to her delight, that he wasn't drinking or smoking. But watching him with those types gave her pause. Truth be told, neither Clifton nor Constantine knew anything about the life Winston lived outside of their house. She asked herself if he had been home when she left. She hadn't checked; she had just assumed he was. When did he sneak out? She thought maybe he had been home but once she had left, he had snuck out too and caught a ride with one of his friends. He'd have beaten her to the gas station easily if he were in a car.

Sure that it was Winston, she bounded up to the car, feeling for the first time the unforgiving hardness of the cement pressing through her shoes, against the bones of her feet.

"Winston!"

The laughter ceased and one by one the cigarettes that had been lit fell to the ground and the bottles that had been opened disappeared behind backs.

Though he tried to play it cool in front of his friends, Constantine could see the shock written on his face. "Wha yuh doing out in de street dis time a night?" she demanded.

Winston thought to ask her the same question but didn't want to make a bad situation worse. Plus he already knew the answer. He was home when his mother left storming out of the house. Had he known where she was headed, he would have suggested his friends take him in another direction.

Constantine almost read his mind. Neither one of them should have been here. Thankfully, she wasn't the one being interrogated. And she silently communicated that sentiment as she waited for his response.

There really was no right way to answer that question. He was going to be in trouble regardless, so Winston just chose the truth. "I was just hanging out with my friends. I didn't . . . I didn't know you would be over this way."

"Let's go." Constantine popped Winston on the back of his head as he walked away from his friends.

Politely, the one who drove spoke up, "Mrs. Reid, do you want a ride home?"

Though she probably should have taken it, Constantine was so affronted by the boy's boldness that she turned it down. "Yuh been to mi house one too many times tunight already."
The boy held his head down in shame until Constantine and Winston were out of ear and eyeshot.

The fifteen-minute walk seemed longer now that Constantine had calmed down. She could feel the frigid wind whipping through the jacket that was too light to protect her. Her feet were throbbing from all of that stomping earlier and now that she was no longer seeing red, she was taking in the neighborhood, asking herself what she had been thinking. Anything could have happened to her out here and her children would have been left alone, at least for a few hours until their father came home, looking to give her his excuse for the night. Tears, not from the wind, but from guilt and sadness, started to form in the corners of her eyes.

Just as she lifted her hand to make sure none of them fell, Winston turned to her abruptly.

"Why do you stay with him? We all know he's never going to change," he asked with an urgency only years's worth of frustration and disappointment could have bred.

Constantine was shocked by his sudden concern. During the few times when Winston was home, he always acted completely uninterested in what was going on in the house.

She gave him the answer she'd rehearsed over and over in her own mind. "Wha meh a do wid 'im gone? Yuh know ya fadda bring in de muney? How meh would afford fi feed unu, put clothes on yuh back, and keep a roof ovah yuh head wid jus me workin?"

She paused, wondering if Winston was believing what she was saying, if he saw the sacrifices she'd made. "Meh stay wid him fi yuh children."

Winston shook his head. "You could leave if you wanted to."

"Maybe. But it cyan be now. 'im keep givin me pickney fi raise. Yuh an Alton grow big now and can tek care of yuhselves. But yuh sisters and brother still have a way to go. It nah fair fi raise yuh one way and dem anutha . . ."

Constantine stopped short then, sensing, feeling Winston's body tense with resentment, "Meh know meh and yuh fadda made mistakes wid yuh and yuh brudda. But yuh must undastan we t'ought we were doing de best for unu."

Winston stared fixedly down the street, unfazed. It wasn't something he hadn't heard before. No matter how his parents tried to rationalize their decisions, he just knew that they'd abandoned him and his brother and then took them from their family, forcing them into one that had been built without them.

More than most things, Constantine feared that Alton and Winston would never forgive her for leaving them to follow their father to the United States. And that's when it occurred to her that leaving her children and following Clifton was exactly what she had done tonight. Decades ago and even now, she was so preoccupied with Clifton that she occasionally neglected her priorities, her children. More than being a daughter, sister, wife, and even woman, being a mother, for better or worse, took precedence in Constantine's life. Tonight, though, she was stunned to come to the realization that the dysfunction of her marriage had caused her to lose sight of that.

Winston and Constantine walked the rest of the way home in silence. Just before they got to their driveway, Constantine looked up at the living room window. Inside, she could see Noel, sitting in the same place she'd left her, that same worried expression plastered on her face. Once she and Constantine made eye contact, Noel's expression changed from concern to annoyance as she stood and walked away from the window.

When Constantine had a chance to take off the too-thin jacket and rest herself on the couch for a few moments, she realized just how tired she was. It was an emotional exhaustion, a fatigue that could be felt in her cells. So she sat there, frozen. Any explanation she could have offered her daughter became jumbled and unclear in her mind and she told herself it was all for the better. She couldn't handle two children interrogating her about their father in the same night.

***

Months later, Constantine would learn just how strongly her husband's behavior was affecting not only her decision making but her health too. After the syphilis scare, she made it a point to go to her doctor more frequently. That diagnosis had shown her the importance of catching illnesses early. And instead of taking the approach of so many Black folk around her, who would rather not know, when Constantine noticed any irregularities in her body, she ran to the doctor.

Like any mother with six children, the days when she didn't feel tired were few and far between. Still, as the days and weeks passed, she recognized that what she was feeling wasn't regular tired. She could never seem to get enough rest or sleep. Then came the headaches, which she had never suffered from before. And finally, the need to get up three or four times a night to use the bathroom. Losing even more sleep in her exhaustive state was the last straw. She made an appointment to see her doctor.

Doctor Shapiro nodded, a bit nonchalantly as Constantine listed her symptoms. It wasn't until she got to the urination part that he raised his eyebrows. He held his hand up to stop her. "I want to run a blood test to make sure everything is alright."

Dr. Shapiro told Constantine that he wanted her to go without food or liquids, with the exception of water, for the next eight hours and then return to his office where he'd conduct another test. She did. The nurse drew blood and she waited a week for the results.

A week later, Dr. Shapiro called her in. "Mrs. Reid, the blood test revealed that your blood glucose, your sugar levels, are too high. Based on your numbers, it seems that you have diabetes."

The next sound punctuating the room was Constantine's scream. She didn't know much about diabetes but she'd heard horror stories of women and men losing limbs or dying from the disease. And despite how she'd behaved at her mother's funeral, she wasn't ready.

Dr. Shapiro, who had been a bit distant during this visit, suddenly appeared next to Constantine, gently rubbing her back as she sobbed.

"It's going to be okay, Mrs. Reid. It's going to be okay." That was all he could manage to say before her wailing started again.

When Constantine's occasional sniffles were the only sounds she emitted, Dr. Shapiro started explaining. "Mrs. Reid, diabetes can be a very manageable disease. If you just make a few changes to your lifestyle you can live a very long and healthy life."

Constantine wiped her eyes, looking up into Dr. Shapiro's. "What cause dis?"

He sighed again, "Well, it could be a number of things. Diet, genetics . . . family history. Even something as normal as stress can cause your body to have an abnormal relationship with sugar."

Of all the things the doctor listed, Constantine knew that stress was the biggest culprit. Between her son's marriage, the death of her mother, raising six children, and worrying about her husband's whereabouts, stress had become her normal. "Is probably de stress."

"You know, Mrs. Reid, we all have stress in our lives. But some of it we can eliminate. And now, for the sake of your health, it's time to do it."

There was no way Dr. Shapiro could have known the effect of his words.

Constantine had every intention of keeping this news to herself. But from the second she stepped in the door that afternoon, Pearl sensed that her mother was ill at ease. "What did the doctor say, Mommy?"

Constantine pretended she didn't hear her.

Pearl stepped in front of Constantine's face, "Mom, did you hear me? What did the doctor say?"

"Yuh mus know everythin nah?"

Pearl stood silently, waiting.

" 'im tell me say meh haf diabetes."

Pearl gasped.

"But 'im tell me de disease is manageable if meh mek a few changes. He give me some papers and tell me about some classes meh can tek."

"I'll go with you."

Once a week for the next month Pearl and Constantine attended classes, where they learned what type of foods to avoid. Seeing some of her favorite dishes on the list, she saw that it was more than just stress that had contributed to this disease. Years of eating like an American, consuming greasy meats and cheese, white rice, flavoring her food with coconut milk and butter, had had something to do with her recent diagnosis as well. It was evidenced in the amount of fabric she needed to buy whenever she made a dress for herself. She felt it in the minutes it took for her to catch her breath after climbing a flight of stairs. What had once been a source of pride, a sense of prosperity in America, had now become a serious health issue.

In addition to the ways in which her teacher had instructed her to improve her diet, they stressed, over and over again, the importance of physical activity. In Jamaica, when people got enough exercise from walking and working in the island heat, exercise wasn't hard to come by. But cleaning her house, cooking and riding in a bus or a car when she needed to be somewhere, it wasn't difficult to live a life lacking in physical activity. Thankfully, the teachers weren't suggesting she do anything strenuous. Just thirty minutes of something that caused her to work up a sweat, at least once a day. Hearing this, it was Pearl who suggested they work out fifteen minutes in the morning when they first woke up and then fifteen minutes in the evening before they went to bed.

"I'll do it with you."

And, as Constantine knew she would be, Pearl was true to her word. Every morning, without fail, Pearl would knock on her parents's door asking the same question.

"Mommy, you ready to work out?"

Afterward, Pearl would wash up while Constantine prepared breakfast.

In a few months's time, with the changes in her diet and the increase in physical activity, it wasn't long before Constantine noticed the reemergence of her clavicle bone, before she had to take in dresses that she'd worn for years.

Still, with the changes of her new lifestyle, she knew that if she stayed with her husband, it would all be in vain.

1968, Forty-eight

Three years later, Maxine was about to start school. Constantine had debated whether or not she was going to homeschool her like she'd done Pearl or send her out into the world. Raising her sixth child at nearly fifty years old, the mere thought of spending her days chasing and begging the girl to do her schoolwork was tiresome. Her youngest was too strong-willed and would do better if she were in a structured environment, with instructors she didn't call "Mommy." Having all of her children out of the house during the day gave Constantine a bit of a breather. Still, Maxine had proven to be quite the social butterfly and theatrical. It never occurred to Constantine that her children would thrive in the world of theater but Maxine loved being the center of attention on stage. And every year since she'd first began, she came home with some type of paper detailing her role in the school production of whatever play they were putting on that semester. First, it was *The Nutcracker* and then a role in *Sleeping Beauty.* Constantine marveled at Maxine's level of comfort with all eyes on her.

Her youngest's performances made Constantine wonder if her other children had hidden artistic gifts she had missed over the years. She remembered that Winston took a great interest in illustration and had been quite good at it. But he was grown and out of the house now. He had graduated and started working at the post office, a good government job. Boysie, who was distracted with sports and girls, wasn't interested in picking up another hobby. So that left Noel and Pearl.

"Girls, how unu feel about learning fi play de piano?"

Constantine had settled for what she felt was a refined instrument, a status symbol. Noel had other ideas in mind. "I'd rather play the drums."

"De what?!"

"The drums." Noel stared at her mother blankly.

"Yuh mus be kedding. Dere's nothing ladylike about bangin up drums. De piano is bettah."

"But mom, I'm not interested in the piano."

"Well, is my muney ah pay fi de lessons dem. And meh tell yuh mi nah pay fi no girlchild tuh play de drums."

Shrugging her shoulders in a moment of defiance, Noel said, "I'd rather not take lessons at all then."

Constantine huffed, annoyed at the fruitless protest. "Noel, yuh ah go study de piano. Dat's it!"

Noel, who was increasingly moody and just beginning to test her voice as a young lady, still knew when it was time to stop.

"I think the piano would be nice." Pearl said.

Constantine smiled, nodding at her.

"Das mi girl."

A week later, the three took the bus together for their first lesson. Though Noel was anything but enthused, Pearl, sensing how much this meant to her mother, was excited to get started.

When the three walked into the spacious studio, with mostly blank, white walls and six pianos in the expansive space, Pearl felt a clenching in her stomach. Hearing the beautifully complex sounds that came from the large instruments, she doubted whether or not she'd ever be able to produce them. After walking throughout the entire space, they finally reached the woman they were there to see. Miss Newsome, a short, thin White woman, who looked fragile in stature, stood from her own piano bench to greet them.

"Hello, you must be Mrs. Reid. These are your daughters?"

"Yes, this is Noel and this is Pearl."

She shook their hands in a surprisingly firm manner before instructing them to take a seat, one at a time, next to her on the bench.

Miss Newsome was patient and had a soft, soothing voice. As she waited for her turn on the bench, Pearl looked over to see the look of satisfaction on her mother's face. She knew Constantine appreciated the tone of her voice. While her mother spent a majority of her time hollering and screaming at her husband, she was always preaching to her daughters about the importance of being soft-spoken, especially in the company of White folks.

Though Noel had no interest in the piano, the second Miss Newsome gave her a command, she was able to execute it to perfection. Standing a few steps away, watching it happen Constantine was so proud of her eldest girl. Despite her early success, as soon as she finished the chords, Noel's face returned to the same disinterested look. Then it was Pearl's turn to try. Miss Newsome gave her the same simple chords she'd given Noel but Pearl didn't take to it as naturally. Comparing herself to her older sister and the sounds she'd heard when she walked into the room, the seeds of doubt grew into weeds, choking out the capacity to make any progress that day. The rest of the lesson was a struggle.

Later, when they'd gotten home, Constantine, who'd noticed Pearl's discouragement, called her into her bedroom. "How yuh did feel about de lesson today?"

Pearl's eyes shifted nervously, not wanting to relive what she'd regarded as an embarrassment. Not only had she humiliated herself, but the whole thing had been made that much worse because her mother was watching. But instead of expressing all of this, Pearl, in true preteen fashion, said, "It was okay, I guess."

Constantine would have to drag it out of her. "How yuh mean, yuh 'guess'?"

"It was just all right. It was too hard for me. Noel should be the one to take lessons."

Constantine smiled, sighing a little. She pulled her middle daughter closer to her. "If yuh wan play, Pearl, you'll get it nah. Yuh can be just as good as yuh sister maybe even bettah if yuh practice."

Constantine watched as Pearl's face turned more hopeful, hearing and internalizing her mother's words. "So tell meh do yuh wan continue on wid de lessons dem?"

Pearl nodded.

After two months of weekly lessons, Noel's consistent apathy, despite her natural ability, made it impossible for her to ever enjoy, not to mention, master the piano. Finally, Constantine came to the conclusion that there was no point in her continuing to waste her money on lessons for Noel. But Pearl continued while Noel came straight home from school and slept. Meanwhile, with her mother's encouragement and her own diligence and dedication, it wasn't long before Pearl became an exceptional player.

One day, as Constantine watched Pearl rehearse from the corner of the room, Miss Newsome left the bench to stand next to her. "Pearl shows such great promise."

Constantine nodded, pleased.

"She's really talented but if she's to have any chance as an accomplished pianist, I would strongly suggest you think about buying a piano for your home. So she can get some extra hours of practice in."

It made sense. Constantine didn't know how she was going to pay for such an extravagance but she'd find a way. "Wha's de bes' brand of piano?"

"You'll want to get a Steinway."

"And about 'ow much dem cost?

"You can get a good one for a little less than a thousand dollars."

The number was higher than she imagined but it didn't shock her. She knew, cleaning a few more houses and maybe even some help from Clifton, she could pull this off in a few months's time.

That night when she got home she told Clifton about her plan to buy the children a piano for the house. At first, he was a little hesitant until she told him they could use it to practice until they got good enough to perform in church. That was all the convincing he needed; watching his children play in church would impress the congregation and that would reflect nicely on him too. So he agreed to help her. He didn't have the whole sum but he committed to five hundred dollars. And Constantine, without a job at the time, would have to raise the rest.

Constantine wasn't exactly happy about going back to domestic work, but it was the quickest way she knew to make money. Just as she had years ago, she noticed that her employers, White folks, all had pianos of their own in their homes. And not just pianos. They had winding staircases, stereos, and fine china that it was her job to dust. After all the years she'd spent in this country, Constantine was still amazed at the type of wealth some people got to enjoy. Somewhere between mopping and dusting, Constantine looked at her surroundings and felt the pressure of the floor against her knee intensify. She wanted her daughters to live like the people she worked for and not like herself, scrubbing and laboring past fifty years old. She'd have to make sure she told the girls to marry White men. At least that way they wouldn't find themselves in the same position.

After three months of laboring, Constantine was finally able to afford the piano. She selected a white console one with gold trim and lettering. She decided she was going to put it in the corner of her living room, where the rest of the children could see and hear Pearl while she practiced. Constantine hoped that after seeing the new purchase, Noel would feel more inclined to play along with her younger sister.

When the instrument finally arrived at their home, Noel marveled at how beautiful the white and gold looked together. She posed for pictures on the bench. But she hadn't changed her mind. Her heart was still set on the drums. Pearl, on the other hand, sat down immediately, appreciative and grateful that this expensive and beautiful gift was just for her. Plus, she enjoyed looking over at her mother, slouching on the couch, eyes closed, humming to the music she created with her own fingers.

Eventually though, Pearl's passion for the piano was replaced by a more pressing priority.

***

After she gave birth to Maxine, Constantine assumed that menopause wasn't too far behind. But she was mistaken. Her period became a terror. Each month was heavier than the last. She bought the thickest sanitary napkins on the market, changing them every hour and still soaking through them, often soiling her clothes. She was so exasperated by the condition that she expressed her frustrations to virtually any other women who would listen. Pearl heard her mother on the phone, one day, with one of her friends describing the condition to Gladys.

"Yuh know meh haf tuh wear diapers now? Das de only ting that will hold de blood dat rush outta me. Meh went to the doctor and 'im tell me say meh haf fibroids and need a hysterectomy. Meh nah want no man cut me, especially taking out everything down dere."

At eleven-years-old, Pearl didn't know what a hysterectomy was. And though it wouldn't have surprised Constantine, Pearl didn't want her mother to know she had been eavesdropping. So she asked Noel instead.

"Do you know what a hysterectomy is?"

"Um, yeah, I think that's when the doctors remove all the feminine organs. Why?"

"I heard Mommy on the phone. She said the doctors want her to have one since she's bleeding so much."

"What?" Noel knew her mother bled heavily but she never thought she'd have to undergo major surgery. "Did she tell you she's having the surgery?"

"Uh, no. She wasn't talking to me. I just heard her on the phone, a few minutes ago."

Noel walked swiftly out of the room, Pearl following her. They found their mother in the kitchen. She'd since hung up the phone and was putting the finishing touches on the dinner she was fixing for her family, complete with butter and flavor. She'd prepare something healthier for herself later.

"Mom, are you having a hysterectomy?" Noel didn't have time for niceties or pretending she didn't know the extent of the situation.

Constantine turned to Pearl. She had thought it odd that Pearl wasn't in the kitchen with her. Now she knew why. Constantine sighed and shook her head in mock disapproval. In reality, she was happy to see that they were so concerned.

"No. Meh nah having ah 'isterectomy. Mi doctor 'im wan me do it. But meh tell 'im no. So das dat."

Noel, satisfied with the answer, left the kitchen almost as quickly as she'd come in. It wasn't her scene. But Pearl lingered, helping her mother with her healthy dinner, wondering if the doctor would ultimately prove to be right.

Several months later, it became clear that he was. In one of the stretches where she and Clifton were getting along, they sat in the living room talking about the evening news. Pearl was in there too pretending to study the notes on her sheet music. In the middle of their conversation, Constantine stood up, "Oh, meh haf tuh get up now or meh ah go mess up dis couch."

She ran to the wooden staircase, making her way to the bathroom. Clifton and Pearl weren't too concerned; this happened often with her and they knew she'd come back in a few minutes having washed up. But this time was different. When she got to the landing, Clifton and Pearl heard what sounded like a full cup of water being slowly poured out onto the floor.

Clifton and Pearl were racing each other to the staircase. He made it there first, shouting at Pearl to move out of the way. When he reached the staircase, he paused, shocked by what he saw.

Constantine was standing there, frozen and frightened in a pool of blood the size of a large dinner plate. Clifton, in an attempt to spare Pearl, hit the light switch so she wouldn't see her mother like this and be traumatized by the scene. He told her to go back to the living room, and he carried Constantine, who was much lighter these days, upstairs to the bathroom. He undressed her and helped her into the tub. Constantine was shaking so he rolled up the bottoms of his pants and got in with her. He took her wash cloth and rinsed off the blood that was caked on her legs and had splattered onto her feet. Once everything externally had been rinsed off, Constantine had calmed down and she washed herself while Clifton went into their bedroom and selected some new clothes for her to wear to bed. Confident that she'd be okay in the bedroom by herself, Clifton cleaned up the stairs.

Within the week, Constantine was in the hospital. She'd finally come to the point where she realized the fibroids were affecting the quality of her life. She was raw from having to wash and rinse blood from in between her legs 3-4 times a day. Her hands ached from scrubbing blood stains from her dresses. There were a couple she hadn't been able to save and threw them away. And she was tired of feeling like she was on the verge of passing out every day.

When she came in for her consultation before surgery, the doctor admonished her.

"You know you should have done this a long time ago. You were in great danger of losing too much blood to function."

All Constantine could do was shake her head. He was right but until she saw all the blood on the stairs, she hadn't understood the severity. She had the hysterectomy and after a few days in the hospital, she was sent home to recover.

It wasn't until she was home, trapped in her bed, waiting for her body to heal, that she remembered why she had been so hesitant to have the surgery in the first place.

After nearly a month of being completely bedridden, she was able to get up and fix dinner for her family. But that sapped her energy and she had to return to bed shortly after, feeling too exhausted to eat.

Since Constantine had purchased the piano she had kept up with a little of her domestic work on the side so she could afford to send Pearl to her lessons. But since her mother had been ill, Pearl hadn't asked for the money. She didn't even bother to ask her father because she knew the answer would be no. So she just stopped going. Plus, she felt it was her responsibility to be there for her mother. After years of shadowing Constantine in the kitchen, Pearl was the one to prepare her mother's meals, feeding her when she was too weak to sit up and feed herself. For weeks, as she busied herself following her mother's instructions feeding the family and taking care of Maxine, Pearl's face was fixed in a concerned frown, wondering if her mother would ever return to her normal self.

As she slowly gained her strength back, Constantine started to take notice of things other than her physical pain. She called Pearl to her room. "Yuh know meh nah hear yuh playing de piano anymore. Why is dat?"

Pearl shrugged her shoulders, not really having thought about it. But Constantine required a better explanation. She knew how much joy playing the piano brought Pearl and she wanted to know what had happened to make her stop. Constantine stared at her daughter, never breaking her gaze, waiting for her to answer.

"Well, you're sick," Pearl blurted. "I should be focusing on taking care of you, not learning how to play the piano."

That statement broke Constantine's heart and then warmed the shattered pieces. "Pearl, yuh know how much meh love fi hear yuh play piano. Yuh playin would help me get well."

Pearl heard her mother but she had already assessed the situation differently. Even more than Constantine would have liked to hear the music or more than Pearl wanted the lessons, she realized her mother needed someone to look out for her, as she'd done for them all of these years. "I'll start playing again when you're back to yourself. I promise."

Pearl was true to her word and Constantine's healing was soundtracked by her daughter's musical stylings.

***

Though Pearl sought first to please her mother, she also cared about her father's opinion. And when he was home, she'd often find herself looking for ways to impress him. She had her chance one day when one of the Jamaican members from their church visited their house with his daughter. The girl was a year younger than Pearl but they didn't know each other that well.

The girl's father said that she was going to show Clifton something. Pearl was standing nearby so she would witness it as well. "Mi daughter can read good, ya see? Watch dis." His daughter opened up the Bible and started reading a passage. Clifton nodded his head as she read each word perfectly. When she was finished, her father clapped his hands excitedly. "Look dere! De girl, she smart, yuh see."

Clifton was impressed. But he also didn't want to be outdone in his own home. Seeing that Pearl was sitting there, he had his friend's daughter hand him the Bible and he thumbed through it looking for a passage for Pearl to read. Thrusting the Bible into her hands, he said, "Here read dis nah."

Although she had had none of the practice and preparation the church girl had received, Pearl focused her eyes on the verse her father had pointed to and started with the name of the book and verse as she'd learned to do in Sabbath school.

"Romans twelve, verse four. 'For just as each of us has one body with many members, and these members do not all have the same function, so in Christ we, though many, form one body, and each member belongs to all the others. We have different gifts, according to the grace given to each of us. If your gift is prop . . . prophes-ee-ing . . .'"

First, Pearl felt the blood rush to the surface of her skin as she stumbled over the word "prophesying." Then, shortly after, her father's disappointment radiating toward her. It was a difficult word for an eleven-year-old. But Clifton didn't consider that. She had embarrassed him in front of one of the church members.

"Das enough!" He snatched the book back from her hands. "Meh so ashamed of you, yuh cyan even read de Bible."

Pearl stood, her hands frozen in the same position they had been when they were supporting the book. She felt a pricking in her heart and then heat spread to her face. Tears sprang to her eyes. And before she cried in front of her father or his friends, she spoke, the words burning her throat: "Excuse me, I have to use the restroom."

She ran straight past the bathroom door and flung herself face down on to her bed. The tears she'd managed to hold back before streamed down her face with chest-raking sobs to accompany them. Pearl wasn't just crying for today's incident. She was crying for all the times she'd felt like there was nothing she could do to gain the approval of her father. The two had always had a distant relationship but she'd never before heard him say that he was ashamed of her. The fact he had said so in front of company only added betrayal to her sorrow. Pearl kept replaying the exchange in her mind, her sobs getting louder with each rewind.

In her haste to get to her room, Pearl had forgotten to shut the door. And it wasn't long before Constantine, having already greeted their guests, walked past her. Hearing Pearl's tears she felt a pang in her own heart and stepped into the room to investigate.

She sat at the foot of the bed, "Pearl? What's wrong, nah?"

Pearl rolled over to confirm that she'd actually heard her mother speak. For the first time in a while, she didn't feel like talking to her. She took her time getting herself together so she could speak through her sobs. Pearl knew her mother wasn't going to leave the room without an answer.

"Daddy's friend Brother Morgan brought his daughter over so he could show Daddy how well she reads. And I guess Daddy wanted to see how well I could read too, so he handed me the Bible. And I was reading it just fine until I got to a word I wasn't sure how to pronounce. I was trying to sound it out but before I could even finish, Daddy snatched the Bible out of my hand and told me he was ashamed of me . . ."

Constantine wrapped her arms around Pearl's shoulders. She sighed in frustration, angered by Clifton's insensitivity. But as many times as she'd slipped and spoken negatively about their father in front of them, she tried, this time, to exercise a little empathy.

"Pearl, ya fadda nevah read too good, yuh know? Until today, 'im haf mi fi read his mail. But him was able tuh mek it in dis country, not being able tuh read."

She could see her words were working. The tears that had stained Pearl's face started to dry as she listened, intrigued by this new information about her father.

"And yuh know why 'im come 'ere to dis country? To mek a bettah life for yuh bruddas and sistahs dem. Meh trying fi tell yuh ya fadda came here so yuh wouldn't haf to go truh the tings him went truh not havin a good education. The same for me. Meh nah go as far in school as meh would like. But we come 'ere so unu can haf a chance to bettah yuhself. Yuh undastan what meh say?"

Pearl thought for a second and then nodded slowly before asking, earnestly, "If I can read better than him, then why would he say he was ashamed of me?"

Constantine sighed again. She knew the answer but she wanted to make sure she explained it in terms Pearl could understand. "'im nah mean dat. He jus wan yuh tuh get bettah. Tuh get so where yuh nah stumble over de words dem. Maybe he went about it de wrong way . . ."

Pearl nodded.

". . . but even t'ough it seem like 'im harsh, 'e wan de best for yuh."

Constantine left out the part about the fear Clifton had probably felt hearing his daughter stumble over the word. True, he was concerned about what his friend was going to think. But she knew that he, no doubt, saw himself in her mispronunciation. He saw himself having to ask his wife to read letters for him and ask strangers for directions when there were signs that indicated where he needed to go. He heard her stumble over that word and he worried that all the work he and Constantine had put into raising their children up right, in the right country, had been for nothing. Perhaps if he were home more often, he would know that Pearl was so determined to please her parents that she didn't need shaming as an incentive to do what they had asked of her.

"Pearl, meh know yuh read very well. Yuh were jus nervous. Try it again."

Pearl reached for the small pocket-sized Bible on her nightstand she had been given as a baby, during her christening, and read the verse over again. When she got to the word "prophesying," she stumbled again. But instead of panicking, she pointed to it and Constantine helped her sound it out. She finished the verse. Constantine asked her, "Now, what yuh tink dat does mean?"

Pearl skimmed over the verse again. "Well, maybe that everyone is different and we can all do something for God but it doesn't have to be the same thing?"

"Exactly. Das what it mean. Is one ting tuh read, Pearl, and it's another ting tuh be able to undastan wha chu readin. That likkle girl downstairs probably didn't know what de hell she read."

The petty remark didn't exactly represent Christian principles but it put a smile on her daughter's face.

1969, Forty-nine

Living in America it wasn't hard to see that White people had it made in this country. This was particularly clear to Constantine, who spent significant time in White people's homes, dusting their expensive furniture, mopping their marble floors, and vacuuming their carpets that were so plush it felt like she was walking on mattresses. From the time Noel was born, she started thinking about the type of life her daughter would have as a woman in America. How it would be different from hers in Jamaica. There was so much more here for them. But they were still women. Black women, as they would be known in America, with their own unique set of struggles. She figured, long ago, if there was one way for her daughters to avoid all of that it would be for them to marry White men and live lavishly. Her daughters could choose whether they wanted to educate themselves or sit back and raise their children in the home. If they married the right man they'd have an option.

Constantine used to think she'd send them back to Jamaica to marry Indian men. They were taking over the country anyway. But there was no need for all the hassle if they could stay right here in the States. That was a thought she had been mulling over for years; but one day, frustrated with her own husband, she let it slip.

It was the weekend and Noel was lying around while Pearl was trying to help her mother clean up. Pearl was pulling the blanket Noel was lying on from underneath her. And her older sister, attempting to annoy her with defiance, refused to move.

Pearl sighed, frustrated, "Ugh! Noel, move! You see I'm trying to clean up. Someone has to. You're too lazy."

Noel laughed at the fact she had been able to frazzle her sister by literally doing nothing in a house that was already spotless. Her brothers joined her in laughter.

"You think it's funny to be lazy?" Pearl shouted.

Constantine intervened before Pearl became too flustered. "All right. Das enough nah! Pearl, yuh sister nah lazy. But meh ah tell yuh if yuh girls want to lounge around de house an' pass yuh work on fi somebody else tuh do, all yuh mus do is marry a White man."

Noel tore her face up, sitting upright, suddenly enthralled by the conversation. "Why do you say that?"

"How yuh mean, why meh ah say dat? Is de trut'. 'ow many years meh been in dis country clean up, mop up, sweep up after de White people dem. Yuh know how much nice tings meh did see inna dem houses? Plenty tings."

Boysie looked at his mother, disappointed by her naivety. "Mom, you think you know these White people. These White men are doing some of the foulest things to their wives, no better than the Black men. They step out. They hit their wives. They're no angels either."

Constantine was silenced for a moment. She'd never considered that White men were men just like the ones she'd known and the one she was living with now. She'd always thought no one could top Clifton. Still, even if they were all the same, there was at least one difference between her husband and a White man.

"At least wid de White man dem, yuh know everything yuh need an wan' would be taken care of. Who cares what him do in de streets as long as yuh haf a nice roof ova yuh head. Yuh can send yuh children to good schools, unu eat well. Yuh can buy whatever yuh want. Who cares what de man dem do? Das a good life."

No one spoke. They all knew she was just talking. Their father was far from rich but they'd never gone hungry and had access to everything they needed. And yet, they all knew the nonsense about her not caring what her husband did was anything but the truth. As much as Constantine pretended, they'd all seen the arguments, the fights, the way she chased after him, searching for proof of what she already knew was true. Their lives were colored by their mother's caring.

Constantine, knowing what each of her children was thinking, shifted the subject. "Well, if yuh mus marry a Black man mek sure 'im haf light skin and nice hair so unu kids come out cute. Mi wan' pretty grandbabies. Yuh see like Alton son Lem. Him dark but 'im hair just like his fadda an mudda, wavy and nice."

Noel rolled her eyes. She always tuned her mother out when she started speaking like this. Listening to her, you would swear that Constantine herself was fair skinned. But like her husband and most of her children, she was not. Noel, who nearly matched her mother in complexion, had never been made to feel unattractive. She couldn't even remember her mother lauding one child's beauty over another. She just chalked the backwards comments up to Constantine being out of touch. In years to come, she would recognize that while her mother didn't speak with a fake British accent like her father, she too had been overly influenced by not only colonial rule but also America's twisted perception of Black people. Now, she dismissed the remarks, shaking her head.

When Constantine talked about her daughters with men, she was envisioning a future far, far off. She'd already had a son marry too early and it wouldn't be long before Winston followed in his footsteps. Though she had plans after her children left the house, she didn't want to rush them away.

But they were already of that age.

Noel and even little Pearl were showing interest in boys. Both Clifton and Constantine laid down strict rules, not wanting to have to extend their parenting years, being forced to raise grandchildren. The girls weren't allowed to leave the house after school, accept phone calls from boys, or have boyfriends until they were eighteen. They couldn't go out on dates, and they certainly couldn't accept gifts from boys. It was the way every girl in Jamaica had been raised. But these measures were considered extreme in America. And while they didn't necessarily work all that well in Jamaica either, it was the only way Clifton and Constantine knew to at least attempt to keep their children from harm. For girls who were barely allowed to leave the front yard during the summertime, no one was surprised. They simply found ways to bend the rules a bit.

Though Pearl did her best to follow her mother's instructions, she knew that all of her siblings "dated" before they'd turned eighteen and it hadn't seemed to hurt anybody. No one had gotten pregnant and they all had been crafty enough to get away with it.

And once she noticed Peter Nichols walking the hallways, she knew it was her turn. Peter was biracial. If she'd never seen his parents, she would just assumed that he was a light-skinned Black boy. But one day she looked into the car he'd just left and saw a White father and a Black mother he resembled. This fact intrigued Pearl even more because of what her mother had advised when picking a mate. Peter, with hair that was more curly than coarse and skin light enough that she could see freckles, was the best of both worlds. She assumed, like her mother had taught her, that because Peter's dad was White his family had money. Pearl had been eyeing Peter for what seemed to her like eons. In actuality, it had only been about three weeks. But during that time, he had noticed her too. And on the day when she was least expecting it, on a day when she had finally convinced herself that Peter wasn't interested, he walked up to her in the hallway as she was chatting with some friends in between classes.

"Pearl?"

She was in the middle of a sentence but hearing a male voice call her name, she turned around suddenly, wondering what this boy could want. She was shocked to see it was Peter. She had spent so much time studying him that she hardly realized that she had never heard him speak and certainly not her name.

"Hi, Peter." His name, which she had never uttered out loud, nearly got stuck in her throat.

"Can I speak to you for a second . . . alone?" He muttered the last word so her friends wouldn't hear.

Pearl hadn't even told her friends that she liked Peter, it was that precious of a secret. She'd had such a hard time fitting in with the students during elementary school that she still didn't trust people easily and didn't want this information blasted all over the hallways. And she wasn't going to give them any clues now. So instead of speaking within their earshot, she pointed to a spot a couple of steps away, turned and excused herself from her friends, and walked with Peter until they were far enough away that no one else could hear their conversation. Still, many followed with their eyes.

"Okay, I know we don't really know each other that well but I've noticed you in my English class and . . . I mean, you seem like a nice person, a nice girl. So I was wondering if you'd like to eat lunch with me . . . at my table today."

Pearl's smile spoke before she did. Seeing that she was flattered by the invitation, Peter relaxed.

"That would be great. Thank you," she said. Then she flinched. Should she have thanked him? Did it make her seem overly grateful?

Peter chuckled. "Okay, great. I'll see you in a couple of hours."

"See you then."

For as much as she was able to concentrate in the classroom, Pearl should have just gone to the cafeteria, sat down, and waited for Peter there because that's where her mind was.

That day at lunch Pearl and Peter had an awkward but eventually pleasant conversation. Realizing they could smooth out any kinks between them, they continued eating lunch together for the next few weeks.

Finally, after about a month of doing this, Peter wanted to make their budding relationship official. "Pearl, you know I really like you, right?"

She nodded sheepishly, trying to mask the grin that had just spread across her face. "Yes. I like you too, Peter."

He returned her toothy grin. "Well, good, because I wanted to ask you if you'd like to go steady?"

Instantly, Pearl nodded, not for a single second considering her parents's rules. "I'd love to."

As soon as Pearl finished her sentence, Peter produced a small, velvety box from his pocket. Not knowing exactly how to present it, he thrust the box into Pearl's hands. She opened it, hearing it creak as she separated the lids from each other. Inside there was gold ring with a red stone in the center. The gold wasn't real and neither was the jewel but to Pearl's untrained eyes, it looked expensive. And she couldn't wait to get back home to tell her sisters and brothers that their mother had been right about White folks having money. Peter wasn't even grown, didn't have a job, and still he was able to give her a ring. And then Pearl hesitated. The only rings she'd heard of men presenting to women were engagement rings. Surely, Peter wasn't trying to propose marriage.

"What does this mean?"

"It's a promise ring."

Pearl nodded in relief. While other girls her age fantasized about getting married soon, Pearl had learned from Alton that getting married before she'd even gotten out of high school, only to end up divorced a few years later, was not something she wanted.

A promise ring seemed like a step in the right direction without requiring too much, too soon.

Pearl was so elated with Peter, their relationship, and the ring, that she didn't even think about what her mother would say about him or it. She decided instead of hiding it any longer she was going to finally share her good news with her. She figured Constantine would take such joy in seeing Pearl happy and knowing that her new boyfriend was rich that she would have no choice but to allow her to continue seeing him.

Luckily, Noel saw Pearl before Constantine did. "Hey Pearl, how was schoo—wait, what's that on your finger?"

She grabbed her younger sister's hand, holding the ring up to her face so she could get a better look.

Pearl smiled, trying to snatch her hand away in mock annoyance. "Peter gave it to me. It's a promise ring."

Noel raised her eyebrows, impressed with the pull her younger sister had over the boys. "That's nice, Pearl!"

"Thank you."

Noel gave her some time to relish the moment before presenting her with the unpleasant reality. "You better not let Mommy catch that on your finger."

Pearl sighed. "You think she'll be upset? She always talks about men who can buy us nice things. And Peter is not all White like she said but his father is. I would think she would be happy with that."

Noel shook her head, reminding herself that her sister hadn't lived under their parents's watchful eye for as long as she had. "She's talking about when we get older. You heard her say we can't date until we're eighteen. Plus, I know for a fact she won't let you keep that ring."

Pearl started to panic. "Well, what am I supposed to do with it? I can't give it back to him. He'll think that I don't like him anymore."

Noel thought for a moment. "Listen, take it off now and put it in your purse. And once we get home I'll tell you what to do with it."

When they got home Noel directed Pearl to a picture hanging in their shared bedroom. "You need to put this ring somewhere where Mommy won't find it. You can hang it on the nail that hangs the picture frame in our room."

Pearl did as her sister instructed. Every day when she got home from school, she ran straight to her room, telling her mother she was in a rush to get out of her school clothes. She'd take the ring off, kiss it, and place it on the nail. Then in the morning when she got up for school, she'd put it back on so Peter would see her wearing it.

This plan worked for two weeks until one morning Pearl overslept. Waking up late, all she had time to do was throw on her clothes and slick her hair back in a quick ponytail. She forgot the ring.

And on that very same day, Constantine decided it had been too long since she'd dusted the house from top to bottom. She turned on some music and went about the business of cleaning. She started with the living room, continued to the dining room, and eventually made her way up to her children's bedrooms. She always started with the boys's rooms because they needed the most work. Thankfully, because they'd heeded her messages about cleanliness and keeping a tidy space, her daughters didn't follow their brother's example. She hummed the tune to a song whose lyrics she'd forgotten as she dusted their dressers and the little end table in between their two beds. Just about to leave the room, she noticed she hadn't dusted the picture hanging in the corner.

She walked over to it swiftly, planning just to run the duster across it briefly before moving on to her and Clifton's room. She brushed the top of the frame when she heard a slight tinkling sound. Her eyes scanned the frame trying to locate the noise. She searched for a few minutes, beginning to lose interest until the sunlight hit the dangling ring. Constantine picked it up, examining it. It was not real gold, and trying it on, she realized it wouldn't fit any of her fingers. It had to belong to one of her daughters. She tucked the ring in her dress pocket and went about doing the rest of the housework. The interrogation would come later.

By the time they arrived home from school, Constantine had a whole plan orchestrated in her mind. She'd start with Pearl. The ring could have been either hers or her sister's but she knew Pearl was the most likely to divulge quickly and honestly, even if it didn't belong to her.

Constantine met her at the door. Pulling the ring from her pocket, she held it up to Pearl's face. "Wha's dis?" She watched as her daughter's eyes widened in terror.

"It's a ring."

"Yes, meh know dat much. Where yuh did get it?"

"Um, a boy at school gave it to me."

Constantine's own voice climbed a few octaves as she parroted her daughter's words. "A boy at school?! What boy?"

"His name is Peter Nichols. He and I are . . . um . . . seeing each other."

Constantine released a sardonic chuckle. What did this little girl know about seeing someone? A boy. The only places Pearl was allowed to go were to school and church.

"How yuh mean 'seeing'? How yuh fi see him and focus pon yuh school work?"

"Just at school, just during lunch time. I'm still doing well in all my classes."

Constantine nodded stiffly, breathing a sigh of relief. Just as she parted her lips to lay into her middle daughter, reminding her of the rules that she'd broken in both having a boyfriend and accepting gifts, she remembered a very similar scenario with her own mother, all those lifetimes ago. She had never forgotten how Grace Ann blew up when she simply told her she had an innocent crush on Tawkins in primary school. And though now, as a mother, she could understand Grace Ann's reaction, she also recalled the shock, disappointment, and even betrayal she felt when her mother dismissed the very feelings she had come to treasure. Constantine remembered how that one conversation informed her behavior when it came to discussing men with her mother. After Grace Ann shut her down that day in the kitchen, the two didn't talk about men again, seriously, until she was pregnant and her mother was trying to convince her to marry Clifton.

Constantine reasoned that since Pearl had made it this far before she even mentioned a boy, she deserved credit and a listening ear, lest she repeat the same mistakes she'd made with men. The ring would still have to go though.

"Yuh mus return de ring to de boy tomorrow."

Pearl's face broke in disbelief. "I can't give it back to him! He'll think I don't like him anymore. It'll hurt his feelings."

"Meh nah care if 'im feelings hurt. Yuh cyan keep de ring."

"Why not?"

"Meh nah wan' any daughter of mine accepting gifts from no likkle boy. 'im give yuh a gift den 'im ah expeck somethin' in return. And meh know yuh nah haf no muney. Haf yuh given dis boy anythin'?"

Constantine tilted her head, eyeing her daughter knowingly.

"No, I haven't."

"Good. Mek it stay dat way."

Pearl realized this was a battle she was not going to win. She reluctantly gave in. "I'll take the ring back to him tomorrow."

Then Constantine walked to the living room, speaking to Pearl over her shoulder. "Tell me bout de boy nah."

Pearl's mood lightened as she bounded behind her mother. "Well, his name is Peter Nichols. He's in my grade and he's in my English class. You know, Mom, I think you would like him."

Constantine raised her eyebrows, amused. "Why yuh tink meh would like 'im?"

"Well, because he has a nice, fair complexion. His mother is Black and his father is White."

Constantine raised her eyebrows and tilted her head slightly, not in approval but in genuine interest.

"So when yuh say yuh seeing dis boy, wha dat mean?" Constantine held her breath as she waited for her daughter's answer.

"He's kissed me on my cheek a couple of times and we hold hands but that's about it."

"About it?"

"No, that's it," Pearl said, chuckling nervously.

"Well, das good. Yuh know dese boys dem can be sneaky. Dem will say anythin' tuh mek yuh open yuh legs tuh dem. But mek meh tell yuh. Yuh may lay down feeling good but yuh wake up feeling like a dawg. Yuh undastand me?"

Pearl didn't really know what her mother meant. She knew she was referencing sex. They'd discussed that before. But the part about lying down feeling good and waking up feeling like a dog, she didn't quite grasp. Still, she nodded anyway.

Constantine softened a bit. "If yuh go too far too soon wid de boys dem yuh could find yuself in a situation where yuh stuck. Yuh could end up pregnant. Or, the way de men dem stay, yuh could catch a venereal disease. But even if neither of dose tings dem happen, having sex change up everythin'."

Noel, who had heard this conversation before, had joined them in the living room to sit in and see what her mother was going to say this time. Each lesson on dating and men was always different, always a new bit of insight that Constantine wanted to impart on her girls before she sent them out into the world.

"People dem always talk bout sex feels so good. Dem right, it feel good, yes. But yuh mus be careful who yuh does give yuh virginity to."

Constantine watched as her daughters leaned in closer.

"Men can haf sex wid any woman and get up and go bout dem business like it nevah happen. But we?" Constantine lifted her voice for emphasis. "We get attached too quickly. And when yuh open yuh legs tuh de men, yuh given dem everythin' There's nothin else yuh can give dem. So yuh mek sure it's de right man."

Both Pearl and Noel nodded. And since Constantine saw that she had their attention she added,"Meh know yuh hormones dem a rage on in unu bodies. And it's hard tuh resist temptation. Meh know. Meh nah come into dis marriage a virgin but dat is what meh wan' fi you two. Try an save yuhself for marriage. But if yuh cyan, come tuh me. Tell me before yuh do anything so meh can mek sure yuh protected and know what yuh doing. Unu undastand?"

Like her mother before her, Constantine wanted to ensure that her daughters didn't find themselves pregnant, trying to learn a new person before they had the chance to know themselves. And as much as she idolized her mother and knew she had wanted the best for her, Constantine realized she'd have to be more open, honest, and direct with her own children if they were going to avoid the same hurdles that tripped her up.

"And yuh know anotha ting. Please, please fin a man who respeck unu. Dere plenty men jealous ah de same woman who lay up next ta dem inna de bed every night. Das how yuh fadda him stay. Noel, when yuh was a baby meh tell him say meh wan start up mi own hair business. Paid de muney fi de classes dem. And de man sit right up at de table dere and tell me no. And meh, followin' behin 'im, meh nah do it. Yuh know how much muney meh coulda mek wid a salon? Meh coulda haf somethin fi pass down to unu. And 'im know it too. But meh mighta one day mek more muney dan him! And he cyan tek dat. But das why meh a tell yuh fin' unu someone who nah stifle yuh. Watch de man who seek fi control yuh, yuh mus run from dem."

Pearl and Noel, who had seen their mother's words mirrored in her marriage all their lives, knew she was telling the truth.

1970, Fifty

Last year, Clifton and Constantine both beamed with pride as they dropped their third son, Clifton Jr. off at the bus station where he was headed to Oakwood College in Huntsville, Alabama. Clifton told everyone he knew that his boy was going to school. For them, having come from so little in Jamaica and enduring grueling and sometimes demeaning work in the United States, it was with swelling pride that they enrolled their son in college to study psychology. For Clifton, who could barely read, having a son who bore his name go to college in America,was something he'd dreamt of but never prepared himself for the enormity of the feeling. It was during that sweep of emotion, that he told his youngest son, with tears rimming his eyes, that he was proud of him. As he boarded the bus, Constantine pretended as if she wasn't crying as she waved good-bye to him from the parking lot.

But the very next year, when it was time for his daughter to follow in her brother's footsteps, Clifton's reaction was entirely different. Noel had never really considered continuing her education after high school. She planned on living with her parents for a couple more years and then getting a job, preferably in a department store where she could be in charge of designing window displays. She hadn't mentioned her plan to anyone; but by the winter of her senior year, her father's words would change it.

One afternoon, Clifton and Constantine were sitting at the dining room table going over their mail together, when a bill from Oakwood came to their attention. Clifton opened it up and nearly spit the juice he'd just taken into his mouth, all over the paper. Constantine had been the one to help her son fill out his college applications and look for loans to help finance his education, so Clifton was a bit naive about the actual costs. That first tuition bill didn't taint the pride he felt for his son; it just removed the rose-colored glasses he'd been wearing.

And it reminded him that Noel would be graduating from high school that same year. Thinking about two children in college at the same time, beads of sweat started to collect at his temple. Leaving him to figure it out, Constantine got up from the table and went back into their bedroom to see if she could get a little bit of rest. Clifton remained at the table, rereading the numbers on the paper in his hand, hoping that they would change.

When Noel came home from school that afternoon, bringing the winter air in the house with her, Clifton called her into the dining room to discuss her future. "Noel, come siddown 'ere for a minute nuh."

She eyed her father suspiciously, wondering what he wanted. The two weren't necessarily accustomed to having heart-to-hearts at the dining room table . . . or anywhere for that matter.

"Yes, Daddy."

"Yuh know youse a high school senior now. Meh wan know haf yuh started tinking bout what yuh wan do after school."

Noel relaxed, realizing he didn't want to talk about anything too serious. "You know Daddy, I hadn't really thought about it too much. I was just going to get a job, maybe decorating the store windows downtown, and then move out in a few years or so."

Though Clifton should have been relieved by her answer, he took the opportunity to lecture her further. "How yuh mean yuh nah t'ought about it much? Yuh almos' eighteen, a grown woman now. From when meh was a likkle boy, just tree or five years old, meh know what meh wan be. First, meh wan be a lawyer. But meh nah haf de education fi dat. So meh say meh wan be a driver. And that's wah meh come to dis country and do."

Noel nodded, unimpressed with the story she had heard too many times before. Desperate to end the conversation she said, "Well, I think I still have enough time left to decide what I want to do."

Clifton's temper started to flare. "Yuh know is good yuh nah wan go to college like yuh brudda. Meh glad fi dat. Yuh nah haf no plan. Yuh would just go dere, waste up mi muney and come home pregnant. Meh nah pay for nuthin like dat." Clifton flung his hand into the air and let it hit the table with a thud for dramatic effect.

What Clifton hadn't known about his daughter was that she was stronger than he thought, stronger than her mother had been at that age and more like himself than he realized. Living in a house as dysfunctional as hers, Noel had learned from a very early age to tune out what was hurtful and harmful to her psyche and embrace what she could use. What she would take from this conversation was the negative decree he'd tried to place on her life and use it as motivation. Rather than discourage her, the fact that he believed she wasn't college material or would leave only to return pregnant, was all she needed to hear. And while this was the complete opposite of what he'd hoped to accomplish in this conversation, the seed had been planted.

And so Noel decided then and there, though it had never been a consideration, that she was going to go to college just like her brother. She didn't know what she was going to study, or if she would even enjoy the experience. She was going to enroll with the sole purpose of proving her father wrong.

And while she had made her decision, she still didn't have a response for her father's tirade. Anything she said would have been disrespectful and she had been groomed not to talk back to him. So instead, she stood up slowly, pushed her chair back in and went directly to her parents's room. Most children would have been broken by Clifton's words. Even if they had come to the decision Noel had, there might have been tears of dejection and disappointment in knowing that their own father didn't think them capable. And though Noel was wounded by his comments and would speak about them decades afterward, she had no tears to give her father. She was more motivated by disgust and indignation. And those feelings only yielded scowls.

She barged into her parents's room not bothering to knock. "Mommy, can you help me get into college like you did, Boysie?"

Constantine, who was sitting on the bed, checking her latest receipt from the grocery store to see if the cashier had swindled her, leaned back slightly, surprised at the inquiry. She'd asked Noel before if she wanted to go to school and had gotten a vague answer. So she'd left it alone, assuming she wasn't interested in continuing her education. She figured that she'd stay home and get married instead. Constantine saw nothing wrong with that as long as that's what she truly wanted to do. But today, looking in her eyes, she could tell something had shifted.

"Of course meh can help yuh. Meh nevah know yuh did wan go. Yuh nevah say nuthin about college. Wha' change yuh mind?"

"I had never really thought about going. You know school has never come particularly easy for me and I thought there wouldn't be any point in me choosing to continue on with my education after high school. It didn't seem to make sense. But just now Daddy called me into the dining room to tell me that he wouldn't waste his money sending me to college anyway because he was sure I was just going to wind up pregnant."

Constantine felt a rage rise from her belly all the way up to her forehead, producing an instant headache. She saw that behind Noel's own anger, her father had cut her deeply.

She looked into her daughter's face and saw her own, the day Theophilus informed her he wouldn't be paying for her to attend teacher's school. The corners of her lips twitched and then twisted as she remembered the scowl her father had worn when he told her he wouldn't pay for her additional schooling for the very same reason Clifton had given Noel. Grace Ann had been powerless to help her back then. But Constantine was living in a different day, in a different time and thankfully, she was in a position to do something.

So Constantine did for Noel what she wished Grace Ann had done for her. She didn't bother Clifton with this process; but once Noel filled out and sent her application, Constantine helped her fill out her financial aid forms. When she learned that the government wasn't going to pay her nearly enough to get through school, she went to the bank and took out a second mortgage on the house. And in the summer of that very same year, she and Clifton were back at the bus station sending their son and daughter off to Oakwood.

Constantine waited until the bus pulled away from the curb and out of her line of vision before she sobbed. She cried for the sense of justice that had been restored, for the completion of a goal it would take her daughter to manifest.

Clifton, who didn't fully understand her tears, patted her on the back as the two made their way back to the car, the triumph of their accomplishment tainted by the necessity of saying good-bye.

Now that four of Clifton and Constantine's six children were out of the house, there was less to distract Constantine from her husband. They were fighting more than ever about money, particularly with two children in college, his philandering and everything in between. The moments when they were civil to one another were virtually nonexistent now. Every day Constantine prepared herself for war in her own home. And none of this went unnoticed by Pearl and Maxine.

Pearl, in her thirteenth year, had seen her parents argue all her life, with few glimmers of hope in between. But now, with the heightened sensitivity and awareness of puberty, she realized that those glimmers, which were coming less and less often, represented freak accidents rather than any actual hope of reconciliation between her parents. The arguing that had perturbed her before, now made her feel anxious and unsafe. So she took measures to be away from home as much as possible. She enrolled in after-school programs and elected to attend summer school so she could be away from her feuding parents.

Pearl wasn't the only one trying to avoid the house in an attempt to escape their volatile household. Clifton was also spending more and more time away. If Constantine weren't so consumed with thoughts of what he might be doing and who he might be doing it with, she would have reveled in the independence. Instead, even the quiet of his absence troubled her.

In all the years they'd been married and all the times she'd questioned him about his loyalty to her, Clifton never admitted to anything. Constantine didn't need his validation to know the truth but a bit of proof came one day at church.

Constantine opened her eyes one Sabbath morning and felt her body sinking deeper and deeper into her mattress. The last thing she wanted to do was prepare Pearl, Maxine, and herself for church. She looked over at the crumpled sheets next to her where Clifton rested just hours ago and she knew the thought of skipping would remain just that. Someone would have to be on their deathbed before he'd allow any one of them to miss church. So she painfully lifted herself from the comfort of her pillow and went about the business of waking the girls.

Two hours later, when she was sitting in the pew at church, she realized she'd been so busy scrambling to get out of the house that she'd neglected to use the toilet that morning; but now, the feeling hit her. For the second time that day, Constantine lifted herself from another comfortable resting place and made her way to the restroom. After she'd finished in the stall, she stood in the mirror, letting her eyes linger on her face as she washed her hands. She looked as tired as she felt.

Just as she was sighing and shaking her head at the sight, Betty Schaffer, who was at least twenty years Constantine's senior, walked into the restroom. Constantine smiled quickly, hoping Betty wouldn't strike up a conversation.

Sister Schaffer's eyes darted nervously around the restroom. "Oh . . . Constantine . . . how—how are you today?"

"Meh doing fine, Sister Schaffer, just a likkle tired."

Constantine watched as Sister Schaffer nodded sympathetically before looking upward, clearly contemplating something.

"Connie . . . you know, I saw Clifton out driving the other day."

Constantine nodded, not sure why the woman felt the need to report a sighting of her husband.

"Well . . . he wasn't by himself. There was a . . . a woman with him." Sister Schaffer whispered the last part of the sentence, barely able to utter the indiscretion inside the four walls of the church.

Constantine was looking down into the bowl of the sink, unable to muster the strength to turn and face the woman. As the shame and humiliation roared and reared in competitive surges in her body, she knew there was defeat on her face. And just like Betty couldn't help but share this story, she knew she'd be eager to tell the other church ladies about Constantine's pathetic reaction.

Her fatigue, the news and the inevitable spreading of that news made

Constantine feel as if she was going to vomit. Instead, she calmed herself, swallowed the salvia, tinged with the taste of bile, and smoothed her clothes before turning to face Sister Schaffer.

"Tank yuh fa de information. Happy Sabbath to you." Then Constantine walked out of the restroom, leaving Sister Schaffer standing there, confused.

She kept up her act of coolness throughout the rest of service, partly because she knew Sister Schaffer was waiting and watching, anticipating some type of breakdown or outburst; and also because in that church pew, next to Clifton, she'd slipped into a comfortable state of numbness. Later, when she had more energy, she'd confront her husband.
After sunset, he left the house and returned, hours later, more jovial than usual.

Constantine wasted no time. "I spoke to Betty Schaffer today."

Clifton nodded, already anticipating the fallout from Constantine's tone. "Um-hm."

"Say she did see yuh de udda day."

Clifton's ears perked and he looked up, waiting for the dramatic reveal Constantine had become so famous for.

"She tell meh say she did see yuh wid ah nex woman."

Clifton reacted a little too quickly, kissing his teeth for too long. "De woman confused nuh. Meh neva had anudda woman wid me in de street. Mussa been someone else's husband she spy."

"Meh sure yuh know de woman she ah talk bout. Probably know 'ar biblically too. Mek me ask yuh somethin, is dis why yuh nevah have no muney for de children yuh have in dis house? How many more women yuh haf out dere? How many uh dem sit up inna de car yuh carry me and de children in?"

Clifton walked upstairs away from his screaming wife. Constantine followed him. The two reached the bedroom, where Clifton had started to take his clothes off, trying to get ready for bed as if they weren't having a discussion.

"While yuh run roun' trying fi impress de church people, is dem who spot yuh in de street." Constantine guffawed dryly. "Yuh nah fool nobody nah longer. Meh cyan wait fi see how yuh a go explain dis one. De people dem barely know yuh haf kids in Jamaica yuh nah see. Now yuh come tuh dis country and spreading yuhself even furda."

Clifton turned to her swiftly, contorting his face in anger. "Woman, shut up yuh noise nah!"

But the portal had been opened. Constantine had years's worth of anger and betrayal and disappointment to convey. Clifton walked toward the linen closet in the hallway and Constantine followed him, still prodding. "Meh nah undastand how yuh call yuhself a man ah God de way yuh run around town acting like a dawg. Meh hope yuh pray de Lord Jesus haf mercy on your soul."

At those words, Clifton grabbed the iron from the linen closet and turned to face his wife. "Wha yuh say to me?"

Constantine saw the iron and looked at it unfazed. She had so much adrenaline coursing through her body, she doubted she'd even feel the blow.

She repeated herself, more slowly this time. "Yuh nah hear me? Meh say, how yuh can call yuhself a man a God when yuh run round 'ere offering yuh dirty self to any 'oman breathing?"

Clifton lunged toward her, his breath labored. But instead of using the iron he still had in his hand, he pushed her and she fell backward into the wall at the end of the hallway.

Hearing the thud, Maxine ran out of her room, hoping that if her father saw her face, he'd stop. He didn't notice her presence. She watched as her father stepped toward her mother, who was attempting to collect herself. Maxine, acting quickly, ran in front of him.

"Don't touch her!" she cried out, attempting to make eye contact with her father.

Clifton paused for a second, seeing his daughter then he made a move to sidestep her. "Girl, move out de way!"

"No!" She hollered back at him.

Enraged by her disobedience, Clifton raised the iron to strike his youngest daughter. Constantine jumped up, running toward him. She grabbed his wrist before it had a chance to connect with Maxine.

"If yuh touch 'ar, meh promise yuh nah mek it truh de night." Constantine spoke softly, her eyes conveying the truthfulness behind her threat.

Clifton dropped his arm and the iron fell to the ground seconds later.

The next morning Clifton left the house early and Constantine sent her children off to school. Once they left, she wept. She had come to accept the abuse she had received from Clifton over the years but never had he raised his hand to any one of their daughters. He was the one who took over disciplining their sons once they got older and they had received plenty of beatings over the years. But the girls were different. It had never occurred to her that staying with her husband might have placed her daughters in danger.

When Pearl and Maxine came home from school, Constantine was thinking in the dining room, having already prepared dinner. Pearl came in and stood next to her mother's chair, looking down at her sunken frame.

"You need to divorce him."

Constantine quickly turned to face Pearl, unable to believe the words that had come from this child. When had she become so bold? Pearl's face remained resolute. After the shock subsided, she nodded her understanding.

If her daughter's words weren't enough for her, the next week she went to go speak to an attorney. Waiting in the drab, gray, and black lobby, she thought about how often she'd fantasized about this day. Just the thought of beginning what was surely going to be an arduous journey caused her to sigh. Still she knew in this type of exhaustion, there would eventually be triumph. She thought about the number of years she had wanted to divorce her husband. Maybe it started the first time he'd kicked her, causing her to lose their child. Or the time she learned that he had lied to her about his other children. She couldn't remember. But as often as she'd considered it, there was always something that held her back, the notion that her kids needed them to be together under one roof or that she wouldn't be able to make it without his financial support. But seeing Clifton charge after their daughter when she had done nothing but try to defend her suddenly allowed her to align her priorities properly. She was doing more harm than good waiting for Clifton to be a better man.

"Mrs. Reid." Mr. Smith, the man she hoped would be her attorney, peeked out of his office and called her name, letting her know he was ready to see her.

Constantine made a mental note to change her name back to Johnson when this was all over. She collected her things, stood up, and joined the man in his office.

"How can I help you today."

Constantine didn't know how to ask for a divorce with tact, so she just said it straight out. "I need a divorce but meh don wan mi husband to know that I'm filing just yet."

"Mrs. Reid, are you in any danger?" The divorce attorney, whose nameplate read Ethan Smith, posed the question with such little concern and emotion that he didn't even lift his head to ask it.

But Constantine took the question seriously, asking herself how Clifton might respond if she told him she was contemplating getting a divorce. Knowing his temperamental nature, there really was no telling. Things that set him off one day, he'd ignore the next. But announcing that she wanted a divorce would present a whole new set of challenges. One of them would have to move out and he was just vindictive enough to make her leave their home.

So Constantine responded, "Yes."

When she did, Mr. Smith looked up from his paperwork, his eyes peeking over the rim of his glasses. This clearly wasn't the first time he'd heard her type of story.

"Would you like for me to send law enforcement to your home?"

"What would they do?"

"Well, they would serve your husband with the papers and then escort him off the premises."

Constantine shuddered at the thought. Still, she was honest with herself and Mr. Smith.

"Yes, meh ah need the police."

During the rest of their visit, Mr. Smith asked her about the nature of their marriage why she wanted a divorce, had her husband expressed interest in one, what assets did she feel she was entitled to, would child custody be an issue. Constantine could have been in there for hours discussing the reasons she and her husband never should have been together but she kept it as brief and as succinct as possible, recognizing that the more she said about him, the worse it reflected on her for having stayed nearly thirty years. Plus, looking at the top of Mr. Smith's head as she spoke, she realized he had tapped out again, listening only for key words.

Within three weeks, while Pearl and Maxine were sitting around the house on a Sunday afternoon, there was a knock at the door. Mr. Smith

313

had called Constantine the night before telling her the police would be there sometime that day. She had been jumping at any and all noises in anticipation of the inevitable drama.

Clifton didn't flinch, assuming his wife was going to answer the door. When he saw she made no movement, he jumped up from his seat, unaware that his life would be forever changed by what was on the other side of that door. Two policemen greeted him. Clifton's stomach dropped and he felt the blood rush to his face as he wondered which one of his children were in trouble or danger. Then he ran down the list of the things he could have possibly done to bring them to his doorstep. Whatever it was, Clifton knew it was time to perform.

To convey some type of good breeding, he spoke in his British accent. "How can I help you today, officers?"

"Are you Mr. Clifton Reid, sir?"

"Yes, that is me."

"Mr. Reid we're here to serve you with divorce papers . . ."

The tact and decorum he had intended to present disappeared instantly.

"Whaaat?!"

"Mr. Reid, your wife has filed for divorce and we have a court order from her attorney requesting that you vacant the premises upon receipt of this notice."

The officers stepped across the threshold before Clifton could close the door in their faces. Once they were inside, assuming ownership and leadership of the space, one of the police officers closed the door behind them. Clifton experienced a flash of gratitude, not wanting his neighbors to see the policemen darken his doorstep. Having calmed a bit, he found words to articulate his disbelief.

"Meh nah curr what de paper dere say. Meh nah leaving de house after meh work all mi life fah it. Meh pay all of de bills here, mi wife haf no right to it."

"Sir, it says here that the wife is the primary caregiver for your children, is that correct?"

"Well, yes but . . ."

"Well, until your case can be presented to a judge, your wife is entitled to the house for the sake of the children."

Clifton threw his hands up in the air, looking around for Constantine for the first time since the officers had showed up.

She was in the corner of the living room, her face at rest, looking past her shocked and now legally estranged husband. She hadn't even bothered to send her children upstairs to their rooms. They sat in stunned silence, watching the day they'd thought would never come, almost outside of themselves. Constantine wanted her daughters to see that she had finally come to her senses and was practicing the same principles she had been trying to instill in them about demanding respect from the men in their lives.

After arguing back and forth with the officers, one of them finally said, "Listen, Mr. Reid, I know you don't want to leave your house but you really have no choice today. You can grab a couple of things and walk out, on your own accord, with dignity, or we can handcuff you and escort you downtown."

That did it.

Clifton wasn't fond of the idea of being arrested but he would have fared better in jail than he would have in front of the court of public opinion. It would only be a matter of time before the whole town, including his church members, knew that he had been arrested and thrown out of his house. They would all jump to conclusions about what it was exactly he had done, likely making the situation more dramatic and salacious than it already was. No one would blame Constantine. And so, flashing her a look of pure disdain, he made his way upstairs to their bedroom, to collect a few of his belongings. The policemen followed him.

Constantine wondered where he would go but then she reminded herself that now it was no longer her concern. The days of wondering about his whereabouts were over. She'd have to train herself to stop worrying about his actions. He'd finally have the freedom to do what he'd been doing all along.

Once he was gone, Constantine searched the upstairs, looking for the things he had taken with him. With the exception of his toothbrush, there really was no dramatic difference. He'd left the drawers open in a sign of defiance but they were all still mostly full. She looked around what used to be their bedroom, closed the door, lay across the bed, and cried. They were soft, slow-building sobs that she tried her best to stifle so as not to alarm Maxine and Pearl, who were no doubt waiting for her to emerge. She wept for herself. For the time she had wasted, the dreams she had sacrificed, and the way she had allowed herself to be dishonored for decades. She cried for the dysfunction she had allowed her children to witness and for the discontent she felt knowing that, in a perverse and confusing way, she loved him despite his mistreatment of her and all of his flaws.

In the following months, Clifton and Constantine were called to appear in court. Constantine only asked for the house, child support, and that Clifton continue making payments for Boysie and Noel's education. All she would have to prove was that she was still raising their children, deserved to maintain full custody, and was in need of the house for that reason. While she knew the truth and what she was entitled to, the thought of standing in front of a judge arguing this nearly made her break out in hives. She hadn't migrated to this country to interact with the legal system, just as she'd never had to do so in Jamaica.

Constantine knew that anyone who knew the realities of her marriage, as she and Clifton did, would not have hesitated to give her everything she asked for. All the evidence was there. But she also knew she wouldn't be judged by an insider; an impartial judge would hear her case and everything was at stake. She doubted that Clifton would apply for custody unless he simply wanted to spite her. He could prove that he was better suited financially to care for Maxine and Pearl but it would be unheard of for the judge to grant sole custody, especially girlchildren, to a father. Her struggle would be to keep the house.

The day of her hearing, Constantine wore a stark white skirt suit. Superficially she believed it would make her appear more innocent and angelic. She took one last look at herself in the hallway mirror before reaching for the doorknob. As her hand hung suspended in the air, a voice stopped her and told her to pray.

Disregarding the color of her skirt, Constantine knelt. As soon as she reached this vulnerable and humbling position, she felt tears spring to her eyes. She whispered the words, "Fadda God bless mi today in de courtroom. Mek meh tell mi side of the story so clearly dat de judge him cyan help but do what's right in de divorce. Please God, don mek me lose dis house. And Lord above all else Jesus, let mi keep de girls dem unda one roof. Let de trut' be told an help me emerge victorious. Let the words of my mouth and the meditation of my heart be acceptable in thy sight. Oh Lord, my strength and my redeemer. It's in yuh son's Jesus name I pray. Amen."

Constantine stood slowly, brushing any hint of dirt away from the suit. Thankfully, she had just mopped the floors and there was none.

She went back to the mirror and retouched the areas of her face that had been smudged before heading out the door.

Later that evening, when Constantine returned to the house, she knelt at that same spot and thanked God for answering her prayer.

1972, Fifty-two

Though he'd always lived like a bachelor, Clifton found that the actual life itself was rather lonely. There was no one to come home to. He had to fix his own meals. And most of all, he noticed, more so than ever before, just how much his children preferred their mother over him.

Whenever Noel or Boysie came home from school for their Christmas or summer breaks, he had to beg and bargain to get them to come over to his apartment. And when they were finally there, he employed tactics to make them stay. He cooked food that they all loved but only their youth could stomach. He told stories they'd heard a thousand times. He tried to shame them with talk of mortality and honoring one's parents. He pulled out playing cards, a checkerboard, and his favorite, dominoes. It didn't matter that Noel had never learned to play and Boysie wasn't particularly interested. In his yearning for company, he grasped for straws.

It was with the knowledge that she'd be trapped that Noel, during the final days of her Christmas break, ventured over to Clifton's apartment one evening. The holiday had already passed and Clifton told her that he wanted to cook dinner for her before she went back to school.

When she got there, not only had her father not started cooking dinner, he told her to make herself comfortable while he hopped in the shower. Noel sighed, settling in front of the television he'd set up in his halfway decorated living room. She'd just found the program she wanted to watch in the meantime when the phone rang.

Normally, she would have ignored it. But Clifton, fresh from the shower heard it too and called out for Noel to answer.

"Hello," Noel said.

There was the distinct sound of heavy breathing on the other end.

Noel, irritated now, asked "Hello?" louder and more sternly than before. The person on the other line cleared her throat before speaking. "This is Eleanor Hayes . . . who am I speaking with . . . is this Noel?"

Noel relaxed, realizing that this was one of her parents's friends, probably someone from church.

"Yes, this is Noel. Who would you like to speak with?"

"Well, I called to speak with your father. But now that I have you on the phone, I just thought you should know that you have a little brother on the way."

Noel clutched the receiver tighter as she felt it slipping from her grasp.

"I'm sure you'll be hearing from me soon," the woman said coolly before Noel was jarred by the sound of the dial tone.

She stood stunned for a moment, still processing what she'd just heard. Just as she managed to move to place the receiver back in the cradle, her father came bounding out of his bedroom, freshly showered and smiling at the thought of spending time with his daughter. "Who call?"

Noel turned to him slowly, her eyes narrowing. "A woman named Eleanor Hayes . . ."

The comfortable smile Clifton wore turned stale, his lips eventually resting in an uncomfortable twist.

". . . she told me that I have a little brother on the way."

Clifton moved quickly, stepping toward Noel, his arms outstretched as a peace offering. "Okay, okay . . . come siddown 'ere. Mek meh tell yuh wha' happen."

Noel reluctantly followed her father to the couch. She heard the laugh track from the show she had wanted to watch minutes earlier and resented the fact that she found nothing funny in this moment.

"Dis 'oman . . . she invite me to 'ar 'ouse. And when meh get dere . . ." Clifton paused for a moment, reaching out to touch his daughter's hand as a gesture of comfort as he said the next words, ". . . she rape me." Noel, shocked not only by her father's brazenness but also by the fact that he took her for such a fool, snatched her hand away from him in disbelief.

Clifton stared at her, desperately waiting for a response.

319

Speaking softly and slowly, so as to pad the harshness of her words, Noel looked directly at her father. "Daddy, don't repeat that...that story to anyone else."

Though Noel had recently transitioned into adulthood, and would have been allowed to use the word "lie" she still had enough respect not to outright accuse her father of lying. After all, "story" was particularly appropriate in this context, given the tale her father had just spun.

Clifton understood the meaning and appreciated the respect, though he questioned whether his daughter thought he deserved it right now. True, he and Constantine had been divorced for going on two years. But until he remarried, according to his beliefs, he wasn't supposed to be having sex. And though Clifton, in his moments of true honesty with himself had to admit that his children knew him to be less than a beacon of morality, he still felt the obligation to at least put up a good front. And a baby when he was still newly divorced wasn't the best way to represent the standard he only pretended to uphold.

After she left her father's apartment that evening, Noel wrestled with the decision of whether or not to tell her mother about the new sibling she had on the way. She knew Constantine would pretend like she didn't care, only to agonize about it for weeks. And while she would have wanted to shield her mother from this agony, there was no way an entire human being could remain a secret.

As she was weighing the decision, she did tell her siblings. One by one they shook their heads in a combination of astonishment and disgust. Still, somehow the thought of their father having a child in his sixties didn't seem that much outside of the realm of possibility. It was quintessential Clifton Reid.

Months later, Noel calculated that her younger brother would be arriving soon. Thinking about the ways in which complete strangers had humiliated her mother in the past with information she should have known, Noel reasoned that it was time to tell Constantine that her ex-husband was going to be a father again.

This time, home briefly for spring break, Noel sat on the edge of her mother's bed watching her tidy her already neat bedroom. Constantine swept the linoleum floor so briskly, Noel was sure she was developing calluses on her hands. Constantine stopped moving briefly to survey all she had accomplished. Watching her, Noel was assured that there would never be a right time. This was their life and all they could do was acknowledge it for what it really was and seek to move forward.

"Mommy, I want to tell you something."

The bristles quieted against the floor as Constantine braced herself for bad news.

"This past Christmas when I was over Daddy's apartment, a woman called and told me that she was expecting his child, that I had a little brother on the way."

Constantine scoffed before she began sweeping again.

Noel sat, waiting for her mother to continue.

"Meh and de man divorce now. 'im can do whatever and whoever 'im like." She paused to sweep before interrupting herself again. "Da man in him sixties and him still run round go chase women! Jeezus, 'im nausty, yuh see?!" Constantine bit her tongue after that, lest she say anything else about Noel's father.

But later, left with the deafening silence of her own thoughts, Constantine wished this baby had popped up sooner, before she and Clifton were divorced. The child would have served as evidence that she wasn't crazy or paranoid and her husband was exactly who she always knew him to be.

Though Clifton had been ordered to pay child support, now that he no longer lived in the house she was responsible for their mortgage. Constantine had started a job working at a local hospital and though it paid a bit better than the domestic work she was doing in people's homes, it wasn't enough to take care of everything comfortably. So she decided to get on public assistance. Welfare.

Constantine had once pitied the women she'd known who relied on it. And she was always grateful that was never her situation. But these days, with children in college and two on their way, Constantine wasn't above it. As hard as she'd worked in this country, they could help her out for a bit. On welfare, Constantine was able to make the improvements on the house that she'd always wanted to make while Clifton was there. With the supplemental income, she patched up their old furniture or bought entirely new pieces. She had someone come and pave the walkway, like she'd been begging Clifton to do for years now. His money always seemed better spent elsewhere. The house was looking so nice that Clifton had no choice but to notice.

One day, after Pearl and Maxine got in his car, he could no longer stifle his curiosity. "Meh see yuh mudda makin some improvements to de house dere. How she afford all dat?"

Maxine and Pearl hadn't been sworn to secrecy. But they didn't need to be. "She just has a good job now." And he remained perplexed at what he regarded as her newfound sense of autonomy.

1974, Fifty-four

All the years Pearl had spent in summer school had allowed her to graduate high school a full year early. And she followed in her brother's and sister's footsteps and enrolled in Oakwood College. Like Noel, Pearl wasn't particularly interested in college initially but she realized that it would be a great place to get away from the chaos and dysfunction at home and also find a husband. He'd be someone educated and since Oakwood was a Seventh Day Adventist college, he'd also share her faith. So in 1974, after Boysie had graduated, Pearl and Noel rode the bus back to Huntsville by themselves.

Boysie came home and got his own apartment, so that just left Maxine and Constantine in the house together. As much as she'd loved raising all her children, Constantine, with grandchildren now, lacked the patience she needed to deal with the mood swings and manners of a teenage girl.

In the home stretch of the journey of raising children to adulthood, Constantine found that Maxine certainly wasn't going to make that last lap easy. And while her hormones produced an ornery nature and slick mouth, Maxine was perceptive enough to see and empathize with her mother's fatigue. Constantine had spent every single year of her adulthood raising at least one child. And though her mother never told her so, Maxine felt a great pressure to grow up and give her mother the peace that had been evading her for the past forty years.

Dealing with Maxine, Constantine thought of an adage she'd heard repeated throughout her childhood about two grown women not being able to exist peacefully in a house together. Her own life had disproved the theory; but what was true was that a little girl pretending to be a grown woman in the face of a real one could result in a homicide. And Constantine wouldn't be the victim.

Thankfully, before it got to that point, Clifton offered a solution.

He came over one day, suggesting that they send Maxine to a private high school in Cicero, Indiana. Constantine had her reservations, but figured both of them could use a break from one another. And she agreed. No one had really asked Maxine her opinion about going away for school. But if they had she would have gladly obliged. Being away from home, away from people who knew her father and his reputation, who knew that she was his child, was just the type of escape she had been looking for.

The year they sent Maxine off to school in Cicero, Noel graduated college. Despite his initial feelings and outright discouragement, Clifton was proud of his daughter for having earned her degree. He arrived in Huntsville, Alabama, for her graduation, with his mustache freshly shaped, dressed in his finest suit. On campus, he staged an impromptu photo shoot with his newly accomplished daughter. He boasted to anyone who would listen that not one, but two of his children had graduated back to back and Pearl would be next. Clifton insisted on meeting some of Noel's professors. And as she stood there, having made the necessary introductions, she rolled her eyes as she heard her father lie to impress these educators.

"Yuh know when Noel come tell me say she wan go to college and study. Meh did know we nevah had de muney but yuh know de Lord provide. He work a miracle so meh could pay for 'ar education."

Noel had spent years watching her father lie to people he felt inferior to, but she never got over the boldness of his untruths. The Lord had indeed provided but He certainly hadn't used Clifton to do so. The suggestion was insulting to all the work she and her mother had done to get her to this point. But she dared not confront her father and discredit him in public. So she simply shook her head, letting his pride flourish under falsehood.

Though he pretended he had, Clifton hadn't forgotten about what he'd said to his daughter during their conversation years ago. And while he couldn't acknowledge or even apologize for the way he'd spoken to her, he tried to make amends by arranging for the two of them to visit London as a graduation present.

Whether it was the air across the water or because he felt free from the responsibilities of his real life, visiting his relatives overseas, Clifton was different in London. And Noel preferred this version of her father. While he annoyed her with his showboating, she enjoyed seeing Buckingham Palace, Big Ben, and the changing of the guard with him. Having grown in a colonized Jamaica, she found he knew more about the country than his shoddy accent let on.

Throughout her entire childhood, comparing her father to her mother, she'd thought no one was more strict and rigid with their religious beliefs and practices, until she met her uncles in England and discovered her father was more liberal than she'd imagined. She left London with a newfound appreciation for the man.

When she got back to America, a rude reality awaited her.

Once she left London, Noel set about the arduous task of securing a job in her field, interior decorating. She went on interview after interview only to hear manager after manager tell her, in one way or another, "You're very talented but we're looking for someone with a bit more experience." When she explained that she had been in college for the past five years, studying, they wished her the best of luck and showed her to the door. After months of job searching, still living under her mother's roof, Noel was ready to branch out. She had given up the dream of becoming an interior decorator and decided to settle for any job that would allow her to move out of the house in which she'd spent a majority of her life. Like so many of her siblings, Noel attempted to avoid the drama of her home. And so, during her summers in college, she traveled, visiting friends who lived all over the country and getting a summer job in their cities so she could both enjoy herself and save some money for school. She had tasted a bit of independence and she wanted that for herself now that she had graduated.

Once she procured a job at a local hospital downtown, working as a respiratory therapy assistant, she started saving money for the next step, moving into a place of her own.

With Maxine in high school in Cicero and Pearl in Alabama, Noel was the only other person in the house. Since she knew it would be the first time Constantine would ever live by herself, Noel wanted to prepare her for the transition. "Mom, how would you feel about me moving out in the next few months or so?"

Constantine bristled at the thought but she suppressed the feeling. She knew it was important that women these days find their own way. And she vowed to be there to help her daughter do so.

"Meh tink it's good yuh get yuh own place and pay yuh own bills."

Noel took her mother's words to mean just that. So she found a place to live, believing she had Constantine's blessing. Having just started a new position, with student loans closing in on her, Constantine cosigned for the apartment and Noel paid the first month's rent as a deposit.

During the whole process, Constantine said little to nothing about the move. She merely provided her feedback when Noel went shopping, buying odds and ends for her new place. Weeks before she was set to move, she helped Noel organize, label and box her belongings.

Everything was going according to plan until moving day arrived. From the moment her feet hit the floor that day, Constantine felt strange and unsettled. As Noel started moving boxes to the car, the reality of the situation started to hit her. She looked around saw herself in that house, alone for the first time that day. And she imagined herself trying to find her way around in the darkness without her mother, husband, and children. She was lost both in identity and purpose. The thought of being confronted with that person, without distraction, for the first time, was terrifying.

Constantine knew then that she couldn't allow this move to happen. She had to do something to get her daughter to stay. She reasoned it would have to be something drastic. After all, a deposit had already been paid. She watched anxiously as Noel carted box after box to the car. And suddenly she started to feel nauseated. And that's when it occurred to her. She'd fake a sickness. A big one. With this thought the nausea subsided and Constantine leapt into a performance so convincing she shocked herself.

Noel trotted back in the house, excited about starting over in her new apartment. "Okay, Mom, I only have one more box left. You want to ride over with me and help get the big stuff set up?"

Constantine nodded feebly as she watched Noel run up the stairs and grab the last of her belongings. As Noel was coming back down the stairs, Constantine waited until she cleared the landing to start her scene.

Leading with the fleshiest part of her leg, she flung herself on the ground. As she was going down, Constantine grabbed on to the end table's edge, causing a few knick-knacks to hit the floor for effect.

"Oh!"

Noel dropped the boxes and ran to her side. "Mom! Are you okay, what happened?!"

Once her daughter was in the right position, she clutched her chest so tightly the jagged sides of her nails snagged the fabric of her dress. Constantine spoke in a hoarse, staccato, still holding onto herself. "Mi . . . chest . . ."

Noel cradled her mother's upper body in her arms. "Your chest! Oh God, let me call the ambulance."

Constantine broke character for a moment. Her voice was too strong as she nearly screamed, "No!" The last thing she needed was another bill. Catching herself, she softened her tone, "Jus stay 'ere wid me."

And that's exactly what Noel did and not just for that night. She lost her security deposit at what would have been her new apartment, unpacked all of the boxes she and her mother had diligently filled over the past few weeks, and moved back into her childhood room. It would be months before she came to the realization of how her mother had played her. Constantine never mentioned it and never had another cardiac episode again.

1977, Fifty-seven

Pearl had been in school for just a year before she came home and announced that she would be marrying her college boyfriend, Clark. From the times she'd met him before, during the holidays, Constantine approved. But that didn't mean she wasn't watching him, making sure her daughter had chosen well. By this time, Alton was on his second marriage. Thankfully, his current wife seemed like she had a bit more sense than the first and, in the five years they'd been married, they already had two sons, living in California. In both Alton's marriages, Constantine hadn't had much of a say. But this wouldn't be the case with Pearl, or with any of her daughters. This was the first big wedding for her children and she knew she'd have a hand in the details so she was delighted when Pearl came and asked for her mother's help. As the planning and preparations for the wedding increased, Constantine found that she had to interact more with Clifton than she had in the past few years.

She'd forgotten how obnoxious and overbearing the man could be, strutting around bragging about how he was paying for everything. One night, during the week of the wedding, Constantine, Noel, and Pearl were coming from the rehearsal dinner in which Clifton had been particularly annoying. Since the dinner had ended, Constantine had not stopped complaining about him. In the car on the way home, she was talking a mile a minute.

"Yuh see how 'im stan up dere and puff 'im chest out like he ah really do somethin. Yuh would think is 'im dat getting married."

Noel and Pearl rode in silence, ignoring their mother's rants.

It continued even when they got home, Constantine walked throughout the house disrobing and preparing for bed, still talking about him, the focus shifting from him peacocking at the dinner to his flaws in general.

"If de people dem knew how 'im stay dey would ah nevah listen tuh him carry on suh. All de times 'im ah choose fi spend 'is muney on de women in de street over 'is own pickney dem. Mi wonder what dem would have to say 'bout dat!"

Noel noticed that Pearl was starting to grow as tired of the soliloquy as she was. This was supposed to be a joyous time and even this new life that Pearl was trying to create with a man was being marred by her parents's relationship. And Constantine and Clifton weren't even married anymore.

Finally, Noel had had enough. "Mom, how long do you think you're going to allow him to control your life like this?"

Constantine was stunned into silence, her mouth hanging open.

Noel continued, "It's over. It's done. You two aren't together anymore, you don't have to worry about him anymore, and yet you *still* spend so much time thinking about him. You already gave him almost thirty years of your life. How many more are you going to give him?"

There was too much truth behind Noel's words for Constantine to refute them. So she stood, still and silent in this truth, wondering what it meant that she was still talking about Clifton after they had been divorced for almost eight years. As much as she tried to convince herself that he was no longer her concern, nearly thirty years of destructive habits and twisted thoughts were hard to abandon.

Then Constantine shifted her train of thought from her own accountability to address the daughter who always seemed to find a way to expose a new weakness. "Ah, chil' please. Yuh talk but if yuh knew like meh . . . if yuh lived it, yuh ah chat bout de man too."

It was no secret that she hadn't forgiven him. She didn't know if she'd ever be able to. But she too was disturbed by the amount of time she still devoted to thinking and speaking his name. Later, reflecting again on Noel's words, Constantine understood that the divorce hadn't done anything to resolve any of the wounds that she'd carried and nursed for decades. That would be another journey in and of itself.

1980, Sixty

As the years passed, Constantine knew that if she were ever going to have a life untainted by her ex-husband, she'd have to keep herself busy. Since her mother had died she hadn't visited Jamaica much. So she made plans to go there. And then, in between she visited her grandchildren: Alton's sons, Brenton and Kyle in California, Winston's only son, Winston Jr., in Indianapolis, and Boysie's young children, James and Nicole, to occupy her time.

When she was at home, sitting still, she watched Noel. Her eldest daughter seemed happy enough; but she wondered if watching Pearl get married troubled her at all. Constantine wanted to broach the conversation without making it feel as if she was pressuring the twenty-seven-year-old. Both the Lord and Constantine knew that it could wait, if at all possible.

One evening, she decided to check in. When Noel had just come home from work, she told her to come sit down with her in the living room. "Yuh know mi been meaning to ask yuh somethin."

Noel nodded expectantly.

"How yuh did feel at Pearl's wedding? Yuh feel yuh shoulda marry first?"

Noel nodded, but in understanding not in agreement. Though she hadn't been expecting the question, she could sense that her mother had been watching her more closely than usual, sticking by her side during Pearl's wedding. "You know, I do wonder sometimes when it'll be my turn. But I was happy for Pearl and I'm not going to rush into something just to be married. I want it to be right."

Constantine beamed internally but nodded coolly. She felt like a sage teacher watching her pupil pass an important test. She knew that there had been plenty of moments in her life when she hadn't made the right decisions as a mother or as a young woman. But if she could at least teach her daughters to pick good men, then she would have done something right. The last thing she needed was yet another generation of Johnson women suffering at the hands of their spouses. And so she commended her daughter.

"Good. No need fi rush. Twenty-seven is still young, yuh know? Nah bodda chase de men dem. Dey will be dere. Tek yuh time and mek sure he's a nice man."

Constantine thought for a second. "Mek mi ask yuh anotha question, yuh still saving yuhself?"

She knew Noel to be honest and if she'd said she was a virgin, it was true.

"Yes, mom, I'm still a virgin." Noel said, rolling her eyes a bit, anticipating the day that would no longer be the case.

1981, Sixty-one

The time would come sooner than she expected. A year later, a man named Dewayne started working at the hospital in the respiratory therapy department with Noel. She thought he was attractive but stories of him being connected to several women around the hospital made her stay away. During her very deliberate attempt to avoid him, Dewayne had noticed her anyway and he had no intention of keeping his distance. He just knew that he would have to bid his time.

After weeks of watching her, Dewayne finally saw an opportunity. Noel was having a conversation with one of their coworkers about a doctor's obligations.

"A doctor has to stop and help someone in danger." Noel said to one of her coworkers.

"Yeah, I think they're bound by the Hippocratic Oath, right?" the coworker asked.

"Right. That's it."

Dewayne, who had been standing on the perimeter of the discussion, spoke up. "Actually, no, you're both wrong."

Noel sighed, rolling her eyes. Not only was this guy a womanizer, he was nosey and conceited too. She didn't plan on acknowledging him any further. But her coworker was interested to hear his thoughts.

"How so?"

Noel tore her face up, wishing her coworker would ignore him.

"The Hippocratic Oath is a vow of all the things doctors should do when treating patients and practicing medicine but it doesn't say anything about being required to help people in the street. And there are no legal consequences if a doctor violates the oath." As he spoke, Dewayne studied Noel's expressions carefully, amused rather than insulted by the contortion of her face. When he was finished speaking, a sly smirk spread, turning the corners of Dewayne's lips.

"I don't know about that." Noel said, eyeing him suspiciously.

"It's okay to be wrong."

Noel felt her face get hot. "I'm not wrong and furthermore, we weren't speaking to you."

"I believe your colleague asked for my input and I gave it."

"Well, I'm done with this conversation."

Noel spun on her heel and started walking away from this smug man.

Dewayne, seeing that he was about to miss his opportunity, followed behind her.

"You know, I'm coming over your house for dinner this evening."

Noel stopped dead in her tracks. "What did you say?"

Dewayne's smirk turned into a full-on smile. "I'm coming to your house for dinner this evening. What's your address?"

Noel was shocked by his presumptuous demand. In any other circumstance, she would have never entertained such a ridiculous offer. But today, she considered it. This was one of the perks of still living with her mother. She was in no immediate danger. Not wanting Dewayne to get too cocky, she only nodded slightly before writing her address down on a slip of paper that he had conveniently fished out of his pocket.

It wasn't until she walked away from Dewayne that she realized how absurd the whole thing had been. But by this time her curiosity had been piqued. They'd have dinner and he'd meet her mother in the same evening. She knew that if Constantine had any reservations or objections, she wouldn't hesitate to share them.

Noel rushed home from work that evening to prepare her mother for the strange man that was on his way to their home. "Mommy, we're having company for dinner. I know it's kind of last-minute, but he invited himself over."

"How yuh mean 'im invite 'imself over?"

"Well, we were having a discussion at work and when it ended, he told me he was coming to dinner. I was so shocked I just ended up giving him our address."

Constantine raised her eyebrows in intrigue. What type of fresh man was this? But because her daughter, who had always had a level head about herself, had given him their address, she was at least partially interested. "Meh a go call yuh brudda jus in case de man crazy."

Constantine nodded in approval at her own suggestion before moving to the kitchen to prepare a meal that would require minimal effort but still impress their guest for the evening.

Winston showed up a half an hour later. "Noel, so what's this Mommy tells me about you having a man over here tonight?"

"He's a guy I work with." Noel left it at that. Telling Winston a stranger had invited himself over with no notice would not go over well.

The doorbell rang sooner than she expected, at seven forty-five. Noel had told him to be there by eight. Thankfully, he wouldn't catch her unprepared. While her mother finished dinner, she'd already showered and changed out of her work scrubs. Not knowing really what to expect on the other side of the door, she wore a perplexed expression when she turned the knob. But when she opened it to reveal Dewayne's face, framed by a pair of oversized glasses, her expression softened and transformed into a sincere, welcoming smile. She noticed that he carried a bottle in his hand.

Seeing Noel's eyes sizing up the bottle in his arms, Dewayne turned the label toward her. It was sparkling grape juice.

"I wasn't sure if you drank or not, so I figured this would be a happy medium."

Noel smiled, grateful that she wouldn't have to tell him that she didn't drink and certainly not in front of her mother.

"Good choice. I don't drink really. Come in."

Dewayne followed her into the living room.

She hadn't mentioned that she lived with her mother and she was anxious to see how he'd react to the news that they wouldn't be alone. "My mother's almost finished cooking and my brother's here for dinner tonight. The dining room's back this way."

When they rounded the corner, they were greeted by the sight of Winston, seated at the head of the table, his hands clasped. He wore a gold chain nestled in his thick, black chest hair. It caught the light from the small chandelier above the table.

"Winston, this is Dewayne." Noel looked from one to the other, hoping both men would find a way to keep things civil.

Dewayne, at the other end of the table, nodded in acknowledgment, "Nice to meet you, man." He knew immediately that Winston, in a tank top that displayed his bulging muscles, was there as a very effective intimidation tactic.

Constantine had heard the doorbell and the brief introductions. Now she was anxious to meet this man. She quickly washed and dried her hands before stepping into the dining room.

Seeing her enter, Noel shifted the attention from Winston to her mother.

"And this is my mother, Ms. Johnson."

Dewayne extended his hand to greet her. "Nice to meet you, Ms. Johnson. Thank you for having me over on such short notice."

Constantine raised her eyebrows again as she smiled. This red-skinned man had the nerve to make a joke about his own rudeness.

But by the end of the evening, after asking all types of questions about his family, his education, and his opinions, Constantine had determined that she liked him. He was ballsy but respectful and seemed pretty intelligent. But he was still a man and there was no way she could be persuaded after one night. She'd known men who wore masks for much longer than a single dinner.

***

After that first dinner and several dates later, Dewayne made a habit of spending time with both Noel and Constantine, getting into mock arguments with his girlfriend's mother.

One evening, as Constantine sat at the dining room table gushing about the recent wedding of Prince Charles and Diana. Noel and Dewayne rolled their eyes at the other end, unamused.

Completely comfortable at this point, Dewayne blurted, "I don't know why you care about those people anyway."

No matter how many times they play fought each other, Constantine was always taken aback by the boy's brazenness. "But why yuh ah worry bout wha meh ah care bout?"

"You think those British people care about Black folks?"

"How yuh ah know dem nah care? Everythin nah 'bout Black an White, wid yuh fair skin self. Meh was raised ah British citizen. So meh care what de people dem in England ah do."

"You were only British because they colonized the islands and brought Africans over as slaves. You think those same people care about Blacks today?" Dewayne chuckled for dramatic effect. "You go over there and see if they treat you like a citizen."

Having had enough and realizing that Dewayne had a point, Constantine attempted to end the discussion. "Oh boy! Shut up yah noise."

Dewayne bucked at the command. He'd had several tense discussions but he had yet to master the art of Jamaican discourse. So he took offense to the phrase. He'd always found "shut up" to be demeaning and dismissive. "Please don't tell me to shut up. I'll be quiet but I won't shut up."

Constantine nodded, but she made a mental note. Now that she knew the word bothered him so much, she was determined to use it again. Staring at him from across the table, she paused for dramatic effect, narrowed her eyes, and said it again, slowly, enunciating and pronouncing every syllable, "No, meh say. Shut. Up."

Dewayne was on to her game. And so he responded to his elder, his girlfriend's mother, with, "No, *you* shut up."

Constantine's eyes widened and then narrowed as she measured this young man up and down. She didn't say anything else but smirked and chuckled under her breath..

Noel didn't find it so funny. Later, as she dropped Dewayne off at his apartment, Noel was uncharacteristically silent. Dewayne, sensing her change in demeanor, asked what was wrong.

"I didn't like the way you told Mommy to shut up," she answered.

He smiled slightly, seeing that she really was upset. "Your mother was obviously testing me, Noel. I asked her very politely not to speak to me that way and she kept on. What was I supposed to do?"

Noel sighed, "I don't know but not that."

1983, Sixty-three

After a year of dating, Dewayne and Noel were engaged. While

Constantine was excited about the union, when Noel told her father about the engagement, Clifton had a completely different reaction. Though he had met Dewayne on several occasions and thought he was at least decent, he assumed that Noel wouldn't take him seriously as a Baptist, or at least force him to change his denomination for her.

"Yuh say Dewayne is a man of God nah?"

"Yes, Daddy he believes in God, he's a Christian."

"But not an Adventist."

"No, he's not. He was raised Baptist."

Clifton kissed his teeth dramatically. "Him nevah tink about converting for yuh? Yuh sure 'im love yuh?"

Noel, losing her patience and manners, rolled her eyes openly. "Yes, Daddy, I'm sure he loves me. I never even thought of asking him to convert. Convert for what? He's a Christian."

"Well if 'im not an Adventist, yuh nah get married at the church."

Noel, looked her father, unmoved. "That's fine."

Clifton, surprised that this didn't give her pause, decided to try something else. "Well, meh cyan walk yuh down de aisle at a church dat not Adventist."

Noel thought for a second about the seriousness of this threat. She didn't know if her father was bluffing or not; but with everything else she had to plan and worry about, she didn't have time to stress about his inevitable shenanigans.

"I'm sure I'll be able to find someone else to do it, Daddy." With that, she stood up, leaving him dumbfounded and disappointed.

A week before her wedding, after she'd asked Boysie to walk her down the aisle, she learned that unlike her college tuition, Clifton was bluffing this time. Though he would have preferred Dewayne convert, he wasn't going to miss an opportunity to be seen and have his picture taken in a tuxedo as he walked his daughter down the aisle.

Dewayne and Noel chose ambiance over affiliation and decided to marry at an ornate Catholic church. After the ceremony, Constantine pulled Noel to the side, with one last bit of motherly advice before she became a married woman. "Listen, mi know yuh still a virgin. And it might be more dan yuh can handle yuh first time. So mi haf somethin for yuh. Here," she said, placing two large white pills in her hand.

Noel looked down at the pills, confused. "What is it?"

"Is muscle relaxant."

"Thanks, Mommy, but I won't be needing that."

"Yuh sure? Tek dem jus in case."

"No, Mom. I won't need them. I'm ready."

Constantine relented, realizing, yet again, that her children were no longer babies. They didn't need her like they used to and she was having to let them go at a pace that was much too quick for her.

Luckily, she wouldn't have to live on her own for much longer. The same year Noel got married, Maxine, who had enrolled in school as a nursing student at the request of her father, decided the program was not for her and she left, moving to Maryland.

Not wanting her mother to be alone, in her later years, Maxine invited Constantine to live with her. She was stunned by the offer. Maxine had been the most difficult and headstrong child in her younger years. And now, she wanted them to live together as two grown women. Though she had some doubts, she didn't want to stay in their family house without her children and she accepted the offer, appreciative.

Time had helped the both of them. The years she was in boarding school and then in college had done wonders for their relationship. They no longer bickered incessantly. Maxine had matured and even apologized to her mother for making things so difficult when she was a teenager. And the elder woman, unburdened by her marriage and with no children to raise, was far less high-strung.

Constantine treasured the chance to leave the state of Indiana and some of the reminders of her troubled life there with Clifton. Sadly, she found that the impact their marriage and its dysfunction had made extended far beyond the limits of Indianapolis.

When she got to Columbia, Maryland, she was immediately taken with the size of the condo Maxine had purchased for just the two of them. "Why yuh buy dis 'uge place for jus de two a we?"

"I wanted to buy a big place. That way, if my sister's husbands mistreat them, they'll have a place to go."

Constantine pursed her lips and nodded solemnly, feeling a pang in her heart.

Though she was rather fond of the idea and considered it both considerate and brilliant, it saddened her to know that her youngest daughter had so little faith in marriage, having watched her parents's own, that she was making her life choices on the assumption that her sisters's unions would be filled with strife.

Thankfully, the only time Maxine's sisters would need her house was when they came, with their children, to visit her and Constantine.

More than her daughter's view on marriage and trust in men, there were more ugly, more glaring reminders of their past lives.

One day at the mall, all the way in Columbia, Maryland. Maxine and Constantine noticed a woman was staring at them from several feet away. They couldn't place her from that distance but it was clear, she was eyeing them. As the woman moved closer, she stared dead into their faces. And then sinisterly, her lips twisted and she erupted with a sick, hollow laughter.

Shocked by her outburst, Maxine looked intently at her for the first time. It was then that she finally recognized her. Tracey Armstrong. They were about the same age. The two didn't know each other well but she was the daughter of Clifton's steady girlfriend from before he and Constantine had divorced and certainly afterward. It was common knowledge. There were no words exchanged; the woman just stood in the middle of the mall, laughing, stopping occasionally to look and shake her head at the two of them. Constantine and Maxine walked past Tracey as if they didn't see her laughing hysterically at their expense.

Later, Maxine asked, "Did you know who that was?" Constantine answered shortly, "Yes. Meh remember."

Aside from that one unfortunate reminder of what she'd left behind, Constantine loved Maryland more than she thought she would. In addition to being with her daughter, her nieces, Daphne and Manetta, had also relocated to the state. After visiting the more common Caribbean immigrant location of New York City, the two opted for the clean, suburban life over dirt and grime, hustle and bustle.

Constantine was grateful for their choice. The three would often sit around and reflect on their island childhoods and, most preciously, their mother and grandmother. With the exception of her trips to Kingston, it had been years since she'd had the opportunity to recall their memories in this way.

Manetta had opened a daycare in her home and Constantine would often spend the entire week over there, helping her with her business before coming home to spend the weekends with Maxine. She spent the rest of her time flying all over, visiting her children and grandchildren across the country.

1985, Sixty-five

In one of her visits back to Indianapolis, Noel surprised Constantine with the news that she was expecting."You're the first person I told outside of Dewayne. I'm about three weeks along."

The news of a new grandchild never got old. Tears came to the corners of her eyes as she congratulated her eldest girlchild. "Just mek sure yuh tek it easy now, Noel."

It was a warning she would have issued to any expectant woman. She knew firsthand how fragile this time could be.

Noel's doctor had told her she could live and move normally. And with her mother there, she felt particularly comfortable. With Constantine cooking and cleaning for her and Dewayne every day, Noel went about tackling the home improvement projects that somehow seemed to keep getting pushed further and further down on her to do list.

A week after Constantine arrived, Noel was replacing an old shower curtain rod, with Constantine serving as her spotter. Reaching up to put the rod in the hole, drilled into the wall, she felt a tearing somewhere in her abdomen.

Hours later, in Maryland, Maxine awoke from her sleep, disturbed.

She'd just dreamt of a child dressed in what looked like a wedding dress, lying in a casket. As she slowly recalled the details of the dream in her conscious state, she realized it was a message. She immediately picked up her phone to call Noel's home, knowing, at once that her sister was pregnant and the baby was in danger.

"Where's Noel?" she asked when her mother answered.

"She and Dewayne stepped out for a minute." Noel and Dewayne had just left to go to the hospital to see about the bleeding she was experiencing. Constantine knew as well that she had probably lost the child but she didn't feel it was her place to tell Maxine. She'd have Noel tell her what happened when she got home.

Maxine sighed, thinking for a second that her traumatic dream may have been wrong. Still, she decided to ask anyway. "Was Noel pregnant? Did she lose a baby?"

Constantine fell silent on the other end of the line. When she was finally able to speak, she said, "Yuh haffa speak to yuh sista when she get back."

Maxine hung up the phone and went back to bed, unable to fall asleep.

1987, Sixty-seven

Noel would hold two more embryos in her hand before she birthed her first child. After suffering the agony of those losses, wondering if they'd ever be able to have children, Noel and Dewayne decided to share the news of their latest pregnancy with just a handful of people. The rest learned she was expecting during her sixth month. They didn't even find out the sex of the baby, not wanting to be further attached should another tragedy occur.

As soon as she learned, Constantine, came back to Indianapolis again to be with her daughter, regardless of the outcome. When Noel was in her eighth month, it was Constantine who had a vision about the baby to come. Grace Ann visited her to issue a warning. In the dream, Constantine saw a child dressed from head to toe in pink standing up in a crib. And as she watched the baby bounce and babble, she heard her mother's voice say to her, "When de baby born, rub 'ar chest down wid Vicks."

A month later, Noel gave birth to a baby girl she and Dewayne named Valerie. Then a month after that, the doctors diagnosed her with asthma. Constantine understood what her mother had meant then and she followed her instructions. The process reminded her of the way she'd treated Alton with the ganja tea when he was first born. Vicks certainly wasn't marijuana but Dewayne, extremely protective after having suffered great losses along with his wife, still thought it was too strong for a newborn.

"Noel, you have to tell your mother to stop using that Vicks on Valerie. The chemicals are too potent for her skin."

Noel didn't necessarily agree but respected her husband and this new protector role he'd adopted, so she passed the message along to her mother. Having raised six children, Constantine didn't take kindly to the novice questioning her judgment. "De man nah undastan Vicks is used fuh healing. The poor child cyan breathe. Dis ah help 'ar."

"I know, Mommy. I don't think anything's wrong with it but that's his daughter, his first child. He has a right to say what he does and doesn't want for her."

Constantine nodded in understanding, not wanting her daughter to have to choose between her mother and her husband. She said nothing more but continued following Grace Ann's instructions. When she bathed her granddaughter, she simply used more baby lotion to mask the smell.

Years later, by the time Valerie was in elementary school, she'd outgrown the asthma. Naturally, Constantine was convinced it was because she had followed her mother's instructions.

She stayed with Noel and Dewayne for months after Valerie was born, making sure that her daughter had all of the help she needed. And when she felt like Noel had developed a rhythm and routine of her own, she left to allow her to truly find her own way as a mother.

1989, Sixty-nine

Less than two years later, Constantine was back in Indianapolis for the birth of Noel's second daughter, Vara. Unlike the months devoid of conflict or contention after Valerie's birth, this time Noel and Constantine ended up bumping heads. As she'd done before, Constantine essentially moved in with Noel and Dewayne to help out with the new arrival.

Though Noel had found a stride with Valerie, Constantine knew all too well how things shifted and changed once another child was introduced. And Noel was appreciative for her mother's help. Constantine assumed that, after Noel had the chance to heal, she should be able to show that appreciation by returning the favor.

A full month after she'd given birth, Noel, in need of a break, left the two girls home with Dewayne while she took her mother to the grocery store. They had just come back to the house and Constantine, as she was in the practice of doing, sat down at the dining room table to review the receipt from the day's purchases. She was always certain that cashiers were out to steal from her and even if it was the difference between some pocket change, she was not going to stand for it.

Today, she noticed that the saleswoman had shorted her seventy-five cents. Constantine never learned to drive, and so she would need Noel to help her get her few coins back.

"Noel, look here. Yuh see de 'oman ah cheat me seventy-five cents?! Can yuh believe dat? Is nearly a dollar and she tink meh nah notice it. Yuh see how de people dem try and tek advantage of people once dey get up in age?"

Noel nodded, half-heartedly. "Yeah, Mommy, it's a shame."

"Well, yuh muss run meh back tuh de store so meh cyan show 'ar de mistake and she can give me mi muney back."

Noel sighed, having had enough activity for the day. "Mommy, you want me to run you to the store for seventy-five cents?"

"Yes. Meh know it's not a lot of muney but it's de principle. Meh haf fi let 'ar know she nah get away wid stealing from me."

Perhaps it was her immigrant background that gave her such an appreciation for money, no matter the denomination. From the time she'd gotten to America, where saving money was the primary goal, Constantine would stop, sometimes in the middle of the street to pick up pennies, telling herself, and eventually her children and grandchildren, that pennies made the dollars. She had conditioned herself so well, that even after she'd made it, with plenty of money saved in the bank, she still stopped to pick up change.

"I understand. But you know, it would cost me more in gas to drive back over there than the seventy-five cents you lost?"
"Meh will give yuh de gas muney den. Let's go."

Noel shook her head, exasperated. "Mommy, I really don't feel like going back out. Can't it wait until tomorrow?"

Constantine couldn't believe what she was hearing. All she had done for her daughter throughout her life and in the past two years, especially, and here she was telling her she couldn't do her the simple favor of driving her back to the store. "No, it nah wait till tomorrow. Yuh gon tek me or what?"

"No, Mommy, I'm sorry. I'm not going to take you back to the store."

Constantine felt her blood boiling. "Yuh so ungrateful!" She accented the sound of the "g" so Noel could feel her disappointment.

Noel, seeing that her mother was choosing to be dramatic, just shook her head and walked away, deciding not to participate in the production. Constantine stood, unable to move, fuming at her daughter's insolence. Despite the rage that made it difficult to think, she eventually settled on a course of action, a way to punish her. She followed Noel into the living room to make an announcement. "Meh nah sleep at a place where meh nah respecked. Meh leaving tonight."

Noel wanted to chuckle at her mother's childish theatrics. Instead, she managed a respectful, "Okay."

Constantine, who was set to return to Maryland, the next day called Winston to ask if she could stay with him for the evening. He didn't answer. Aside from Noel, he was the last of her children living in the city and she didn't have any friends there anymore. The only other person she knew in town was Clifton. And though she certainly didn't want to call him, she'd already told Noel that she wouldn't be spending the night there. Her pride wouldn't allow her to back down on her word. So she called Clifton and asked him to pick her up. She explained that she and Noel had just gotten into an argument and asked if she could stay the night at his apartment. He agreed.

As Constantine sat in the car on the way to Clifton's house, entertaining small talk, she wondered if it would be possible for them to maintain a friendship with one another. Just because their marriage hadn't worked, didn't mean that they couldn't be civil and cordial. She reasoned that they had spent too many years together, working hard and raising children, to be on the outs with one another so often. She appreciated him letting her stay with him and thought that this might be the first step in rebuilding, or building for the first time.

When they got to the apartment, Clifton poured her some of the sorrel he'd made and offered some of the chips he'd let go stale on the top of his refrigerator.

"No, tank you," Constantine said, "Meh jus wan go to mi bed and get some rest before mi trip back in de mawnin'."

Clifton nodded. He turned heading toward the linen closet. Constantine sat down on the sofa, waiting for him to come back and inform her of her sleeping arrangements. But when he returned, he had a different type of announcement.

Clifton walked back into the living room naked as the day he was born, standing with his legs shoulder-width apart. His only accessory was the self-assured grin painted across his face.

It took Constantine a few seconds to process what was happening. When she regained some of her composure, she screamed: "What de hell yuh a do?!"

Clifton's face broke in shame and he ran to the kitchen, adjacent to the living room, trying to hide himself behind a dish rag that proved too small.

"Wha—meh tought—when yuh called for mi tuh pick yuh up, me tought yuh . . . maybe . . . wan get back tugetha."

Constantine shook her head, disgusted and appalled by the man's gall. Still, even in her shock she had words for him. "Yuh tink meh would want yuh afta all des years? Yuh could barely stay home when we were married! Only de Lord above know where yuh been stickin yuh ting since we divorce. No meh nah wan get back tugetha!"

With no other choice, Clifton turned around, exposing his ashen backside, and made his way back to his bedroom.

Left alone in the living room, Constantine tried Winston one more time. Thankfully, he answered. She told him she was at his father's house and asked him to come pick her up.

"Mommy, what are you doing at Daddy's apartment?"

Constantine sighed, disappointed with her own poor decision making. "Meh had a fight wid Noel and meh couldn't stay dere. So when yuh nah answer, meh ask yuh fadda if meh can stay wid him. But . . ." She paused, wondering whether she really wanted to divulge this information to her son. ". . . it nah work out."

Winston was more than frustrated, certain that his parents were going to bring even more hell into each other's lives if they reunited. But he didn't ask any questions. He assumed, since she was asking him to come get her, she'd realized the error in her ways and she'd be on her way back to Maryland the next day.

When Constantine did get back to Maryland, it would be months before she would speak about what happened that night. And Clifton, in an attempt to preserve his pride, would never mention it. Constantine eventually told Maxine to boost her own ego, relishing in the fact that Clifton still wanted her after all these years, and to share in his humiliation. She couldn't bring herself to tell Noel though, because she knew she would see it as a lesson. That night Constantine learned just how costly seventy-five cents could be.

1993, Seventy-three

Even though she lived with her mother, Maxine was still a very young and vibrant woman. So it was only natural that she was dating. She just had to be respectful of the fact that her mother was living in her house. If she was seeing someone, they had to take her out. And if she were going to bring a man home, he had to be someone she was seriously considering or someone she wanted her mother to approve of before she proceeded.

So Constantine knew that when Maxine brought Rohan home, it was someone she wanted her to vet. He was Jamaican and that caused Constantine to raise an eyebrow. She thought it was no coincidence that both Pearl and Noel had married American men and they seemed to treat her daughters well. She assumed Maxine would follow the same pattern. She playfully scolded herself for not knowing better. Maxine had never done anything like her two eldest sisters. And so she brought this Jamaican man to meet her mother.

Constantine watched him closely. He was a bit too charming, with a bright smile and several children throughout the city. He immediately reminded her of Clifton. Constantine had heard theories about girls subconsciously choosing their fathers and she realized now that, in many ways, Maxine had unknowingly done so herself.

Rohan's saving grace was that he had at least been honest up front. Telling her and her daughter about his children wasn't going to elevate him in their eyes, but he told them because his children were a priority for him and that spoke volumes. And though she figured Rohan had a great heart, she didn't know how a relationship, let alone a marriage between the two of them, would work. But she didn't tell Maxine that. She had seen, on more than one occasion, what happened with her children when she tried to dissuade them from certain people. They usually ended up pursuing them with even more vigor. And this time, she decided to let Maxine make her decisions, even if she didn't agree with them.

For the past year or so, Constantine had heard Maxine make more and more mention of having children, how she wanted a daughter, how she was going to dress her and style her hair. She always spoke about children, in the feminine, as if she were having them soon.

Constantine would always say, "Yuh talk lik' yuh carrying now."

Maxine would respond, "No, I'm not pregnant. But it could happen sooner than later."

Constantine assumed that she meant she wanted to have children after she married Rohan but Maxine meant exactly what she'd said. She wanted to have children and knew, just like her mother did, that the two wouldn't work long term in a marriage. She'd seen Rohan could be a good father and so she chose him for that role. After about a year and a half of dating, Maxine came home and announced to her mother that she was expecting.

Everything was going according to Maxine's plan with the exception of one thing, her child's gender. Unable to wait nine months to find out if she was having a boy or a girl, she asked the doctor to tell her. And when she said boy, she realized there was another feeling she was experiencing along with the inevitable happiness.

For weeks, she couldn't determine what it was. Why she was so shaken by the thought of raising a son? And then it came to her. Her son would eventually grow to be a man. And Maxine didn't regard men in the highest light. In fact, she found them, for the most part, untrustworthy. Realizing that the feeling of uneasiness wasn't directed at Rohan, it wasn't long before she realized it was the seed her father planted that had grown into a weed, snuffing out the happiness from what was supposed to be a joyous occasion. Clifton was the reason she'd purchased a condo, three times too big for herself. Clifton was the reason she'd never been ready to commit fully to a man, and instead opted to be a mother. She'd seen an example of a great mother and knew it could be done. But she didn't have a model for relating to a man in a long-term, committed, mutually respectful relationship. Maxine could have gone to therapy to try to work through her issues but she didn't need to pay someone for months to tell her what she knew, in her heart, she needed to do. She'd have to go to the source.

Two months after the birth of her son Qadir, she invited her father, siblings, cousins in the state, and Rohan's family to be a part of his christening ceremony that she had arranged to take place at her house. She figured as her son was being dedicated to the Lord, she could begin to heal from the scars her father had left. The whole week before Clifton got there, Maxine rehearsed the speech she was going to deliver to him, over and again in her head. She didn't know how he was going to respond to a confrontation that had been a lifetime in the making. But she knew it was something that needed to be done not only for her own mental stability but so she could raise her son as a healed woman.

After Qadir's dedication, Maxine decided now was the time to speak to her father. She pulled him aside, away from all the guests who were in her home for the day. And the two sat down in the courtyard located at the back of her condo.

"Daddy, you know I don't know how you're going to take this but it's important that I speak to you about something."

Clifton nodded quickly, trying with the impatience in his body language, to rush her into saying what she had to say.

"When I found out I was having a boy, I was mostly happy but there was a piece of me that was disappointed."

Clifton perked up. He assumed that she was disappointed because she'd gotten pregnant without being married. Maybe she was going to offer an apology, one he would graciously accept. He waited silently, fully listening now.

"For a while I couldn't figure out why I felt this way about having a boy. And then I realized, he would grow up into a man. And my track record with men hasn't been the greatest . . . starting with you."

Clifton's eyes bulged. And if he hadn't caught himself, his mouth, which dropped for a second, would have caught flies. He was too shocked to articulate a single word. Maxine was his baby girl, the child he had spoiled. He couldn't fathom what possible issue she could have had with him.

"I know you and Mommy didn't have the best marriage. But it wasn't until I grew up and left the house that I realized how much your marriage affected me, I couldn't speak to you about it as a child; but now that I'm grown, with a son to raise, I know for myself, it's time that I say something."

Clifton sat terrified into silence. In all of his years of being a less-than-stellar husband, it never occurred to him that it might negatively affect his children, their relationships, or the way they viewed him as a father. His relationship with his wife was just that—something his children should have had no thoughts or opinions about. He told himself that because he provided for them, he was doing his job as a father. He thought, foolishly, that that was enough. He didn't consider and couldn't fully comprehend what years of watching him disrespect and degrade their mother had done.

"Daddy, you know I don't know if you realized that all throughout school I was teased because of you. From elementary school and even in boarding school, everyone seemed to know that you were stepping out on my mother. And not just stepping out—stepping out with women in the church, women we all knew. It was embarrassing to have to hear all that gossip as a child. And I know all children go through trials but the things I saw and the things my siblings saw in our home were not normal and they weren't healthy. They left scars that linger until today. Do you know what it does to a girl to see her mother crying? Do you know what it does to a girl when she realizes her father is the one who's causing her mother this pain?"

The question was rhetorical but Clifton wouldn't have had an answer for it anyway.

Maxine continued, "I know you might be wondering why I'm telling you all of this now. I'm telling you this because it's my turn to raise a son. And I intend for him to be the kind of man I wish you could have been for your wife and your children. The only way I can do that successfully is if I come to him with a clean and open heart. I have to clear out all of the resentment and bitterness I've been harboring toward you for years now. And I want you to know I'm not expecting an apology. I'm just letting you know I forgive you and I love you."

It had been Clifton's practice over the years to deny negative claims made against him. They were too hard to stomach and easier to deny completely. Instead he chose to deflect back on those who launched the attack. He had trained himself to block out the past, burying it so deep that he had almost forgotten it entirely. But this time was different. Maxine wasn't accusing him, she wasn't yelling or bashing him. She was doing something for him that he hadn't had the courage to do for himself: offering forgiveness. Every one of her words pierced his heart and he knew she was telling the truth. He had been trying for the last few minutes to stop the tears that threatened to fall down his face. But as he prepared himself to speak, to respond to her graciousness, they flowed. Some ran down his cheeks, some fell into his bristly mustache, and others dropped onto his dress pants, leaving markers of their presence.

After a few seconds, his throat had stopped burning and he was able to speak, in a barely audible whisper. He grabbed Maxine's hand and holding it, said, "I'm so sorry. I'm so sorry meh hurt yuh."

Maxine had said she wasn't expecting an apology, not to trick him into offering one, but because she meant it. True forgiveness didn't require one. Still, she appreciated what she could see was authentic remorse. "Thank you, Daddy."

She hugged him tightly before leaving him in the backyard. Once he was sure she was in the house, Clifton bowed his head, and covered his mouth trying to muffle the sobs. Looking at his own hands through clouded eyes, feeling the full weight of his aged body, hearing the foreign sounds of his own cries, Clifton was confronted with himself. He had been lying for so long and so well to those around him that the image of his true self had become distorted and morphed in his own mind. And now, being forced by his daughter to stand in the mirror, he was both mortified at the sight of what he'd allowed himself to become, and relieved to know Maxine still loved him anyway.

**

Early the next morning, after everyone had been sleep for hours, Constantine crept into Maxine's room, flipping on the light switch to wake her. "What yuh did say to yuh fadda yestuhday?"

Maxine squinted as her eyes adjusted to the light. She propped herself up on her side, waking and preparing herself for what she knew would be an intense conversation.

She gave her mother the highlights, repeating the parts she found particularly poignant. When she was finished, Constantine shook her head over and over, punctuating the movements with an occasional "umph."

"Yuh know, 'im just left mi room, talkin bout it still. Meh nevah see de man cry lik' dat in all mi life. Yuh nah disrespect 'im, right? Meh know bettah dan anyone the man nah perfect but 'im still yuh father."

In the past Maxine might have rolled her eyes at this statement she'd heard her mother make thousands of times over the years. But now with a child she hoped would one day grant her that same kindness, she understood precisely what she meant by it.

1998, Seventy-eight

Four years after Qadir was born Maxine and Rohan had another son, Jermaine. Where Qadir was mild-mannered and obedient, Jermaine, from infancy, was headstrong and defiant, choosing to suffer the consequences afterward. Constantine warned Maxine that the stress and heartache she'd caused her as a child would come back to her. With Qadir, she thought she'd evaded the wive's tale. But Jermaine proved karma's memory is long. It was after Jermaine's birth, raising two children with two completely different personalities that she began to understand her mother just a little bit better. Why she'd made the decisions she did, how challenging it must have been for her raising six children, all different from each other, while she was worrying about what her husband was doing in the streets. Maxine wished she had this type of clarity and understanding when she was a child. She wouldn't have given her mother such a hard time.

2002, Eighty-two

That Christmas, Clifton, Constantine, and all of the children and grandchildren met at Pearl's house in Arizona, where they were going to participate in a gift exchange. Months before they all arrived, the children arranged to buy their mother a ring with their names engraved next to each of their birthstones.

Christmas Day had lost much of its luster since Grace Ann died. Still, Constantine didn't want to taint the day's festivities, so she sat back away from the children and grandchildren, spread out across the entire living room, smiling and laughing as they learned the identity of their secret santas. She watched the scene somewhat removed from the room as she thought of the words her granddaughter Valerie had said to her during one of their late night conversations about her marriage. The girl, who was still in elementary school at the time, hearing just some of the horror she'd endured with Clifton, sat quietly for a second before looking up hopefully, "Well if you hadn't married grandpa, you wouldn't have all of us." She scoffed when she'd said that and scoffed again that Christmas morning. While her children were the greatest parts of their union, still if she'd known when she was pregnant with Alton, all those years ago, how it would turn out, all the ways Clifton's actions would wage war on her mind, body and spirit, she would have made a different choice.

As much joy and purpose as her children had brought into her life, she knew she could have done better for and by them if she were married to someone else, or had she decided to raise her children alone. More than robbing her of her sanity, constantly worrying about her husband, took her focus off her priorities and kept her from being the mother she could have been. And that, more than the cheating and the abuse, she could not forgive. Replaying all of this in her mind, Constantine's face turned sour.

Much later that evening, after all of the grandchildren had opened their gifts and the family had eaten dinner, Constantine sat at the table snacking, watching her grandchildren zoom past her spot in the chair. Gradually, each of her children in attendance gathered around Constantine at the dining room table. Beaming, Maxine said a few words before removing the ring they'd purchased from the faux suede box and placing it on her finger.

"If you look mom, you'll see that it has all six of our names and birthstones on it."

Constantine held her hand out, staring at the ring, not saying anything for a few seconds.

Maxine looked nervously at Pearl and Noel, wondering if they'd made a mistake and picked something their mother found ugly. They all exchanged worried and confused looks. Just as she was about to ask her mother whether or not, she liked the ring, she watched Constantine cover her mouth, still staring down at it on her finger. Maxine stepped even closer to her and she could see the streams of tears running down her face.

For a moment, Maxine shocked by the sight, stood paralyzed, not knowing how to respond. She looked up, once again at Noel and Pearl for guidance. They two were frozen, watching their mother in disbelief. Noel had told Maxine that she'd seen their mother cry at Grace Ann's funeral. But it wasn't something she'd witnessed with her own eyes. And there was a big difference between a funeral and a piece of jewelry, one of many rings Constantine had accumulated over the years. Abandoning her own confusion, she stepped forward, rubbing her mother's back and asked softly, "Mommy, are you okay?"

Constantine, sniffling, said, "Meh jus love my ring and me cyan believe unu did dis for me."

Maxine frowned. "What?"

"Meh nevah know unu love me dis much."

Maxine fell silent, saddened by the fact that for all she had done and sacrificed for her children, her mother still questioned her abilities and their love for her.

Later, gathered in Pearl's room, away from the rest of the family, Maxine, Pearl, and Noel talked about Constantine's tears. "Maxine, have you ever seen Mommy cry like that?" Pearl asked.

"Girl, no. Never. But what got me was her saying she didn't know we loved her that much. How could she think something like that?"

"Right!" Noel said chiming in. "I've seen her cry but I would never expect to hear her say that. I never thought she doubted herself like that. You know she's always been so strong."

"Well, she had to be, Noel. Now, that she's older without those same responsibilities, away from her husband, she can finally just be herself," Maxine offered.

They had learned a long time ago that their mother, subject to manipulation and occasional pettiness, wasn't a superhero. But in their minds, Constantine was always rock-hard and self-assured, even when they all knew she was dead wrong. She didn't break down or exhibit any type of softness. She didn't have time to. But seeing her like that, so insecure, they were reminded that before she was a wife or mother, Constantine was a woman, subject to frailty and vulnerability just like the rest of them.

2003, Eighty-three

Years after Maxine's relationship with Rohan had run its course, she realized she was ready to be married to the right man. And so she asked God for a man who would approach her, love her children, and treat her properly. Months after she first said the prayer, Ivan showed up at her doorstep, sweat rolling down his bald head as he picked her up for their first date. Maxine had known Ivan for years but he had been married and then when he divorced, she had been with Rohan. The timing never seemed to properly align, until now.

Constantine liked Ivan almost immediately. He was different from the men Maxine had dated in the past, drastically different. He was more conservative, when the others had been liberal, more religious when the others had been more lackadaisical. And he was ready for commitment, when the others had procrastinated. There was a goodness and decency about him that Constantine couldn't help but like. And she knew that Maxine was going to marry him. Now that she was in her eighties, she found herself thinking more and more about her children's welfare once she was gone, and Ivan seemed to be the type of man who would take good care of her daughter and her grandsons whether she were there to watch him or not.

After a relatively short courtship, the two decided to get married at the justice of the peace before they had the big, white wedding in front of both of their families. When the time came for them to pick a date, they settled on one in the middle of July when Clifton's side of the family was having a reunion in the city. Maxine figured that all of her siblings would be in Maryland for the reunion and they could kill two birds with one stone. Her father could walk his youngest daughter down the aisle in the presence of all his brothers and sisters, who'd traveled all over the world to be there.

While Constantine both admired and applauded Maxine for taking the necessary steps to forgive her father, it was a decision she hadn't made for herself yet. In fact, for the past year or so, thoughts of Clifton consumed her. She kept playing the most painful, the most humiliating parts of their marriage over and over in her mind, transporting herself right back to some of the lowest moments of her life. Seeing Clifton, once or twice a year, as she had become accustomed to with the arrival of more and more grandchildren, Constantine loathed the fact that he had the nerve to play victim in their divorce. She'd heard him telling one of Alton's sons how horrible divorce was and how he'd never wanted one. He didn't bother to mention the role he'd played in making it necessary. And she knew if he were to be so bold as to lie to the innocent fruits of their hopeless union, he had certainly done the same with his own siblings, who were coming into town.

Knowing that Clifton's siblings were attending the reunion and many of them the wedding, Constantine decided to invite them over to her house for dinner so she could clear her name from the half truths she knew Clifton must have told. As a staunch Christian, Clifton had been vehemently against their divorce and she was sure he'd told his even more conservative family members that Constantine had requested it simply to spite him. The divorce had been classified as a "no fault," so she knew he used the phrasing to his advantage, though there was plenty of fault he could have assumed. With this dinner, Constantine was going to take a page from her brother-in-law's book and tell all, expose everything so that they would know that not only was the divorce not her fault, she had both biblical and legal reason to leave him. More than anything, she wanted to present something to counter the saintly pictures Clifton had painted of himself.

Constantine had Maxine tell all of her aunts and uncles to come to the condo the two shared together.

She thought this session would serve as some type of cathartic vindication. But she was wrong. As the time for the meeting neared, she grew more and more anxious. With an hour before the group's arrival, Constantine moved about the kitchen slowly, as she finished up dinner, sure that she was going to vomit and ruin the meal before they got there. Taking a family reunion as the time to express her personal grievances felt wrong. But it was too late to cancel. They were already on their way. Constantine figured that by telling her side of the story, she'd make him look worse. And using the reunion as opportunity to besmirch their relative would say more about her character than it did his.

She started to shake thinking about what she was going to say. She wondered if they would believe her or cling to whatever half truths or full lies their brother had told them. She thought for a minute that they might misinterpret this dinner to mean she wasn't completely over Clifton, that the only reason she cared so much was because a part of her still wanted to be with him. She wanted to let them know it was he who should be trying to get into *her* good graces. Still, there was a lack of closure, some untold truths that troubled her. And she needed to talk to the people who may have believed them.

Constantine wished she didn't care. After being divorced for nearly as long as they were married, Clifton still had a power over her. She hadn't learned to break free. And because she hadn't learned how to heal herself, she found it much easier to replay, rehash and recount his shortcomings.

Unbeknownst to her until that day, Constantine didn't have the same stomach for revenge as she did when she was younger. The mounting pressure of having to speak to Clifton's family was starting to take its toll. By the time the doorbell rang, announcing their arrival, Constantine, regressing to childlike reflexes, panicked and ran downstairs into the basement to hide.

Luckily, Noel saw her shuffle down the stairs. As Dewayne opened the door to let her guests in, Noel followed behind her mother quietly. When they were both down there alone, she asked: "Mom, what are you doing? They're here."

Constantine was hyperventilating and shaking slightly, "Meh cyan do it. Meh tought meh was ready fi talk tuh 'is people dem but meh nah do it. Just tell dem meh sick or somethin and apologize fuh me. But meh cyan go up dere righ' now."

Noel looked at her mother in near horror as beads of sweat were starting to dot the top of her forehead. Completely unprepared to deal with the situation, Noel ran back upstairs to get Dewayne.

The two excused themselves and ran downstairs.

"Connie, what's going on?" Dewayne asked. "Your guests are upstairs waiting for you."

"Yuh wife nah tell yuh? Meh nah go up dere! Tell Clifton people dat meh sick. Meh cyan talk tuh dem tunight."

Constantine paced back and forth across the basement floor, stopping occasionally, to pass her hand over her forehead, collecting sweat.

Noel tried to reason with her. "Mom, you can't just have those people sitting up there when they came all this way to see you. You have to go up there. I don't know what you're going to tell them but you can't hide down here in the basement."

Constantine just shook her head. "Yuh nah hear meh say meh cyan do it?"

Dewayne, who had stepped aside, frowned at the scene in front of him. And then, more to himself than a comment to Constantine, said, softly, "I've just never seen you weak like this."

Constantine stopped pacing and looked up at her son-in-law, stilled by his words. Seeing that he'd captured her attention, Dewayne pushed further.

"You've got to pull it together. These people came to see you. You should go speak to them. We're right here. Nothing's going to happen to you."

Constantine nodded solemnly. She took a few deep breaths, wiped the sweat from her face and climbed the stairs.

The kitchen was right on top of the basement stairs. She'd have no time to run in another direction before they'd have a chance to see her. When she opened the door and saw them all sitting at the kitchen table, waiting patiently, expectantly, she smiled in greeting as her stomach dropped.

Noel, realizing that this was something her mother needed to do on her own, she, without announcement or fanfare, excused herself from the dining room. As Constantine took her seat at the round, glass table in Maxine's kitchen, she thought for sure Clifton's siblings could see her heartbeat through her clothes. Placing her palms, face down, on the table, she relished the coolness of the glass for a second before she began speaking.

"Yuh know meh just call unu here today fi tell yuh mi side of de story. Meh nah sure wha yuh brudda . . . Clifton had to say bout de divorce but meh want tuh clear some tings up."

For as much as she said otherwise, Constantine cared deeply about people's impression of her. And she didn't want her reputation smudged even in the eyes of her former in-laws. She thought it might be better to begin with a question. "Did 'im tell unu why we split?"

Some of the siblings nodded. Constantine sat in silence, waiting for someone to share.

His baby sister, Mary, was the first to speak. "Well, yuh know it was long ago but 'im tol me dat it was a no-fault divorce. That yuh request it for no reason really."

Constantine shook her head sternly. "De judge rule it a no-fault divorce because meh didn't wan embarrass 'im by letting de guhvament know de way him stay. But even de Bible say dere plenty reasons we shoulda divorce."

She paused, waiting for them to draw their own conclusions. Sure that they know what she was speaking of, she continued, sighing, "Meh jus don' wan unu harbor any animosity tward me, fi unu look pon me as a stain on de family. Meh stayed long as meh could fi mi children dem."

Mary was the first to speak up again.

"Meh nah blame yuh. Meh love mi brudda but meh know how de men dem stay. Yuh stayed til yuh pickney dem grown. What else can yuh do? Meh know yuh a good mudda and a good wife. Mek yuh catch yuh rest now, cha!"

Constantine chuckled at Mary's comment, at the unwarranted fear she'd felt earlier. She never considered the fact that Mary's womanhood and recognition of the truth might override her own brother's word.

The next day, Clifton and Constantine, sitting in different pews, watched their youngest daughter get married.

***

Since Maxine and Ivan had been married months before they had their official ceremony, by the time they exchanged vows in front of their family, they were already expecting their first child. Having two boys already Maxine had dreams of having a daughter. And so during one of her ultrasound appointments, they opted to learn the sex of the child she was carrying. The nurse told them they were finally going to have a little girl. She knew immediately what she was going to name her. Right there in the doctor's office, Maxine said, "Ivan, I was thinking we should name the baby after Mommy."

"I think that's a great idea. Can she have my mother's middle name?"

Maxine agreed.

When they got back to the house, they found Constantine sitting at the kitchen table, eating a banana. They both joined her, smiles on their faces.

"Mommy, the doctor told us we're having a girl!" Maxine announced, a teary, joyful expression spreading across her face.

Constantine shifted the banana to the side of her mouth to reveal a grin of her own, accented by her signature gold plate.

"And we're going to name her Constantine Victoria after you and Ivan's mom."

The corners of her mouth twisted as tears started streaming down her face. She had never been particularly fond of her name as a child or even an adult but knowing that something she had done had inspired them to name their daughter after her was an honor so meaningful and humbling that she could only express her gratitude with tears.

A few months later, shortly before Maxine was due to give birth, she and Ivan decided to move their family to Indianapolis. Constantine was ready to go back to Indianapolis and Maxine wanted to be close to her mother. Constantine was going to go ahead of them and then Maxine and her family would join them once she'd had the baby.

Despite having spent the better part of her life there, Constantine didn't feel any particular way about Indianapolis as a place but the thought of living so close to Clifton again produced a visceral reaction. Now they would be forced to face each other for more than the week they usually saw each other during family reunions. Things had simmered down between the two of them, not because they liked each other any better but because now they were too old to exhibit the same passionate detest they once had. Living in different parts of the country had been good for them. She was sure now that the move back was going to disturb the pseudo peace they'd found.

One day, as Constantine was packing up her things, she thought about the unfortunate and drama-filled run-ins that awaited her. And speaking to no one in particular, she started ranting. "Meh nah move back to Indianapolis fi fight wid da man, yuh know? Meh nah do it again. If him tink 'im ah go stress me like 'im did when we married, he got anudda ting coming."

Maxine heard her mother's broiling soliloquy from her room across the hall and came in to see who she was talking to. She peeked around the doorway and saw Constantine neatly folding clothes and placing them into her luggage. Her movements were calm, almost serene, but her mouth moved feverishly. It sent a frightening chill down Maxine's spine and she stepped into her Constantine's room to calm her down.

"Mom, who are you talking to?"

Constantine was startled out of her bitterness as she saw her daughter, swollen with the granddaughter who would carry her name. As she opened her mouth to answer Maxine's questions, the resentment returned. "Meh jus sittin in here tinking about yuh fadda. Meh nah want 'im stress me when meh reach Indianapolis."

Maxine's heart sank. "Mommy, aren't you tired of going through this over and over again in your mind?"

"Meh tired in general."

Maxine sighed. This was not the first time her mother had spoken like this. And while she had spent months trying to dismiss the severity and the morbidity of the words, she figured, at this point, she needed to fully understand what she meant.

"Are you tired to the point where you're ready to go?"

Constantine paused for a moment, not wanting to pain her daughter with the truth, but she told it anyway.

"Yes. Meh just pray de Lord spare mi life till dis baby get here."

"Listen, if you say you're tired, I need you to really work toward forgiving Daddy. Do you know what I'm saying?"

Constantine nodded but Maxine pushed her point. "I need to know that when you go, you're going to the right place. And you can't go to the right place if you have hatred in your heart for Daddy. You have to find a way to move past it."

Long after Maxine had left her room, her words rang over and again in Constantine's ears. She knew she was right and chuckled at another one of her children raising her. And though she didn't know how she was going to accomplish the enormous feat of forgiving a man whom she felt had wasted so much of her life, she agreed with Maxine that it had to be done.

The day Constantine left for Indianapolis both she and Maxine, who had waddled out of her house, felt that this good-bye was different than any other they had experienced since they had been living together. Even though Maxine knew her mother was going to be apart from her for only a short time, she didn't want to let her go. She knew, on some level, that she wasn't going to see Constantine in the same condition again.

Constantine felt the weight of this departure as well. The two women hugged one another tighter and longer than usual. And when they pulled away, not quite breaking their embrace, Constantine looked hard at Maxine, trying to embed her face into her memory. They both knew it would have been too painful to say what either one of them was thinking, so they just stared.

As she and Ivan pulled out of the parking lot in front of Maxine's condo, on the way to the airport, Constantine craned her neck to look at her daughter for as long as she possibly could from the backseat.

When they were younger, Constantine used to see Noel's daughters each and every summer. But as they transitioned into middle school and later high school, the visits became less frequent. Still, the bond that had been established after all those road trips and months Constantine spent at their house had cemented a bond between the three of them that neither time nor distance nor puberty could destroy. The girls were ecstatic to have their grandmother living with them in the same state, under the same roof, even if it was only temporarily. Valerie, at sixteen, thought about sharing all the high school happenings, crushes, and teenage drama with her, just as she'd done when she was in elementary school, hoping her grandmother would be more receptive to talks about boys than she had been when she was in second grade.

Constantine was introduced to their new teenage life the day she landed in the city. Valerie and Vara made Noel promise that she would bring their grandmother to them as soon as possible, so the two rode straight from the airport to North Central High School, where the two sisters had just watched a basketball game. The girls walked up to their mother's car and immediately started screaming with delight as they saw their grandmother's smiling face, beaming back at them from the front seat. They were so preoccupied in their excitement, that it took them a full minute before they actually opened the door.

Once they were inside, Valerie and Vara leaned over from the backseat hugging Constantine, who was dressed from head to toe in a casual, creamy winter-white ensemble. Constantine felt full seeing how much these two still loved and valued her presence in the same way they had when they were children.

Until Maxine and Ivan got to Indianapolis, Constantine shared a room with Valerie. She said her body was too old to sleep in the waterbed her granddaughter used, so Noel had Dewayne blow up a queen-size air mattress for her. In the mornings, Valerie would awake the sounds of her grandmother's heavy breathing as she did her daily exercises. And in the evenings, as they'd done from the time she was old enough to understand, the two stayed up long into the night talking. Over the past sixteen years, it seemed like Valerie had heard all of her grandmother's stories. But she gladly listened again, in her head silently finishing the lines Constantine never deviated from.

Days after Constantine arrived, the girls were on Christmas break and though Valerie didn't have to be at school the next morning, Constantine was always the one telling her they'd stayed up too late and it was time to go to sleep. At her grandmother's prompting, Valerie turned off the light. Even though she was saddened by the end of story time, she looked forward to hearing her grandmother's whispered prayers. She'd hear the names of her cousins, her aunts and uncles, people she'd never met. She could make out the words "bless," "Lord," "keep," "forgive." And then the closing, "Let the words of my mouth and the meditation of my heart be acceptable in thy sight. Oh Lord, our strength and our redeemer. In Jesus Christ's name I pray, amen."

With those fervent whispers, so comforting and passionate, Valerie felt so connected to God, she'd forget to say her own prayers. She was debating whether or not she should tell her grandmother she had been listening to her conversations with God for years now, cherishing those moments nearly as much as the stories themselves. A small, unobtrusive voice said, "Say it now before it's too late." And she obeyed.

"Grandma, you know, I love listening to you pray."

Constantine chuckled, tickled by this sudden admission. "You know meh used tuh feel de same way about mi mother. Dere's a song, yuh know, yuh fadda play it sometime called . . ."

"'If I Could Hear My Mother Pray Again'?" Valerie asked it as a question but she knew the answer. Years ago, she'd heard Constantine humming the Mahalia Jackson song at the table, entranced by the music and she never forgot it.

"Yes, dat's de one. Meh did love dat song. Lord willin, meh will see mi mudda soon. Meh jus pray God spare mi life till dis little girl born safely."

Valerie rolled her eyes. For as long as she could remember, her grandmother had been talking about death like it was around the corner, bringing it up at the most inopportune times, taking the sweetness out of their shared moments. Since she was being honest tonight, she decided to tell the truth one more time.

"I really wish you wouldn't talk like that."

Constantine chuckled again, sensing her granddaughter's annoyance. "Meh know yuh nah like it. But tomorrow nah promised tuh yuh or me."

"I just don't like to think about you dying. What am I going to do when you're gone?"

Constantine, smiling in the darkness, said, "I'll be your guardian angel."

The image satisfied Valerie and she sighed heavily before wishing her grandmother a good night.

Minutes later, the heat of the room had clogged Valerie's nose. She reached for the Vicks that she had resting on her headboard and she rubbed a line of it on her upper lip. Constantine smelled it immediately.

"Is Vicks dat?"

Valerie smiled in the darkness. "Yes."

"Give me some, meh wan rub it on mi chest before meh go tuh sleep."

Valerie reached over and handed the jar to her grandmother. As Constantine took it from her hand, she thought about the baby she had dreamt about standing in the crib wearing pink. She remembered how she had used Vicks then to heal her and now here she was a teenager, handing the jar of it to her. Constantine marveled at the passage of time and thanked God again, silently this time, for the way He had seen fit to bless her family.

***

For the entire first week Constantine was in Indianapolis, she had been able to successfully avoid Clifton. And she was thankful for it. Not only because she didn't want to deal with the drama their encounters usually brought but also because she remembered Maxine's words. They'd eventually have to have a conversation. And no matter how he acted during that conversation, she'd have to forgive him—for her own sake.

That conversation came sooner than Constantine expected when Clifton came over to Noel's house, unannounced. He said he was there to see his daughter and granddaughters but he knew full well that Constantine was in town and he wanted to see her too. Though they both had received every sign, warning, and suggestion that they should not be together, they had children, grandchildren, and great-grandchildren that bonded them forever. So they always seemed to find their way back to one another.

Constantine didn't know when she'd see Clifton and hadn't mentally prepared herself to speak to him. But when he walked through the door, she knew it should be tonight. After he'd spent a couple of hours chatting with Noel, Dewayne, and the girls, just as he was about to head home to his apartment, she asked if she could speak to him privately. The two went downstairs to the family room while the rest of the family were upstairs in their rooms.

When they sat down on opposite sides of the couch, Clifton looked at her expectantly. He prayed this didn't turn into an argument, though it had been so long since they'd spoken, he didn't know what they could possibly argue about. Then again, conflict and tension had never eluded them.

Constantine started the conversation with a statement of fact. "Yuh know we shoulda never marry."

Clifton nodded, agreeing wholeheartedly. "Meh jus wan please Mudda Johnson."

Constantine found herself softening, thinking of the way he'd cared so much for her mother. "Meh know yuh did luve 'ar. But all de tings we did go truh. Yuh tink it was worth it?"

"No, it nah worth it." Clifton's head hung slightly as he realized the weight of those words and the memories, actions, and shared pain that they held.

"Meh used to tink if we did stay together, it would be better for de children dem. But watching me and yuh argue and fight with one anudda was no way fi dem tuh grown up. Dey did see too much. And meh know dey did hurt from it."

Clifton nodded silently, not wanting to sit through another conversation like the one he'd had with Maxine years ago.

"And de children dem wasn't the only ones hurt, yuh know. We nevah love each udda when we get married but meh still never expect fi have a husband who love to play wid women in de church and in de street and anywhere yuh find dem. And meh knew de whole time. And wha nearly cause meh fi lose mi min' is dat yuh nevah admit it. For nearly thirty years yuh nevah tell de truth. Instead, yuh try and mek mi believe is me who crazy. Meh used to say all de time, is not de cheating dat bodda me. And it wasn't. It was de lies. Yuh cut me twice. Once when ya step out and den tuh come back and mek mi believe is meh who off mi head. A doctor actually tol me that if meh nah leave yuh, meh woulda go crazy."

Seeing that Clifton was still, listening without trying to defend himself, she continued.

"Meh nah understand how a man could behave like yuh and call himself an Adventist. Everyone knew what yuh was doing. And meh sit up dere every week in fron a dem people who know mi husband steppin out. It was humiliating. For de longest time, up until just a few weeks ago, meh never know how yuh could carry on suh. But now meh realize, meh haf to tek responsibility too. De girls dem used tuh ask meh why meh stay wid yuh and have a whole 'eap of chirren. And meh couldn't really tell dem why. Meh realize den, meh allow yuh tuh control mi life. And it continue after we divorce. Meh would spend 'ours tinking about everything yuh did do tuh me when it dun long time now."

For the first time since they'd met for ice cream that day, Constantine wasn't trying to get answers or understand his behavior. She just wanted to be heard, to be honest about her feelings in front of the people responsible for hurting them: Clifton and herself. She really didn't care how Clifton would respond. She needed to purge herself of this bitterness before she left this world. And sensing the finality of this conversation and the resolved calmness with which she spoke, Clifton was receptive.

Constantine continued. "As bad as de marriage was, meh realize, it was yuh who brought me to know God. All de time we did spend in church, meh learned fi call on God when I had no one else tuh talk to or when meh did feel like I couldn't do it no more, it was de Lord who helped me. Yuh know we nevah go to church regularly growing up. If it hadn't ah been for yuh, meh woulda nevah known to turn to de Lord during those times."

Clifton aspired to bring people to Christ. He went about the mission of spreading the gospel by inviting people to church, quoting scripture, and shaming people who didn't believe as he did. He never imagined his own shortcomings would be the vehicle that saved his wife. And though it wasn't something he'd brag about, he knew better than to question the way the Lord decided to use him.

Finally, he spoke. "Meh know meh wasn't de bes husband. And meh sorry for dat. Even doe we shoulda never marry, yuh was a decent wife tuh me and a good mother tuh mi chirren dem. And meh sorry me nah return de favor. But meh wan yuh know meh love yuh as de mudda of mi chirren. And meh know mi actions embarrassed yuh but yuh brought honor to mi name in raising de kids dem so well."

Constantine's heart fluttered at the sentiment. So much of the anger and resentment she'd directed toward Clifton was because she felt like he didn't recognize, realize, or appreciate what she did as a wife and mother. And despite his words today, she knew he never would. Still, somehow whether through age, maturity, or honesty he was saying it now. And while it came much later than she would have wanted, it still mattered.

The two sat in silence for a while as their words worked as a salve for some of their old wounds. In the quiet, they both replayed bits and pieces of their life together. All Constantine could do was smile slightly to herself. It had taken most of her life to get to this point of honesty and forgiveness and she couldn't understand why she hadn't at least attempted to do this earlier. Immediately, she could feel the lifting of the burden she had carried most of her life.

When they had both said everything they needed to, Constantine walked Clifton to the doorway. There, Clifton lingered a little bit longer, making small talk. Constantine sat on the bottom step listening. As they were saying their good-byes, Valerie walked past the top of the stairs and stopped to admire the strange scene of her grandparents speaking cordially to one another, even smiling in each other's direction. In the rare moments Valerie had seen them alone together, usually by force, they bickered and nitpicked at one another. And though she didn't know why they were being so civil, she was grateful they were coexisting in peace, even if it was just for a moment.

"Oh, Connie. Yuh know, me haf someting for yuh. Meh lef it in mi car. Lemme run out and get it."

He came back with a wicker basket overflowing with fruits, nuts, and fragranced soaps. Clifton hadn't really forgotten the basket. He left it in the car because he didn't know what type of mood he'd find Constantine in this evening. And if she were unkind or unpleasant, he was planning on gifting it to someone else.

Constantine looked at the basket and smiled. It reminded her of the one he'd brought to her house soon after they'd started dating. She opened her arms wide to accept the large basket.

"Tank you."

"Merry Christmas."

Clifton bowed a bit before he went back out into the Indiana winter they had come to know so well, on his way back to his apartment.

Just a few days after Clifton and Constantine's conversation, Little Connie was born. Constantine took the fact that her life had been spared until her namesake was born as an answered prayer. And now she was returning to the Lord again, asking that he keep her until she was able to see her last granddaughter safe and healthy in Indianapolis.

On the phone, days after Maxine delivered the baby, Constantine told Maxine, "Meh know meh just ask for God to spare mi life so meh could see de day de baby born but now meh wan see 'ar in person. Hold 'ar, ya know? Meh know de Lord is tinking that I'm so presumptuous that I'm going to ask 'im a nex time. But meh haf fi ask."

Maxine smiled over the phone at her mother's excitement. She was happy to hear that she had something to look forward to. "How are you feeling, Mommy?"

"Meh doing okay. Just tired of the prickin and pokin and all a de pills dem. Meh run out a mi insulin all togedda."

"Mom, why haven't you been taking your insulin?"

Constantine shuddered. She hadn't meant to say that and worry Maxine with her health when she needed to be thinking about her baby and getting rest. She went silent on the receiver, hoping her daughter would change the subject.

"Mommy, you have to take your insulin. How long have you been off it?"

"A couple weeks now." It had been a full month but a couple of weeks sounded less severe.

"Oh! You have to get to the doctor. Can you put Noel on the phone? I want to talk to her about getting you an appointment."

Constantine rolled her eyes. If she couldn't keep up with taking insulin, she certainly didn't want to see a doctor who'd just scold her for it. But she knew there was no point in arguing, so she called Noel into the room, so the two could intercede for her. They scheduled an appointment for Christmas Eve.

Early that morning, on the day of her appointment, Dewayne and Constantine left out for the doctor's office. Constantine sat in the waiting room chatting with her son-in-law, wishing she were spending her Christmas Eve somewhere other than this sterile space. When it was time for her examination, the nurse asked if she wanted to go in by herself or with her son-in-law.

"Meh nah haf nothing fi hide from 'im," Constantine responded and she walked into the room and made herself comfortable on one of the chairs, surmising that she was too old to hop up on the raised table.

The doctor came in shortly afterward. He wasn't particularly friendly, but not rude either, just straight to business. While his demeanor might have bothered her any other time, today she regarded it as a blessing. Hearing that she was off her insulin, the doctor wanted to test her urine for any irregularities. Constantine had just gone to the bathroom before she left the house and didn't have anything to give. She sat in the restroom for several minutes completely unproductive. Finally, Dewayne knocked on the door.

"I have a suggestion. But I'd have to come in. I'll wait til you're decent."

Constantine pulled up her pants quickly and opened the door.

"Connie, let's try this." He turned the faucet on at the sink and closed the door behind him. Within another few minutes, it proved successful. Constantine came out of the bathroom, warm cup in hand asking, "Who taught yuh dat trick?"

Dewayne smiled. "Just something I picked up."

The doctor came back in the room shortly after. "Based on the preliminary tests we've done, everything appears to be fine. But you will have to start taking your insulin again."

Constantine nodded solemnly, mourning the end of her freedom from the needles that had been a part of her life for decades now.

After the appointment, Constantine and Dewayne walked back into the house, jovial, laughing with one another. By this time, Noel and the girls were up and it was just about time for lunch. The night before, Constantine had made a chicken potpie and so she asked Valerie to dish her out some. The two sat at the dining room table eating and chatting a little bit. After a lull in the conversation, Valerie noticed her grandmother slumping in her chair, snoring softly.

She tapped her asking, "Why don't you go lie down."

Constantine smiled in agreement.

Valerie cleared her grandmother's plate from the table before she joined her in their shared room. She scooted past the air mattress that took up all the floor space, climbing into her waterbed. She turned on the tv in her room and the two of them watched a couple of episodes of *Fresh Prince of Bel-Air*.

Constantine chuckled, "That Will is so silly." Within the next few minutes, she was sleep and the soft snores that she was emitting in the dining room morphed into loud, distracting, gurgling ones. Valerie who was also trying to nap, along with the rest of her family, found herself increasingly irritated by the noise. And then, as if a prayer had been answered, she didn't hear it anymore.

Two hours later, stirring from a restful sleep, Valerie heard Noel say from her bedroom across the hall, "Dewayne, wake Mommy up and have her take her insulin."

Dewayne stood in the doorway and called out, "Connie."

She didn't respond.

Dewayne called out louder and then stepped into the room. He leaned over the air mattress to shake her gently out of her slumber, and then, crawling onto it, he continued shaking her and calling her name.

By this time Valerie sat up in her bed and Noel came running from her room, into the hallway.

"What's wrong?" Noel asked.

"I can't wake your mother up," Dewayne said.

Valerie watched as her father checked her grandmother's pulse and then start performing chest compressions and mouth to mouth. In between breaths he told Noel to call 911.

In her shock and panic, Noel asked, "What's the number?"

Valerie, who was sitting on her bed, watched the whole thing, her mother losing her senses, and her father performing CPR, like it was a horror film, playing out in slow motion in front of her eyes. Both she and Vara, who had also come out into the hallway, said the digits slowly for their mother: "9-1-1."

As Noel was dialing, Dewayne continued alternating between compressions and mouth-to-mouth. After several rounds of this, vomit leapt from Constantine's mouth.

Valerie took that as a sign that she was breathing and functioning normally again. But Dewayne still couldn't hear a heartbeat. Meanwhile the 9-1-1 dispatcher was providing instructions, which Noel repeated to her husband.

"The paramedics are on their way but they said you need to move her to a hard, flat surface," Noel said.

Dewayne lifted and carried Constantine out of the bedroom and to the living room floor, just across from the dining room where she had eaten chicken potpie earlier. On the phone, the dispatcher told Noel that Dewayne should remove any clothing blocking her heart. So he took off her blouse and continued compressing. The dispatcher told Noel that included her bra. Dewayne hesitated a second, looking down at his unresponsive mother-in-law on the floor. Valerie repeated her mother's instructions frantically.

"Daddy, they said you have to take her bra off."

"I heard her! Just give me a second."

He took the bra off and resumed compressions. Minutes later the ambulance arrived. Valerie watched what seemed like a pack of paramedics move swiftly and deftly up the stairs into their living room. Aside from the fact they didn't remove their shoes first, it seemed like they'd lived and known the house as well as she did. She was thinking briefly about the mud and snow they were tracking into the carpet, when she realized she hadn't seen her sister. She walked back down the hallway and found her hyperventilating in her room.

"Vara!" She called her name in concern, putting her arms around her. "You have to calm down. We can't have two people going to the hospital today."

She grabbed her hand and the two sat in the doorway of their bathroom. Valerie put her sister inside, closer to the toilet while she looked down the hallway. She heard the paramedics shout clear three times as they used the defibrillation paddles on her grandmother. She watched Constantine's body convulse unnaturally three times before it returned to the floor, limp. The repeated shocking of her body had become grotesque. And though Valerie wanted them to bring her back, she also wanted them to stop handling her.

After the third time, she called down the hall to her mother. "Is she breathing?"

Noel, looking over Constantine's body, said no.

Valerie knew then that her grandmother was gone. But when the paramedics placed her on the gurney, whisking her into the back of the ambulance, she bustled through the house with her mother, sister, and father, throwing on clothes quickly and jumping into the car to ride to the hospital.

Once they'd gotten to the waiting room, Dewayne started calling Noel's siblings to let them know that their mother had been taken to the hospital. By the time he had reached all of them, an older woman, dressed in all white came walking out of a corridor and said that the doctor was ready to speak to them now. They all followed her into a room marked "Consolation." Inside it they sat until the doctor came in and told them what they already knew to be true.

Noel crumpled into Dewayne's arms, and Vara threw herself onto Valerie, sobbing. A single tear fell down Valerie's face as she stared into the distance at nothing in particular. In the midst of all the wailing in the room, she reached into her coat pocket. She felt a bit of plastic graze the pads of her fingers. Wrapping her hand around it, she realized it was one of the strawberry candies Constantine always carried with her to regulate her blood sugar. Valerie unwrapped it and put it in her mouth.

Later, the same woman in white came back into the room and asked the family if they'd like to see Constantine. Valerie tensed, unsure. But Noel immediately said yes and the four of them followed the woman down to a room where Constantine lay on the table, the glasses that she'd fallen asleep in still on her face. She looked like she had hours ago when she was snoring on the air mattress.

"Oh, Mommy..." Noel cried, pulling the sheet up to cover her shoulders. "I don't want her to be cold in here."

Valerie looked at her mother with pity. She was already struggling to recognize the reality of the situation.

After they all had a chance to look at her for a bit, Noel occasionally reaching down to touch her mother's arm, or face or hair, the woman in white asked if they wanted to pray. None of them had any real desire to pray but they agreed and joined hands, each looking down at Constantine on the table. The woman said kind words, all of which Valerie resented at the time and didn't remember later. When she was finished, Dewayne closed out the prayer the way Constantine would have. "Let the words of our mouths and the meditations of our hearts be acceptable in thy sight, Oh Lord our strength and our redeemer. Amen." Afterward the woman gently ushered them out of the room and back into the hallway.

The car ride home was silent with the exception of Noel's sporadic comments. "I didn't want to have to leave her there. She's going to be cold in that room."

Valerie knew her grandmother wasn't there, just her body. Still, she didn't know where her grandmother was at that moment so she prayed that God would send her some type of sign to let her know that she was okay.

That evening Dewayne tried to distract his daughters with cartoon Christmas movies and letting them open their Christmas gifts. Valerie and Vara appreciated their father's efforts and tried to humor him but in the background they listened as their mother made calls to her siblings telling them, "Mommy's gone."

They all went to bed early that night. The girls slept in their parent's room. Valerie woke up before her sister to a cold feeling on her leg. She ran her hand underneath the covers, down her leg and grabbed a penny that was lying under the sheets. Valerie held it in her hands thinking of all the times her grandmother had admonished her to pick up pennies she saw. She thought about the time just a week ago, when Constantine had bent in the middle of an intersection to pick up a penny lying on the ground. And Valerie smiled, knowing that the penny was her sign that her grandmother was fine.

As much as Valerie wanted to avoid talks of death with her grandmother, it was a good thing they'd had those morbid conversations. After she passed away, Noel, who had never entertained those conversations, didn't know where to look for her mother's final arrangements.

"I don't even know where Mommy put any of her burial paperwork."
"Let me look," Valerie told her mother, confident that she'd be able to find them.

Valerie promptly went to the closet in the guest room, retrieving her grandmother's security trunk. Noel had the key and the two found everything they needed.

Constantine had regarded her funeral as her last hurrah, her final dance at the club. And so she left explicit instructions she wanted followed for the day. She wanted her hair styled in an updo. She had selected the bra that would not only display ample cleavage, but would also prop and form her breasts into the triangular shape she preferred. When she moved back to Indianapolis, she had been sure to pack a gold and white dress, cape, and slippers in which she wanted to be buried. In a decision she made for her mother, Noel placed the ring bearing all of their names on her finger.

Within the week, family had come in from across the country to say good-bye.

The day of the funeral, at the tail end of December, the sky was overcast and rainy. Constantine's children rode in the customary limo to the service while the older grandchildren, cousins, nieces, nephews, and others rode in their own separate cars.

As with most funerals there were moments that elicited wails and sobbing, particularly when Noel's childhood friend sang "Don't Cry for Me." Then there were moments that seemed completely out of place. Strangely, a woman from Circle Center, who admitted to the entire audience that she didn't know Constantine, stood at the podium and sang "I Won't Complain" loud and off-key for what seemed like ten, full minutes. There were even moments where Valerie was sure Constantine had sent some comic relief. At one point during the ceremony, Valerie and Vara were holding their newest cousin, baby Connie, as someone offered a prayer. In the middle of it, the little girl, less than two weeks old, let out a loud and long fart. It was impressive for the days-old infant. But it also reminded Valerie and Vara of their grandmother's presence. Constantine would have been pleased with Little Connie's participation in the ceremony and would have uttered her motto: "Let it be free wherever you be for that was the death of poor Mary Lee."

After everyone had spoken, the minister announced that it was time for final good-byes. Alton walked up to the casket and laid his hand on top of his mother's. Winston, who had never been to a single funeral, did not break tradition to attend his mother's and sent his only son as a representative. Boysie, with tears in his eyes, kissed his fingers before touching them to his mother's cheek. Noel stood in front of the casket shaking her head from side to side. Pearl went up with her husband and only caught a glimpse of her mother before she turned away, unable and unwilling to stand the sight of her mother unmoving in her sparkling dress. When Maxine went up to the casket she tucked one of Baby Connie's bibs near her mother's arm.

After the children, it was the grandchildren's turn. Dewayne walked with Valerie and Vara on either side of him, grasping them tightly just in case either one of them felt faint as they approached. When they got to the casket and peered down, Valerie noted that the woman inside vaguely resembled her grandmother. She looked different even from the woman who had been lying on the table who they had to leave her at the hospital. Her skin seemed to be stretched too tight and the wrinkles that once decorated her face were gone. Unable to help herself,

Valerie reached in to touch her grandmother's hand. On contact, she gasped, withdrawing. Constantine's hand, also devoid of its wrinkles, was so hard it was more like a mannequin's than a person's. It would be months before Valerie would remember what she'd known the day her grandmother passed. That the body in the casket was simply the vacant vessel that had once housed her grandmother's spirit and her soul. It wasn't really her at all. But that day, she bent down into the casket and kissed her grandmother's shell good-bye and silently told her that she'd see her again.

Shortly after they went back to their seats, the funeral home administrators came up to the casket, gripping the handles. Qadir, Jermaine, Valerie, and Vara stood behind their mothers, aunts, and uncles in the front row so they could take a last glimpse of their grandmother. Valerie wrapped her arms around Qadir's shoulders, both of them crying along with their mothers as they lowered the lid to the white, gold, and pink box.

Minutes later, when the family arrived at the cemetery, they were exceptionally grateful that Constantine had decided that she wanted to be buried in a vault in a wall instead of in the ground. It was raining so hard that had they lowered her into the earth, they would have been slinging mud on top of the beautiful coffin she had so painstakingly selected. Instead, the funeral home workers, slid her into the vault and placed a plaque in front of the open space. The family said one last prayer and they all touched the plaque, some kissing it before they got into their cars and headed back to Maxine's house.

By the end of the week, everyone was leaving to go back to their homes. Having to say good-bye, even temporarily, was more difficult than it had ever been. And they vowed to get together soon.

***

In the weeks and months after Constantine's passing, she visited her children and grandchildren. Boysie's son James hadn't been able to make it to the funeral and she visited him in a dream, showing off the sparkles of white and gold in the dress and matching cape she wore before she told him that she was proud of him. Later, she visited Qadir in another dream, showing him a phone with a cord that extended to the heavens. She told him that he could use it anytime he needed to speak to her. She visited Valerie and the two of them went flying over all of the places that had meant something to the both of them.

She even made time to tease her ex-husband. After the funeral, he'd hung an old picture of Constantine up in his apartment on the wall between his living room and kitchen. It stayed there for only about a week. Clifton eventually took it down, telling Noel that it seemed like she was haunting him, her eyes following him throughout the apartment. She and her siblings suspected it was Clifton's own guilt that had him so paranoid.

More than anything, Constantine wanted to see her namesake. One evening, when Maxine was feeding Little Connie in the nursery, she saw her mother clear as day walk into the nursery to peer into Maxine's arms, smile at the bundle she held, then walk out again.

Long after she'd visited everyone else, she had yet to appear to her eldest daughter. Noel had heard from Valerie and Maxine how Constantine had come to see them and she had been waiting, anxiously, wondering when she'd have a chance to see her mother.

Months after her funeral, she got her chance. Noel dreamt that she was walking hesitantly into the funeral home, the same place where they'd eulogized her mother. The coffin was still in the middle of the room. The lid was open and as she got closer, she saw that her mother was sitting upright inside of it.

Noticing her daughter, she called to her. "Come! Sit an talk wid me for a while."

The two chatted, talking and laughing. After a few minutes, suddenly Constantine yawned. "Meh tired now." She grabbed the handles to close the lid on her own coffin.

Not wanting to relive the pain of that day, Noel screamed, "No, Mommy, don't!"

Constantine paused for a second, confused by her daughter's protest. She looked at her, her hand still on the handle and said, "Oh no, meh fine. Meh like it 'ere."

And Noel, satisfied with her answer, nodded and let her mother be free to rest.

Acknowledgements

Thank you God for my gifts, the power to bring them to fruition, and the positive impact they'll have on others.

My mother, who let me know, time and time again, that my words and my voice were important.

My father, who fostered my love of reading and told me, before anyone else, to write a book.

My sister, Vanessa Wells, for making this whole book and my entire life so beautiful. Thank you for being a perfectionist when I couldn't care less.

To my sister-friend, Whitney aka Coco Amazon, who was the first to read this book and shed real, thug tears when she finished.

To my Aunt Myra, Aunt Pauline, Uncle Son, and Cousin Daphne, who filled in the gaps. Love you all!

To my aunts, uncles, and cousins. So much of this was done with you all in mind.

To Soils, whose work ethic, creativity, and support inspires me. Thank you for waiting so patiently to read this.

To my editor, Elizabeth Smith, who helped tighten this up, who believed in and was invested in this story and character from the first e-mail. Thank you!

To my MadameNoire loves, past and present, thank you for showing interest in this story and asking when it was going to be done.

To my Big Daddy. Thank you for your courage, hard work, your lessons, your love, and for getting better with age.

And lastly, to my grandmother, my guardian angel. Good lookin' out.

Made in the USA
Charleston, SC
26 January 2017